AEGIS

R.L. Arenz III

VRÆYDA
LITERARY

VRÆYDA
LITERARY

An Imprint of
Vræyda Multimedia Inc, Langley
www.vraeydamedia.ca | www.rlarenziii.com

Editing by Lis Goryniuk-Ratajczak
Cover by Marissa Wagner
Cover Photography by Sebastian Staan

Printed in USA
Second Printing, 2016 10 9 8 7 6 5 4 3 2 1
ISBN: 978-1-988034-12-6 (Paperback)
ISBN: 978-1-988034-13-3 (eBook)

Vræyda Literary brings authors to your event. For information, to bulk purchase or book an event contact literary@vraeydamedia.ca.

To my mother, Jo Anne, who introduced me to the magical world of books and always believed I would one day contribute to the literary universes.

PART ONE: LAKE GEM

I

SKiPPiNG

Thursday, April 25, 2024
10:02 a.m.

Newnans Lake used to be public access. Once the surrounding private property, conservation zones, and protected forests were purchased, Jim Stevens went to work. Lake cleanup removed alligators. Through the creation of miniscule dams, the flow of water was measured and chemically corrected in order to create and sustain the artificial oasis. The largest aspect of renovating a natural body of water was removal of centuries' accumulation of sediment. Mr Stevens refused to feel daunted by his chosen task. With the same stubbornness that built his company, he mustered on until the lake flowed with the pristine blue waters of a paradise.

After the hardships encountered in purifying the newly christened Lake Gem, which played to the crystalline aspects of water and homophone of Jim, the surrounding areas purchased were fenced in with a ten foot tall stone wall. From his company, Mr Stevens promoted a handful of foreman into the dual role of initially managing the construction of the perimeter wall and new homes before they transitioned into onsite security guards.

Jonathan Ross was one such foreman.

He and his family moved to the eastern side of the lake, to an alcove cul de sac permitted the blue collar workers to be part of the lavish, extravagant lifestyle of corporate aristocracy. As far as management was concerned, the workers' seclusion in a dead end was an additional perk. Less chance of normal traffic making the necessary turns to arrive in that segment of the community.

Dead enders. Blue collar families located in the Turn Alcove were situated at the dead end of streets to ensure their segregation from the affluential citizens. The nickname grew in use with the younger generation.

Dead Enders became the name the kids from 'The Turn Alcove' were called in their community's school, which that morning, several Dead Enders were skipping.

Bare back seared as he lay upon the pristine sands of the shore. Infantile waves lapped at the sands. Cotton candy clouds diluted the sunshine to a comfortably warm glow. Tan arm lay draped over Kyle's face as the sounds of Sandy and Clay splashing in knee deep water echoed. Sage sat nearby building a detailed sandcastle. Three males without anything in common except for the lone, young woman. Sandra.

Sand cascaded down Kyle's back as he sat up. Sandra and Clay wrestled out of the sparkling water with a wet thump upon the bank, before rolling. Sage let out a holler as his castle masterpiece was reduced to sprayed sand, before being pulled into the fray. Elaborately sighing, Kyle shook his head adamant even as Sandra grabbed his calf. Without initial intention, all four became wrapped into the frenzied wrestling across the shore.

"You cheater!" Kyle kicked from beneath Clay, who laid several powerful blows across his face with clenched fist. One such kick knocked Clay backwards onto his rear where he laughed loudly, the tangles of black curls plastered to his dark complected forehead. Finally disentangled, Sage stood and marched down the sandy shore. Dark mutterings followed in his wake. Sand fell from Sandra as she stood, ragged cut jean shorts showing the flawless legs of a cross country runner.

"Boys ..." The single word carried equal parts exasperation and ownership. Amusement stretched her lips wide which was concealed as she turned her head to follow after Sage.

With a sigh Kyle flopped back onto his elbows before he noticed Clay staring a bit too hard at his sister's backside. Another kick lashed out and sent a wall of sand across Clay, who sputtered and climbed to his feet.

"If you weren't Sandy's brother, I'd kick your ass", Clay grumbled between spitting sand from his mouth. He rose with a glare and turned to look across the lake, his back to Kyle, who merely smirked. Sandra and Sage walked around a copse of trees and disappeared.

"I don't understand what she sees in him. He ain't special." With a grumble of discontent Clay reentered the water and relaxed to float. All the while he continued to mutter.

"I say the same exact thing about you, you tool", Kyle continued to smirk as he spoke. A ball of wet sand, formed into a misshapen missile, hit Clay in the face. Hoarse cry and Clay went under water before he stood with a sputter of outrage. The red faced Clay splashed like a drowning bull determined to reach the china shop. Chuckling, Kyle leapt lightly to his feet and gave Clay a two finger salute, both middle fingers extended purposefully. Leaving no doubt to the gesture.

"Come on lover boy. Catch me if you can!" Never goad someone capable of crushing your skull with their bare hands. That was advice Sandra often gave Kyle in regards to Clay. Then again, Kyle wasn't exactly defenseless. The four possessed a secret.

The Dead Enders weren't normal.

Not in the typical sense but in the hushed whispers slowly infecting the world.

GETAWAY

For decades, whispers of people with powers circulated the globe. Eyewitnesses propagated. Always the friend of a friend of a friend's cousin as the source. Every year announced more sightings.

Brian Keyes was a silent man. Ten years with the post office, sorting and stuffing boxes. No wife or kids lived on McGinley farm south of Atlanta. Co-workers, neighbors, and fellow parishioners described Brian as quiet but willing to help if needed. Mostly kept to himself. Or he did until half the employees were let go due to ongoing mistakes by management. Enough suspicion was cast upon the lower level workers, while the postmaster retained her position.

A protest grew outside of the post office, the laid off with their families and friends, Brian Keyes one of the affected workers. The hours ticked by, celebrated by a new round of shouts and chants. Brian waited. Waited for the postmaster. When she finally arrived with a police escort, the sun was halfway home to the western horizon. She shouted venomously at the workers. Each retort another accusation to bolster her public defense the local news stations were called into attendance to witness. The postmaster played to the cameras.

Slow strides barely rippled the crowd as Brian maneuvered to the front. Breath came quickly, face grew blotchy. Only a few people separated Brian and the postmaster. With a final dip of his shoulder he stood at the front of the barricades. The footage couldn't be contained. Shouts raised to screams on the videos as men and women scattered. When the view became clear again the carnage was easy to see amidst the maddened commotion.

Brian Keyes screamed. Fire squelched from his gaping mouth as flames licked across his clothes and body. Then all flame seemed to inhale back within Brian for one long breath of incredulous reality. An explosion of liquid fire rode upon the pressure waves from where Brian Keyes once existed. Those closest to the explosion were killed from the combination of pressure waves and all consuming flame. Including the postmaster. The authorities attempted to cite a form of spontaneous human combustion. Perhaps a rare form of ketosis that created and released acetone in greater amounts than normal. Maybe his skin and clothing were dusted by magnesium and all it took was a static charge. It didn't matter. The world discovered the truth. Supers were real and they were here.

Another swing of Clay's bowling ball sized fists missed wide again. Kyle slowly circled the older boy as he waited for an opening. Again a swing and again a miss. Legs bent at the knees before Kyle launched forward to tackle Clay round about the waist. Branches snapped and grass flattened as the two rolled into the foliage. Kyle found his feet first to dance out with a left, right, left combo, fists smashing the rising face. A cocky grin filled Kyle's face at the sight of blood appearing from Clay's nose as he danced backwards.

"All I have to do is hit you once", Clay wiped the blood from his upper lip, a smear across his right cheek like half forgotten warpaint.

"That's what you say to all the girls, eh Clay? You charmer."

"Your sister doesn't complain." The grin stretched across Clay's face as Kyle stepped forward, right arm already cocked back for the swing.

Too late Kyle realized he got suckered. Knuckles connected with his nose. Bone crushing force launched him backwards to snap a sapling, a hand's width dimension, in half through the ferocity of the punch. A groan accented the scene of the newly flattened clearing by their fight. Brief though the skuffle may have been.

"You broke my nose. Bastard." Blood dripped from beneath his hands as Clay ministered to his nose. Not for the first time, Clay reset the cartilage with an audible pop. Kyle stood slowly with blood dripping from his own nose, across both lips, and down off his chin to drizzle crimson on his tanned chest. Clay rolled his eyes and stomped back to the bank of the lake.

"You were anyone else, your head would've knocked clean off!"

"The punch still hurt, man. You know I don't break easy anymore. Be proud you almost broke me and did break a tree. That's something, right?" Kyle couldn't quite keep the hint of mockery from his voice.

"Whatever."

Kyle went down the embankment and knelt in the lake. Water gently lapped his cupped hands while he scrubbed his face and chest clean. Gently though. The first splash was cold against his inflamed face. Tepid lake water turned frigid upon his heated, swollen skin. Face throbbed in time with his pulse. Yes he was able to take a beating without breaking.

Did the blows still hurt? Holy mother!

Satisfied he was sufficiently clean, Kyle took a seat in the shallows as tadpoles and minnows scurried from the disturbance of their water.

"I found the probabilities that the two of you would fight very likely. This is why I'm the brains and you the muscle. The memory and mind is mine, Hugin. You are the thought that leads to action and reaction."

"Get off it Sandy. And stop calling me Hugin. That nickname

is lame, sis." The sand was cold on Kyle's back as he stretched out in the shallows. Eyes closed, he relaxed. Easily he imagined the overprotective look often worn on Sandra's face. Older than he was by seven minutes. That shouldn't count. It did. With a sigh he muttered, "alright Sandy, what else do you want to do for fun on your birthday?"

Joyous sound of laughter rang out in a clear, pristine tune that was both happy and musical. People never talked about that moment of pure fulfillment. Pure joy was a mythos many sought to obtain. The pursuit of happiness. A wave of warmth settled over him. Prompted by the sensation, Kyle opened his eyes with expectation to find his twin. Expectation surrendered to knowledge. Just as Sandra wasn't standing beside him, she was still in attendance.

Gifted by a form of telepathy, Sandra Ross learned she was different. The ability wasn't only being able to sense emotions or intent, but the capacity to know memories and exact thought. Once, she likened it to tuning an old fm radio where all she needed was tune in to the individual and listen. With her capabilities Sandy was able to connect people, almost anchoring a piece of her psyche, or soul, with them. This offered the chance to exist within others' minds. A deeper connection with a few loved ones. Influencing or outright control of another sentient being was easily within her grasp.

However, she refused to cross the morally ambiguous line, no matter what.

Sensations danced across his skin, instantly bringing goosebumps. Felt like a blind, maniacal man's deluded braille journal. A glance to the shore revealed Sandra was psychically speaking to her boyfriend. Clay folded his arms and nodded in silent conversation that Kyle wasn't privy to. While Sandy walked with Sage, her best friend, she remained protective of her little brother. As always. Independent and passionate, Kyle experienced Sandy without her guard up. Of course at that moment Clay probably wished he was the BFF or the one Sandy defended. A smirk crossed Kyle's face as he imagined the scathing verbal beatdown Clay currently received.

"I'm sorry Kyle", the words were painstakingly extracted from Clay, like a root canal without local anesthesia. Kyle grinned so wide his face hurt. Rising from the water he joined Clay who stood on the embankment, hands planted defiantly on hips. With hand extended, Kyle smiled demurely.

"No worries. We're all good." The wait for Clay to take his hand wasn't a long one, not with Sandra viewing what they were both doing. Inevitably they shook, marking an external peace for Sandy's sake. Of course Clay attempted to crush Kyle's hand to dust with his enhanced strength. Anyone else would have the bones in their hand reduced to powder from the power in Clay's grip. Not Kyle.

Where Clay quickly discovered an innate strength greater than anyone else and Sandra learned how to delve into the secret machinations of a mind, Kyle's abilities manifested slowly. His first fist fight gave him a split lip and bloody nose. In the next fight he was punched repeatedly in the face and yet wasn't injured the second time. Another incident where he received a slice across his palm as he foolishly attempted to learn how to juggle. Instead of mastering the skill with tennis balls he unwisely used pocket knives. A boy's prerogative. His hand healed. Even camping offered pain as Kyle more often than not inevitably received a burn.

With every wound came a reveal. Each injury sustained was never duplicated. His body healed faster and evolved to ensure Kyle was never grievously wounded in the same manner. Slowly his body changed to limit the severity of repeated injuries. Even his speed, strength, and stamina increased to make Kyle stronger and faster than the average person.

They both released one another's hands while still eyeing each other. The gentle pressure in his head was alleviated. Sign that Sandra moved elsewhere. Probably back to Sage and their conversation. From the look on Clay's face it seemed they both reached similar conclusions. Left to their own devices they returned to the water for a bit of swimming as the sun beat down from above.

"What was that crap about probabilities? Sounded like Sage spouting off." Clay dove beneath the waters after his question, resurfacing moments later.

"Probably plugged into Sage as she was talking to us. Although that's gotta burn. Knowing your girl needs more 'intellectual stimulation' than what you provide." Quickly Kyle closed his eyes as Clay flippantly splashed water toward his face.

"Ha ha ha, let's all laugh at the dumb jock."

"You said it, not me. Can't blame me for agreeing with you."

"You really are a son of a-"

"Careful Clay, that's Sandy's mom too", Kyle smirked.

With a sigh Clay lay back, floating. Content to leave well enough alone, Kyle bobbed along like a cork freed from a fishing line. This was Sandra's day, her sweet sixteen. Born at 11:57 p.m. on the twenty-fifth, she was only seven minutes older than he was, born on the twenty-sixth at 12:04 a.m. In celebration she asked her twin, her best friend, and her boyfriend to skip school and have a day of freedom from supervision and expectation.

Silence was a nice change Kyle admitted. Relaxation without the continual vigil from adults constantly watching. Maybe he should ask for tomorrow to be another skip day. Lips stretched in a grin knowing he wouldn't. Today would be more special without duplication. No, he would allow his sister to enjoy her singular and unique day. A faint hum was heard in the distance.

"Ah hell, security is headed our way in their little patrol boat!" The mocking tone was dispelled even as he grabbed Clay by the arm and pulled toward the shore. The two were the apparent targets. Hopefully Sandra and Sage weren't visible. The little boat made an impressive amount of distance, closing quicker than anticipated. Feet dug into the sand as Kyle dragged his sister's boyfriend along.

"Come on, do you want to get caught?" Kyle shouted in exasperation.

"My father is a shareholder. You really think I would be in trouble? Not my problem if they catch you."

Both hands reached up and grabbed either of Clay's ears. Pulling the bigger boy downwards, Kyle snarled.

"How do you think Sandy will react when you let her brother get caught and most likely herself and her best friend? Just because we aren't rich with our futures mapped out before we could walk doesn't mean we don't matter. So stay if you think Sandy will forgive you. I don't give a flying monkey's turd." He released his hold on Clay and sprinted for the tree cover as the patrol ship, a fiberglass dinghy, puttered to shore with a trolling motor.

Amusement flickered across his face when he heard the loud curse from Clay followed by a less than graceful escape from the clearing. The breakneck pace slowed just long enough for Clay to catch up. Then their escape began anew as the sound of pursuit grew behind them.

"Stay close to my back. I'll break trail through some thickets. Use me as a shield so stay real real close. If they want to follow, they're gonna regret that choice."

With those words spoken softly, Kyle turned and plowed into the brush. Palm fronds whipped with the speed of their passage, thorn bushes sought purchase on unblemished skin, and countless spider webs engulfed faces as the two flew as quickly as their feet could carry them. Kyle was unbothered by the potential pests. Skin refused to allow minor wounds to afflict him. Clay was not as lucky. A palm frond caught his right ear in a slicing motion as they scurried. More than one thorn embedded in his legs as each grunt marked yet another thorn.

Behind them the screams of the security team was hilarious. The guards must have rushed in with fervor in their attempt to gain notoriety by apprehending either trespassers or delinquents skipping school. Their determination left them a dozen yards into the bushes where vines encircled and thorns pierced them. Emasculated shrieks cried for help that would not come.

After several more minutes the two broke free, arriving on one of the many hiking trails. Standing in feigned boredom was both Sandra and Sage. Sighing with exaggerated motion Sage looked between the two.

"What took you two so long? Doesn't matter, we're headed back to my place. Are you two coming, or going to keep playing tag in the bushes?"

The four headed to Sage's house.

FAMOUS

Thursday, April 25, 2024
7:33 p.m.

Brilliant purple blended with navy blue. Narrow splashes of white clouds festered on the horizon, from white frills to darkened outlines in the distance. The ever present hum of insects created a static background noise recognized only by absolute silence. Not to be quieted by more than a moment, the insects renewed their cacophony. Deep croaks signaled the many frogs on the hunt.

Stretched out on the couch, Kyle revelled in the soft embrace of the cushion. Socked feet perched on the glass coffee table before him. On his lap sat a plate of pizza rolls which quickly dwindled in number. The love seat on his left and twin lazy boys on his right matched the same white hue as the couch. With a wiggle, he sank deeper into the plush couch.

"Don't eat in the living room!"

The french doors to Kyle's left echoed with Sage's rapping knuckles. Through the glass panels of the door the young man glared as Sandy stood behind him with a grin. Fingers jabbed pointedly at the white fabric of the living room furniture before he pointed to the cream colored rug.

A sigh of resignation joined hands tossed into the air in surrender in an overly dramatic reaction. The quick movement caused the plate to wobble from Kyle's lap. Quick reflexes caught the plate without spilling any of the rolls. Another thump sounded as Sage flopped his forehead against the door.

"I meant to do that. Just wanted to see your heart stop." Sheepishly Kyle rose and moved to the counter that ran off the same wall as the television. Muttered agitation from Sage outside was easily heard within. The plate was tossed to the marble countertop and a stool pulled out.

With the seat taken, Kyle observed Clay in the kitchen as he searched the cabinets. Shaped like a 'U', the black speckled pale counters were immaculate and free of clutter. Unless you counted the hershey bars and a pack of marshmallows that Clay retrieved from the pantry. A toss of a pizza roll into Kyle's mouth followed by a swig from the blue sports drink as Clay continued the hunt in earnest.

"What exactly are you looking for", was mumbled around a mouth full of food. A single glance of annoyance was shared by Clay before he went back on the hunt.

"You looking for the graham crackers", Kyle questioned between bites.

"Yeah. You know where they are?"

"Of course."

"Well? Where are they?"

"At the store."

"I swear I'm going to kill you one day."

"You'll try."

Clay turned back to his search while grumbling at the legality of murder. Amused, Kyle tossed the next to last roll into his mouth before the windup. The last roll was thrown with a pretty good impersonation of a pitcher firing a fastball. The roll splattered against the back of Clay's head. With a turn Clay prepared to throw one of the chocolate bars into Kyle's face. But Kyle was already slipping through the door to the back porch.

The sound of the local news station reached the porch. The anchors droned on with a monotony that tried to lull Kyle to sleep. No emotion, only a repetitively robotic pitch without variance. On the deck, Kyle unceremoniously flopped into one of the wood slatted rockers.

"Aren't we a lively bunch", remarked Kyle.

Returned to his own rocker, Sage grunted as he opened his laptop. From her perch on the railing, Sandy shook her head with a smirk. A history textbook cracked open next to her while she thumbed through a second book. Legs swayed front to back while she read.

"Are you really doing homework? The whole point of skipping is to not do school work", an exasperated sigh escaped Kyle as he leaned back and closed his eyes.

"Not really homework. Although I will be using the idea for an assignment."

"Homework."

"No, not homework. Personal study."

"That you're going to use for a homework assignment."

Sandy stuck her tongue out as her response. Computer clicked as Sage's fingers flew across the keyboard. Each individual press of the key merged with the others for a continuous litany. The constant sound was quite soothing when combined with the light breeze that swept across his face.

"You know, you probably should be studying", Sage spoke over the incessant caressing of the keyboard.

"I don't want to."

"Well your grades aren't exactly stellar." Eyes opened as Kyle sat up and stared at Sage.

"You hacked into the school records again didn't you?"

"Not like it's hard."

"Then change my grades while you're in there."

"That would be wrong."

"What do you think hacking into the school is?"

"Informed information gathering. However, I can tell you we have a test tomorrow."

"Sweet, a pop quiz. Good looking out."

"Mrs. Hall announced the quiz yesterday."

Laughter escaped Sandy while she set the book aside. The hairband slipped off her wrist and used to tie her hair up into a ponytail. Standing, Kyle turned his chair around with his back to Sage in irritation as he flopped back down. Sandy couldn't help the smile.

"So what exactly are you studying? For fun", Kyle questioned.

"I'm so glad you asked. The comparison between cultures separated by hundreds of miles, or even different continents. Specifically their mythos. How most cultures believed in a form of an afterlife. Or how spiders in nearly every civilization are often represented as tricksters. Buried in the old tales must be some truth."

"No, don't start that theory again." A pout appeared on Sandy's face until, finally, Kyle gave in and waved her onward.

"Come on now. You can't tell me that the idea isn't interesting. Evolution occurs over thousands of years. So what if the heroes and gods of mythology were the first supers. How amazing would that be?" Eyes rolled again at the often repeated idea from his sister.

"So that means I'm a god." From behind Kyle, Sage interjected.

"A god of sloth and spray cheese, maybe." Kyle twisted and glared from over his chair as Sage continued his typing. With a hop off the railing Sandy stood on the porch.

"No, we aren't gods. But what if there's truth in some of the old myths. Like a contest between Athena and Arachne. What if these figures actually existed? And what if just one of them evolved enough to survive to today?"

"Does this mean I can have a three headed dog?" Exasperated

at her brother, Sandy grabbed the textbook from the railing and tossed the book which hit Kyle's chest with a thump. As he rubbed the point of impact Clay stuck his head out the door.

"We're famous. We made the news."

The three from outside went in and stood in the pristine living room to watch the news segment. A report of several lawsuits against Jim Stevens for discrimination. Several families were in the process of buying a home around Lake Gem. But once Mr. Stevens found out that one of the family members was a super, the sales were terminated. The story wasn't surprising to the four.

Jim Stevens was a bigot.

Other stories drifted from the speakers as Kyle thumbed through the textbook absentminded. According to the news anchor, large lots in downtown Gainesville were being purchased while several meetings between investors, city officials, and the Chamber of Commerce unfolded. Samuel Abernathy was looking to create a megalith, a building unlike any other. A massive tower so large, the building would in essence be its own little, self contained, city. A technological wonder was how the anchor described it.

Head shook in exasperation while Kyle sighed. Of course they used the excitement of the new building to bury the previous story. A page fell from the textbook in his hands, a piece of notebook paper with the rendering of a massive spider. Below hung a silhouette of a woman on marionette strings.

The picture and book was snatched from his hands by Sandy who stowed the picture back into the textbook.

"Come here babe", Clay said as Sandy slipped into his arms.

With a roll of his eyes, Kyle followed Sage back to the porch. Paused on the deck, Kyle glanced back to the doors. The news reports were coming more frequently. Stories of supers becoming the norm. Ahead, Sage reached the end of the dock.

The dock poised over the lake ran to the back patio of the house. Standing sturdier than the other houses in the dead end cul de sac, the home was designed to represent what was attainable by the blue collar work class employed by Jim Stevens. The idea was to dangle the carrot tantalizingly close so the blows from the whip barely registered. And the plan worked pretty well. Sage's parents put in the time for the prestigious house among the Dead End. All too frequently Sage was at the Ross house to eat dinner and do homework. In the evenings Kyle and Sandra walked the few blocks back to his house.

The dock creaked with his weight as Kyle walked along its length. Sage stood with the last rays of the sun cutting a shadowed profile along the wooden boards. A nod between them acknowledged one another as Kyle stopped beside his friend. Mosquitos swarmed the two but found no purchase on Kyle. Instead they renewed their efforts upon Sage. Heavy hung the scent of bug spray, state sponsored cologne of Florida. He smirked and turned to recount the joke out loud. Concerned concentration added premature lines to Sage's sixteen year old face.

"What's with the face?"

"I'm not sure." The frown deepened as Sage absently waved the mosquitos from his shaved head. For a moment Sage's future was a close call. More than enough mosquitoes swarmed to haul his skinny frame from the dock and into the night. A good thing he wore massive flip flops on his clown sized feet. Kept him grounded. An elbow dug into his ribs.

"Were you imagining me getting carried away again? Because I swear, everytime you wear that goofy smile, Sandra tells me that's what you're thinking of." Eyes narrowed as Sage looked at Kyle in careful observation before a wide grin flashed pearly whites.

"You ever worry what will happen when people find out the big secret?" An arched brow questioned from Kyle.

"I don't have to wonder, I have my calculations for that. I can tell you one thing, the reveal won't be pretty. Not for me."

"You always have me around. And Sandra too. Even Clay, just because he wants to stay in my sister's good graces." Flickering yellow pinpoints blazed to life around the lake. Eyes followed the release of swarms of fireflies nearby. Kyle almost shook his head. Many times in childhood his parents told the twins about chasing and catching fireflies in mason jars. An activity that died with fireflies. Humanity wanted to control everything so tightly that, when life threw a curveball, humanity decided to change games midswing. So they created more fireflies to release into nature.

They were wrenches, tossed by the fickle timing of evolution into the well oiled machine called humanity. Like the fireflies, supers were entering a world not fully prepared for their introduction. However, nature only needed a little time to eradicate the firefly swarms once again. Fish swam near the surface, tails raising ripples from the surface as he wished for his fishing pole. Frogs croaked with excitement. Wings flapped on the breeze as bird and bat tracked new prey and cast shadows over the pair on the dock. Spiders finished their webs. Even the females of the firefly species prepared to feast on their own, specifically the males.

How dangerous would the real world be to a fledgling subspecies? Afraid to even ask the question, Kyle kept the grim contemplation to himself as several fireflies drifted by the pair, their bioluminescent light flicked sporadically. Unfortunately all four of them witnessed how their peers reacted.

IV
NEW KiDS, OLD MEMORY

Thursday, August 31, 2023
1:18 p.m.

"I don't care if you're a new transfer or not! Get your butt out to the track field and start giving me laps! Three more years of this Bobby. All you have to do is not strangle one of these idiots or drop from a heart attack. Three more years and we retire … Where the hell are you going son? The track field is on the other side of the gymnasium! I swear they are trying to kill me …" Coach was always yelling at kids and mumbling to himself. He wasn't old, barely greying at the temples, but his eyes said he was close to a nervous breakdown. Tricks the kids constantly played on him didn't help..

"Whatever man." The grumble came out after Kyle turned around. Run track. That wasn't going to happen. Walk track, yeah. Red hood cast his face in shadows even as he began to plod around the circuit. Every few steps he tried to kick a clump of red clay free, but to no avail. Switching schools always sucked. Usually right in the middle of the school year. That's what happens when your father follows the construction.

This time was supposed to be different. New opportunity that was going to be permanent. Finally putting down roots. Might have made a difference if he and his sister were still in grade school. Sweat began to trickle along his back and ran down his spine. With a frustrated curse he pulled the hoodie off and tossed the garment across the chain link fence wrapped around one side of the track. A glance at his phone showed he'd only been walking for ten minutes. The period was going to be a long one.

Interlocking his fingers on top of the short, blonde crew cut he sported, Kyle continued to stomp around the track, slowly closing on another student. The other guy was wearing black jeans with a blue University of Florida jersey several sizes too large. Scrawny but nearly Kyle's height. Picture perfect rendition of a string bean. With the gap between them disappearing with every step, Kyle matched his pace to the other kid.

"Hey", a short word of greeting in case the other kid didn't want to talk to Kyle.

"Hey."

"I'm new here. My name's Kyle. Kyle Ross." Hand was extended in offering.

Ignoring the attempt to shake his hand, the other kid increased his speed to distance himself from Kyle. With shoulders shrugged Kyle let him go. He wasn't about to beg someone for small talk. Another glance at his phone said only three more minutes passed since last time he checked. This was going to be a long, long period.

Feet shuffled in a trance. Heel toe, heel toe, repeat. The well worn paper back flipped beneath his fingers. Homer's The Odyssey was one of his favorites. Heroes and villains, failure and success, sacrifice and reward. The story spoke to him even before finding out he was a weirdo. His sister was too, but their parents only knew about him. That was the real reason they moved so much.

His parents didn't want anyone to find out their son was a freak.

The family moved every time there was an incident. Sandra was the one who caused the problem last time. The attempt to make two boys forget what they saw worked too well. Their entire memory was erased. Immediately their parents assumed Kyle was responsible. He took the blame to cover for his sister.

It was bad enough that the disgust and loathing on his parents' faces was impossible to deny. He could take it, and he did. The most recent transfer was the fastest yet. All that was what plopped the twins into the new community school within Lake Gem Estates. Jonathan Ross went off to work before the siblings woke and returned after they went to bed. Christy Ross always made her first drink of the day as the final bell at their high school. Tipsy was the only way his mother could look at him without seeing a monster.

The phone was pulled from his pants pocket again. Four more minutes. This wasn't even possible. Somehow he must be in some form of time dilation because every long minute seemed an hour. Even the skinny kid couldn't take the monotony. A rapid path was blazed from the track to the locker room doors at the back of the gym. Even as he slipped in the doors a group of four guys, big enough to be seniors, followed closely. Kyle closed his eyes as feet continued their autonomous pace.

"Not your problem Kyle. You don't even know if there's gonna be trouble. They might be friends. They could just really need to hit the bathroom. Maybe …"

From within his head he heard another voice.

"Brooooooo. Tell me you aren't just going to let that happen."

"Get out of my head Sandy! Focus on yourself."

"I've already read this book. Anyway the teacher isn't even going to test us. Her thoughts are on the last pile of essays she burned over a bonfire one Friday night while drinking chardonnay. So I'm safe bubba."

"You aren't going to leave me alone are you?"

"Nope."

"Unless I go see whatever is happening in that locker room, right?"

"Correctamundo."

"I hate you sometimes."

"Love you too Huggin."

Annoyed, he snatched his hoodie from the fence and headed for the locker room doors. If he went in and found some weird crap going on he was going to make Sandy pay. All he wanted to do was finish school as quickly as possible and join that new academy in Saint Augustine. The one for supers. The military was already a serious option for escape. But if this academy proved to play out, he could be among others with powers and still make a difference for the country.

At the entrance he pushed slightly and met resistance. The door wasn't locked but there was definitely someone on the other side keeping him from entering.

"I swear if I get expelled, I'm blaming you Sandy."

Even when his twin wasn't actively listening to him she still was present. The way she explained it one day only gave him a headache. Made the twin thing even more spooky.

With a grimace Kyle looked to make sure no witnesses were around before he lowered his shoulder and rammed the door. The kid on the other side flew across the room and Kyle staggered in. Two of the kids were busy shoving Kyle's track buddy into a locker while the third attempted to close the door.

"Really guys? Stuffing him into a locker? Isn't that the nineties calling for their cliches back? And P.E. lockers? You can see through the grates, he wouldn't be in there half a period. What's happened to bullies? Every school I go to, y'all get stupider and stupider. First punched says what?"

"What?" The bully released the locker door after catching a fist to the face.

"They always fall for it." He grinned in self amused satisfaction. Then the two released locker boy and rushed Kyle, slamming him back and raining blows down. Yeah they weren't going to break anything but a punch still hurt. Somehow he managed to free an arm and shoved the one on his left backwards until he hit the bolted down benches and fell over hard. The other kid was shoved halfway into the locker then Kyle slammed the grated door twice. The bully fell to the floor even as the one holding the door ran for help.

"Well this is gonna suck. You good?" He took a seat waiting for the inevitable coach, then the Dean, and finally a suspension or expulsion. The skinny kid looked around the room before turning once more to Kyle.

"You're one of them. One with abilities." The kid's monotone voice spoke calm words, not questioning, which made Kyle frown. Suddenly the kid froze all motion. The slight rise and fall of his chest betrayed the slightest movement. That was it. Mouth opened to speak to the kid. It wasn't necessary. Sandra whispered in his mind.

"You and Sage go back to the track. The bullies apparently disagreed with themselves and fought. You two have been walking this entire time. When school lets out he's coming over. Sage is one of us. Oh and you owe me baby brother. Again."

He shook his head in annoyance before he stomped back to the track. Behind, Sage closed the gap and this time matched his pace with Kyle's.

"I'm … a … well, I'm Sage. I can see numbers. I understand numbers. You feel no pain or something?" The youth looked worriedly at Kyle who shook his head.

"Na. Still hurts. I kinda get used to something really fast. I get punched in the nose. The next time nothing breaks. Still hurts though. I adapt. Sandy, my sister, she can slip into peoples' heads. As you've experienced by now. And I'm Kyle, nice to officially meet you."

The two shook hands for the first time.

SCHOOL'S OUT

Thursday, August 31, 2023
3:21 p.m.

School released for the day as kids streamed from their final classes. Any self respecting student flowed with traffic to escape campus. Final class for Kyle was science. A little torture before class released. When the bell rang he was the first out the door. One of the perks of being at the back of class. The sleeves to the hoodie were pulled up to his elbows while the hood perched precariously on his head. Kids swept by mercilessly as he stopped at the flagpole alone. No Sage or Sandra.

"Sis, where you at? What about Sage?" A shrug settled the black backpack across his shoulders while his hands shoved deep into his jean pockets.

"I'm stuck signing up for a partner. Sage should be nearby. Hold on ... He's in the library. He's not alone." Urgency was imparted by Sandra's volume. Some unknown reason blocked tonal inflection. The easiest way to decipher subtle emotion or intent in the tone deaf world of psychic communications was to listen to volume and enunciation. Even then, knowing the person was the best chance to

understand.

When Sandy said he was in the library it meant more than merely where Sage currently stood. What she was saying was put your weirdo butt in gear and go to the library. Sisters were always bossy, older sisters the worst. Even if she was only seven minutes older and a day. However he wasn't going to argue. At least not now.

Trotting through the grass to avoid the continual migration of students from the school he pushed through the front of the main building to the entrance. The front steps were taken two at a time, the mold on the concrete being dangerously slippery. Both doors were pushed open as he entered the building again. Two massive halls ran right and left while the bank of lockers littered the opposite wall like recesses in a reef. Beige linoleum streaked with black scuff marks clashed with eggshell hued walls that once were a brilliant white. Yellow light aided in the feeling of ancient ruin the school echoed.

"That's what happens when you use some abandoned building. You live with the specters of ghosts past." Fruitlessly Kyle scanned doorways for a directory to the library. Without any guidance from the oddly silent Sandy, he was faced with a decision. Which creepy as hell hallway was he to go down. With school dismissed half the lights in the building were extinguished by an automatic timer. The old building lacked many windows which only added to the eerie sensations climbing his spine.

Along clang echoed down the halls, the sound of a symbol crashing in the band room. Closely following was the spatter of what might have been a row of books hitting the linoleum floor. With his head on a swivel Kyle followed the ringing reverberation from the symbol.

"What kind of evil would put the library next to the band room …", he muttered incredulously.

Turning at an open door he poked his head in and glanced around. This was most definitely a band room with instruments scattered. As he pondered the noise he heard after the symbol the sounds of scuffling erupted behind him. Quickly he moved across the hall and entered a different room. Immediately he was stopped by a counter with a small chain holding a sign that said "Closed".

If you get hit enough, or throw enough punches, you learn what a body shot sounds like. You hear a hard enough body shot and your ribs ache in sympathy for the punched or an appreciation for the puncher. The crashing shelves and books only added to the audial carnage. The chain links parted easily as Kyle stepped around the counter to the scene.

Three guys in blue jeans and button down shirts lay scattered about the small library. Agriculture types. Boots with dried mud and jeans with so much starch they could stand on their own. Course right now they adorned mannequins of flesh, laid in pools of books crashed upon their unconscious forms. Kyle took all in with a glance. Even the statuesque jock standing between himself and a huddled Sage.

"Hate to give you bad news but Sage is coming with me", words tumbled free from Kyle as he sized up the bigger kid. Wide shoulders, long arms and legs, perfect complexion. This wasn't so much a kid as a young adult with narrow hips and enough muscles in his chest he probably popped the tops from soda bottles using only his pectoral muscles. Of course Kyle's luck meant he would run up against the human personification of Atlas, the titan holding the world on his shoulders. That was the way his luck ran.

"Listen, I don't want any trouble. I'm just going to grab Sage and leave. Not starting anything." Kyle eased closer to Sage while speaking softly to the glaring giant.

"You've got trouble if you think you're going anywhere with him." Piercing green eyes drilled into Kyle as the giant took a single step forward.

"Alright Goliath. Here we go. Two men enter, one man leaves. Welcome to battledome b-", Kyle was cut short as the giant grabbed the book trolley beside him and effortlessly raised the rolling shelf high before slamming Kyle in the chest. That must be what an insect feels like when hit by a VW bug. Hard enough to hurt like hell, but only a bug so you won't die. Unless you die of shame. When you have just been laid out by someone stronger than you very few options are available. Play dead, stand up and have the same thing done to you again, or do something unanticipated.

Arms pushed him to his knees as the bottom of his sneakers braced against a bottom shelf. Legs tensed and Kyle kicked off the bookshelf in a lunge at the other fighter. Arms wrapped around the slender waist and he tried to find footing as he slipped on magazines and books scattered about them. Blows rained down upon his back trying to dislodge him. To no avail. Then the strikes grew more powerful, Kyle's torso becoming a bongo drum. There was only one question. Would the drummer pounding incessantly tire before the drum broke?

Not willing to wait and find out, Kyle wrapped his arms tightly around the other boy's midsection, tucked his head to the side, and lifted with all his might. While his abilities made him more durable, they also supplied him with greater strength. Muscles grew by tearing then repairing even larger than before. And his body was designed to adapt.

And so, when Kyle flipped his opponent over his head he failed to remember in that moment his own enhanced strength. Which wouldn't have mattered if the other guy let go. He didn't. The full momentum of the throw tossed both into the bookshelf behind Kyle. And through it. They crashed into a second shelf, both still vying against one another in determination to win.

Abruptly Kyle released and covered his ears trying to ward off the head splitting siren screeching in his ears. Beside him the other guy was in an equally pained situation. As suddenly as the noise appeared it was silenced. Two faces looked down at the fighters, lips moving but nothing overcame the ringing in his ears.

"Why are you upside down?" Seemed a valid question at the time. Sage reached down and pulled Kyle to his feet. Upright again he almost swung on the other guy until Sandy intervened by helping him stand. Confusion stretched across his face.

"Both of you just shut it and follow us. We have to go, unless you fancy detention until you're a senior citizen." Sandy glared at both fighters. Not able to offer a better alternative, all four escaped down the hall and out into the pre fall afternoon. Not that Florida ever experienced fall, just a season with empty promises that floridians considered as the worst part of hurricane season.

Through the woods they staggered and ran until the school was no longer in sight. Hands clutched a tree trunk as Kyle slowed to a stop gasping for air. Smugly he found pleasure. The big guy was equally winded. With a push from the tree Kyle squared up against the giant who mirrored his movements. Fingers clenched and breath grew faster. Heartbeats accelerated. Pupils dilated. And then Sandy stepped between the two males with a playful shake of her head.

"Stop the testosterone kegger. You two are both idiots." She turned and jabbed a finger into Kyle's chest. "This is Clay. He's a friend of Sage. Sage is his tutor and Clay keeps an eye out for him. He's a friend." The glare of doom made Kyle realize he didn't take his time in judging the situation. In classic Kyle style he punched first and let Sandy ask the questions later. Eyes dropped as quickly as clenched fists. The giant, newly introduced as Clay folded his arms over his chest and grinned smugly. Until Sandy turned on him.

"And you! You think just because you have super strength you can fix everything with a punch. Well, you can't! Guess who saved Sage earlier in the day? Sure wasn't you, the pretty boy. It was my brother. So before you get cocky you should realize you can't fix every problem with a punch." The height difference between Clay and Sandra was almost an entire head. Nose bumped against sternum. However, in that moment Clay backed down.

"You do realize I'm standing right here … right?" Heads turned to Sage who was waving his hands for attention.

"I mean, thanks for the help. But can we not talk like I'm completely incompetent while im literally five feet away?" Volume raised as Sage spoke until the final few words came out in an almost scream.

Four very different people looked between themselves. The situation just experienced was inconceivable, fantastical, and completely ridiculous. That was high school. Tradition started that day as the four walked to Sage's home after school.

BOAT PARTY

Thursday, April 25, 2024
8:13 p.m.

Seemed like forever, but it was less than a year. Bonded by mutual understanding and united against the social hierarchy of high school, the four became inseparable. There was also the secret of what they were that drew them together. All of them were freaks. And yet only Kyle was exposed by the truth's revelation. A burden he shouldered that none of the others were able to fully appreciate. After all, he was the one capable of adapting to anything thrown at him.

The final slice of the sun was fully gone, the last vestige of light quickly surrendered to the darkness. A houseboat slowly cruised across the lake. Its passage shattered the glassy surface of Lake Gem. Ripples distorted the stars in the heavens. In the distance thunder grumbled in discontent. Sage smiled and motioned to the boat trudging along.

"My idea. I wanted Sandra to have fun and just relax. That's the perk of free tutoring, people owe me favors." Pride at his birthday present colored his words with self worth. A gift for sure. To just be normal for one night.

"She'll love it." Kyle reached over and squeezed Sage's shoulder before standing straight. A little two finger salute and then he was walking back up the dock where Clay and Sandra walked attached at the hip. Stopping, he moved to the side as Clay continued along to join Sage at the end of the dock. The dim starlight glinted off the gold around Clay's finger.

"Pansy." Clay shouted over his shoulder without turning.

"Loser."

"Cry baby."

"Silver spoon douche." Kyle grinned as Clay turned and grabbed his chest in mock pain.

Turned around he reached out and took Sandy's hands. Fingers found the gold band and design. Sheepishly she tried to pull her hands away, but Kyle held firm.

"It looks good on you. On him that ring is a collar, so pull the chain for me a few times. Seriously though. You deserve to be happy. As to why it's with 'Dingo ate yo baby' over there, I'll never understand. You could have done better. You could have done a lot worse too. Don't tell him I said that or your troll collection will meet the garbage disposal." Arms pulled her into a hug as she smiled into his chest.

"Just a promise ring. I'm not marrying anyone anytime soon, Kyle."

"Yeah I know. But Clay's too stupid to understand the difference. Ow!" A punch glanced against his shoulder as he stepped back and feigned being wounded.

"Tonight is also my gift. The three of you go have fun and hang out with other kids. I'm going home. Stop, don't try to talk me into coming. Go have some normal fun without me. If I hang around things always become strained. People believe I'm different, I don't care. Tonight is about you having some fun. You fun. Now go." Hands released hers as he stepped back motioning her along. Hesitation was momentary before she turned to join Clay and Sage as the boat neared.

The trio climbed aboard and the houseboat headed for the center of Lake Gem. Music drifted on the wind even as it began to gust. The smell of rain rode the breeze. With a final glance he turned to head home.

"Hey! So you don't think I forgot about you, I left your present on the bed. Don't open your gift until four minutes after midnight or I'll find out." Sandy's voice faded from his mind. With a shake of his head Kyle slowly walked home.

VII
NO PLACE LIKE HOME

Thursday, April 25, 2024
10:37 p.m.

Home was never inviting when Sandra wasn't around. Either his parents were withdrawn and distant with a hint of fear or they were jovial, loving, and kind. The difference was his sister. When they looked at him all they saw was something different. A freak of nature. When they looked at Sandy they saw the personification of good.

Quietly he snuck in the back door and walked barefoot down the hall to his bedroom. The trick was to lift the handle as you turned. The door didn't creak that way. Safely in his room he turned the lamp on and sat on his bed. Beside him sat the present from his sister. A smile stretched his face as he raised the box and shook. No clue as to what the gift was. He gave up and set the box on the desk. For a moment he was tempted to open it early, but she'd know.

Flopping back on the hand me down comforter too large for his twin bed Kyle looked at the ceiling.

Stretched out like a canvas were articles and magazine covers. Each piece based on The Citadel. Saint Augustine was home to the first permanent base for the Protectorate, a branch under the

Department of Defense. With the surge in new cases of supers, the decision was made that teams would be formed from other 'gifted individuals' specifically for handling the sensitive cases that were quickly becoming commonplace. The world was in motion and governments hurried to catch up. Newspaper clipping spoke of tryouts for the team, the vision for the Protectorate, even an article on Anastasia Island was now the base of operations for the first of many units stationed around the country.

A poster covered the door of his closet, a hole cautiously cut around the doorknob. Jon Franklin, a.k.a. Champion, the first member of The Warriors. The official name of the team based from Anastasia Island needed to be strong, a sign that the team would fight for the people. Champion embodied all that the Warriors were to be. Strong, handsome, and determined. The stern lines of his face were softened by humility and caring reflected in his dark eyes. Unseen wind flared the cape out to trail behind him. Black suit highlighted by yellow lines that converged on the chest into a Spire. Warriors of the Spire.

A final look and Kyle rolled to his side. Eyes stared at the box for minutes before he finally sighed. Time to turn out the lights and sleep. His hand dropped to the cord and prepared to pull free from the outlet. A flash of searing pain speared his chest. Fire burned through him and Kyle thought he was dying. Vaguely he heard the muffled thump as he fell from the bed. All he could do was writhe in agony. Mouth opened in silent scream.

And then sweet relief as unconsciousness claimed him.

NiGHTMARE

Fog obscured his vision even as he blinked in slow confusion. Nothing was able to be seen in the blanket grey. Hands rubbed his eyes ineffectively before he continued to glance around like a lone top. Spin after spin. Still nothing came into focus. Tendrils of fog clung to his hand then passed through the mist. With no other idea he cautiously stepped forward through the fog. Each step gave under his bare feet bringing to mind he wasn't even sure if he was wearing clothes. Fingers tried to feel his body. The fog clung to him with more consistency. Almost as a membrane.

"Kyle."

At the sound of his name he twisted to find the source. Nothing. Just more grey mist. As he prepared to turn back in the general direction he originally faced he caught a flicker. Eyes narrowed as he squinted at two forms stumbling through the fog.

"Clay? Sage?"

"Is that you Kyle?"

"Where the hell are we?"

Hands lanced out taking Sage and Clay by the arms. Felt weird, like the undulating body of a snake. Inconsistent. Their faces were before him, but he couldn't focus on the details. Only the vague general outline. If the outline was done on an etch-a-sketch, shaken clear, then sketched again. Everything was fluid.

Another being approached. At first there was a feeling, familiar and warm. The mist rolled in upon itself to create a simile of a figure. Distinctions never came to be, just an unfinished form constantly folding back on itself in perpetuity. Even in a shapeless silhouette, Kyle recognized Sandra.

"*Kyle … Clay … Sage …*" The depth of emotion washed over him and pressed Kyle deep beneath the waves of loss, desperation, and fear. He knew without knowing. The faint memory of pain lancing through his chest brought his hand up to probe the spot. Yet that precise point, as well his form, was inconsequential. Mouth moved without words as he tried to speak. Fingers brushed his mute lips in an achingly empty caress.

"*Listen to me. I don't have much time. I was a fly snared in a web I couldn't imagine. It's over for me now. Don't talk, listen! Sage. Never doubt your mind. Follow your own path. I will always be here for you. Always. When you feel lost listen. You will find the way. I love you. You are my best friend.*" Unfallen tears from shifting mist couldn't give the release Kyle needed as Sandy and Sage merged leaving his sister before Clay.

"*We will never have our life together. That doesn't mean our love was any less real. I dreamed a thousand life times in your arms. I held hundreds of our children in my dreams. And not once did I ever feel unloved. You are my strong man, my rock. When you are lost, think of me. At those times let my memory be your anchor. I love you.*" Two pillars of mist converged until only a single whirlwind remained.

Lightning played across the grey heavens in a wondrous and frightening display. Patches of thick fog became tossed by the unseen storm. The whirlwind that was Sandra spun closer. Even as the malevolent tempest clawed at the cohesive mist that made his form, he strained toward his sister.

"*Brother! Fight for what you want! Remember who you are and never forget that part of you that always fights for those who can't! Always stay passionate and when you need me, I'll be your calm center. The spider got me Kyle. Don't let it get you. Don't let it get you!"*

Lightning forked across the sky in greater intervals and longer duration. A design of a web became noticeable even as the whirlwind Sandra was tossed ruthlessly from sight. A presence unlike any he ever felt lowered from the heavens. Unable to resist, Kyle was pressed into the ground. The pressure built over him, his mind screaming as his vision cracked spiderwebs across his sight.

Unseen fangs dripped saliva laced acid on his neck. The mirror shattered, the shards raining upwards into the storm. Freed from the mist Kyle fell into darkness. And fell. The sound of his body crashing to the bedroom floor was the last thing he heard.

IX

AWAKE

Friday, April 26, 2024
3:52 a.m.

The sound of muffled cries bled through his closed door. Angry shouts were delivered to the officers tasked with delivering the unfortunate news. His parents railed. Their daughter, Sandra Ross, died hours earlier. A party was hosted by a minor on his father's boat in which she was in attendance. Several of the minors partook of the liquor aboard. One thing led to another and several youth began playing with the spear gun. Tragically the gun went off. EMS said she didn't suffer. The spear pierced her brain. Her body continued to survive several more minutes before she expired. Time of death was listed at four minutes after midnight.

Another wave of wails escaped his mother while his father rocked in shock.

Kyle sat on his bed, the opened birthday present in his lap. The box revealed the newest issue Warrior boots from the catalogue. Kevlar weave and shock absorbers, just for starters. They cost a fortune. A literal fortune. The card inside read simply, "To my baby brother. You'll need these at the academy. I will always be there to protect you, Hugin. P.S. that nickname rocks."

The irony was not lost on Kyle. But his sister was gone. Tight grip clutched the boots to his chest as he rolled onto his side and let the tears escape with silent sobs that rocked the bed.

PART TWO: THE ACADEMY

CAMP OUT

Sunday, June 22, 2025
9:53 p.m.

"Are you telling me you never ate a s'more?" Incredulous at the very possibility, Clay rolled from his sleeping back and moved to the trunk of the old granddaddy oak. With the nylon rope untied he slowly lowered their packs from where they hung over a massive branch. A grin stretched across Kyle's face while Clay gathered the three ingredients for a s'more. Head turned to point out the madness that Sage never ate a s'more in his life. Eyes fell upon an empty patch of grass, where his twin should have sat. She wasn't. A year after her death and he still sensed her presence. Too often Kyle forgot he would never have that chance to talk with her again.

"Is the marshmallow supposed to be covered in fire?" Using a stick, Sage pointed to the flaming white lump that quickly turned into a charcoal brisket.

"Of course it should be on fire! You don't get that ooey gooey taste if it's not done right."

"Don't forget third degree burns from eating something that was just aflame." Helpful input from Kyle was not appreciated by Sage if looks were any indication.

"The marshmallow melts the chocolate and the second graham cracker goes on top, like this. And voila! Now tell me you haven't been missing out with this bad boy." The smore was held out. Between the expectation and fierce determination, Sage didn't have a chance at talking his way out of trying a bite. Tentatively he took a small bite. After a few thoughtful moments he took another bite and devoured half the s'more. Satisfied he corrected a terrible wrong in the world, Clay made one for himself.

Laid back on the sleeping bag Kyle turned his eyes from the bare ground only to stare at his boots. The boots. Clean black sheen reflected the firelight. Everyday since his birthday he wore them, giving them a workout. No scratch or indention from use marred their beauty. Like the idea of becoming a hero. No, a superhero. The dream was a foolish aspiration. Ultimately, he was just one among many applicants. What chance did he have?

Dark thoughts plagued him. Everyday since Sandy died, Kyle often found himself questioning if there was more he could have done. If only they didn't skip school, maybe she would have not gone on the boat. Or he should have joined them and been able to stop the accident from occurring. Always the game of 'what if'. What could he have done differently to save his sister?

Without speaking to the s'more devouring duo, Kyle slipped into the woods on socked feet. Hints of moonlight shone through the thick canopy above. Enough to recognize general shapes and outlines but not sufficient illumination to see the details. A harsh bark of laughter erupted from him at the ironic metaphor that was now his life. Everything turned topsy turvy and all he could do was march onward into the unknown night.

Or at least until his face ran right into a low hanging branch. Staggered backwards, his arms windmilled in an attempt to regain balance. Would have worked if, in his backpedaling, Kyle's heel didn't catch on an exposed root. Down he went in a hard collision with the ground. Slowly he regained his breath while he lay unmoving on the forest floor. The quiet was eerie.

For the first time since Sandy's death, he was truly alone. No condolences or looks of sympathy. Certainly no one judged the tears that tracked from his eyes. Just the empty forest and Kyle. A vacuum in time and space that offered no judgement to the weakness he exhibited. Without worry he would be seen, Kyle allowed the destruction of the emotional dam.

"Why? Why?" A mantra chanted in confusion. The single most important question of his life and he possessed no adequate answer. He rolled to his hands and knees before sitting back on his heels. The gentle sound of her voice muted, the mental image of Sandy escaped. Rage surfaced at the injustice. Right fist lashed out and struck the ground. Not content with a single hit, Kyle squeezed both hands into fists and drove punch after punch into the unyielding earth. All his strength fueled every devastating blow. Teeth clenched against the scream which threatened escape.

Seconds turned to minutes. Hands grew numb from the onslaught. Breath gasped from the exertion. Freed groans encircled him in a wall of turmoil that Kyle was unable to escape. Nor did he believe he deserved to. The erroneous thought he could have saved her if only he went on the boat that fateful night. Fingers clawed deep furrows in the packed dirt. Anger, loss, and guilt swirled around as Night Terrors. Haunted specters of the past circled round and round, their taloned claws tore pieces from him until all that remained was a broken, bleeding shadow of a man.

"Sis … I need to talk to you, see you. I can't do this without you. I'm not strong enough." Desperate, he searched the surrounding darkness for any sign. Nothing. Shoulders sagged as dejected acceptance settled over him. The faintest fluctuation in the darkness before him drew his attention. Shadow within shadows moved. An outline formed by the little light that filtered through the branches above. Hope leapt in his chest as the shape coalesced into a human being.

"Sandy …" Right hand extended for the being to take his hand.

The final few paces confirmed the identity. Arm collapsed as all energy drained. Clay knelt beside him, a hand reached out and steadied Kyle.

"I wasn't spying on you. I just thought maybe you wanted, or needed, a little company." The two young men remained in that position for a long time. The sounds of the forest slowly buzzed back to life. Angrily Kyle ground the palms of his hands across his face which eradicated the tears and their tracks.

"I can't hear her anymore. Why can't I hear her?" Voice trembled under the emotion which threatened to break him. Pleading eyes looked to Clay.

"Don't try to hear her voice. Doesn't work. What you need to do is focus on a memory. Remember the last time we camped out here? All three of us were playing the brave protector. We were idiots, well … still are. But that's not the point. Remember she used the flashlight to look around. A few birds and squirrels bounced around. Man, when she flashed the light on the ground and all those little pinpricks of green appeared? What did she say?" Clay arched a brow while he waited on Kyle to remember.

"Yeah, I remember. She said those were spider eyes that caught the light. And that the only reason we saw those little reflections was because the creepy crawlers were watching us." A slow smile spread across his face even as Kyle rubbed his eyes clear again.

"Who knew you were capable of being insightful?" Amused, Kyle questioned rhetorically.

"Nah, I stole the line from one of the tv shows always on during the day. I only remembered two things. That was the first one. The other was, ' the test results came back and you are not the father'. Glad I picked the right one", Clay smirked as he stood and offered a hand down for Kyle.

"You know that I'm here for ya, no matter what, right?"

"Yeah, I understand that now", mumbled Kyle.

"Good. We need to go back before Sage eats all my s'mores. I swear half of my supply is already gone. *Sage!* Put my s'mores *down!*"

NOT A GOODBYE

Spring 2026

"Now just you remember, college is supposed to be fun." Clay shook Sage's shoulder, attempting to knock sense into him. "We already figured you are going to be at the top of the class academically. So stretch your legs a bit. Don't be afraid to take chances. And don't keep that nose buried in a book! Remember the honeys, and you're the bumblebee."

Eyes rolled while Sage broke away. As always, he was dressed in blue jeans and a jersey. However, instead of the traditional Florida Gator paraphernalia, he wore a Golden Knight shirt. UCF Golden Knights.

"Come on man, be excited! I'm excited for you." Very lightly, Clay punched the jersey. Hand rubbed the spot that was hit while Sage turned to look at Kyle.

"Do you have any advice for me? Other than trying to pollinate the campus?" Eyes cut sideways as Clay laughed which caused Sage to shake his head in utter hopelessness that his friend would ever grow up.

It could have been any day of any week. The three stood on the dock in back of Sage's house. Boats scattered across the lake fishing.

Predominant blue skies only clarified it wasn't the grey canvas of winter. And Kyle was here with Clay and Sage. It could have been any day. But wasn't. There should have been four of them.

"My advice? Don't try to get noticed. But don't hide either. Just do what you're supposed to do. Find friends on your own terms. And don't let anyone peer pressure you. You've seen how this douche tries to pull us into trouble." The expected shove brought a smile to all three of their faces. Kyle lost his first.

"If Sandra was here she would say, If you want a friend, be friendly. You were her best friend. She'd want you to live a full life. Don't hold on to a ghost so tightly that you miss the life in front of your eyes." Her death was always a sensitive subject. But Kyle needed to say the words. Hands tucked into his pockets, Clay walked back the way to the house nonchalantly. Two sets of eyes followed his retreat. Head nodded in agreement with what Kyle spoke. With a sigh the two young men leaned against the railing on the dock.

"I see her. Sometimes. You understand?" The words clawed their way from Sage who caught the bare hint of Kyle's nod.

"I mean, nothing like straight jacket in a round rubber room sorta way. Kinda like a mirage. Or seeing a memory play on a screen in my mind. Like right now, I can picture her right here with us. Almost as real as you and I …" Throat caught on the emotion that welled up within Sage. An arm reached out and wrapped around his neck as Kyle pulled him into an embrace.

"She is here. Right here with us. As long as we keep her memory alive she'll continue to live. In and through us. She loved you. I was her brother, so she had to love me. Clay was the one she was attracted to. But you, you were the one she chose as confidant and companion. As her best friend. And as her friend she wants you to live your life. Be happy. If you do that, you'll uphold her memory." Arms tightened once more before he released Sage. Both looked away and cleared their throats. Maybe they even wiped their face, though neither would ever choose to recall. Man status and all.

Up at the house, Clay went inside which gave the two a few more minutes alone. Movement drew his eyes as Sage walked to the end of the dock. There was no urge to join yet his feet moved unbidden to stand beside him. Without needing to look Kyle knew what Sage lightly traced with fingertips. Their initials. From that first day years ago. Eight letters temporarily immortalized in wood.

Immortality was a lie. Wood inevitably crumbles. Memories grew threadbare. Everything ended. Even so, the engraved handiwork of his twin lasted longer than she did. Cruel twist of fate. Life was fickle with a horrible sense of humor.

"I remember when you told us we had to carve our initials on that piece. Something about the angle being perfect for longevity versus other board locations. I couldn't follow your mind then, still can't now. You are an enigma my friend." A half smile was offered to Sage. They were each different but Sandra united them in a way they couldn't divide. And he was fine with that.

Absently his hand trailed along the wooden rail until he felt depressions. Curious, he leaned forward and picked out several deep holes encircling a central point in unknown design.

"Sage, what is this?" One hand motioned for a closer look. Both men bent over the intricately purposeful carving. A frown creased Sage's lips as he straightened with a shrug.

"I'm not sure. I've never noticed. Of course that doesn't mean it hasn't been here the entire time either." Foreign thought gnawed at Sage as his face revealed his uncertainty.

"I smell smoke so you must be thinking. What aren't you saying, Sage?" A long pause hung heavy between them.

"Sometimes I dream of Sandra. She asks me how my day is. One dream we may be at the lake swimming. Another fishing. Still another we would be reading and discussing opposing opinions. I know the dreams aren't real but … still feels real. She said something to me last night that I was supposed to tell you and Clay. Her message was 'I cut the strings so you can pull the thread'. And no, I have no clue what that means." Shoulders shrugged sheepishly at his dream while Kyle grinned.

"You got me. I haven't the foggiest idea what that means. Maybe you should stop eating spicy food before bed." An elbow dug into his ribs. With a laugh he shoved Sage before he turned to the design one more time.

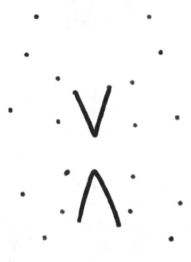

Brow furrowed at the marks. Then Clay shouted from the house. Time to go. A sense of finality settled on his shoulders. With his departure he made the choice to leave his old life behind. Memory of his sister would live on. But he swore never to return.

HEiGHTS

Thursday, November 19, 2026
2:07 p.m.

The Direhawk sliced through the heavens effortlessly. Capable of MACH 5, the Protectorate's chosen jet usually strolled along at MACH 2. Instead of being a typical jet, the Direhawk could also hover on vertical thrusters. The options between a standard takeoff and vertical takeoff expanded its potential.

Rows of seats lined both sides of the rear fuselage. In one of the seats Kyle sat.

"One more flight. Damn silver wings." The straps of the parachute were snug but he still squirmed. Still, he was feeling green around the gills. If man was meant to fly they'd have wings.

Beside him Clay pretended to be asleep. Lucky bastard loved this. Unlike Kyle, Clay loved the swing lander and the two hundred and fifty foot parachute tower. Kyle despised heights.

Across the open aisle, Gale fiddled with her hands. At least he wasn't the only one not looking forward to jumping out of a perfectly good plane. It was unnatural. But it was necessary to continue in the apprentice program. And Kyle was willing to endure several minutes of terror to succeed and become a Warrior.

Outside the plane would be nearly a dozen other Direwolf jets loaded with equally excited and terrified apprentices. A slight vibration thrummed through the soles of his boots. With a glance down, Kyle focused on his footwear, a silent promise to Sandy that the boots would see him through to being a superhero.

As long as he didn't splat on the ground.

The instructors wandered up and down the aisle checking gear and the recruits they were attached to. Cold sweat appeared on Kyle's forehead as he nervously wiped it away. An elbow dug into his ribs as Clay stretched as though waking.

"We there yet", asked Clay.

"You missed it sleeping beauty. You failed to jump so you're out of the academy." Kyle smirked as he spoke. Finished with his impromptu stretch Clay straightened in his seat and glanced at Kyle's off hued pallor.

"It will be fine, man. If Gangsta, who is afraid of climbing a ladder, can manage to pass, you should be fine. Anyway, four times without a hitch. This will be fine too."

"Did you just compare me to Gangsta? I'm not that afraid of heights. You just jinxed me. If I die I'm haunting you for the rest of your life."

"Please, you'll be fine. You have two things going for you."

"What's that?" Eyebrow arched with Kyle's question.

"Well for one, blondes bounce, because they're airheads. So they may survive. Two, you are like Humpty Dumpty. Plus even if you did land on your head you'd be fine. Can't be brain damage if there isn't a brain."

A scathing glare was shared by Kyle. It wasn't funny. The idea of being conscious while hitting the ground and somehow surviving sounded worse than dying. There was always the thought in the back of their minds that they could fail and be drummed out of the academy.

Eddie Banks, one of their bunkmates, earned the nickname

Gangsta for being the opposite of the stereotype. From a white collar family, Gangsta made it to the academy because of his sister. Stephanie Banks was a founding member of the west coast Protectorate team, the Hellhounds.

Gangsta's sister's status as a big league hitter entitled him to a golden ticket. All he needed to do was make it through the four years at the academy without quitting. Wouldn't be drummed out, no matter how bad he was.

Didn't earn him any friends with the other apprentices or the instructors. The rumor was he would either quit or have an accident. While Kyle didn't believe that would happen, he still decided to keep an eye out for Gangsta.

A red light illuminated the interior. The signal to stand and grip the hand rail that ran along either side of the rear fuselage. Instructors went up and down the aisle securing the apprentices' static lines to the central steel cable. The line would deploy the parachutes after about a five second freefall.

Kyle learned those five seconds felt like an eternity. And while falling you couldn't even hear yourself scream.

After thirty seconds the red light turned green as the rear hatch lowered. The apprentices began the shuffle forward. A slow meandering stagger step drilled into the apprentices as they neared a step into oblivion. Clay shouted over his shoulder to Kyle behind him.

"Remember! If your chute doesn't deploy, go head first!"

It was the only time Kyle ever shoved someone out of a plane. And then it was his turn.

With every jump, Kyle found himself identifying with dogs, when their owners pointed to the front yard while the door opened for their departure from the perfectly good house. And the ones with their heads out the window as the wind flapped their cheeks wide in distorted appearance. Especially the dogs in harnesses, pulled along forcibly by their owners. The straps of his own harness dug in as the chute opened above.

Held aloft on the chute, Kyle was given a panoramic view of Saint Augustine, the coast, Anastasia Island, and the unending oceanic blues. It was beautiful and nauseating simultaneously. Hands gripped the toggles tightly as he directed the steering lines.

Kyle chuckled at the realization that entered his mind. He was a marionette on strings to a master manipulator. But in reverse. Instead of being the puppet, he was the master. With hands gripping the toggles it was he that controlled the parachute.

And so he did.

The blue sky was filled with dozens of other parachutes at the mass deployment of the freshman apprentice class. It was almost cathartic. Wide expanse of the vista and the miniscule points on the ground reminded Kyle of his own insignificance.

Already he directed himself toward the northeastern stretch of beach on Anastasia Island. As he floated among his fellow apprentices he chuckled at their appearance. A smack of jellyfish. Weird name for a group of a particular species. Mildly he wondered if he could convince the instructors to let them use pink parachutes. Then they would be a flamboyance of flamingos.

Still chuckling, he landed on the sand. After he absorbed the initial impact on the balls of his feet, Kyle rolled to his side allowing the falling motion to spread the force of his landing throughout his body. With one toggle released as he stood, he pulled the other in and moved quickly downwind of the collapsed canopy. The brakes were secured and Kyle bent to ensure there was no trapped air in the canopy. Lines were looped and the deflated canopy pulled into his arms as well as the D bag, bridle, and chute.

With equipment stowed in his arms he remained vigilant of the skies as he headed south. There was no desire to have someone land on him because of inattentiveness. From the left Clay trotted over with his own burden. The idiot was grinning ear to ear.

"That was awesome! How was it for you?" Clay smirked as he asked Kyle.

"Actually, that was my best night jump ever."

"It's daytime dude."

"Not for me. Because my eyes were closed."

A bark of laughter escaped Clay as the two joined the mini caravan of apprentices. Seconds later voices rang out and people pointed to the sky. Hand raised to his eyes as Kyle searched for what caused the commotion. Moments later he saw a body descending through the sky. No parachute was deployed. The apprentices held their breath in hope that disappeared when the body hit the water. The ocean sprayed into the air from the impact. Gale joined them. Tears streaked her somber face. Disbelief covered Kyle's face.

"Who was it?" Shivers wracked Gale and her voice cracked as she answered.

"You know how the instructors were pressuring Gangsta to quit voluntarily?"

"Yeah."

"And how he was told if he didn't quit he would have a training accident?"

"Yeah ..."

"His parachute didn't open. The reserve was never pulled. Died on impact."

Joviality vanished from the faces of the two men.

It was the first time Kyle questioned the Protectorate.

And it wouldn't be the last.

IV
THANKSGIVING PARTY

Thursday, November 26, 2026
5:07 p.m.

Run. And Run. Followed by more run. When legs trembled and body quivered with exhaustion, run some more. The beautiful ocean vista meant less than nothing. Instead of a breathtaking beach with warm sand that sought to embrace you they were faced with cold ocean spray that leeched all warmth from their bodies. Salt from the ocean irritated skin to cause uncomfortable rashes. Feet wrinkled and blistered. Whether from saturated sweat or the dampness of their oceanic run, it didn't matter.

And just as they thought they finally were used to the run, a new aspect was introduced. And the run began anew.

Spring flowed into summer and onward to fall. Winter finally appeared, late as she often did. Randomly and unanticipated. One moment the runners were wrapped in sweltering heat and the next instance panted breath frosted with every jogged step.

The normal bustle of the Academy dissipated earlier in the week as recruits and soldiers alike were granted leave for the holidays. Thanksgiving. No forced marches from dawn to dusk or ruck marches through the elements. Responsibilities and duties were assigned to the personnel that remained, but large portions of the day would be free.

After nearly nine months both Kyle and Clay were comfortable with their schedules but more than happy for the reprieve due to Thanksgiving holiday. Each was presented with the chance to go home over the break. Neither accepted. The question was, why return? Sage moved to Central Florida with a full ride to college. And Sandy was gone. Both agreed the trip was worthless.

The dome tent flapped in the brisk wind. Already the sun dipped beneath the seawall at their backs. The beach was bare of civilian guests. One of the perks of the military privatizing Anastasia Island. A few of the base personnel and other apprentices headed in their direction with similar ideas. Rucksacks, coolers, and light chairs brought out for the weekend.

Down the shore Clay played football with some of the others. Their laughs, shouts, and hollers were heard despite the cold wind that muffled the sounds. Several gnarled logs were already arranged around an open pit. Grey remnants of a previous bonfire still existed within. Quick, tents were rolled out and set up. Chairs became sentries next to their owners.

Gale brought several pieces of firewood over to the pit and tossed them in. A shy smile was shared with Kyle who stood watching. Cut off jean shorts paired with a bikini top was the dress for the ladies, although most already wore dark hoodies against the chill. With one hand Gale reached in and lightly gripped one of the pieces of wood. A low hum was heard as her hand went in and out of focus. Like an eye exam, is number one better than number two. One? Or Two?

Hand pulled away as black smoke coughed flame to life. Another sideways smile was cast at Kyle who only shoved his hands deep into the pockets of his sweatpants. It still amazed him when he watched another super use their power. Like Gale. The ability to agitate the molecules in her epidermis allowed her to create vibrations.

Enough vibration caused heat, and hence the fire.

Randomly he decided to stroll south along the beach for a few more minutes of solitude. Bare feet clawed impressions into the packed sand. A black tank top, a size too big, flapped with the evening wind. With unconscious habit his hand idly scratched his jaw. A few months earlier he signed up to have his comlink implanted rather than carry as loose equipment. One of the benefits was always having communications. Another bonus was access to the artificial intelligence program. Most of his classmates limited their interaction with the computer program, but Kyle found something comforting in the foreign unknown.

"Apprentice Ross, why do you not interact with your peers?" The voice heard sounded feminine. The A.I. sounded gender neutral to most of the other recruits. Not to Kyle. On more than one occasion he even believed the AI joked. When mentioned to others he received odd looks. He no longer talked about it.

"Evening Munin. And I'm not avoiding them. I just … prefer my own company." Even in his own mind the words sounded hollow and unconvincing.

"According to my observation, Apprentice Tanaka was attempting to create dialogue with you. Why did Apprentice Ross retreat?" The dang program needed to leave well enough alone. Clay rode his back enough on the same subject. Recently, the same woman too.

With a frustrated sigh he stopped and looked at the darkened horizon. Daylight vanished even faster than it seemed possible. Losing the bronze rays to see by was a decent metaphor.

After his sister's funeral, Kyle was unfocused and lost. Every day filled with constant reminders of the loss. His parents drew even more distant. Demeanor grew frigid, and they weren't winning any friendly contests before the death. Tolerated was the word that best described Kyle's existence. And so he withdrew, only spending time with Sage and Clay.

School was a bothersome necessity. Graduation was the only reason he stayed. With his diploma he could apply to the Academy on Anastasia Island. To become a member of the Protectorate and the local unit named the Warriors. He was determined to do his part and keep his promise to his sister. Classes were doubled so he could graduate early. Every night Kyle fell asleep looking at the boots of a superhero. The last thing received from Sandy.

Days blurred into weeks. Weeks merged with months. Until finally he completed the necessary credits to attain his diploma.

iNTERRUPTED

Thursday, November 26, 2026
6:04 p.m.

"So this is where you went off to." Playful tone escaped as Gale walked up on Kyle lost in distant memory. Surprise and unexpected appearance made him flinch, a shot of adrenaline coursed through his veins in reaction.

"Yeah. Just wanted to walk and clear my head a bit." The stars were bright, her skin a pale white beneath the luminescent glow. The sands reflected the light hue giving an ethereal feel. For a long moment his eyes were trapped by her gaze. Warm brown eyes so large the inherent danger if he fell into the windows of her soul would be all encompassing.

"Apprentice Ross, may I suggest you clarify your statement before Apprentice Tanaka chooses to leave." A birdsong mechanized voice whispered in his comlink from Munin.

"Yeah yeah." His head nodded once.

"Yeah yeah? Um, what does that mean? Nevermind, I'll let you return to your head clearing." Turned to go with the hood cloaking her face in shadow, Kyle reacted by reaching out to snag her cool hand in his.

"I didn't mean yes …"

"So you meant no?"

"No, I mean yes. I mean, wait what was the question?" Flustered, he couldn't stem the babble.

"I asked … where you went. You said you were clearing your head. I was going to leave you to your privacy … if that's what you want." One hand was entwined with his as her other laid gently upon his chest while she looked up with hypnotic eyes of glowing green. His eyes blinked and once more he got lost in twin pools of mahogany. The hood was slipped back before her chin was cradled in his hand. His thumb lightly drew across her lips playfully as they both stepped closer.

"That's not what I want." Words betrayed him. Velvet skin beneath his hand tormented him. Wonder filled him. What did her lips feel like? What did she taste like? His face slowly lowered as her eyes closed. Breath intermingled as the barest of sensation ran from his lips and down his spine.

"Where are you bird boy?" Clay shouted as he walked upon the intimate scene. Both Kyle and Gale jumped back like they touched an electrified fence. The silence weighed heavy, the uncomfortable kind. Cheeks turned red as Gale pulled her hood back up.

"Um, I'll see you at the bonfire Kyle. Hey Clay." A distracted flicker of fingers was all the acknowledgment Clay received while Gale hurried her retreat. However, she did look back at Kyle twice.

"Man, I didn't know. If I thought you might be macking with Gale right now I'd of set up a 'do not disturb' perimeter."

"The hell you would have. More like selling tickets to the show."

"Hey, don't mock my scheme. You would have your privacy and the others, a show. Provided they purchase a ticket from me. Binoculars are extra. That way the audience wouldn't be too noticeable."

"Your careful consideration is heartwarming." Kyle clutched his chest in mockery.

"Hey now! I look after my boy. Ten percent of the ticket sales are yours."

"And your generosity knows no bounds."

"That's me. Considerate, heartwarming, and generous."

A noncommittal grunt escaped Kyle as he lowered his frame to the sand. With much less grace, Clay flopped down on his side. They remained that way for some time. The silence was neither deafening or uncomfortable. That rare ability to be in someone's company without the need to fill the quiet with incessant ramblings. Wasn't always so.

REPUTATIONS

Thursday, November 26, 2026
6:27 p.m.

"I wonder if they brought stuff for s'mores …" The sound of his back flopped on the sand as Clay rolled from his side to gaze into the night sky. Kyle turned his head to hide the amusement stretched across his face. Never doubt the other man's ability to narrow any moment down to the all important question. Any food?

The surf gently cascaded onto the beach with a peaceful cacophony that kept neither beat or continuous expectation of sound. A general rhythm that refused to follow the simplest cadence of pattern. The beauty of chaos in all her revealed glory. From his back Kyle scoured the sky and the uncounted stars. When still a child he would sneak to the roof, of whatever place his family lived in at the time, and stare at the stars for hours. Nothing like feeling infinitely inferior on the majestic scale of the cosmos. The perk of being miniscule was the fact he was merely a blip on the grand scheme's radar. Even he couldn't screw up any event to shake the pillars of history.

Content with the knowledge life would continue despite his actions, or lack of, Kyle turned his head as Clay stood. Sand cascaded from the other man's grey sweat pants and shirt. A subtle tension drifted into the silence between the men. Cautiously intrigued, Kyle sat forward with elbows leaned against bent knees. Willingly he waited for Clay to broach the subject.

"All this wasn't my dream. Being here, training to fight, learning when to fight. None of this was what I planned for myself." Hand waved nonchalantly at the dark horizon as an all encompassing gesture for the Academy. Throat cleared with a chest rattled cough before Clay continued while he faced rolling waves.

"A house and kids. That was my future. With Sandra." Another paused moment as emotion was carefully battened down. A slight quaver still resonated in Clay's voice.

"I'm haunted by your sister's ghost. Each choice I make reflects the man I was supposed to be. The man who married Sandra. She's gone and I'm stuck here. Lost in perpetual hell. Not because of Sandy but because of me. I'm trapped between the man I should have become and the man I've tried to emulate. I'm either an unrealized husband or a copy of your aspirations. And I'm neither."

Stillness settled over them as Kyle waited for the announcement he now suspected was imminent. The academy was his dream, not Clay's. Lips remained sealed to allow one of his best friends to pour out his heart uninterrupted.

"I can't go back. Without her, there's nothing to go back to. And I signed the same contract as you did, Kyle, so the next decade will be in the Protectorate. Just not here. Not with the Warriors."

The words tumbled free. With the revelation off his chest Clay assumed the burden lifted. However, all they did was curve his shoulders inward under the weight of guilt. The choice to abandon Kyle. Hands pressed into the sandy carpet of the beach as Kyle stood and walked around Clay who refused to turn and face his friend in the moment of betrayal. Either side of Clay's head was grabbed by Kyle who pulled the taller man's face down to his level.

"About time you realized that. You need to find your way, so do it. And don't think you are losing me as a friend because you are not my friend. You're my brother. My family. That means you're stuck with me for the long haul. Wait, I've got something …" Hand released its hold on Clay's face as it delved deep into the sweatpants' pocket. Kyle pulled his hand free and opened it, palm up, before Clay. A bronzed, five pointed star rested there. The wreath encircled star was perched on by an eagle which rested upon a central bar that read 'VALOR'.

"The one item my father treasured above all his other possessions. His Medal of Honor. The day we left he must have stuck this into my boot. Along with a note. 'You never know what you are made of until you enter the Crucible. You never know who you are until you pass the Crucible.' Right now, this turmoil you feel, this is your crucible. Listen brother, I'm here for whatever you might need." Kyle pulled the bigger man into an embrace. Long moments passed before they finally parted. A last gesture, Kyle took Clay's hand and pressed the medal into his palm before he closed his fingers around it.

"Keep it." A hard lump formed in his throat. Kyle knew there was one more announcement to come.

"I'm transferring up north. New York. A fresh start, you know? No ghosts everywhere I look." Shame etched deeply on Clay's face. A fist lanced out sharply and careened off Clay's bicep that elicited a short bark of surprise and pain. Hand rubbed bicep as Clay stared at Kyle who smirked as he turned away with a wave.

""Come on Lurch. We've got a celebration to throw and a reputation to make. Give them a legend to retell every year." A hurried flurry of feet scattered sand as Clay caught up. The two men returned to the bonfire surrounded by a small representation of first year cadets. With a shake of his head Kyle watched as Clay headed for the s'mores which were in the process of being made. A grunt escaped when he sat on one of the oversized logs used as a makeshift bench. Smoothed from nature's fury, Kyle slipped down the side of it choosing to lean against it instead. The sand made for a more comfortable seat anyways. Returned with s'mores in one hand and drinks in the other, Clay passed a bottle while he kept both s'mores. The bottle was tipped for a deep draught before Kyle paused in mid swig.

Across the bonfire Gale watched him with a chilling expression. Firelight glinted a weak, sickly green reflection across her eyes until she blinked. The mirage of jade disappeared into brown eyes and a demure smile hidden by the curtain of her hair as Gale turned to speak to one of the others near her.

A chill crept up his spine as he remembered the flashlight and spiders.

HERO WORSHIP

Unconsciously aware, Kyle found himself sitting in a grey mist. Head turned on a swivel at the barest movement. Four sets of eyes glinted from the depths of obscurity. Without moving he tensed as the creatures approached into sight. It wasn't four creatures but a single one. A spider the size of one of the coolers that littered the beach walked forward on eight slender legs. Fur bristled on the appendages that moved ungainly. Malevolence oozed from the dark intent reflected in the arachnid.

As Kyle prepared to rise, another figure appeared behind the large spider. A hissing sound reverberated from the spider as its front appendages rubbed together. Another noise drifted from the femine figure outlined in the fog as her feet rustled the grass.

Once the spider heard the noise behind, it scurried away to once more disappear in the mist. Tentative steps drew the woman closer. Features that were once unformed finally smoothed into a visage he recognized.

"Sandy."

The youthful form of his sister closed the distance and wrapped her arms around Kyle. Reciprocating, Kyle tightened the embrace. Soft words whispered into his ear.

"You have to go back. It's coming, for both of us. Go back. GO!" Dainty hands, he remembered oh so well, shoved against his chest. As he fell back the vision of Sandy spun on one heel and ran back into the mist.

Butt hit the sand. Eyes blinked several times before he knew he wasn't hallucinating. Sand, fires, tents, and his fellow freshmen were all around. A shiver wracked Kyle and he exhaled a shaky breath. Hand swept across his face roughly rubbing away confusion.

A dream. Only a vivid dream as he dozed fireside in relaxation.

With a glance to the ocean he saw fog as it rolled inland. Too many horror stories began with fog.

Leaned back against the log he slipped from, Kyle noticed a figure droping from above. Heart beat fast as pulse raced upon recognition.

The Champion. Firelight cast angles on his face, sharp features accented by shadows. Cool breeze ruffled his dark hair. He wore the black uniform engraved with the golden Spire upon the chest. Every one of them at the academy aspired to wear the uniform. To be counted among the Warriors.

Here he was, the Champion, descended from on high to consort with mere mortals The breeze that chilled the freshmen left no mark on the Champion. Only the black cape humored mother nature with ripples.

Half the apprentices surrounded him while the other half remained frozen in place. The Champion was the first superhero. What they all aspired to be. A deep voice boomed.

"Glad to see so many recruits. I just wanted to stop by and congratulate all of you for making it this far. You, big man. Are you shooting for a spot with the Warriors?" The Champion looked at Clay who opened his mouth but nothing came out. A good natured chuckle rolled from the Champion who nodded.

"Don't worry about it son. Happens to all of us", his hands opened wide to make himself part of the statement. Up front Gale raised her hand in an attempt to catch the Champion's attention.

"This isn't class. Put your hand down and speak", Champion said with a smile while he waved her forward. Clearly nervous, Gale spoke anyway.

"What's your favorite part? As a warrior. What's the worst part?" Slowly he scanned the crowd, his gaze locked on each for a moment then moved on. The ease of his smile pulled them into his confidence.

"This, right here. What you are building everyday with one another. A family. That is, without a doubt, the best thing the Warriors have given me." Almost every head nodded in agreement with his words. Less than a year at the academy and each of them felt the bonds the Warrior spoke of. Then Champion lowered his voice so that all needed to lean forward to hear his following words.

"The worst part also begins right here. Not all of you will make it to the Warriors. Some of you will become Guardians, which is just as important as being a Warrior. Some will wash out. And some will not make it through training. It happens sometimes, and it hurts regardless. Those that do muster through graduation and make the teams will find a camaraderie closer than family. Unfortunately, the danger we face exacts a price. Friends will die."

All listened in rapt attention, leaned forward to hang on his every word. Again, Champion scanned the freshmen with a sad smile on his face.

"Embrace life. Grow stronger together. Always look out for one another. But this is the holidays! So enjoy your downtime and have fun with traditions handed down to you by those that came before. I look forward to serving with you. Happy holidays." With that, the Champion flew away.

Excited voices contended to be heard as all were starstruck.

The crowd dissipated back to their original places. Hands pressed back against the log to stand. Nonchalantly Kyle moved to the depression where his hero just stood. Clay joined him.

"Can you believe it? The Champion just told us good luck", Clay gushed.

"I know right?" Dropped to a knee, Kyle pulled something half hidden within the sand. Hand raised and offered the device to Clay.

"What do you make of this?"

"A tracker."

"Really? You don't say? Of course it's a tracker you buffoon. But why? That's the question", Kyle shook his head at his friend.

"So they want to know exactly where we are", Clay shrugged as though the matter was settled.

"But why?"

"I don't know. Though he did say something about embracing traditions."

The two men looked at each other without an answer. Commotion behind caused both to turn. A large group of apprentices emerged from the trees that lined the beach. There was no way to identify who they were as the fog rolled across the beach. However, one did stand out. Compared to the group the lone figure stood tall, nearly twice as tall as the other students with him. There was only one person at the academy with that size and stature.

"That's Goliath", Clay pointed out.

"Thanks captain obvious."

Realization gripped both men simultaneously. The reason for the locator and the appearance of the senior class meant only one thing. A yearly tradition at the academy between seniors and freshmen.

Initiation prank.

Other freshmen were slow to react as the seniors shouldered weapons. Macy, a long legged freshman who always wore a smile, raised a hand to wave. A pop sounded and she jerked her hand back. In the firelight the center of her hand oozed a dark green. Time froze as all eyes watched Macy. Hand dropped limply at her side and she staggered. Three more pops coincided with an equal number of green smears across her exposed midriff.

When she collapsed the spell was broken.

The senior class opened fire on the freshmen. Immediately Kyle and Clay dove into the sand, random shots sprayed sand into their faces. Nearby Gale and two other girls also laid prostrated as freshmen jumped around and tried to avoid the projectiles.

"Clay, Gale, we need to make a break for the trees", Kyle shouted. Together they rose to their feet and ran. Behind the two men, Gale let out a screech. Paused, Kyle backtracked and looped an arm under her shoulders. On the ground lay the two other girls splattered with green goo. With a grunt Kyle shuffled with Gale until two more hits stiffened her body before she went limp and crumpled to the sand. Clay tackled Kyle as rounds buzzed over their heads.

The rounds flew through the air to splatter on the freshmen. The two men finally realized what the seniors were using. Paintballs filled with an instantaneous neurotoxin. Designed to be absorbed through the skin, the thickened gel was a paralytic. The dropping freshmen were proof to its potency.

Low to the ground, Kyle and Clay sprinted for the cover of the trees. Several other apprentices split off and ran for the treeline. As Kyle and Clay reached the edge of the trees there were the sounds of more firing. Those who entered before the two men cried out before they fell silent.

Ambush.

Groups of seniors were on either side of the attackers on the beach. Too late to retreat. Teeth grit in anticipation of being hit. Best chance of escape lay in the accelerated charge into the seniors who fired with abandon. A hundred paces in and they finally ran into the shooters.

Startled at the sudden appearance of Kyle and Clay, their shots went wide.

Determination drove Kyle forward as Clay outpaced him. A sting at the nape of Kyle's neck flushed hot then immediately cold. Body grew numb as he stumbled. Coordination failed and his foot caught on an exposed root. Arms didn't work so he slammed into the ground hard. A brief glimpse of Clay's back showed he escaped. Not Kyle.

Arms and legs lay immobilized as Kyle tried to muster strength into action. It didn't work. Instead he lay dormant until one of the seniors found him. Roughly he was dragged back to the beach and dropped among the group of freshmen caught in the trees.

Eyes flickered to movement and saw what the seniors were doing. One by one each freshmen was stripped of all clothing before being raised up against a tree trunk. Duct tape went round and round until the apprentice resembled a silvery sheened mummy. All except for the head.

Another apprentice was stripped, Kevin, and the process began anew. Sympathetic pains ran down his spine. Poor bastard. Kevin was a very hairy man. On top of that there was also the adhesive tape wrapped around his groin.

Kyle was determined not to end up like that.

Several minutes passed as he laid there. None of the other freshmen stirred. Only eyes darted to and fro. The fog thickened as it encroached further inland. A new sensation stirred upon his skin. Pins and needles puckered his flesh as feeling returned.

Half the senior class lounged around the campfire and enjoyed the supplies the freshmen class brought. The other half grew complacent. Secure in their own superiority they left their paintball guns on the nearby sand. The largest of the group paced about as he raised a bottle of liquor to his lips. Goliath thought he was invincible. Soon Kyle would disprove the foolish notion.

Nerves screamed as feeling returned, his fingers flexed to see how much control he possessed. Not enough to matter. Epiphany slapped Kyle in the face when he remembered the embedded comlink. Quietly he whispered.

"Munin. Are you there?" A moment of silence sank his hope. Then he heard the voice of the AI.

"Literally? I am not. Technically? I am."

"Gods … can you help me or not?"

"I have been ordered to remain silent over the duration of the hazing incident. I cannot inform instructors or any other authority."

A frustrated sigh escaped. Of course there were orders in place. The group of seniors returned and grabbed another young man for his turn. Rage at his slow acting ability consumed him. Then his jaw vibrated.

"However, I have no orders pertaining to other freshmen. Specifically Clay Issacs." Lips almost pulled back into a smile.

"Brilliant. Can you open a secure channel between us?"

"Already done." A new voice vibrated in Kyle's ear.

"Looks like they bagged and tagged you. I think I'm the only one who got away. I'm at the edge of the treeline. What are they doing?" Amusement was easily heard in Clay's voice.

"See for yourself", Kyle spoke quietly. Sharp eyes scanned the trees and finally saw Clay barely peeking from cover.

"Wow … that looks rough. Oh, poor Kevin."

The group of seniors doing the work joined the other group around the campfire. Carefree, they believed they were safe. At least there was a momentary reprieve from naked apprentices being duct taped. As the two men observed, they both came to the same conclusion.

The senior class acted like a pack of dogs. Together they were ferocious. But they all looked to the alpha of the pack. The strongest of them all. Goliath.

"You know, if we drop the giant and then strafe the rest, they're gonna break and hightail it out of here", muttered Kyle.

"Of course that's your plan. You want to fight the biggest, strongest, and meanest person I've ever met. Why the hell am I surprised? You have a plan? That doesn't involve me being beaten to a pulp." The sound of exasperation was easily heard in Clay's voice. Kyle actually did manage a smile that time.

"This is what we're gonna do …"

VIII
LEGEND OF THE FLAMINGO FLAPPING FLORIDA MAN

November 26, 2026
9:32 p.m.

"That's a terrible plan", gripped Clay.

"Yeah, maybe. But look at it this way, you will become legendary."

"Not how I planned to be remembered."

"If only Sandy and Sage were here to see this."

"If they were here we would have a good plan. Not this hairbrained, completely ridiculous, asinine plan."

"Yeah, maybe."

While Kyle explained his idea Clay moved north of the firepit while he remained hidden in the treeline. South of the fire laid Kyle. The last several minutes Kyle tensed muscles to warm up for the action. Fog created a hazed blanketing on the beach

For a brief moment Kyle remembered the vivid dream. The mist that swirled echoed the fog that embraced the beach. A chill ran up his spine as though something or someone watched him.

And then it was go time.

"Caw-caw! Caw-caw! Caw-caw!"

A figure broke from the anonymity of the foliage. The voice cried out in horrible mimicry of a crow. While that was disconcerting, it wasn't the oddest aspect. In each hand Clay held a palm frond as he flapped his arms. Even more disturbing than the high pitched caw-caw. Stiil, it was the third thing in combination with the other actions that made for a sight Kyle would never forget. No matter how much he may drink to erase the imagery.

Palm fronds flapped the cold air while Clay continued to shriek. A randomly sized figure eight was created as Clay ran in circles. A silent curse escaped while Kyle wished he was able to record the scene.

Clay was butt naked.

Every senior stood dumbfounded by the display before them. Some shook their heads in horror as others laughed uncontrollably. More than a few of the women in the group grinned with obvious appreciation for Clay's build.

Without waiting, Kyle forced his body into a leopard crawl across coarse, cold sand. In only a handful of seconds he reached the paintball guns. Each hand grabbed one before he rose unsteadily to his feet.

The guns were lined up straight at Goliath. Several rounds flew out and smashed into the back of the giant's head. The senior class pivoted to see Kyle before them. With a roar Goliath charged. Two rounds splattered on Goliath's forehead. To his credit, the giant managed two more strides before falling face first into the sand.

The conundrum was etched on their faces. Attack or retreat?

To offer more time to decide was not in the plan. As quick as he could Kyle feathered the triggers and strafed the group. As easy as shooting fish in a barrel. Now he understood the antiquated saying. They scattered like cockroaches, frenzied scurry for safety.

By the time the survivors disappeared into the trees over two thirds of the senior class lay motionless on the sands.

With a palm frond over his groin and the other at his backside, Clay joined Kyle.

"I don't see them coming back", said Clay.

"I agree."

"Now what?" A smirk stretched across Kyle's face at the question.

"Now we give as well as we got. Let's pull all of our people into their tents. Then cut down our classmates. As for the seniors? Payback."

The next morning the apprentices stirred from their tents and saw a spectacle. Trees held the seniors securely to their trunks. In a pile before them were the seniors' clothes.

Later that day Champion addressed all four years of apprentices in general assembly. Hazing and pranks were not acceptable and would be dealt with severely. Possibly even expelled from the academy. Afterwards Clay let his frustration out.

"Hypocrite. Says don't do it but he helped the seniors with that tracker." With a frown Kyle shook his head.

"I'm sure it was an accident. I mean, this is the Champion we're talking about." The two looked at each other with polar opposite opinions. Shoulders rose and fell as Clay shrugged.

"Well, that's not my problem. Hopefully New York won't have questionable incidents and accidents."

The two decided to agree that they disagreed.

PART THREE:
THE WARRIORS

TWiLiGHT

Thursday, April 25, 2030
7:35 p.m.

What is a superhero? Someone willing to stand up for others through strength of character and conviction and blessed with abilities beyond a baseline human.

Kyle was a superhero.

He stood on the beach, sand enveloped his shiny black boots, a woman and child frolicked in the evening surf with nary a care in the world. The setting sun hovered on the horizon, clouds gently caressed the dying light and were rewarded by an infusion of color that transformed the billowing forms into hues of violet and deep crimson.

A brisk wind swept across the muted waves and wrapped the sodden dress about the woman's curved form. Black hair, salted by the sea, fell in raven ringlets across tanned shoulders revealed by the spaghetti straps of the amber sundress. The young boy played alongside his mother, the shaven head a shade darker than the rest of his bare body. A mirage of steam hissed from his tired body as the woman wrapped him in the hem of her dress and carried his diminutive form to the wet sand before sinking into a feigned pose of relaxation. Long, tapered fingers lightly caressed the boy's fevered brow.

"I'm sorry. Freedom comes with a price", whispered words rolled from the woman as her lips tasted the salt of her own tears.

Kyle walked closer before he knelt beside them. Olive eyes searched his own pale blue before they turned to watch the final vestiges of the disappearing sun.

"You don't have to stay", she said. A sad smile played across his lips as her velvet tone wrapped him with emotions and urges not his own. The desire to rail against the dying sun and scream in impotent fury that masked a deep set, desperate need to find a buoy in the ocean of desperation. However, there would be no salvation. Tears were blinked away and fell unbidden upon shaven cheeks.

Today he was a superhero.

DAWN OF A WARRIOR

12 hours earlier ...
Thursday, April 25, 2030
7:35 a.m.

Today he was a superhero..

He stood on the beach, sand enveloped his shiny black boots laced to the knees. The newly risen sun cast its warm light upon the golden accents engraved upon the black armored suit. A spire of gold pierced the left breast of dark armor directly over his heart. The resemblance to the Citadel on Anastasia Island was not lost.

Newly promoted from apprentice to the Warriors meant he could now wear the symbol of the Spire. Lines of gold stretched from the sigil and ran from the artistic depiction throughout the entire suit of black. The uniform worn by all Warriors. Warm fingers caressed the symbol with awe.

Yesterday he was an apprentice.

Today he was a superhero.

Not just any superhero but one of the Warriors of Anastasia Island. With nearly a decade of tradition and legacy, Kyle was honored to call the Olympus Spire home. A Protectorate bastion of defense against domestic threats.

A clench of his jaw activated the comlink embedded in the bone. A slight hiss whispered the activation from the filaments wrapped around the ear drum.

"Time?" The words were a bare whisper.

"7:37 a.m. Journeyman Ross." The emotionless tone of Munin purred, audible only to Kyle. With a smirk he gave the rising sun a final glance before he turned to leave the beach. Dune grass sought purchase but found none as he quickly retraced his steps through the scenic foliage before the boots found the boardwalk that led to where the Spire pierced the heavens above. The silver sheen of modern architecture reflected the sunlight in prismatic glory.

"It would not make a favorable first impression to be late, Journeyman Ross." A chuckle escaped Kyle as the boots touched the paved section of the walkway leading to the main entrance of the Spire. Paused to allow a troop of jogging freshmen to pass, he shook his head at their apparent youth and newb status. A smirk stretched across his face at the knowledge that they lacked any idea what the next four years would be like.

With an easy pace he continued forward near the entrance to the Spire, eyes taking in the Guardians stationed on either side of the doors. Their gaze pierced his skin, accusatory and envious with an overwhelming sense of responsibility and duty. They were the ones who graduated from apprentice but didn't make the team for Journeyman.

It was a possible reality for all the apprentices should they not prove themselves.

The sheer, glass doors slid open without a sound, cold air ruffling his blonde flattop, barely regulation, and gave him a slight shivered chill at the temperature difference. The front desk sat in isolation, the lone crescent desk flanked by more Guardians who missed nothing with their eagle eyed stares.

The uniform granted Kyle unaccosted passage while the A.I.

approved of his credentials and clearance. For without the necessary authorization, the Guardians would have apprehended him forcibly. Or at least tried. The idea of the Guardians attempting to stop him brought a grin to his face.

"I calculate a forty seven percent chance of success against your unauthorized entry." Munin's silent words were like an internal monologue by an angel on his shoulder. Perceptive of her.

The lift doors opened on the elevator as he crossed the threshold. Imperceptibly the doors closed as the lift raised on magnetic rails. The glass walls of the cubicle offered a clear view of the lobby while he rose past each subsequent level.

The distant grey marble of the lobby floor caused a momentary thought of 'what if'. A fall from those heights, already seven levels up, would be unpleasant yet survivable. Kyle hoped he made the team by being top of the class, but knew the likelihood of his promotion was due to his ability. The codename left no doubt to what he truly was.

Aegis. Shield of the Gods.

It was fitting that he was bulletproof, or nearly so. A literal shield between the gods and their foes. The thoughts swirled and he hoped he was wrong. That he wasn't a sacrificial lamb used to cover others with the protective qualities of his body. One day he hoped he would stand among the pantheon accepted as an equal based on merit and skill.

The doors silently opened on the top floor. As he stepped out it was like he entered a fairy tale.

A table sat at the center surrounded by chairs of finely lacquered mahogany that matched the pristine tabletop. The one way, floor to ceiling, windows offered a majestic view of lush Anastasia Island and the crystalline Atlantic Ocean to the east. Boots sank half an inch into a deep burgundy carpet that enveloped his boots as though a welcoming cushion made of soft, billowy clouds.

Breath caught in his chest as the reality finally began to sink in. Finally, he was a Warrior. No, not just a Warrior but a member of

Alpha Team. Pulse raced to the rapid beat of Kyle's heart while his mouth grew dry. This was real.

A throat cleared behind him, a rasping cough carefully cultivated to shock by its nearness. Instinctively he turned and found himself staring into a chest. Or was it a wall garbed in the Spire emblem? A glance up and his mouth went from cotton dry to desert parched with nary a hint of moisture.

The giant before him was pale as milk. A crown of hair so dark it had highlights of blue shimmered in the sunlight piercing the room. Eyes of equal darkness gazed upon Kyle as though a cat with a mouse. Instantly, he felt the first true pangs of fear, in years, travel down his spine with an involuntary shiver that was very perceptible. Colorless lips stretched impossibly wide over sharpened teeth that looked as inviting as a two week starved hyena.

"Jack, I see you've met the newest member of the team. Welcome aboard Ross, or do you prefer Aegis?" A deep voice echoed from behind the massive wall that was Jack Harrington, aka The Hound, who still stared with soulless eyes and alabaster skin.

Without sound the Hound, for Kyle didn't believe he could ever humanize the man with the name Jack, circled him and took a seat at the table. There stood The Champion, Jon Franklin, leader of Alpha Team. An average sized man with dark hair and brown eyes, the Champion was the face of the Warriors since the beginning. An easy smile creased his face causing dimples to appear while the man reached out a hand for me to grasp.

Kyle's hero wanted to shake his hand. A euphoric haze surrounded him as his right hand was wrapped by Champion's own. White teeth flashed, nearly blinding Kyle who was starstruck in frozen fangirl mode. His left hand clasped Kyle's shoulder as he steered the newest Warrior to a vacant seat next to the Hound. Personal preference of seating forgotten as the chair touched the back of his legs.

"Ross, sir. Or Aegis, whichever is fine sir." Champion's hand patted Kyle's shoulder while a smile that revealed bemused acceptance that this was the reaction he would always receive. As the Champion moved to the head of the table, though that was impossible for a round table, Kyle idly wondered if this was how his father felt when he was presented the Medal of Honor by the president.

The doors to the lift opened once more and two figures eased to the table with fluid grace.

Henry "the Tank" Kitridge was a squat, barrel chested man with a darkly bearded face that appeared to have gone twelve rounds against a baseball bat. The man moved to the opposite side of the table and sat across from Kyle. The chair creaked in protest at the Tank's girth.

Beside Kyle perched Ellen "Starburst" Paige. Dainty hands lightly drummed on the armrest as a tight lipped smile was offered in greetings. The angular lines of her face were reminiscent of an elf. The prominent blonde widow's peak was pulled back into a tight ponytail that rested just above the collar of her outfit in straight uniformity.

"Anything new, Franklin?" The voice that escaped sounded like a mountain avalanche. The gravelly bass timbre sounded as rough hewn as Tank looked. Champion shook his head in the negative.

"Nothing new to report. Team two is still in Orlando. Looks like the Intel we received was wrong." The Hound leaned back in his seat before he turned his massive frame to look at Kyle with a feral grin that glinted eerily as he spoke.

"Of course it was. Came from the flatliners." The Champion shook his head in silent reprimand. Flatliner was the derogatory term for baseline humans, those who weren't Supers.

Fingers tapped the tabletop to gain the team's attention. Once all were focused once more, Champion continued.

"The Liberators, our brothers in New York, are still reporting missing precogs. And empaths. Charlatans and telepaths. They believe there may be killers that are specifically targeting them. Or a more powerful precog knocking off the competition. Working theories with no hard evidence."

With a slight frown Kyle leaned to his right, unconsciously putting a few more inches of empty space between him and the giant. Tank watched with deep set, unfathomable eyes. Starburst shook her head at the Hound's antics which set the end of her ponytail into a bobbing motion above the nape of her graceful neck. Champion sighed audibly and opened his mouth in retort to the obvious issue but never got the chance.

The lift doors opened a final time and Hallan Branch spilled out. The milken eyes contrasted deeply with his dark skin. However, it wasn't his blindness that was offsetting but his ability to see everything at once. The different levels of levity and animosity fled the table as the Wizard turned sightless eyes to the team with an announcement.

"Fed-X just turned themselves into the New York Protectorate. Catch 22 himself. Just gave himself up after a decade."

An audible gasp of disbelief rippled through them all, none greater than Kyle who grew up reading about the clashes between the Protectorate and Fed-X who both fought for what they believed in. Each side looked at the other as the villain while believing they were the heroes and every super was faced with a choice for what they believed in. The Hound slammed an angered blow to the tabletop even as Champion rose to his feet with a warm smile.

"Stop it, today is a momentous day. The day Fed-X accepted the truth that the Protectorate is the righteous and just branch of Supers. We should celebrate." The team at the table wore different expressions, Starburst watched Wizard as though she knew there was more to tell.

And so it did.

"Catch turned himself in but he's blowing up the airwaves." The Wizard swallowed, his Adam's apple prominently rising above his collar.

"Information streaming on almost every channel while also flowing through space. I can barely see through the patterns.

There's a power spike right where he said there is." Hallan waved a hand through unseen obstacles before him as he inspected the invisible. Fingers jabbed the air before him. Kyle stared in confusion which prompted Starburst to lean over and speak quietly.

"That's his gift. Somehow he's able to manipulate the electromagnetic radiation, to see different frequencies and oscillations. Between his brain and eyes he's able to filter through and understand things without needing a computer or tv. All this information that floats all around us is there for him to see and rifle through. See his hands? Think of it as an interactive three dimensional display that only he can see and hear. And only he can interact with it. Everything that transmits passes before him. He's a receiver that deciphers transmitted signals."

Kyle nodded though he could only grasp a rudimentary idea of the process she described.

"Now I see. A woman on Catch's team named Pulsar. She's very good, almost as good as I am. One of the reasons they've stayed off the grid so well. She's sending out some kind of automated signal in a pulse pattern. Hold on."

The team quietly watched and listened as Wizard worked, his hands weaved invisibly through patterns and frequencies only he could see. And then he turned to his left as fingers pulled at some unseen thread of information that caused Hallan to release a soft gasp. A hand flicked at the space before him as he turned toward the table and the rest of the team.

"Computer, pull up reports from the gulf of Mexico. Anomalies in sonar frequencies. Overlay with discoveries of dead whales and dolphins. Now one more layer, news of rabid bat attacks."

The computer brought three holograms to life over the table, each unique layouts of western Florida and the gulf. Yet as the holograms merged a pattern was seen in waves of oddities occurring from a singular, central point. Taurus Island, Florida.

Champion rose from his seat and leaned forward, palms flat on the tabletop as he scrutinized the hologram layout that writhed slowly as time progressed forward. Eyes narrowed darkly as he turned his head to Wizard, eyes still locked onto the display, and questioned his friend and ally.

"So you believe Catch turned himself in to bring attention to this situation? Instead of coming south and Fed-X handling it themselves?" Wizard nodded slowly to the question and knowing what the follow up would be, he chose to answer it before it was uttered.

"These reports seem to agree on two things. One, the source of this phenomena is strengthening in power. And two, whatever, whoever, this is will peak in the next several hours. And when it does it could very well kill anything within range. And possibly destroy all infrastructure as well."

A thrill of anticipation and forewarning ran up Kyle's spine with the next words spoken.

"Warriors, we leave in ten."

NOTHING GOOD COMES FROM HEIGHTS

Thursday, April 25, 2030
8:32 a.m.

The seat's restraints dug deeply into the uniform he wore. An assault rifle rested within the boot attached to the wall behind him. As did his shield, shaped similarly to a deputy marshal's badge. A heater shield design that narrowed to a point at the bottom.

His first day as a Warrior and they were being sent with the QRF, Quick Response Force. On the opposite wall, across the row from Kyle, sat Starburst in quiet conversation with Wizard. Catching Kyle's gaze, she faced him as her hands tested the seat restraints against her chest. "Don't overthink things Journeyman. Just do what you're told, follow orders, remember your training, and don't try to be a hero." She turned back to her quiet conversation. His dismissal was without a second thought.

Their jet was just one of several that departed Anastasia Island. Shortly after they departed Team 2, led by Titan, left Orlando en route to the location. They would be arriving mere minutes before Kyle's group from the Citadel.

Already closing in on the island, they began to listen in to communications. The island seemed to be nearly abandoned, only a few signs of human life and residency. At Wizard's request, the computer activated a projector into the central aisle which allowed the team to view the live feed from Team 2.

As they watched, the jet began to fly erratically, the force of the maneuvers slammed the team into their seats and against the restraints that held them in place. Suddenly the floor ripped away from the jet, three members of Team 2 being sucked from the plane even as the jet slammed to the ground in a roll. The wings wrapped around the body of the jet for a bare moment before the fuel reserves exploded, ending the footage.

Kyle released a shaky exhale, unaware of the fact he held his breath at the catastrophe witnessed. A look across the aisle and he saw Starburst grow even more pale as Wizard closed his eyes.

He wondered briefly when the blind man closed his eyes if he was able to cut off the stream of information he saw without the use of his eyes. Kyle figured that the constant barrage of information would drive one mad. All eyes fell to Champion who wore a determined expression which galvanized their failing courage and shaken disbelief.

As Champion studied the holographic display, Kyle fidgeted in his seat. While he didn't personally know the Warriors that died there was still a pang of loss. Those were superheroes like him. And they were snuffed from this life like feathery dandelion seeds tossed by the wind.

A chirp across the comlinks echoed in Kyle's ear as Champion spoke to command and gave them a sitrep. Eyes closed as Kyle listened to the report. An acknowledgement of civilians was given. At the end Champion recommended an air strike if their team failed. Head turned so Kyle could look at Champion. The Warriors were there to eliminate the threat, not kill innocent civilians.

When Champion finished his report, Kyle interjected.

"Sir, I didn't sign up to murder innocents." With a turn of his head, Champion looked at Kyle with guarded eyes.

"Neither did I, son. But sometimes there's collateral damage.

And sometimes we must acknowledge the necessity for evil actions. For the greater good."

Heavy silence descended on the team. Before Champion could rouse their spirits with words their jet joined the others in evasive maneuvering as an unseen attack rose from the island with lethal intent. One moment saw Kyle pressed back against his seat. Blood tried to drain into his feet as Kyle fought to keep his eyes open.

And then the next moment the restraints valiantly denied gravity. Belts dug into uniforms and the flesh beneath as the force of the maneuver sawed the restraints into flesh. His head began to pound as the pressure beat with the force of a jackhammer behind his eyes. A great shudder tore the jet, black smoke rolled through and made visibility impossible. Heat licked at his exposed skin as he breathed in tendrils of smoke that choked lungs. Another explosion shredded the ceiling of the plane, the smoke sweeping from the ship as flames engulfed the cockpit.

Munin echoed in Kyle's ear yet a different sound blanketed out the words with a high pitched squelch that grew in intensity with every second passed. Through determination he forced his eyes to look up at the holes in the ship. He was gifted with a sight that confounded his senses momentarily.

Above them was a landscape surrounded by water. Other jets flew by while rotated belly up. One crashed into the side of a business. As their jet rose to meet this land of reverse Kyle realized the truth.

They were the ones upside down.

With moments left before their ship crashed he couldn't help but laugh at the absurdness of the situation. Somehow the computer managed to remotely rotate the ship and pull the jet up out of its steep dive. But not enough. The jet hit hard enough to snap the nose off, the shattered wreckage flew by above them. Then the wrecked ship crashed through a glass lobby of a several story building. Finally darkness claimed Kyle into unconsciousness.

IV
DREAMSCAPE

The cloying scent of rotting flesh invaded his nostrils. With a gag, Kyle woke. A grey mist encompassed him and the darkened clouds hung low in the sky. Sickly grass cushioned his backside where he laid. A groan escaped as he stood.

Turning in a circle to find his bearings did little to help his disorientation. An open meadow of dying grass rose waist high. Around the perimeter were ancient trees partially hidden by the misted breath oozing from the forest. An ominous presence stretched from trees and caressed bare meadow with cold fingers.

A chill caused him to shiver. It wasn't the cool temperature or brisk breeze. No. It was the lingering touch of death. The sensation of being watched and hunted. Trees cracked and shattered as something headed for the meadow.

Quietly he crouched down, half submerged in the field. The fog thickened as though a red carpet unrolled for a celebrity. But in the barren land there was no joviality. Vigilantly Kyle remained hidden within the grass and fog. Air shimmered and condensed into the figure of a woman. Detail was hard to see through the low visibility. However, he didn't need sharp eyesight to see the creature that emerged from the woods.

A spider, larger than a man, skittered forward into the field. It approached the woman who stood with slumped shoulders and bowed head. When the creature reached the woman, it circled her twice before stopping before her. The woman dropped on her knees with head barely visible.

"I did what you wanted me to. Please … please let me and my son go."

The creature chittered as its body vibrated. Then the voice came out. Honeyed tone, sickly sweet, fell from the abomination.

"You are free when I say you are. First there is one more thing that needs to be done."

At that moment the breeze started to rise in strength. Unable to hear the words snatched by the wind, Kyle crawled forward slowly and quietly. After a minute of tensed approach he could finally hear the conversation. The woman begged her case between sobs.

"You said we would be free if I did what you said." The creature rose to its full height as the words were spat out.

"Foolish girl! I could snuff the light out of your soul with a single gesture. With a sweep of my leg I can take your boy and use him for sustenance as I slowly drain his life. Now you know what I want from you. Do it and I shall grant you safe passage across the mists of the veil. Disobey me and I will visit upon you pain unimaginable. Torment unfathomable. Do you understand?"

The woman sobbed as Kyle moved even closer.

"I'll do it. I promise."

"Yes. Yes you will. Be thankful I have my eyes on a prized prey or I would have taken you for myself."

A dried stick snapped from beneath Kyle's body. With a blur of motion the creature leapt forward as Kyle clambered to his feet. All he had time for was to watch the woman disappear as eerily as she appeared. Then one of the creature's legs swiped at Kyle's head. The force of the blow sent him cartwheeling through the air, pain lanced his face.

When Kyle's body hit the ground darkness surrounded him.

DUTY

Thursday, April 25, 2030
5:12 p.m.

Drip. Drip. Drip.

Droplets of water cascaded down to splash upon his face. The coolness brought him from the fog that enveloped his brain. Heavy eyelids opened as clumsy fingers depressed the restraint release and slid from his seat to collapse in a puddle. Hands formed a ladle and he scooped the water like a shovel to splash onto his face. Gingerly he rubbed away the crust upon his upper lip. A sneeze sent a clotted glob of blood from his nostrils and down his chest.

Groggily he used the seat to get his legs back underneath him and stood. Slowly he turned to assist his teammates. Tank was still suspended with his torso gripped by the safety belts. But at some point as they crash landed an obstacle took off the bottom half of Tank's seat. And his lower extremities with it.

Turned from the grizzly scene he went next to Starburst. Her chest still rose and fell to a shallow rhythm while a blood trail ran from her eyes, ears, and nose. A hand raised to his own and found that he shared the same injuries as the petite woman. Wizard still remained whole and was currently awake. Currently he struggled, fingers seeking to detach the harness that kept him in place during the crash.

A look at the ruin of the ship and he nodded at a decision made while Wizard attempted to raise anyone on comms. With arms slipped under Starburst's shoulder and knees, Kyle stood and moved to one of the great rents in the jet. Careful of the edges they slipped into the ruined lobby of the building they plowed into.

"We should move out of the wreckage. Take up a position in the lobby somewhere unseen. You manage to raise anyone on that?" With lowered voice Kyle nodded slightly at the portable communicator in Wizard's hand. As gently as possible, Kyle crouched down and laid Starburst behind the alcove of the desk that once served a purpose as a welcome station. Now it worked rather nicely as a barricade.

"Nothing, like our communications are being jammed. I can't reach anyone with this", Wizard tossed the communication device and dropped below the top of the desk to hold his side gingerly. "And I think I have a few broken ribs." With a shake of his head the fog wore off nearly completely. Pointedly Kyle looked at the comatose woman to ensure there was no miscommunication that Wizard should stay.

"I'm grabbing some gear. You stay with her."

Quickly he crossed the lobby, boots ground shattered glass into a marble floor and etched deep scratches across its surface. Careful to avoid the jagged edges and not risk injury Kyle crept back into the ship. Of course that would be the perfect ending for a perfect mission, accidentally falling on the serrated edges of the ragged openings. Survive a crash and die from clumsiness.

Boots stepped back down into the pool of water. He collected a medkit and tossed it over his shoulder before grabbing two assault rifles. Another slip through the sharpened edges of the hull again and Kyle paused to look and listen down the street.

Shouts and screams were intermingled with explosions and gunfire. With a deepened frown he moved back to settle behind the confines of the desk. Body popped as he squatted down beside Wizard.

"Our communications are down. Starburst is out. And you are injured. I hear a battle going on a few blocks away and, unless the enemy decided to fight amongst themselves, we have friendlies there too. Maybe they have a way to extract the two of you. See what you can do for her and keep your head down. Don't be a hero."

The irony caused Kyle to smirk at using the last thing Starburst told him. And then it was time to move. With rifle shouldered he eased from the shell of the building and glanced down the streets. Just that morning the city appeared well kept, wholesome and unblemished. But after the course of a small amount of time the conflict already ravaged portions of the streets and buildings.

Cautiously he eased south and kept the rifle at the ready while he avoided the debris that littered the earth. It wasn't until he went a block south and two more blocks east that he reached the site of battle. Half a dozen entrenched Guardians fired on a couple of men. One easily kept the troops down with some form of energy blasts that were fired from glowing hands. The concrete barriers the troops used were being destroyed with every energy blast. The other man was engaged with Champion and the Hound.

Frank Baxter used to be a pitcher in the Major Leagues with a fastball that broke records for quickest pitch ever. Three years of pitching no hitters came crumbling down when at practice one day he discovered a teammate was sleeping with his wife. He threw the ball with such force that the ball obliterated his friend's skull. Going on the run, he eventually was said to have joined a group of supers in Florida. And here was the proof as he fired two more chunks of concrete at Champion who weaved through the sky as a distraction. The Hound crept closer behind Baxter in short bursts of speed to move from shelter to shelter and close the distance with the enemy.

One of the Guardians fell with a hole the size of a fist burned through his torso which drew Kyle's attention back to the first man.

With a running jump Kyle launched himself over a pile of rubble. Boots slid across the ground as he shouldered the rifle. Several shots were fired at the enemy who continued to take potshots at the remaining Guardians. A three round burst tracked across the man's back which dropped him unceremoniously to his face where he moved no more.

With Kyle's back turned, Baxter saw him in his peripherals. With a turn the pitcher focused his attention to launch a hand sized chunk of concrete straight at Kyle's back. The impact drove the breath from his lungs and launched him forward to the ground. Vision dimmed momentarily from the missile which slammed into Kyle.

Despite the screams his body offered in protest, he rolled to his side. Through pain fused consciousness he watched Baxter lob another concrete missile at the Hound. The nightmarish Warrior leapt forward and closed the remaining dozen meters between them. The distance between them disappeared with a final rush. The Hound lacked enough time to avoid the blurred projectile he intercepted with his chest. The chunk of concrete continued through the torso and plowed into a wall behind the Hound.

Kyle could see through the Hound's chest cavity.

Champion dropped from the heavens as he used a combination of gravity and his power of flight to accelerate at Baxter. Both fists rammed into his opponent and drove them both to the ground in a heap. Kicked free of one another they both stood and threw a punch. Both landed simultaneously.

Champion's blow landed across Baxter's cheek while his enemy's punch landed on the team leader's left shoulder. Such was the speed of the strike, Champion was knocked an arc across the broken road. Left arm dangled at several wrong angles. Hands shoved himself upright as Kyle staggered over and fell across Champion. Ruthlessly Baxter riddled them with more speeding projectiles which impacted Kyle's back. The thrown makeshift missiles tore through the uniform to create weeping craters in his flesh.

Aegis. His codename.

Ironically, Kyle chose to become what he feared he would be known for. A shield. As a barrier of protection he saved Champion from devastating blows that would have killed him. Instead raised welts and bruises leapt into existence, skin split and blood ran across his back as they skidded across the rough asphalt.

The remaining five Guardians played leapfrog from obstacle to obstacle as they laid down suppression fire. Constantly they moved forward, every second gained ground on Baxter. The pitcher ducked down and reached into the back of a van parked illegally on the sidewalk.

"Yes, let's take him into custody for illegally blocking the sidewalk", Kyle grumbled to himself.

"Al Capone was arrested for tax evasion." The even tone from Munin echoed in his ear.

"Not helping! Not helping!"

Behind the van for a moment, Baxter came back into view. This time he held a young boy in his arms wielded like a shield. Guardians held their fire, unable to get a clear shot. Even over the rapid beat of his heart and the barrage of fire power being released Kyle heard Baxter's shouted order to the boy,

"Kill them all!"

The child, a sickly youth of tender age, screamed in the direction of the Guardians. Sudden nausea and lack of equilibrium gripped Kyle. Sensations denied his attempt to stand. The pressure built in his head and blood dripped from his nose and down his chin.

However, the Guardians were not as lucky.

Even as Kyle watched, eyeballs jerked in a multitude of directions in sockets. The five allies screamed silently as they gripped their heads and chests before exploding like watermelons smashed upon the ground. The boy collapsed into a heap unconscious as Kyle's body ceased to scream at the vibrations that gripped his body in unseen hands.

Baxter bent and collected two more fist sized shards of concrete before he advanced on the two surviving Warriors. Two blurs of Baxter's hands and Kyle fell back. The missiles collided with his face and nearly ripped head from shoulders.

On my back all he could do was watch as Baxter picked up one of the fallen rifles carried by a Guardian before he began his slow walk of triumph toward the downed men. Champion was awake but unmoving. Behind Baxter a familiar woman exited the van and clutched the young child to her chest. Kyle pushed to his knees as Baxter prepared to fire on the still form of Champion. With a reserve of energy he wasn't aware he still possessed, Kyle clambered to his feet. Three shaky steps were taken in Baxter's direction.

The pitcher turned and gave him a mocking smile before firing a round into his chest.

The pain was exquisite. His nerve endings screeched for his body to quit. But despite being rocked back, Kyle remained defiantly upright with his shredded uniform. A second shot was lined up directly at his face. Resigned, Kyle accepted the very real possibility that this was it. This was how he would die.

And then the strangest thing occurred. Guilt overwhelmed him with powerful emotions so deep and soulful that he welcomed death. All emotion fled except for a bone crushing desire to end it all. Death was the only thing he needed, he craved. Behind Baxter stood the woman with the child in her arms.

Her lips moved and her spoken words reflected the emotions that swarmed Kyle.

"I am damned. Blood covers my hands and my victims claw at my soul. Misery calls me home. Death welcomes me with arms open." The woman's soothing voice wrapped around him. The words infected his mind. Kyle's hands searched the ground for a shard of glass, a sharp piece of metal, anything he could use to end my suffering. The torrent of guilt pulled him into a mire more deadly than quicksand. Why did the woman attack him?

The truth was realized moments later when Baxter turned the rifle on himself and fired. The body crumpled to the ground with lifeless fingers that still clutched the rifle.

Numbly Kyle watched as the woman carried her burden westward toward the only thing that laid in that direction. The beaches of Taurus Island. Static hissed in his ear as the comlink came back on line, the weighted voice of Munin echoed from within.

"A stryker jet is recovering Starburst and Wizard. ETA two minutes for rendezvous at your location."

By the time the jet arrived, hovering on its thrusters, Champion was once more standing while cradling his shattered arm. Face pinched with pain as he spoke resigned words.

"We need to eliminate the threat." It took Kyle a moment to realize his idol meant the boy.

"He's just a kid! We can't kill a kid!" Adamant shock at Champion, who ordered the youth's death, shook Kyle.

"We can find another way, a better way!" Eyes followed the woman who cradled her son as she slipped from view.

"Look around you Aegis. We can't stay and find another way. We've suffered heavy losses and we don't know if there are more hostiles. Those are my orders."

"Then you can shove your orders! Or is this how you handle Protectorate issues? Like guys that don't quit from the academy have accidents? Or turning a blind eye to assault? Or favoritism? Is this how the Warriors run things? Killing kids who haven't done anything wrong because attempting to figure out another way doesn't fit your rules."

Kyle advanced toward Champion but stopped when two guardians flanked the team leader. Rifles weren't aimed, yet there was a wariness in their stance. Prepared.

"You're nothing but a green, idealistic rookie with no understanding of what it takes to be a superhero. When you were taking math tests and watching cheerleaders at the high school football game I was fighting people who could burn the skin off me or stopping a super who leaks radiation. Sometimes there is no good choice. No right path."

There was a darkness reflected in Champion's eyes. Regret, shame, and resolve.

"Listen to me Aegis. Everything isn't black and white. This job will put you in situations where sacrifices have to be made for the greater good. That kid has to die. We have our orders. And you will follow your orders." The implied 'or else' hung heavily between them.

Fists clenched as Kyle prepared to argue. There was no way he could stand by and watch as a kid was murdered just because he couldn't control his abilities. It wasn't right. Before Kyle disobeyed orders the comlink crackled with Wizard's voice.

"Terminating the child will most likely create a cascade implosion of the child's abilities in a wave that could very well impact the entire western coast of Florida. The probability the child will die within the hour is extremely likely. His death will still create an implosion of sound waves that will rock the island. However, the damage will be centralized off the shore of Florida."

Turned to look at Champion, Kyle managed to conceal his disgust at the idea of killing a child.

"Sir, I volunteer to stay behind and make sure this ends as quietly as possible." Determination etched upon Kyle's face as he looked to Champion. Pain and loss filled the face of the leader of the Warriors.

"Staying here isn't going to do anything but kill you. Your death will mean nothing. Such a waste."

After several seconds Champion merely nodded wearily before he allowed the soldiers to escort him into the jet.

As Kyle stood there alone in the wreckage of the battle with upturned face, the jet rose on thrusters before it accelerated east. Solemnly, he followed the trail left by the woman and child.

VI

THE BiG BANG

Thursday, April 25, 2030
7:17 p.m.

While the island wasn't large, it was still big enough to make the search for a woman with a child difficult. Boots crushed debris as he followed their last seen heading. Toward the beaches. As he was about to ask Munin for advice the slight waves of emotion washed over him. The woman was near. Kyle used the new feelings that rippled from the mother to hone in on their location. When he found them his own feeling of helplessness momentarily overcame the heartache which echoed from the distraught mother.

She held her child. A timeless melody drifted from her lips as the boy cried out in his sleep. Kyle watched quietly from where he stood. Waves from the tide washed over his boots. A great depth of sorrow filled his being. Whether it was his own, or merely a reflection of the woman's, Kyle knew the end was nigh.

The boy cried out once more, a pitiful sound that heralded the end as his body twitched and skin crawled with unseen force from within. Staggered by the effects, Kyle stumbled in the surf as the boy's small body began to vibrate and nausea escalated to agonizing pain. Fingers clutched at his temples in an attempt to wrest the excruciating pain from within. Yet he failed.

The child's skin glowed as his body vibrated faster and faster in quick succession. The woman leaned down and pressed her lips softly to the boy's forehead. A sense of acceptance washed over Kyle as her emotions reflected outwards.

A sonic wave of sound, with such intensity, flashed out and lifted the Warrior from his feet. The water flashed by as he was bodily launched outward into the waves. As he sank beneath the ocean he caught a last glimpse of the woman and child. And then they were enveloped by energy that rippled out with such devastating force that destruction consumed all.

The waters embraced him.

VII
NEW DAWN

Friday, April 26, 2030
7:57 a.m.

Yesterday he was a superhero.

Today he stood on the beach. Sand enveloped his shiny black boots laced to my knees. The newly risen sun cast its warm light upon his shoulders. The dawn revealed the destruction that embraced the island.

However, it wasn't what was destroyed in the city that left an indelible mark. No. It was the belief in the inherent justice and righteousness of the cause that was shattered. Yesterday the greatest beacon of hope, pride, and personification of good, willing offered to take a child's life. The greatest representative of supers worldwide justified his willingness to murder an innocent child. The epitome of hope was prepared to stain his hands with innocent blood. The so called greatest superhero to walk the earth.

Embittered, Kyle tore the final scraps of the uniform from his chest. The breeze tossed the charred emblem of the Spire into the waves to sink from sight.

Yesterday, Kyle was a superhero.

Today, he was not.

PART FOUR: BYSTANDER

RUN, RUN, AS FAST AS YOU CAN

Friday, April 26, 2030
9:03 a.m.

He was, most definitely, not safe.

The sun rose with rays beating down warmth. Wreckage and destruction revealed in the early morning light was less than was expected, but more than was hoped for. Boots climbed rubble as Kyle pressed through and left the beach behind. Asphalt streets cracked while concrete sidewalks were shattered. Glass shards lay crystalline in chaotic beauty that promised injury to those unvigilant. Black smoke rose to the heavens throughout the city from several fires. Shimmering haze filtered the light as Kyle stumbled forward. Hand muffled a cough and eyes watered from the encompassing smoke.

Ash drifted from above until his bare torso became colored a gray pallor. Through careful steps he backtracked to where the Direhawk jet crashed. There were already scavengers combing over the wreckage. Crouched low, Kyle stayed out of view. Soon enough the Protectorate would send a retrieval team. Before that happened he needed to be gone. But in order to do that Kyle needed supplies from the downed craft.

Several minutes went by as he observed the scavengers. It

became apparent that the downed ship was already stripped when the group separated. Half a dozen moving in another direction deeper into the island and just two pulling hoversleds held aloft by a blower system directed downward and contained by a steel reinforced rubberized skirt around the sled perimeter.

The higher likelihood of finding what he needed lay with following the scavengers with the sleds. Allowing a reasonable space between himself and the duo, Kyle followed as quietly as he could. Just as he began to grow disheartened in ever being led to their ship, the vessel materialized. The boat was ugly. Long and flat it possessed a large fan at back. An airboat to be exact. Not thrilled at the idea nonetheless Kyle continued forward.

With cover growing sparse, he knew eventually the only way to approach was a sprint. And hope neither man would have enough time to bring their weapons to bear. Precious minutes ticked by while he waited for the men to load the vessel. The best opportunity he would get was to wait til the stolen goods were lashed down.

Only when both men's backs were to Kyle, did he sprint forward. He was only a few strides away when the men became aware of his presence. One of the men tried to bring his rifle up Kyle dove for the boat and crashed into them. The armed scavenger flipped over the side as Kyle landed hard on the second man.

Once, twice, Kyle struck the scavenger with closed fist. Each blow connected with his opponent's throat before the other man stood sputtering in the water. Right hand yanked the pistol from the downed man's holster and aimed at the scavenger in the water. The pistol barked first, two rounds hitting center mass of the scavenger in the water. Swiftly Kyle shoved the man from the boat and turned to search for what he needed.

However, he found he didn't need to search. Next to the handle for the rudder was what he desired. A military grade portable jammer. With a larger battery, interior cooling fans, and heatsink the jammer possessed a larger range of jamming frequencies. Exactly what he needed to keep the embedded comlink in his jaw from being tracked.

The device slipped into Kyle's pants pocket as he went to the rear of the boat. Left hand on the stick rudder, he pressed the accelerator to send the airboat from the shore. Angled around he headed east as the boat accelerated. There was a friend in Sarasota that Kyle knew he could wheel and deal with. The haul of equipment in the boat would be a nice bargaining chip.

Several hours later Kyle was driving northeast in a 1987 white SS Monte Carlo. The trunk was loaded down with several crates of Protectorate gear. In the passenger seat rested his shield. More than once he glanced at the contours of the shield and wondered why he brought it. Though when it came time to leave he realized he couldn't part from it.

Taking care, Kyle obeyed all traffic laws as he drove. The sense he was being followed nagged at the back of his mind. The wind whipped through the car, windows rolled down, as he headed north on Interstate 75. A pack of menthol cigarettes sat on his lap as he inhaled the first of many. There was only one person he could trust. It just so happened the man also had the necessary skills to help.

Sage Winters.

Skirting around Tampa and Ocala, Kyle made it to Gainesville in a handful of hours. The car cruised through town where he grabbed food from a drive through and stopped at a city park to rest. There was no way he could drive into the gated community around Lake Gem. Instead he chose to wait and rest in plain sight. Head swiveled at every blare of siren or revved engine.

When evening encroached upon the daylight Kyle headed east on Highway 20 and made a left on 234 into Windsor. It wasn't difficult to find a secluded drive to park the car in. With the car locked, Kyle popped the trunk and pulled out a small nine millimeter and slipped it into his pocket. Two magazines went into the opposite. A red hoodie slipped on and he closed the trunk.

Beneath cover of darkness Kyle headed west through the trees. Eventually he made it to the wall that encircled the community he once called home. With resigned trepidation he climbed the wall to drop into a crouch on the other side. With remembered ease he coasted through the woods. Memories assaulted him as specters of the past replayed in his mind.

Sage, Clay, Sandy, and Kyle owned the woods. All the other kids became enslaved to technology as a biological accessory never a hand's reach away. Not the Dead Enders. They roamed the grounds and explored every nook and cranny.

At first it was the flashbacks of better times that trailed after him. Soon it regressed as eyes darted at every shadow and benign shapes turned malicious. Crouched in a stand of trees Kyle checked the portable jammer. Paranoia tickled his thoughts. The only person in the woods was him and yet, the unshakable sense of being watched infected him.

Hypervigilant, he moved through the forest to skirt areas of population. Homes, new and old, dotted the landscape. Street lamps created halos of prevalent ambient light. The community settled into sleep as the hour neared midnight.

Finally Kyle arrived. Leaned against a tree trunk he looked at the back porch where so many memories were centered around. Meals, studying, the cast iron fire pit … it was the real home for him. Like a distorted mirage seen through the mirror of time, Sage sat in a wicker chair with feet propped against the railing.

Cautiously Kyle approached. At some point the flames from the fire illuminated his approach and drew Sage's attention. A glass tumbler froze halfway to Sage's mouth as Kyle climbed the wooden steps of the porch and stopped across the brazier. The two men looked upon one another for a few moments. Then Sage leapt to his feet and enveloped Kyle in his arms.

"Dude! You were reported dead this morning! I got a call from Clay around lunch telling me what happened. How are you here?" Confusion and relief echoed from Sage as he squeezed Kyle who returned the hug.

"It's a long story. I need your help."

NOT ANOTHER GOODBYE

Saturday, April 27, 2030
12:12 a.m.

"I remember when you and your dad did this", Kyle remarked as he looked around what was once a two car garage. The space was divided in half. One side held Kyle's Monte Carlo, retrieved and hidden within. The other side was converted into a room with a single door. Wood paneling covered the walls.

"Mostly dad. Every little thing needed to be perfect. No gaps", Sage swung the door open and went in. With a shake of his head Kyle followed and pulled the door closed behind. Two generators, a motorcycle, and boxes filled with more electronics than a Radio Shack. The ceiling and wall was covered in reflective aluminum.

"Three layers of aluminum. And now the door. Take a seat by the desk." A roll of aluminum unrolled from above the door. Using a roll of taped Sage secured the border and made sure there was an overlap.

"Dad always told me to make a faraday cage and keep it stocked", finished Sage took a seat at the desk.

"I gotta say Sage, I'd take an eccentric dad over a nonexistent one."

Briefly Sage nodded as he opened two laptops. Fingers flew over the keys as glasses slipped to the end of his nose. Where Clay possessed immense strength and Kyle evolved from every encounter, Sage was able to see patterns. Breaks in programming, repetitive lines of code, designs, and template unraveled before him.

When you're able to design an artificial intelligence with a double helix of code so intricate, hacking a comlink and gps tracker was nothing.

"Have you given any thought to where you will go? What you will do?" Multitasking was simple for Sage. Talking while working was easy for him.

"Well … I can't go back. Too much is wrong with the Protectorate. And I can't exactly pick up my old life as I'm currently dead. All I know is that I can't stay here and I can't return to the Warriors."

Eyes closed and Kyle released a weary sigh before he continued.

"This is the first time in my life where I don't have a destination. In school it was to get to the next grade. After Sandy … well, after I finished High School, I knew I wanted to be a part of the Protectorate. At the academy it was to become a Warrior. Now?" With a pause Kyle glanced over at Sage.

"I don't know who I am, let alone where I'm going."

Several minutes of silence passed before Sage closed the lids of the laptops.

"Done. You are officially free of tracking or transmissions."

Kyle rubbed his jaw while he nodded.

"Thanks man, I owe you one. And thanks again for storing the car. I better disappear while I have the opportunity." Both men stood as Sage frowned.

"You sure I can't convince you to stay? That way you can rest some and eat a home cooked breakfast. Plus I want to introduce you to my fiance, Naomi."

Arms opened as Kyle embraced the other man. In that moment Kyle felt safe. But it passed and the itching sensation of being hunted returned.

"Trouble could come down on you if I was caught here. And you've already done enough. So I've got to decline. Plus I feel like I'm still on the radar." Released from the embrace, Kyle walked to the door and turned the handle. Paused, he spoke without turning.

"Even If I wanted to and it was safe, I still couldn't. Everywhere I'd look would be another reminder of what I lost. What we all lost. Sandy. No way would I be able to handle that. Be good brother. And always ask yourself, 'what would Kyle do'. Then do the opposite because we know I always make bad choices. Take care."

With that said Kyle left. As he slipped back into the woods there was the urge to look back. He didn't because he knew what would be seen. Sage standing alone on the back porch. It would hurt to see that. Instead Kyle buried his emotions. Safer that way.

UNCOMPLICATED OBSCURITY

Friday, April 25, 2036
9:03 p.m.

The memory of the woman and child dying on the beach swelled like the river's waves. Gut churned with a phantom of the explosion's impact, which tossed him into the night time surf. The psychic connection forced him to feel the last moments of a mother's agony at the death of her child. It also awakened the memory of his inability to save Sandy. Utter helplessness to save them left their scars. When he rose to the surface and was greeted by the sunrise, he tossed off the last emblem of his uniform and disappeared. To the world he died that day. A part of him did. Extreme durability forced him to survive. His power evolved from physical damage, to ensure he wasn't harmed in the same manner again. Though his body healed even stronger, his mind retained the fleeting moments of agony and despair of losing a child. The woman's powers left a wound in his own psyche.

Not only was he physically injured during the destruction caused by the child, but broken inside to a degree unfathomable. In that moment of death on the beach Kyle experienced more than he ever wished. Through the emotional, telepathic link he knew what it was to be a parent. To love a child more than the breath in his lungs. The pride and joy as he watched his child grow from a bundle of mewling flesh that did nothing but eat, sleep, and fill diapers. Elation at his toddler's first step. And terror at the child's first injury.

Kyle remembered standing in the doorframe and watching the child as he slept. Unknown dreams caused little smiles in his sleep. A cry roused him from sleep to rush to the child's side and coo gentle lullabies while he stroked fingers back across his kid's forehead. The vain struggle as the child tried to keep his eyes open, but ultimately failed.

Complete shame as he failed the child. Sorrow at not being able to protect his little innocent. And the hope that in the next life, the child would grow to be happy and healthy. When death came and the wave of power shredded his being, only one thought was left. This was his rightful punishment for being an inadequate parent. The blast of soul seared pain filled him and found a home within.

He would never be free. Nor did he believe he should be.

Disillusioned and mourning, Journeyman Kyle Ross disappeared and laid down his proverbial sword. A normal man drifting from place to place and job to job, never staying in one place too long.

Kyle proved to be up for the challenge of a drifter's lonely life. Often he rolled into town and found some form of labor that paid him cash. It was usually enough to sustain him for the duration of his time in that town. But weeks or months later, he grabbed his pack and departed for the next town to remain anonymous in. Until two years ago, when he arrived in Palatka on a Friday night.

In town he found Riverfront park on the Saint Johns River and stowed his pack in the overgrown flowers that marched across sections of the manicured park. Streetlights glowed in a nice ambiance, without blinding any of those visiting in the evening. With a shrug, Kyle pulled the denim shirt closed and buttoned it as he walked from the park to one of the local bars he saw as he arrived. He wasn't necessarily looking to get buzzed. No, history and repetition proved a decent shot at acquiring a local laborer job by mingling and being somewhat friendly. And of course buying a few rounds always greased the wheels of so called friendship and opportunity.

After several hours Kyle watched his money dwindle to nonexistence. Downing the remainder of his beer, he left and headed back to the park. There would be no contemplation tonight, just merciful, dreamless sleep. As he sat among the flowers he pulled out a pack of cigarettes and lit one using a scratched up zippo he carried. With a sigh he laid back, his shoulders and head against the pack, almost disappearing in the bed of flowers and grass. It wasn't possible to see the stars through the street lights. Still he looked upwards. An empty, dark haze that carried no point to focus on. Just an ocean of darkness that swallowed all in its maw.

A sound drew his eyes to the walkway where a man and woman slowly strolled. She was slender, thin shoulders and arms with a face that was plain yet beautiful in its simple veneer. Straight hair danced slowly on the wind blowing in from the river. Laughter rang out from her to pierce the night. A wondrous sound. Pure and free. The man pulled his woman close, one hand falling to her waist. That was when Kyle saw the baby bump. He half nodded to himself as he sank down and lay upon the pack once more. They could have their quiet time, he wouldn't intrude.

In the silence, he heard the couple move down the path and boat ramp to enjoy the views, their voices muffled and occasional laughter filling the void of words. Smoke now swirled upwards to ring the darkness of the sky. Kyle smoked with a wry grin at the blissful ignorance of love. When it was still and quiet all he could see and hear was the woman and the child moments before their death. They were the ghosts that haunted him. But they weren't the only ones. Sandy stood with them and looked at him with blame. As though he should have done more. The constant companions chased away the loneliness. They were always with him.

The butt was stubbed out in the dirt beneath the grassy bed.

With a sigh, he rolled to his side and closed his eyes in weary acceptance. He hadn't drank enough to chase away the dreams and the woman beckoned him forward for a night of tossing and turning.

A night of second guessing.

A night filled with the inescapable deaths of the woman and child. It was his burden to carry. Everyone must bear their own burden and this was his. And so he would continue to bounce from town to town, avoiding people and the law. No way to live, but it was enough. For now.

With eyes closed he began to drift to the hum of the yellow haloed street lamp. Then a woman's scream shattered the stillness of the night. Head slipped from the duffel bag he was using as a pillow. Grunting he quickly pushed himself to his feet and looked around attempting to find the source of the cry. Another cry focused his attention upon the boat ramp and moorings. There, the same couple from earlier were in confrontation with another man.

Trotting forward he swayed from the imbuement of liquor from earlier in the evening. Of course the one time he wished his liver would have worked more efficiently. The attacker lashed out in a strike that sent the young woman spinning from the deck into the water below. With a grimace he sprinted to where the two men still wrestled. The attacker kicked the other man in the gut and sent him falling to his back before leveling a pistol at the distraught man's face.

For a brief second Kyle's mind asked why he was involved. The moment passed with a bone crushing tackle that launched Kyle into the attacker and through the air. Just before hitting the water's surface Kyle heard a roar that was followed by what felt like a mule kick to his chest. Beneath the dark waters was disorienting. A red hue tinged the yellow illumination leaking into the river making it difficult to pinpoint which direction was up. The pounding head from lack of oxygen and heavy drinking made him nauseous. Pain spread from his chest with every beat of his arms to break the surface. And then his head found the open air, a sputtering and coughing gasp for breath as he turned to the mooring where the man was shouting "Elle" with growing desperation.

"Where is she", he asked while treading water. The other man cast him a look of rage and snarled.

"If I knew do you think I'd be up here?" Not able to argue with the rebuttal, Kyle kicked his way to the general vicinity and treaded water as he waited.

"There!" The excited exclamation was followed by the man diving from the pier where the brief glimpse of bubbles had been seen. Fraught seconds stretched into an eternity as Kyle waited and watched, neither head breaking the surface.

Just when he was about to dive down in search of them, their heads finally surfaced.

"Over here." Hands reached up and gripped the wooden dock to pull himself up. Once up, he knelt over the water and held out his hands, taking the woman's wrists as the other man raised her from the water by her hips. As gently as he could, Kyle pulled her up to the pier where she laid down on her side gasping with open lips. Again he reached down and grabbed the other man's wrist preparing to raise the other man when they heard the audible snick of the hammer being cocked back on a revolver.

Frozen in place the three sets of eyes slowly turned to the attacker, freshly emerged from the river. Water dripped from his sodden clothing and Kyle finally got a good look at the man. Name brand jeans and tshirt, threadbare though. Nikes with the soles worn out. Palid, pock marked face with open sores and rotting teeth emerging from colorless thin lips. Eyes were nearly black, the pupils dilated so much the natural eye color was nearly imperceptible. Shallow rapid breathing as the fingers tightened even more on the grips of the pistol, eyes flickered between his victims as the other man tried to speak in a calm, clear voice.

Kyle stayed motionless as he observed the attacker. The other man spoke soothingly. Black veins streaked the hand holding the gun and up either side of the skinny attacker's neck. Realization became apparent of what it was even as the gun began to transition toward the pregnant woman still laying on her side.

The Cape. A popular drug that made you as high as a Caped superhero could fly. It also boosted energy, cognitive abilities, and senses. Some criminals began using the drug to boost their natural skillset. Others used it for the high. And then there were the others who got hooked and disconnected with reality in order to get their next fix.

Like this guy.

Scientists still didn't know if there was any memory from those too far gone on the Cape. For those in the throes, nothing was impossible. Like shooting a pregnant woman for no real reason.

Old instincts honed to razor sharpness, dulled by the rust of disuse, did not fail him. Weight shifted forward as he crouched and sprang on the thrust of his legs. Like a coiled snake he struck, his body moving into the line of the revolver, to become what he once cast away. An Aegis. Like his old superhero codename, he took the rounds fired from the revolver in his chest to protect Elle as she laid with arms wrapped around her midsection in a small attempt to shield her unborn child. He knew it would hurt but he could take it.

The two men crashed together, their bodies once more falling into the water. As they fell the shooter's head cracked one of the wooden struts. In the water he was gripped by the gentle current. Vision grew dark as he slowly sank to the silt covered riverbed. The faint light from above became cloaked by the blood rising from his torso. It wasn't the wounds that held him there, among the debris of the river. A lethargic mood caused by the injuries, the liquor, and the knowledge that if this was his last moments, at least they were heroic.

And peaceful.

A new weight pulled at him and his head broke the surface as the dark haired man hefted him to the pier. Even while he was hoisted up, the darkness of the river swirled under the moonlight. The part of him that chose to set himself apart was still there, under the waters. A baptism through crucible revealed the truth of who he was. He wasn't just the secluded drifter that didn't care, he still possessed the capacity of a good man. Eyes closed knowing that fate interjected on his behalf on the river.

Two years later Kyle was still in Palatka. Frank and Elle took him in like long lost family. Gave him a home. People who cared about him. So he worked construction with Frank and found a measure of peace in his life away from the public. Frank and Elle refused to let him completely isolate, especially when Gabriella was born. Gabby was a whirlwind of activity and love. Even Kyle was not immune to her charms. And so he became Uncle Isle, content to enjoy the simpler way of life. Present but not a part.

IV

AS THE ROOSTER CROWS

Sunday, April 25, 2038
5:12 a.m.

Eyes snapped open. Darkness permeated his vision as he lay still. And waited. Something or someone stirred him from his slumber. Stretched out on the single bed, a sheet lay across his body. With the pace of eroding rainwater his hand climbed beneath the sheet and delved under the pillow. The comforting grip of the 1911 fit his hand snuggly as he flicked the safety off. In silence he laid in wait.

Minutes ticked by in the quiet. Then the noise returned. A light scratch occurred again. This time he was able to pinpoint the noise. Slipped from beneath the sheet he crept cautiously across the wooden floorboards. Careful to avoid boards that creaked, he eased to the door and leaned against the wall beside it. Left hand reached out and turned the lock before he gripped the handle. The pistol was held at waist height as he waited for the next noice.

A shadow blocked the scant light beneath the door. Another light scratch. With a twist and jerk he yanked the door open and leveled the pistol at the interloper. By the faint light of the moon he saw Rusty, the ancient golden retriever, looking up at him. Tail wagged heavily as the dog trotted inside the room.

"One of these days dog …"

The door was pushed shut and locked before he pulled the string from the ceiling. A fluorescent bulb glowed to life. Bright white light invaded the single room cabin. The light swayed and cast harsh light over the room. The old dog moved to the large oval rug in the center of the room and circled it twice before he flopped down with a canine huff.

"Make yourself at home."

The cabin possessed a rustic feel, the wood slats of the floor matched the walls and bare rafters above. Opposite of the door was the bed. To the left was a desk and chair, rows of shelves anchored to the wall. Books lined the simple bracketed racks as packed as a library bookshelf. Retracing his steps to the bed, he flicked the 45 back to safety and laid it on the lone pillow.

The bedside table held an empty water basin and a gallon jug of water. Water was poured into the basin before he wearily splashed water into his face. A towel hung on a nail beside a mirror attached to the wall. Thoroughly he scrubbed his face dry before leaning forward on braced arms.

"Pull yourself together Kyle. It was just a dream."

In all actuality it was a nightmare. However, he refused to give the dream legitimacy. This too shall pass. Often he woke in a cold sweat and fevered mind. Repeatedly Kyle told himself he was safe. As far as the Protectorate, and the world in general, knew Aegis was dead. He wanted to keep it that way.

Moving to the wall opposite of the desk, he collected his clothes draped over one of the two chairs and dressed. Blue jeans were pulled over his boxer brief sleeping attire. A black tank top was slipped on before he sat in the armchair and put on his socks and yanked boots on. Fingers ran down the matte black boots and allowed himself a moment of acute loss.

The boots were almost tossed years earlier for what they represented. A dream of becoming a superhero. Now the dream was dead. As dead as Sandy. She was the real reason he held on to them. A final, physical tether to his twin.

Head shook side to side as he brushed away the cobwebs of sleep and thoughts of Sandy. The face in the mirror was his. And a stranger's. Long hair and beard was a large change from a shaven face and crewcut.

Taking the pistol in one hand, Kyle leapt up to grab one of the rafter beams. Muscles bunched as he raised up and slipped the pistol into a nook. Boots thudded when he dropped from above. With one hand he raised the end of the bed and pushed the fold out bed back into the confines of the beige couch.

A final glance at the room before he turned the light off and pushed open the door. Fingers snapped twice. From the darkness the old dog trotted out as Kyle closed the door. It was still half an hour before sunrise with sleep unattainable, so Kyle went to the chicken coop to collect fresh eggs.

An old rooster waddled into sight as Kyle drew close. Head bowed, the rooster danced as it challenged Kyle. Stopped, he faced the bedraggled bird with annoyance.

"Go on bastard or I'll punt you like a football again."

A few seconds later the rooster charged only to receive a kick that launched it through the air. Wings flapped until it landed. Beady little eyes followed Kyle as he entered the pen. Mason jars of chicken feed sat on a bench inside. The chicken scratch was tossed to the side which drew most of the hens. Erratically they pecked at the feed. With a one gallon picked up from the inside of the coop he swiftly collected the eggs without disturbing the hens too much. The door was closed and latched.

Again the rooster charged and once more it was kicked like a soccer ball. More than a little amusement hit Kyle everytime the bird attacked. The stupid rooster never quit. From the mat of grass Rusty rose and shambled along beside Kyle as they headed for the big house.

The hairs on the back of his neck raised. With a turn Kyle peered into the darkness. Only the insane rooster moved as it flapped its wings and ran in circles. Old feelings clawed from deep within and froze his guts. Eyes shifted from shadow to shadow as his pulse accelerated. Breath came in short gasps.

The moment passed.

Ominous presence vanished. After Kyle calmed, he turned and continued to the big house. The steps of the back porch creaked under his weight. Instinctively he looked back. Nothing. No real danger. He was still safe.

iNTO TOWN

Sunday, April 25, 2038
10:00 a.m.

The crisp morning air still retained a hint of winter's cool. A cloudless blue sky blessed the early day, the sunshine warmed to combat the momentary chill, which raised goosebumps along his bare arms. The black tank absorbed more of the sun's rays, not that the man needed additional warmth. His body learned long ago to appropriately regulate his internal temperature. Among other things. With hands shoved into faded blue jeans, he stood on the grassy knoll overlooking the banks of the Saint Johns River. Pant legs were shoved into scuffed black boots, the single memento of his former life.

Beside Kyle, Baby Gabby bounced on Elle's narrow hip as the thin woman took her husband Frank's hand in hers. The couple smiled sideways as they trotted down the slope to enter the odd combination of Farmers', Flea, and Fishers' market. With a sigh he followed along in their wake to slip behind them within the crowds which milled about the tables and booths at the fringe. The brief smile Frank offered up knew Kyle wasn't a fan of crowds or the public in general. It wasn't any sort of phobia, just a lack of desire to be surrounded by strangers.

Wares were offered. Several sellers held items and shouted their attributes to potential buyers to gain attention. Music plucked invisibly from the world wifi which half a dozen digital players blared from as many tables, their sounds combined in an unpleasant battle that would go on for as long as the solar batteries charged. The scents of cooking food wafted through the people to reach him. An odd combination of breakfast and grilled BBQ, with a hint of marine saltiness. An intriguing aroma that wasn't unpleasant.

Elle knelt and looked at local produce as Gabby toddled upon chubby legs clutching her favorite stuffed animal. A brown bunny absent of whiskers and a face worn almost white by two years of drooling kisses from the toddler.

"Isle!" The child's pronunciation of his name and clasping hand drew a smile from the man as he bent and raised her into his arms. High up, she placed her left arm about his neck and giggled at the new heights that gave her a greater view of the market. He sighed as stubby fingers gripped the shaggy, dirty blonde hair falling to his shoulders in waves. The child's mother smiled with that smirk of unrevealed secrets many women seemed to master. Of course he was pretty sure she imagined him as a german shepherd that just had a toddler climb on top of them and was looking to the adults with eyes pleading for help.

Moving on, the group continued deeper, as the morning advanced forward. The chill was burned off as the heat of the day inevitably marched closer. Thankfully a brisk wind blew inwards from the river and lent a cool breeze to what would otherwise be a stifling experience. Unfortunately the smell of fish was prevalent upon the breeze, the fisher's market bustling with activity along the docks. They headed to the line of barges just off the shore. A dock led to the towboat and plankways between barges, where more stalls were set up along the long stretches of deck.

On the first barge little Gabby called for her pa, so Frank reached over to pluck his daughter from Kyle's embrace. Which was just fine for the tanned man. While Frank was his best friend and boss, and his family were kind and friendly, Kyle didn't care for undo attachments, at least his own personal attachments. That wasn't his life, nor one he could have. Maybe once, but no longer. That life washed away on a beach on Taurus during his first and last mission for the Warriors. They were the southeastern branch of the Protectorate, a special forces group under the Department of Defense for supers. Those individuals who possessed abilities above those of baseline humans.

Once he was a superhero, but no longer.

VI
CONSEQUENCES

Kyle gave Frank a nod and motioned back the way they had come.

"I'm going to grab something to eat. I'll be up there when y'all are done." Elle nodded absently as Frank silently mouthed, "traitor". A smile raised his lips as Kyle headed back to dry ground. Moving through the crowd, he bought a pulled pork sandwich wrapped in aluminum foil and eased over the slope to sit beneath the shade of the trees. Sweat stained the clothing of the crowds as the day crept from comfortable to stifling, even with the breeze from the river. It was only an amount of time before that particular scent was added to the aromas already permeating the area.

With a hairband removed from his pocket he threw his shaggy mane into a loose ponytail as he relaxed and ate the sandwich. Moist and flavorful, he contemplated buying another. Or maybe some of the brisket. Doing so required him to get up from where he was reclining but he was too comfortable. Soon enough Frank and the girls would be done on the row of barges and the stalls set up in irregular lines. The decision to wait was a simple one.

A deep sigh of contentment escaped his lips as he idly scratched the beard several shades darker than the dirty blonde ponytail he wore. Stretched out lazily, Kyle frowned at his boots. They had seen him through school and his first mission. Watched as he ran from his life and his past. Observed him falling into his current home. And still, they survived. The boots chose to emulate their owner in durability and dexterity of use.

Every so often he wondered if he should lay them down. To retire the boots and leave all of the past behind him. But he never could. While they reminded him of life's milestones, both the good and unpleasant, when he slipped them on he thought of her. The boots were a connection to Sandy. While he could part with the boots over the past, never would he be able to surrender them because of who gave it to him.

Dozens of horns blared on the Memorial Bridge in the distance. Thankfully there was a football field's worth of space between the market and the bridge so the noise was annoying instead of painful. Thunder rolled from the sky. The empty aluminum foil crinkled as it fell from his hand.

That was not thunder.

All thought of slumber cast from his mind as he stood. With eagle eyed sharpness Kyle studied the skies in hope to disprove his fear. A speck that could have been a bird rapidly enlarged with the dull roar to confirm his suspicions. One of the jets from the Citadel, from the Warriors, screamed to a hover above the bridge. Without conscious thought he moved to the tree trunk, looking around at the sight that made the crowds around him call out and cheer in excitement. What they didn't grasp, and what Kyle knew to be true, was the only reason the Warriors would be there was for an imminent threat.

They didn't have long to wait.

An explosion rocked the bridge with enough force to send vehicles arcing into the sky among chunks of concrete and rebar. Portions of the bridge collapsed into the river sending a wave of water toward the barges and market. Preceding the wave was the shockwave that knocked people from their feet, shattered glass, and scattered booths and wares alike in all directions. Kyle managed to remain on his feet because of his grip on the tree trunk. Just as the earth calmed, the wave crashed into the market to wash people and stalls in all directions.

Water shook from his eyes as he turned to search the barges roiled in the river. In the chaos, where was Frank, Elle, or Gabby? Screams radiated around him with such ferocity the heat of their anguish burned his ears. But they weren't his problem or his concern.

He wasn't a superhero.

All he cared about was his friends, his close knit family. Vaulting debris and crying people passed as he ran for the pier to find a way to the barges. Outcries for loved ones assaulted his ears, wails of pain, shrieks of hysteria. They weren't his responsibility chanted as a mantra in his mind, as his boots hit the slick grass covered with water and mud.

Boots lost traction and he rolled forward to absorb the fall. A board with nails exposed raked his side, tore his tank top but no scratches upon his skin. Finding his feet, Kyle leapt the final distance to land on the pier. Above a shadow blotted out the noon day sun and he ducked reflexively as a car exploded above, tossed by unseen force. The boat ramp was damaged with boards and moorings missing. It appeared as a half exposed skeleton with bare bone showing where once there was flesh. A dangerous game of hopscotch was played to avoid the gaping holes as he eyed the nearest barge. The tow boat was capsized, no longer connected to the lines previously held.

Sound of clothing rippled by wind heralded the arrival of Champion, the leader of the Warriors, as he landed on the nearest barge. Tall, lean, and dark haired in a flawless black jumpsuit that sparkled in the sun, Champion stood from his landing. Jon Franklin was the posterboy for supers.

A falling tangle of arms and legs crashed into the barge which announced the landing of several more combatants. The flurry disentangled revealed three more individuals. Screamer stood with her jaw unhinged to reveal a gaping maw. Wraith released the tie holding back his coiled dreadlocks that writhed like living cable. Both wore emblems of the Children of the Spider, a political group fighting for the rights of Supers. They were home grown dissidents and radicals. The third to rise was garbed in the jumpsuit of the Warriors. Hawk, a winged soldier recently promoted according to news coverage.

Kyle's pants leg was snagged by a single hand. A man, barely out of his teens with peach fuzz on his chin, cried out for help. One of the boards from the pier pierced his side just above the silver belt buckle around his waist. Above the hum of the din Kyle heard his name shouted. It was close. The first barge that held the supers. Without a second glance he pulled free from the clutching hand. He wasn't a savior. It wasn't his duty. His friends were.

The remaining part of the pier was unsteady, disconnected from the anchors holding it in place. The first barge floated by freed from all lines. It was only a leap away. With a burst of speed he jumped from the end of the damaged dock and rolled across the deck of the barge. Debris grabbed his jeans but he would not be hampered or denied. He stood amidst the wreckage aboard the floating vessel and searched for his friends. Finally he saw Frank waving weakly from a pile of destroyed stalls with blood running freely down his face. His friend would never stay still unless he was with Elle and Gabby.

Between Kyle and Frank stood the four supers as they sized one another up. Adrenaline spiked as he felt the tension of silence amidst the catastrophe. Nearest him was Champion and Screamer, the latter with her back to Kyle. Creeping forward as quietly as he could, he moved even as Champion saw him. Recognition sparked behind the dark eyes. An unspoken expectation of assistance seemed to emanate from the Warrior as Kyle neared within a few steps of Screamer.

Not his responsibility. Surprise colored Champion's features as

Kyle slipped by Screamer to continue on. The momentary distraction cost the Warrior as Screamer released a sonic scream that connected with and sent him crashing into a pile of twisted metal and wood. Somewhere within the wreckage came cries of agony as the force of the attack buffeted those trapped inside. Hawk and Wraith converged with wings and tendrils of braids as strong as cable. Another sprint forward and Kyle passed the fighting to arrive at Frank's side.

"I can't reach them!" Frank was ashen from blood loss, another wound visible on his thigh soaked his jeans with blood.

"Help me please!" Kyle forcibly moved his friend back, concern etched on his face before turning to the twisted metal and wood before him. Inside he heard Gabby crying and then a pale hand stick out from a space in the center. Elle's hand closed with his own with a vice like grip.

"Hold on Elle, we'll get you out." A sharp shard of metal blocked a possible escape. Absently he noticed the slick blood on the metal railing and realized that was most likely how Frank hurt himself.

The edges bit into his palms as he braced his legs against the deck and heaved. Slowly the metal bent as his muscles bulged and sweat sprouted from his forehead down his face. Still he pulled. Grip grew slick and pain throbbed in his hands as blood wept from wounds that opened under his exertion.

Behind him Frank grew excited with a shout of jubilation.

"You're doing it, you're doing it-". The words were choked off suddenly. A glance was spared backwards even as he refused to release his grip. What he saw sent shivers running down his spine. Hawk managed to roll atop Wraith, hands raining brutal blows into his opponent's face. Dreadlocks writhed about seeking anything to bludgeon the Warrior with. One such tendril found Frank's neck and with a jerk launched him toward Hawk in a frenzied attempt for freedom. Without needing to see his friend's face Kyle knew the quick jerk snapped Frank's neck.

Using the emotions that boiled out in a roar of rage, Kyle

managed to snap the railing to open a space to worm out of. A look back for the body of his friend only barely noticing Hawk standing over the still figure of Wraith. Then a sonic blast hit Hawk with such force he was driven into the pile of rubble where Kyle stood. The whole pile shifted across the deck of the barge, a large portion now hanging precariously over the side. Kyle pulled himself back to the hole to see the fear flicker in Elle's eyes before determination replaced the look. Violently she shoved Gabriella through the gap. The toddler was grabbed in his bloody hands and resignation filled Elle's eyes as the pile of debris tipped to pull her into the river. The waters covered her face and she was no more.

A shout echoed around him.

Only later did he realize the howl came from his own lips.

Another sonic concussive wave glanced against his back to send him sliding across the deck. Gabby held close in his arms, Kyle rolled behind another pile of rubble knowing just how temporary it was. A thud beside him caused him to spin as Champion crouched beside him with an arm cradled across his ribs.

"Deserter", he spat in accusation at the man he once knew as Aegis. Another sonic blast hit a nearby mound of debris which elicited shouts quickly silenced in a brutal death. Guilt wracked Kyle as his decision to merely be a bystander and not a combatant shook him. If he only had chosen to intercede initially then maybe baby Gabby wouldn't be an orphan.

The realization struck that choosing to do nothing allowed the events to unfold which cost countless lives. His decision cost the lives of Frank and Elle. No more.

"Take her to safety. I'll handle Screamer, or keep her busy until reinforcements arrive." Kyle placed the toddler in the superhero's arms as he spoke. Champion shook his head,

"No, I'll fight. I'm the superhero that will protect the people."

"You're right! I'm no hero but I want revenge for my friends. And you're hurt. You can't get close enough without being dropped. I can. I can take a blast and keep going." Almost as though to prove his point another blast ripped into another mass of ruined stalls right next to them.

"Go. Take Gabby to safety!", Kyle growled before turning as Champion merely nodded in reluctant agreement.

"For Frank and Elle." With a loose board gripped in his hands he charged over the pile making himself a target as the sound of Champion's cape fluttered behind as he took to the air. Screamer let loose with a blast that missed Kyle. Still it was close enough to leave his ears ringing. The woman was momentarily frozen by indecisiveness. Blast at the Warrior in the sky or the charging man wielding a wooden board like a club. Her pause allowed Kyle to close the distance coming perilously near. She chose the imminent threat and released a short blast at the baseline human rushing her. The clipped blast hit him in his right side. Head swam and his right side grew cold, numb, as he fell to the deck. Nerveless hand released the board as he rolled from the mindless pain.

He laid there on his side all vigor gone as Screamer turned back to the sky. Mouth opened and her jaw unhinged as she deeply inhaled. Rage built in his chest as he gathered his legs. With a mighty bound he dove the remaining distance and collided with the woman as she released her pent up scream. The deck shattered from the power of her bellow while they rolled and she ended up on top of him with legs on either side.

As she inhaled for another blast all he could notice was how young she looked. Too young to be in this life. No gray hair or wrinkles or even the tell tale creases of laugh lines. Then the sonic blast hit his torso compressing his ribs and sternum. Organs pressed against his spine and his sight grew dim. A shadow above them paused before an object detached in freefall. Screamer paused and looked up, trying to scramble to the side as she screamed ineffectually to the heavens. The doughboy, a memorial statue of a soldier in the first World War, crashed into her and through the ship.

Red mist sprayed and then Screamer was gone.

A dull thud landed near him in a heap. The cape fluttered weakly in the breeze in testament that Screamer's final blast was not in vain. A roll weakly to his side, Kyle looked to where the pile that held Elle once sat. Unfocused eyes searched for Frank's body, finally finding it. Seated next to him was Gabby who cried for dada.

Champion lied. The superhero didn't take her to safety. Determination forced himself into a seated position, his mouth open to call out for the toddler. Then an explosion erupted, consuming half the already floundering barge. When the heat and flames subsided enough to see, Kyle felt himself collapse to the deck. Frank's body, along with Gabby, was gone. Only burning wreckage where they had been.

Champion called out weakly. Painfully Kyle rolled over and crawled over to the fallen superhero, a national beacon of all that supers could be.

"Help me", he whispered with bloody froth on his lips. With the remainder of his strength Kyle closed his hands around the other man's neck and squeezed as words escaped between clenched teeth.

"Frank." Squeezed with all his pain.

"Elle." Squeezed with all his rage.

"Gabby." Squeezed with all his guilt.

The rushing water of the river claimed their still bodies as the barge dipped beneath the surface.

JADED

Monday, April 26, 2038
1:24 a.m.

Emergency services were out in force. Paramedics, firefighters, police, and volunteers searched for victims and worked to clear debris and rubble. Clouds hung low in the sky, great and pregnant with the threat of rain. The gods prepared to cry at the tragedy. Tents and pavilions scattered the slopes as families and friends were reunited. Some were filled with joyous cries of relief at finding their loved ones alive. Others were filled with dismay and loss at the death of loved ones. Even more were left waiting with unanswered questions.

The man stood on the muddy bank, a wool blanket around his shoulders. When he was fished from the river the rescuers told him he was one of the lucky ones. He didn't feel lucky. He felt empty. Empty of life. Head hung low with eyes squeezed shut. Remorse, guilt, and shame threatened to overwhelm him. The role of a bystander scarred his mind and soul. He would never forget. Nor would he forgive himself.

Black boots were scuffed. The exterior scratched, lost their luster. But they still served a purpose. And they were functional. He snarled, his face hidden by the curtain of his hair. Once the boots belonged to a superhero. But no more. Once they belonged to a bystander, a mere witness of events. But no more. He wasn't a hero and he would never again be a bystander. So what was left?

As he looked at the crowds of innocents crying out, at the lines of bodies of the innocent dead, he realized what he could become. If he chose.

He wasn't a superhero that saved innocents. But he could give revenge and justice to the silenced voices. And for now, that was enough.

The shrouded man with the boots of a hero walked away.

PART FIVE:
NECESSARY EVIL

AN OLD FRIEND

Saturday, October 20, 2040
4:39 p.m.

The white SS Monte Carlo followed several vehicles behind the Eden Sunrise, a new motorcycle manufacturing company based in South Florida. A massive chassis perched on thirty-five inch mud truck tires. It was a tank of a bike. The Sunrise weaved in and around the traffic on US Highway 301. Three black Hummers followed at a distance. The entourage was headed south. Citra, a small town offering orange groves, receded in the rearview mirror as the separate parties continued for Ocala.

"I'm positive. That's where he's headed." The woman in the passenger seat of the Monte Carlo leaned back after her announcement. The open window tossed the thick wavy hair with auburn highlights scattered within the chestnut hue. Olive eyes closed as she relaxed into the burgundy seat.

Eyes returned to the road as he adjusted his grip upon the steering wheel. Now that they knew for sure where the bike and it's rider were going, they no longer needed to follow. With ease the car merged into the right hand lane and reverted back to the speed limit as vehicles continued around them. Which included the Hummers.

A squelch in his ear erupted as the final Hummer passed.

"What the hell was that Munin?" The right turn signal was activated with a flick of his hand. The gas station was nearly empty as he pulled near the air compressor and vacuum machine at the edge of the pavement. Eyes turned to the woman who napped fitfully before he chose to leave her to peaceful slumber.

Briefly he considered the past, for all of them. Pain from loss left indelible fingerprints on all. For him it was a mother and child on Taurus beach. And a friend, along with his wife and daughter, on the bank of the Saint Johns River. For Lydia it was her own child and husband. Their deaths made her a widow and broke a part inside of her. She never asked about the ghosts of his past and he gave her the same respect.

With the car turned off the door opened and he stepped out to quietly close the door behind. A quick glance skyward confirmed the lack of Sk-Eyes, the surveillance net of drones over most large cities. Black boots laced to his knees was the only article of clothing that stood out. Blue jeans and a black short sleeve shirt made the rest of his apparel normal attire. A good stretch of his arms popped several joints, kinks worked out as he walked to the front of the store and entered.

"It was an old program that you never deactivated." The soft sound of artificial intelligence, Munin, vibrated within his jawbone where the comlink was embedded during his first year at the academy. After his first and last day as an active member of the Warriors, the southeastern branch of the Protectorate, he went to Sage who deactivated the device which silenced Munin and any transmissions from the Citadel. However, with the return to a semblance of his old role, Kyle once again visited Sage who reactivated it with a few alterations. Any contact from the Citadel was blocked.

Randomly he cruised the aisles as he made several selections. Gummy bears, jerky, granola bars and a six pack of water were carried to the counter where an unenthusiastic clerk rang them up.

Behind, the door chimed as another shopper entered. The cadence of steps combined with the solid impact of the boots caused the man to slide a few bills onto the counter before he headed off to the right of the counter where the single occupant restroom was located. The deadbolt slipped into place as he backed from the door.

"What program would that be exactly", he whispered to the disembodied voice.

"The squelch was the warning system employed by you and Master Issacs."

The fluorescent bulbs flickered to reveal dingy walls. Soap scum clouded the mirror over the porcelain sink. The toilet lid was up with the prerequisite floaters belonging to every public bathroom. The boots kicked discarded toilet paper across the floor scuffed linoleum flooring as he moved next to the door.

"Clay", was spoken as a barely audible rhetorical question that Munin chose to answer.

"Yes."

The door's handle was slightly pulled, just enough to click the locked deadbolt. Kyle reached out and extinguished the light. Shadows moved from the gap beneath the door as whoever it was moved back.

"This is the Protectorate. Slowly exit the bathroom. Now." There was no debate in the command.

A muttered curse came from Kyle as he weighed his options. Records of Kyle Ross were classified. But they all said the same thing. Killed in Action at Taurus Island, Florida. April of 2030, ten years previously. The identification and driver's license in his wallet were authentic. Real documents of a real person. However, the pictures were of Kyle. They should pass inspection.

The deadbolt was unlocked. Using the toe of his boot, Kyle hooked the gap and used it to swing the door open before he pulled his leg back into the relative safety and obscurity of the bathroom wall.

"Slowly exit with your hands empty and in view. I would really like to know why you are wearing a dead man's boots." There was a faint rasp Kyle knew all too well. The sound of a pistol as it cleared its holster. With exaggerated movement he moved into the open doorway with his hands held out to either side.

"Probably because the dead man ain't done using them yet." The snarky remark was spoken low as he looked at Clay Issacs who held a pistol clutched in one hand. Kyle wiggled his fingers in an impersonation of jazz hands.

"Surprise." One word spoken created an avalanche of facial reactions in Clay. Shock turned to disbelief. Disbelief morphed into incredulous acceptance. Acceptance transformed into joy. As Clay stepped forward he returned the pistol to its holster even as his free arm wrapped around Kyle. The tight hug was returned and doubled by both. Breaking the hug, Clay clutched Kyle's arms and held him out at arms length as unbelief returned.

"How? Why? How? Why didn't you come back? If Sandy could only see you know! What is this, a ponytail? How?" The rapid fire of questions and the shock on Clay's face caused Kyle to laugh. It seemed as though Clay would never let go, almost as though if released Kyle would dissipate like an apparition from the past.

"I thought you were dead. You let me think you were dead, you bastard." The words were still filled with disbelief, the accusation possessed no anger. The two men embraced again before they slowly separated. The clatter of items came from behind the counter where the clerk huddled amidst a fallen rack of cigarettes.

"Hell ... hey, everything is fine. Just a misunderstanding. Come on let's go." Clay grabbed Kyle and drug him from the gas station, but not before he grabbed his purchases from earlier. Thankfully they remained on the counter in a bag. Outside, Clay waved a hand at the Hummer where a few similarly uniformed people milled about before he followed Kyle to the Monte Carlo.

"So this was you, eh? Just a nice visit to Ocala or you going to tell me you weren't following Henry Abernathy?" Clay leaned against the side of the car, a quick glance in the window seeing nothing of note except the curvy woman sleeping in the passenger seat. Arched brows turned to question Kyle who set the snacks in the driver's seat and snagged his pack of cigarettes from above the sunvisor.

"Someone special?"

"As you said, I'm just out enjoying a nice drive with my friend. Just a friend, who has a knack for finding things. Course I guess the real question is why are you, with a team of Warriors and Guardians, following this, what was his name, Henry Abernathy?" As he spoke Kyle plucked a cigarette from the pack and stuck it between his lips. The silver zippo dug from his pants pocket flipped open and he cupped his hands to puff the ember to life. A long exhale of smoke escaped as he arched his own eyebrows at Clay.

Arms folded over Clay's massive chest as the handle of a sword rode up in it's half sheath upon his back. Furrowed brow over staring eyes as he frowned. Slowly Clay spoke.

"There's been some worry about recent vigilantism. Specifically a man, dressed in what has been reported as being a Protectorate issue battle dress and using a shield, has been sighted around open investigations. Either suspects, badly beaten, appear trussed up for authorities to find or suspects that have no evidence against them suddenly grow a conscience and confess while giving up details not released and evidence that could convict them without a confession. But you wouldn't know anything about that."

"Sounds like someone is doing your job, Mister Excalibur sir", Kyle said as he innocently smoked the cigarette and looked at the sword handle. The two men stood quietly as several semi trucks whipped by on 301, the draft yanking their clothes as the sound tore away any retort from Clay. Shoulders shrugged which caused the hilt to rise and fall above his back.

"Look, I was fine in New York. When Jon Franklin died the south lost their Champion …"

A cough escaped Kyle as he reached in and retrieved the aviator sunglasses from the dash to slide on his face that didn't hide the roll of his eyes. Clay glared into the reflective shades.

"As I was saying, when he died there was a need for another face to take the lead."

"Thank god Excalibur came back to save us."

"I'm not the one who went AWOL and did nothing for a decade."

"You don't have any idea what I went through."

"Of course I don't! I thought you were dead! And you sure as hell didn't do anything to change my mind. I mourned you", Clay accused as his fingers jabbed into Kyle's chest.

Guilt chewed at Kyle as he dropped the butt of the cigarette and ground it out with the heel of his boot. It was impossible to explain why he never came back after resurfacing on the beach on Taurus Island. No way to explain what he endured. Or what he experienced during the devastation. How could he explain that what he trained for, what they both trained for, was a lie? A beautiful ideal at a distance. But up close the ugly aspects were revealed in all their horror.

Words failed to express the memories not his own. To hold your dying child and know you failed at your greatest responsibility.

Quiet stretched between them with neither expounding on their points. A stalemate of sorts. Head turned to look back at the Hummer before Clay's voice intruded on the silence.

"Look, I have to get back on the road. How do I contact you so we can talk?"

"Back to babysitting a killer?"

"Why should it matter to you what I do? You quit the hero business. So stay out. And for the record, Henry Abernathy was found not guilty of his crimes."

"You know he did it." The sunglasses were pulled off as Kyle glared up into Clay's face who just shrugged weakly.

"All I do know is there wasn't enough evidence to convict. Society is regulated by rules. And the rules keep us safe."

"Tell that to the parents of the twenty-three missing person reports that were tied to him."

"Don't get involved, Kyle. Stay out."

A wide smile crossed Kyle's face as he went in for a hug before opening the door to the car.

"I always do", was his response as he climbed into the Monte Carlo and closed the door. Clay leaned into the window, hands atop the door.

"Don't make me do something I don't want to do, because I will, if I have to."

The keys jangled as Kyle started the ignition.

"Here's a little secret between us. Those few times you beat me, when we were kids. I let you. For Sandy. We aren't kids anymore Clay. And Sandy isn't here to stop me. So you do what the law let's you do, and I'll do what needs to be done. Good seeing you brother."

The car dropped into gear and peeled off. In the rearview mirror Kyle watched as his old friend shook his head with sagged shoulders. The squelch in his ear made him shake his head to clear it. That was why he could never go back. The Protectorate operated within the law, even when the law protected monsters.

"It doesn't sound like that conversation went well. Do you intend to stop Henry Abernathy even if Master Issacs stands between you?" The downside to activating the comlink in his jaw was that he was forced to have the internal voice of Munin constantly available in his head. Grimly he frowned.

"Those twenty-three families deserve justice. If they can't have that, at least I can offer them some closure. Judgement."

TiME iS SHORT

Saturday, October 20, 2040
6:33 p.m.

"Kyle, wake up. Something is happening", gently Lydia shook his shoulder rousing him from the brief nap. His hand rose against the weak sunlight that stabbed his eyes with its dying swansong for the day. The knapsack initially made a reasonable pillow where he stretched out on the grass beneath a mossy oak. Now he felt a less compact pillow would have been better suited. A bottle of water was offered as Lydia squatted next to him with a concerned expression.

"What", he croaked as he accepted the bottle and washed the dryness from his throat. With a splash he rubbed away the last vestiges of sleep as he rolled to his feet to glance around the empty stretch of woods. Earlier they found an overgrown road and went down it far enough to be secluded until they knew what their next step was.

Apparently something changed.

Lydia moved to the open trunk of the car. Fit without being muscular, curvy without being voluptuous, she moved like someone accustomed to activity. A grunt escaped as he joined her at the rear of the car.

"What do you sense?" Next to her he saw her eyes closed tightly as eyes flicked quickly behind the lids. Time was what she needed. Hands brushed the loose grass from his shirt and jeans as he calmly waited for her answer. It wouldn't be rushed or focused until individual choices were made.

He once asked Lydia how it felt for her. Countless possibilities danced at the edge of her vision, like shadows in the day. Possibilities of existence floated near the surface of her mind but until someone made a conscious decision she couldn't see what would happen. And it couldn't be focused, just random points of decision weighed with future importance.

That was how they met.

Several months earlier he caught a bigot bully tormenting a small community of supers. The cops found him nicely trussed up and arrested him. At a small deli he was enjoying a meal when she slipped into his booth, olive eyes pleading from the thicket of brown curls. She warned him that he needed to permanently stop the punk once he made bail. That was a line Kyle was unwilling to make.

And three families felt the pangs of loss before the maniac was stopped. The decision he made, of not crossing his moral line, precipitated the choice made by the criminal to extract lethal revenge. Lydia never explained the past that set her upon her life quest, and he never asked.

It was the final time the bell of human decency tolled within him for the evil beings in the world. Some could be rehabilitated for wrong choices. Others needed to be put down. Judgement passed for the innocent lost. And for those yet to taste death.

If all it cost was his peace of mind to protect the innocent from tragic futures, it was a small price to pay.

He was Aegis. The shield of protection for those unable to protect themselves.

And so they followed Lydia's gut instinct and intuition to scenarios where only his brand of assistance could help. Judgement. From the Aegis.

Rumors and folk tales of a man with a shield and unbreakable tenacity began to spread as he travelled with Lydia. Somehow they managed to stay under the radar of law enforcement and the Protectorate. Until two days ago when Lydia woke with that dread filled feeling. Darkness grew to become a blight on the land and cause a wellspring of sorrow. The two headed north for Ocala, the location of the coming disturbance.

The most frustrating aspect was that the law knew who was preying on the innocent. But without adequate proof their hands were tied. By the very same law that was to punish evil. Even the Protectorate and Clay knew who was responsible. Yet they chose not to act. Luckily for all, Kyle was no longer shackled by the legality of the system.

A whimper escaped Lydia as she hunched over the trunk at the waist in pained aftershock. The cost of her gift was she needed to experience the possible future. Perhaps it was the trauma that added the silver in her luscious hair. Strain and pain always left their mark.

Careful not to move her, Kyle lent his hands as support to ensure she wouldn't collapse to the ground. With ease he turned her to where she could sit on the rear bumper and catch her breath. The final rays of light slipped through the trees which brought a chill that shivered his spine. Or maybe all the prescience was beginning to rub off on him. Either way, Kyle knew something wicked this way comes.

"In twenty minutes Henry Abernathy will kidnap two children from a cabin in the Silver Springs State Park. Into the woods … and I know why there is no physical evidence. He's a cannibal. And a monster. Like some kind of horror creature. If you go after him something happens there. It changes you Kyle. But I can't see what." The clipped words whispered from clenched teeth as she raised a hand to his cheek.

"You won't make it in time."

Being told he could make a difference saved him. What he did mattered. And now? There was no way he could stand down. No one told him he couldn't change the future before it was written. The only one in charge of his life was him. And he wasn't going to sit on his haunches and wait. Not today. The duffel was grabbed from the trunk and the lid slammed shut as Lydian hurriedly moved.

"Come on. We have some traffic laws to break." The door was snatched open and he slid in as Lydia jumped into the passenger seat. Dirt and gravel peppered the trees as the car was gunned wide open. With a bark from the tires as the car roared onto the pavement, Kyle unzipped the duffel and pulled out kevlar body armor with steel plate inserts.

"Help me put this on. If he's gone when we arrive I guess I will go hunting." As Lydia assisted, the car screamed down the road. All Kyle saw was the small smile on her face and the blood red highlights in the sky. Sailor's delight supposedly. The full moon would be born in crimson to rise as the hunter's moon. An apt setting for what Kyle planned that night.

NiGHT HUNT

Saturday, October 20, 2040
8:39 p.m.

The mist as he exhaled, frosted in his beard while cold air chilled his bones as he laid among the bushes. Night breeze rustled the forest floor and sent branches swaying as moonlight scattered through the leaves. Illuminated night moaned as the trees stretched. Leaves skittered about, not yet dried brown and crumbled to dust. The 1-4x24 scope remained close to his right eye as he silently watched with both.

Patterns moved with the breeze as the full moon peeked through the canopies above. Two portions of shadow remained fixed. When the wind died, eerie silence came as nature knew there were intruders. The rifle was out of line with the two figures. Instinct wanted to shift just enough to cover the two with the scope and barrel. Sometimes you needed to fight impulses so he remained still, unmoving.

The dark figures did not. Careful steps led them forward. In the frozen night they were the only things that moved. When you were the only motion upon a static background it was an announcement, no matter how quiet you remained. However, the two were not quiet either. Voices carried in the dead of the night.

An exasperated sigh of frustrated disgust was narrowly withheld.

When he attended the academy the sergeants would have murdered him if he was so careless and stupid. Possibly quite literally. The forest breathed again, the wind creating life from darkness and dry dead things. Using the motion to cover his own movement, Kyle eased backwards and burrowed deeper into the underbrush while shifting his rifle slightly. The sound of his movement covered by the moving forest before it held its breath once more.

The poor bastards moved like city boys. Careful not to kick anything big but completely unaware of how to walk in nature. Heel toe, heel toe. Upright with legs extended and torso leaned forward there was no opportunity to step softly. Just the noisome crunch with every stride. Shoulders brushed into branches that scratched against the plate armor they wore. Legs snapped dry thickets.

Wonder at the lack of woodsmanship rattled in his head. Slow, short steps that rolled slowly. Some called it fox walking. The key was a slow and easy pace. Feel with the blades of the feet. And if you can step over it, step over it. Don't step on limbs, branches, or other sticks. While the sound of leaves was a near constant in the forest, it was man that snapped sticks and broke nature's rhythm. And never shuffle stepped. Another secret was to wear socks to soften the sound of the sole of a boot.

Common hunting etiquette was also to stay downwind and never silhouette yourself.

Slow, as the snow melts, Kyle raised the bottom half of the black ski mask over his mouth and nose, leaving only his eyes exposed. A familiar sensation tingled along his spine, hairs raised on his neck. His hand froze near his face as he slowed his breathing and waited. Something more was there. Another presence nearby. Senses screamed of danger as instinct rebelled between staying still or rolling into action.

The two Warriors before him felt the change as they dropped into crouches, rifles shouldered and slowly moved from perceived potential targets. Internally he wanted to shout to be still, but that would reveal his location. Not only to the Warriors but to the predator that was nearby. The wind stilled. Harsh breath echoed from the Warriors.

Finger laid on the trigger guard as he waited breathlessly. Finally the breeze breathed through the forest bringing the ambiance of static noise. The Warriors began moving again as though the threat they felt passed. Not Kyle. Tension burned in his shoulders and worked to the base of his skull. Trigger finger itched, wanting nothing more than to caress the trigger.

A shadow moved to his right, only eyes flicked to look. Nothing. Mind played tricks. Or maybe not. The shadow slipped into a copse of trees soundlessly. Where Kyle and the Warriors believed they were there as the hunters, the stealth of the large shadow that disappeared into the darkness without a noise proved it was the predator.

The two men closed the distance to the thicket of saplings and thickets unaware of the danger. With the barest of movement Kyle placed his finger on the trigger. Action bred action. Inaction bred action. Faced with the dilemma to act first and attempt to alert the Warriors would make him a target. To wait would seal the fate of the Warriors who neared their demise with every ill gotten step.

The night's silence was broken by gunfire, screams, and roars.

IV
RACING THE CLOCK

Saturday, October 20, 2040
8:41 p.m.

The shadow rose, separated from the copse of trees. Silhouetted by the empty landscape behind it, the figure took on detail. The choice of doing nothing was no longer an option for Kyle. The rifle barrel twitched to line up with the figure the two Warriors were still unaware of. A gentle squeeze of the trigger was followed up with two more squeezes, launching fifty caliber rounds through the air to slam into the dark being.

The warriors, alerted, swept the muzzles of their rifles over his position as they searched without discharging. Old technology reinvented with modern resources and advanced designs.

The Girandoni air was one of the world's first air rifles and capable of firing two dozen times in less than a minute. Everything old is new again. So modern gunsmith's took their shot at the convenience and oddity of a powerful air rifle.

Many were successful. One was groundbreaking.

Salazar Bauer, an austrian gunsmith, decided to try his hand at creating a new PCP (Pre Compressed Air) rifle combining the ideas behind the original Girandoni air rifle and a bullpup design made popular by Steyr AUG, while utilizing the top rail feeding from the FN P90. The high pressure tank slipped into the shoulder stock with the attached one hundred round magazine riding the top rail into the receiver along the length of the rifle.

The invention of titan-steel allowed for a much greater psi than standard air tank reservoirs which increased the fps of the bullets. Threaded barrel on the bullpup allowed a barrel extension that made the gun a rifle. Rifled Barrel and a 1-4x24 scope completed the package. With the addition of a suppressor, Salazar Bauer gave the world his repeating, high powered rifle.

When Kyle fired, there was no telltale flash or cloud of smoke. Even the sound of the air rifle was suppressed. However, the fifty caliber rounds slammed into the shadowed figure as deadly as fire from a traditional modern rifle.

The shadow stumbled into the moonlight revealing his identity as Henry Abernathy. Blood stained his disproportionate chest from the wounds. Yet it was the elongated torso with lengthened arms and a gaping mouth of sharpened fangs which glistened in the night that drew the Warriors attention. Their automatic rifles flashed in the night which nearly blinded Kyle to the immediate action that followed.

If only it did.

The physical strength to dent titan-steel was unimaginable from reality. Even Clay would have been incapable of pounding a fist sized section of the plate armor into the Warrior's chest cavity like Henry did. The other Warrior was slammed into a tree trunk with such force that Kyle pretended the fine mist that sprayed him was just condensation.

The tacky texture belied the thought.

Henry raised his misshapen snout, for the lack of a better word, and huffed deeply. Finger froze on the trigger as Kyle internally chanted, "you're a log, you're a log". The undersuit he wore was designed to restrict body odor and sweat from escaping which could be scented by animals. For once he dearly hoped that buying a name brand was worth the extra hundred dollars.

Uncertainty colored Henry's movement as his growing discontent revealed he did not have Kyle's scent. Nor would he find the smell of gunpowder. Another benefit from Salazar's air rifle. Arms ached at the tension of remaining perfectly still. Though he wasn't seen or smelled the threat of discovery loomed too close for comfort. All it would take was for Henry to choose to move in his direction for Kyle to be accidentally found.

And he didn't care to be beat against a tree like a pinata.

An unheard sound caused the massive monster to ratchet his head sideways in concentration. Then in near silence Henry lopped off for whatever it was that drew him from the grisly scene of death.

"That was too close", Kyle whispered to Munin.

"I believe the Warriors would agree." It was a wasted action but he knelt beside both men, or what remained of them. Neither possessed a pulse. Unsurprised he stood with the Bauer air rifle pulled to his chest. Gunfire broke the grim tranquility of the night as screams were silenced ruthlessly. The screams were from the south, toward the Silver Springs State Park.

"He's doubled back. Why would a predator double back into hunters? Especially this predator. If he just kept heading north he could have just circled around eventually and there would be no witnesses placing him out here." With a frown he took a knee as he contemplated his next move.

"Perhaps he believes there will be no witnesses when he finishes."

"That's very helpful Munin. And not very encouraging. No, he came back because he is protecting something. That's why he's on a rampage." The night grew quiet once more. Briefly he wondered if Clay was out there somewhere. If he was still among the living. But there wasn't nearly enough of a fight for Clay to have been killed.

With a turn he rose to his feet and looked north with a frown on his hidden face.

"I don't think he had enough time. He's a monster, so he likes to play with his victims. He didn't have enough time before Lydia warned me. And with me, Clay and the Protectorate." With determined steps he hastened his pace north as eyes fervently searched for any sign of Henry's passing. Alone the monster would most likely have left nothing to track. But with his burden, there was a chance.

"What are you thinking Kyle?" The quiet voice whispered in his head.

"He didn't have enough time. The kids might still be alive."

STEALING THE PRIZE

Saturday, October 20, 2040
9:47 p.m.

Over an hour he searched. The further north Kyle went, the closer he got to Silver River, the more sign of the recent river rise before it slowly receded. Low sections still retained dampness and cypress trees stretched to the heavens with bare roots poised above the earth like fingers driven into the soil. During his zigzag pattern he found no trail of Henry or the children. No prints, bent grass, snapped twigs, nothing to prove the monster passed this way.

Yet instinct drove him onward.

"Munin, is there a way to open communication with Clay without reestablishing contact with the Protectorate", Kyle questioned his internal sidekick. Her reply was long in coming.

"Not in the traditional sense. No." The response was spoken slowly. Stubbornly he continued forward even as his boots began accumulating a layer of mud upon the soles. Frustrated he stopped and scraped the mud free on a rotten log most likely deposited there when the water was higher.

"That's not a straight answer. I need to know how many Warriors and Guardians he has out there. And if Henry has been sighted recently. I can't look for sign and watch my own trail simultaneously. Connect me with Clay." Irritation colored his words as he finally accepted that he went the wrong way. Sometimes instincts were wrong.

The full moon shone brightly as he turned in aggravation. There, along a line of roots that extended from a root ball, was mud. Similarly scraped free as he performed for his boots. Easing down he reached out, fingers prying the mud from the bark. It was still moist. Someone or something left the trace amounts there since the sun set.

Eyes searched other areas around for sign of camouflage passing. Several paces away a slight trace of mud. Swiftly he followed along as eyes searched fervently for the next clue of Henry's passing.

Then he found it. Compressed areas of green lichen along a log to snaking roots from a massive cypress tree. Hints of footfall. Reenergized he quickened his pace to the massive white tree and circled it cautiously. Halfway around, the roots parted in a recess. Silence reverberated. Nothing moved or swayed in the stillness of night.

Convinced it was temporarily safe he ducked into the alcove with the rifle shouldered. Inside he found two young children wrapped tightly in vines and strips of their own clothing. Dirty faces were filled with fear. Hands pushed the hood back and peeled off the mask while the rifle lay suspended upon his chest.

"Do not fear me. I'm taking you home." The words were spoken confidently with the grave power of an adult voice that stated simple facts. Hands freed their bonds. His arms scooped their diminutive forms into his arms and stood, his precious cargo cradled to his chest. As he stepped from the natural cave depression, he froze.

Silence reigned supreme. But instead of the quiet of the woods accented by nature's sounds there was nothing. No chirping of insects nor croaking of bullfrogs.

They were no longer alone.

With the south more than likely cut off by the return of Henry, it left only one option. To flee north.

The time for quiet stealth was passed.

The two children, no more than a handful of years between them, somehow knew they needed to remain silent. And so he moved at a light jog which left a clear trail of mud splattered indentions as clear as day. Even a child could track the trail he left. He possessed only two options. Slow stealth and silence or a hasty retreat that abandoned the care he used to arrive.

Several minutes north he turned east for a few more minutes before he believed they were far enough away to turn back south and the relative safety offered by the Protectorate presence. There was no time to tighten the straps of the gunsling snug. The weapon bounced against his armored vest with quiet sounds. A snarl threatened to mar his face at his mistake but two sets of eyes stared into his face with wide eyed, frightened innocence.

A roar of rage split the night to echo through the woods. The monster found his layer despoiled and his prizes missing. Feet hastened to greater speed, sock covered boots now making noise upon the foliage. The earth dried as the guttural roar shook the night once more. The idea to find a semi defensible spot to make a stand flew in and out of his mind with equal speed, though he did slow.

A group of young trees appeared to his right which would have been an appropriate spot to ambush Henry. Another roar of unfettered rage pierced the woods and decided his course of action.

He noped out. Not today. This was not that day. And he sure as hell wasn't going to play Van Helsing to some sort of werewolf cosplay with two children in tow. Not going to happen.

"I just criss crossed my references there. Think that means I jinxed us and doomed myself, Munin", he panted his question even as he accelerated through the woods.

"Yes."

"Thanks, you're a lot of help you know."

"I know."

Breath came in more ragged as he pondered the wisdom of accessing Munin once again.

"How about that connection with Clay? You do that yet?" Heart pounded in his ears as he neared a sprint. To keep up the neckbreak speed wasn't conceivable. Not with his current load. All he needed was to get inside the Protectorate formation.

A crash reverberated behind him. Dropped to a knee as he turned, eyes scanned to terrain. No one. There was still time. With a hiss between clenched teeth, Kyle stood again and returned to running.

"You kids like the stars", he asked. Two heads nodded yes. If he ended up with the two, they would make great additions to his bobble head collection on his car dashboard. Gasping, he spoke to the kids.

"Let's play a special game then. Both of you start counting the constellations you see between the tree branches and when we're back you tell me how many you saw." Any distraction he could toss at them would work. Or at least hoped.

"Communication established with Master Issacs." The urge to mutter, 'about time', passed without fruition.

"Excalibur, Clay, listen up. This is the man with the beat up boots." The quick pace slowed to a fast walk as Kyle talked. The time for frenzied flight passed with the need for early warning the more important aspect. If Henry caught up as they were running, Kyle and the kids stood very little chance. A moment's notice offered a chance to meet the monster prepared.

"Kyle? How are you talking to me?" Confusion colored Clay's words. At least he was alive though, that's what was important. A deep breath rushed out in relieved relief as Kyle counted the lucky stars for the other man's safety.

"I got Munin to bypass Protectorate channels. Just shut your trap and listen. I have the kids and Henry is on my tail. I need to get to you. Don't shoot me." The last part was said sarcastically as Kyle vigilantly checked behind them as he walked.

"Firing flares. And that's not possible about how this is working. We aren't talking on comms. We have friendlies incoming. Someone rescued the kids, but we are looking at dealing with Henry immediately." Shouts echoed in his head as Kyle searched the skies for flares. The rest of what he heard merely confirmed he wouldn't be shot on sight. Which was always a good thing. Tightly he closed his right eye.

Ahead three flared burst into existence, their red light illuminating the woods with an eerie tiny. Everything wept blood under the harsh glow of the flares that descended on small parachutes. The pace quickened. If he could see the flares, the odds were that so did the monster behind him.

Nearly a minute later the flares died.

With the woods reclaimed by darkness, Kyle blinked at the blindness earned from the light of the flares. Right eye opened to return the night vision that he managed to keep from being denied admission to the flare show. Two visions layered over his sight. The dark and murky blanket of shadows in his left and the detail filled dimmed vision in his right.

Even as the short distance rapidly shrank due to his loping run, Kyle wondered at the meaning of the other man's words. Was or wasn't he using the comlink grafted in his jaw to speak on a separate bandwidth with Clay? Regardless of his thoughts, the game of cat and mouse ended.

A snarl was the only warning he received as Henry launched from the darkness. Taloned fingers pierced the jacket he wore as they drove for his spine. They would have, if it wasn't for the heater shield strapped to his vest upon his back. Razor sharp claws scoured the titan-steel shield even as Henry's weight and force of jump shoved Kyle to the ground.

The children were pressed between his body and the ground, temporarily safe from the monster. However, it was not for long. The deadly blows rained upon the shield, the reverberations vibrating Kyle's spine. Pressure shifted and changed as Henry moved from off his back. Realization hit as the talons gripped the edge of the revealed shield and yanked.

The children were released as Kyle was thrown backwards several car lengths before smashing through brush and snagging bushes. When Henry didn't immediately follow Kyle rolled to his feet, shrugging from the ruined heavy jacket. Instinctively he reacted.

The shield slung from his back and his left arm slipped through the enarmes, leather straps, and clenched the grip bar. Right hand gripped the bullpup air rifle as he sprinted forward. The monstrous form of Henry stood splay legged over the children. Viscous triumph radiated as enlarged hands reached for their frightened, still forms.

Then Kyle rammed him with the shield as he utilized all his added strength and speed to launch them away from the children. The two careened away, Kyle lucky enough to land atop the snarling monster. Legs kicked himself free and Kyle came to a knee, the extended barrel of the rifle resting upon the flat top of the shield.

Henry was fast, too fast. Back on his feet he turned to leap at Kyle. Talons still glistened with blood from those murdered earlier. While the monster was fast he was not able to beat the rapid pull of the trigger. Fifty caliber bullets hit center mass as Kyle feathered the trigger in rapid fire. The force of the rounds knocked Henry back where he fell into a thicket with a crash.

Paused for a moment, Kyle took the opportunity to stand. Cautiously he approached the scene which should easily display a riddled body. There was nothing. Crushed bushes and broken branches. Nearly crouched, he retreated as the rifle remained perched on the rim of the shield. Moonlight sprinkled through the canopy above in a glittering display of light. The wind breathed life with swayed branches and moaned into the night. Every scattering of light which pierced the tree cover danced with new activity.

Movement drew his eye. A branch swayed. Motion on his left

proved to be breeze rustled grass. A tree trunk undulated at shoulder height and Henry dove for him from the height. Falling back he tried to bring the rifle to bear, but wasn't fast enough. The two collided and rolled through the brush as the rifle, no longer tethered to his body, flew from his hand and into darkness. The shield was swung, the right edged point drove into Henry's bloodied chest even as talons raked down the right side of Kyle's torso.

A scream of pain escaped as clawed hands tore through the steel plated kevlar vest to dig into the flesh beneath. Rancid breath washed over his face as Henry laughed in primal glee. They rolled to a stop against a tree with the creature on top. Both hands raised into the heavens before slashing down in speedy strikes to shred Kyle alive.

The shield deflected many blows but did not mitigate their bone crushing power. Unable to push the heavier man away, Kyle became pinned beneath the shield and the ferocious onslaught. Right hand snaked down to his boot, the handle of the dirk dagger meeting his palm. Fingers closed and he pulled it from its sheath. The force of the blows dizzied Kyle as pain wracked his body.

Rebellion at the pained haze which drifted into his mind he drove the pointed dirk up into the side of Henry. The sharp point slipped between ribs as the double edged blade buried deep into the monster. A gasp and pause gave a moment's respite which Kyle took advantage of. The grip tightened on the handle and he twisted before he withdrew the dirk and struck upwards once more. The tip skipped across a rib before becoming buried again.

Another roar escaped Henry though this one sounded different. Pain. So the beast could actually feel pain. Another twist of the blade while Kyle struck out with the edge of the shield directly into the snout of the creature. Body arched as he attempted to hump Henry from his position. Using the buried dirk as an anchor Kyle kicked against the tree and flipped them.

He landed on top of Henry, quickly rising up to rain blows down with the shield on his left arm. His right withdrew the blade to plunge into Henry's chest repeatedly. Despite the amount of damage inflicted, Henry raised up from his back, both hands grabbed Kyle's wrists. Misery filled the monster's eyes as they glared inches from Kyle's. However there was more in the gaze.

A hungering rage.

The beast's strength was greater than his own. Slowly his arms were forced backwards away from his body even as the grip squeezed bones near to shattering. Evil glee filled Henry's face, teeth unnaturally long stretched open in a grin. The struggle for freedom was lost against a foe more powerful than he. So Kyle did the only thing he could think of.

Head leaned down and teeth latched over Henry's nose as he bit down with all his might. Blood spurted dark oil in the darkness of night. Instead of continuing to restrain Kyle's arms, Henry shoved with immeasurable strength which tossed Kyle up and away. Branches broke with his flight through the lower limbs. Then he arced into the ground which jarred his entire body.

Agony screamed as Kyle rolled to his side. The shield remained attached though the dirk was lost. On the ground Henry groaned before rose slowly. Fatigue dulled Kyle's senses.

"Stand up", Munin intoned from within his head.

The beast rose to his full height.

"Kyle, get up now", again Munin echoed.

The moonlight revealed the wounds that covered Henry.

"On your feet now!"

Black stains wept profusely as Henry's head rolled upon shoulders.

"Move it or you are dead!"

Dark eyes stared into the heavens as the beast breathed a deep, shuddering breath.

"You're the only hope those kids have!"

Finally Kyle roused. Hand and shield pressed to the ground as he pushed to his feet. Their eyes met and there was zero question who Henry was killing first. An attempt at a smile crossed Kyle's face. More like a grimace. Death looked upon him from Henry's eyes. Kyle held his hands up in a gesture to stall the beast from advancing and killing him immediately.

"I'm sorry Henry. I thought you were a few fries of a happy meal. I now know I'm wrong." The words hurt to say. Not the apology but the act of speaking. The monster glowered at him but did not yet advance which prompted Kyle to continue.

"Yeah, I now know that's a horrible analogy. You're actually those fries that fall in the cracks of the seat. You know, the ones down there for years but look exactly the same as the day you bought them. Even roaches or mold won't touch them cause they're so bad. That's you Henry. Years old fries, that even roaches will not touch."

With a bellow, the monster charged.

VI
UNEXPECTED REUNION

Saturday, October 20, 2040
10:58 p.m.

"Get down!"

The words barely registered before the body reacted. Instead of diving to relative safety as was seen in movies, Kyle just collapsed. Crumpled to the ground gave him a great view of the destructive power released as Warriors and Guardians unleashed hell.

A dozen points in a semicircle poured massive amounts of firepower into Henry. Staggered back, chunks were removed in grisly fashion before the beast collapsed into the woods.

"Flares. Make sure that bastard is down and stays down." The authoritative command was barked by Clay as he moved next to where Kyle lay in a crumpled heap.

"Sir, we have the kids."

"Standby", Clay ordered as he gave attention to Kyle.

A grunt was followed by swears as Clay probed the wounds on his friend's chest. Bloody furrows ripped flesh. Already the torn flesh clotted. With practiced ease Clay helped Kyle free of his vest and shredded shirt. A small silver cylinder appeared in his hand before a cold spray coated the clawed wounds.

Curses followed as the antibacterial disinfectant spray sterilized the wounds. It may have felt cool initially but now burning hot pokers raked Kyle's wounds. Cold sweat appeared on his forehead and upper lip. The sterilizer now stowed, now Clay pinched the wounds closed before he used a surgical stapler securing the opposite ends closed.

For good measure Clay pulled out a tube of fast drying superglue and coated the ragged incisions.

"Excalibur, he's gone. There's blood everywhere but nobody here." The search detail returned with cautious looks into the woods. Clay stood and gazed about as the next plan of action grew in his mind. Kyle slowly pushed to his feet, shield now tossed over his shoulder by the strap. His skin puckered with goosebumps as the cool wind caressed his bare torso.

"Not my place, but I'd suggest sending a team back to safety with those kids. If I'm not wrong, Henry wants his pound of flesh from me. So use me as bait and take the kids out of here." The grudge Kyle spoke about using was easily evident when he locked eyes with Henry. The night would only end when one of them was dead.

He could agree to that.

Another turn as Clay scanned the area gave him another moment to decide.

"Franklin, get these kids to safety. Then set up a perimeter and reinforce it. I'm going to use this civilian's idea. But if we fail then you and your boys use the quarantined area and turn it into a killbox. I don't even want earthworms to survive. Understood?"

"Yes sir."

The remaining Guardians formed up for a quick march back to civilization with kids in tow. Two Warriors joined the two old friends as Kyle stood. One stood tall and wide, shoulders as broad as a door. Close cropped hair left only a darkened outline. Prominent nose and a face that looked like it went twelve rounds with a sledge hammer, and won. The other was as lithe and agile as grass. Pale eye looked from an equally pale face. Tight, thin lips and a braid tied back so severely she appeared to be in a constant state of discomfort.

"Big man is Exo. He's able to rapidly grow his bones that pierce his skin to form an exoskeleton, hence the name. This barrel of laughs is Spotlight. She can light up the room or toast us like marshmallows over a campfire." Each was pointed to with the introduction. Clay looked to Kyle and motioned.

"This is …", Clay faltered, not wishing to reveal that the former Warrior, Kyle Ross, still lived. Quickly Kyle stepped forward to interject.

"Call me Aegis", he shrugged at Clay who merely raised his brows.

Quick introductions were finished and then he collected the Salazar rifle. The extended barrel was bent in the fight so he removed it before he tied the sling, slashed by Henry's clawed hands. Looped over his left shoulder, it wasn't perfect by any means, but it would do the job. The warriors converged as he stood apart.

"See if you can find his trail. Time to run him down and take him into custody. Or take him down permanently if that's not possible." The two Warriors went back to where the monster was last seen in the brush.

With the small window of opportunity, Kyle approached the team leader.

"What did you mean when you said we weren't talking over comms? Munin bypassed Protectorate channels is all." As he spoke he removed the tank/magazine combo from the rifle and slapped another in. Frustrated he lost his knife he patted the empty sheath on his boot.

"Kyle, the artificial intelligence program has been offline for over five years. And I heard you in my head, not over comms. Like how Sandy used to." The two men looked at one another as each tried to comprehend the meaning from the other.

The words didn't add up. Kyle was in contact with Munin this whole time, and now he was told she wasn't real. Slowly fragments floated into place. Nobody else ever heard a feminine voice. She was always there, in his ear, when he needed her. And her name … Munin. It all made sense. And none of it did.

"Munin, why didn't you ever tell me?" Bewildered, Clay looked on in confusion.

"What are you talking about?"

Head shook again in disbelief as he placed his hand on Clay's shoulder.

"You ever get a gut instinct that didn't come from your gut? An idea that changed your mind for the better?"

"Yeah, I guess. A few times. Actually I've had a few occasions where I made orders on a whim that shouldn't have worked, but did. Almost like I had the secret plans, but couldn't explain how I knew any of it." The poor bastard still looked confused.

"Munin was from norse mythology. So was Hugin. They were Odin's ravens. Sandy used to call me Hugin because I always acted. My thoughts were my actions. She was the one who always had the plan, the mind. And she always remembered everything. Munin isn't here", his finger pressed to his jawbone where his comlink was embedded.

"She's here", his finger moved to his temple.

"And Munin isn't an AI. Munin is Sandy." The weight of the words rocked them both.

For Kyle, the full understanding of what he said was inconceivable. A decade and a half passed since he lost his sister. Fifteen years of loss, regret, and what-ifs. Knees shook before he stumbled to the hard earth. The promise to always look after him rang in his ears.

Pain of loss resurfaced. As though he relived the nightmare. The casket shimmered before his eyes. She was cold and drawn, waxen skin beneath layers of makeup. A false flush of color marred her cheeks. It wasn't his sister. He closed the lid and buried his emotions.

Emotions were interred alongside his sister. Until now.

A hand gripped Kyle's shoulder which brought his back to reality. Next to him Clay swayed in disbelief. The only reason the big man remained on his feet was because of the anchor grip on Kyle.

Shoulders were bowed from the weight of guilt. But no more. She was back. And all the years the emptiness haunted him were erased with the following words.

"Hey boys", her voice echoed within them. Clay was the first to regain his composure.

"How are you doing this Sandy? You're gone, we buried you."

"I don't know exactly. What I do know was that when I died I reached out for you three, and somehow was able to anchor on. So here I am, a spirit or ghost, who is still looking after her boys. My boys."

Tears streamed down Kyle's face while Clay's mouth gaped open in utter amazed confusion.

"There's so much we need to talk about ...", Kyle's words died off as he climbed to his feet.

"Everytime I speak to one of you, or nudge one of you, it gets more difficult. I'm losing pieces of me each time. But I'll give anything to save y'all."

The two Warriors returned. Taking a moment for composure, Clay turned to them first.

"Anything?"

"Nothing. It's like he vanished", Exo grunted out.

Turned around, Kyle looked at the Warriors with an expression of epiphany on his face.

"Looks like the civie has an idea. That bulb gets any brighter, he's gonna blow a fuse", Spotlight remarked sarcastically. Kyle ignored the remark.

"Henry is just a big beast right? What do animals do, especially predators, when they are hurt? They go back to their den or cave. Well, I know where his den is. I say we go and burn him out."

The other three nodded heads in agreement. It was settled. They broke into pairs and followed Kyle's lead.

Often he found it amazing how a flight from danger passed in seconds. The return to the same place stretched into hours. They moved steadily but with great care to be silent. Their decision to go the monster's lair was equal parts bravery and foolish ardor. The Warriors it was for revenge against a man who killed several of their brethren that night. For Kyle, it was all together dissimilar.

Judgement was coming for Henry Abernathy.

The ground changed once more. The tacky texture clung to their boots as they marched ever closer. Curiosity turned Kyle's head to his friend.

"I'm not sure how well these guns are going to work. That monster kept coming despite how much damage he took. But my blade seemed to work pretty well. What is he exactly?" The shield shifted from his back as he slipped his arm into place. Quietly Clay answered the question.

"We call them mutts. We've got flatliners and supes. Some flatliners have been upgrading in order to be on equal footing with us. Well, some nut job has been making mutts. Supers with tech upgrades. Every single time we find one it's because they've gone rabid. Like Henry."

Feet moved quietly as Kyle tried to understand why anyone would want to cut away at what made them unique. It was twice as hard to imagine why a super would do it.

"Why haven't you shut them down yet?"

"Because we don't know who is making them. And the mutts don't exactly cooperate. Something big is happening but no one can put their finger on it."

With hand raised, Kyle motioned for both teams to stop. In a crouch he moved backwards until all four men were huddled closely.

"From what I saw there was only one way in. Halfway around there's a gap", Kyle explained quietly. Clay pointed at the two other Warriors.

"Me and Aegis will cover the rear in case there is a secondary way out. You two hit the front. Spotlight, let it shine. Blast that opening into ash. Hell, take out the entire tree if you can. Exo, watch her back. On your toes." Hand motioned for the two to circle around and move into position. Near Clay, the moment gave Kyle another opportunity to speak before madness ensued.

"I don't think shooting him will be the answer. You handy with that thing? Cause that might end up being the best way", Kyle gestured to the sword strapped to Clay's back. Almost proving the point, Clay pulled the longsword free and held it in his left hand. The right hand held a submachine gun. The smirk was heard in his voice.

"Kind of a stupid idea to call me Excalibur if I don't know how to wield a sword. Don't you think?"

Kyle couldn't argue with Clay's perfectly founded point.

Squatted behind a tree for cover, Kyle watched Clay move a little closer before stretching his body out upon the grass. Partially blended with the palmetto bushes, there was nothing left to do but wait for the Warriors' attack.

Suddenly a flash of light blinded him at the intensity. As the illumination faded Kyle blinked away the afterimages printed on his retinas. Flames licked up the tree trunk as the trunk blistered and groaned. For good measure grenades were tossed in with the mandatory shout 'frag out'.

Another explosion echoed in the woods as shrapnel sought to pierce a body. Anybody.

The Warriors kept their rifles trained on the opening. A nudge against Kyle's leg and Clay motioned toward the tree. The intent was clear. They would each circle the massive trunk in opposite directions until they neared either side of the opening.

Slow step by slow step Kyle eased around his side of the cypress tree. The trunk was charred with little tongues of flame burning sporadically upon the surface. Eyes flickered around making sure there wasn't a hollow or recess that could give escape to the monster. Finally the Warriors eased into view at their stationary positions and the hollow opened.

Taking a knee Kyle looked around the opening but could see nothing but small flames. Nothing moved. A glance at Clay got his attention before Kyle shook his head. No eyes on the target. Each of the others shared his failure. They just couldn't see enough inside.

None of them wanted to go in if Henry was still alive, hurting, and angry. Hand gesture backed Kyle away at Clay's insistence. When the plan of action became clear, it made sense. Arranged in a half circle around the opening of the tree, they opened fire once more at Clay's command.

Twenty seconds of concentrated fire and then silence. The scorched trunk was filled with bullet holes, smoke escaped as the tree exhaled. Clay motioned for Exo to trade spots. Once at the front, Clay slowly advanced as Spotlight slid wide right to maintain a clear line of fire. Crouched close to the tree Kyle strained his eyes to see into the hazed darkness. Concern flickered in his mind as Exo did what he, moments ago, decided not to do.

With the damage done to the tree there were several spots torn open by the bullet barrage. Several were large enough to place your face against and see through with an eye. Enough horror movies were seen in Kyle's time to make his confidence that nothing would happen waver like a kite in high wind.

Exo pulled his eye away from the hole and shook his head at Clay. Still couldn't see anything. A shake of his head before he refocused on the opening as Clay slowly approached. The rent and tear in the trunk released a constant vapor of smoke making visibility even more difficult. They needed eyes inside. So with trepidation Kyle looked at the darkened bullet holes in the trunk before him. Slowly he moved his face closer to an aperture.

A thousand horror movies flickered through his mind. Yet they needed to know. Left eye closed and Kyle exhaled slowly in preparation. The dark pit beckoned. A slight shake of his head and Kyle Leaned in.

The burned lid snicked back and the bright red, hemorrhaged eye stared into Kyle's own with only the shell of the cypress tree separating them.

VII
JUDGEMENT

Saturday, October 20, 2040
11:39 p.m.

Time slowed as he reared back. The rifle was out of line due to the proximity to the tree when he peeked in. Mouth opened with a warning shout. A section of tree trunk exploded outward as a clawed hand grasped Kyle around the neck. The immense strength pulled his face right into the tree before the arm shoved out and yanked back again.

Face turned sideways when the force of the impact destroyed a basketball sized hole as his head was pulled into the hollow. Blood dripped from split brow which, in turn, colored half his vision red. The nightmarish visage of Henry would haunt him for sometime.

Teeth glistened with strands of saliva which dripped from open mouth. A gaping wound where the nose once sat, dark gore pulsed from the cavity. White skull glistened from where bullets split and shredded flesh to hang by the barest connective tissue. Lumps of hair were gone completely, the scalp exposed with cankerous skin lesions.

The moment of promised death neared fulfillment.

Hands pressed against the outside of the trunk, small embers burned palms without notice. Heaving against the more powerful Henry proved futile. A line of saliva coiled on his cheek putrid and slimy. Fang points slightly dimpled Kyle's skin right before the powerful bite that would rip his face from its skull.

Suddenly arms wrapped around Kyle's waist and heaved backward while simultaneously Exo charged through the opening of the hollow, right arm shouldered the rifle while a long, bony protrusion erupted from his left hand in the form of a prehistoric spear fashioned from bone. The spear drove home with the weight of Exo's driving force behind it. Henry slammed against the interior of the tree as Kyle's head felt the cool breeze from outside the tree's cavity.

A sword flashed down, moonlight glinted from the pristine blade. The sword was so sharp that there was nor report of titan-steel hitting flesh. The blade passed clean through the bicep. The hand remained clenched on Kyle's throat as he fell back, his fall cushioned by the diminutive Spotlight.

Gunfire peppered the weakened tree trunk. Several rounds escaped prompting both Kyle and Spotlight to dive flat to the ground. Clay charged into the fray in the darkened recess within the tree. Sword held high and at the ready.

Spotlight gained her feet before Kyle as she sprinted several strides ahead. The full auto firepower released into Henry revealed the scene. Like an old slide projector that flashed every new image on the backdrop of emptiness was Exo and Henry's story revealed.

Rounds hit the monster's torso. Most exited the back with black spray. The flash from the rifle barrel showed the bone spear pulled free of Henry and rammed home through Exo's body. Discarded with as little care as trash, Exo was hurled through the opening to collide with Spotlight. Skewered by the same bone spear that protruded from Exo, the woman Warrior went down hard, still joined with her partner.

Inside, shouts mingled with the sound of bodies colliding repeatedly. With a snarl Kyle charged into the darkness. Eyes focused to see two silhouettes struggling mightily against one another. The sword held between them as each tried to drive the cutting blade into the other's body.

The sword inched perilously close to Clay as he lost the battle of strength. Legs coiled to spring Kyle forward. The shield slipped between the sword and Clay's body just as the sword slammed home to ring against the titan-steel barrier.

Through brute strength, Henry lifted the two men and threw them at the interior wall of the tree trunk. Such force was exerted that they broke through the tree to scatter across the ground. The tree groaned and snapped to topple forward. Clay managed to land a safe distance away though neither Kyle nor Spotlight was so lucky. The trunk fell straight for Spotlight who weakly tried to claw from the path of the falling behemoth. Still speared to Exo, there was nothing she could do. Both Warrior bodies disappeared under the compression of the tree.

A branch as thick as his waist crashed into Kyle, slamming him to the ground mercilessly. A loud snap sounded at the impact. Despite the sudden pain it was the sound of the branch breaking rather than Kyle's own body. Slowly he crawled from beneath the tree limb, his spine and legs alternated between flashes of burning pain and cold needles. Unable to control his own body he spasmed in jerks arced his entire body.

Several body lengths away laid Clay. The sword was embedded across his right shoulder. Blood seeped from the wound but the pressure of the sword kept from more profuse blood loss. Activity near the base of the smoldering trunk revealed Henry's emergence. Ravaged skin and flesh were exposed to the moonlight as blood seeped from nearly every pore.

The monster staggered, almost falling to his knees before seeing Clay. Eyes narrowed before Henry shuffled to the fallen Excalibur. Legs splayed over the unmoving form of Clay before dropping to knees.

Fingers clawed at the dirt leaving furrows as Kyle pulled himself along the ground. Muscles spasmed when he tried to push to his knees. Ahead, Henry gripped the blade and leaned down to saw the sword deeper into Clay's shoulder.

The rifle was gone somewhere, possibly under the fallen tree. All that remained was the shield. Body cried in resistance to the punishment received and rebelled when Kyle pushed unsteadily to his feet.

A sickening sound of bone crunched as the sword bit deeply into Clay's shoulder. And then his arm fell away with fingers twitching lifelessly. The cry of utter loss and surrender in the face of the insurmountable enemy galvanized Kyle. New life energized his bruised and exhausted body.

Somehow one foot after another and then Kyle was in motion.

The shield was reared back, almost held behind his body, and swung with the edge of the shield. The crunch shook Kyle's arm as he felt windpipe, cartilage, and bone crush in Henry's throat. The monster fell off and jerked across the ground before he laid still.

Knees hit the ground next to Clay as Kyle frantically searched equipment pouches that festooned Clay's chest. Finger finally found and closed on a silver canister. Raised so the moonlight illuminated the description, he nodded and pulled the tab. The opening of the bottle was oriented at the traumatic shoulder wound where the arm, just moments before, was connected. The trigger was depressed releasing an aerosol acid compound that burned closed arteries and veins in a chemical reaction.

Readjusted with one knee now over Clay's chest to hold the thrashing body still, Kyle popped the bottom cap off and dumped the powdered contents across the wound. The seal powder dehydrates the blood that formed a jelly like scab. With pressure atop the chalky mound of granulates, the sealer promoted clotting while using the solidified jelly as a makeshift scab.

Hands searched the pouches once more to find the emergency blanket. The silver sheet was stiff. Both hands wrapped around the wrapped emergency blanket and twisted to start the thermal reaction. Miniscule sections of water, salt, iron, and magnesium powder intermingled to create the chemical process. The blanket was shaken out and then tucked against Clay's body.

Fingers lightly plucked the comlink from Clay's ear.

"Warriors down. Henry Abernathy dead. Emergency medical assistance required at this location", Kyle finished before he dropped the comms next to Clay who shivered.

"He's not dead", Clay whispered between chattering teeth.

Kyle looked down at his friend before he squatted and placed a hand against his fallen friend's temple.

"You stay alive. Helps coming for you. As for that monster being alive? Not for long." The shield was retrieved as Kyle stood and moved over to where Henry stared with hatred. Unable to move or even control his breathing, all the beast could do was watch.

"Kyle … don't. This isn't … right. This isn't justice", the words rattled from Clay's chest. Knees dropped to either side of Henry as Kyle straddled the decimated form that refused to die.

"No, not justice. Judgement."

The shield was gripped on either side as Kyle raised his arms overhead. The tear drop design along the bottom of the shield came to a sharpened point. Henry's eyes widened. The point came down into the hollow of his throat. Repeatedly Kyle raised and slammed the point. Blood flew and snarls of unrepentant rage escaped his mouth as his throat grew raw. The shield continued to rise and fall until exhaustion stayed his hand.

The severed head lay away from the body. Eyes stared vacantly into the darkness. Wearily Kyle struggled to his feet and slung the shield, coated red, across his back. His hair was disheveled, wounds marked his body, shirtless, and splattered in blood. The two men stared at one another even as Kyle's chest heaved from the exertion. Clay laid with lost, confusion colored, pain filled eyes that wasn't sure what came next. Or where either of them were to go.

"Judgement is come. All those who believe themselves untouchable will taste judgement. I love you Clay, but never get in my way."

Back turned to his fallen friend as legs carried him north. Sounds of reinforcements echoed to the south. Legs stopped and he turned back, looking past the trees to where the Guardians arrived at the scene.

At least Clay would live.

Twenty-three families got judgement.

And countless innocents were now safe because Henry Abernathy was dead.

Guilt tried to worm into his mind but he shook it off. He could live with guilt if it meant innocents would be safe.

He would live with it.

The darkness embraced Kyle as his blood caked boots walked into its depths.

PART SIX:
GIVE AND TAKE

NEW ALLiES

Tuesday, September 10, 2041
10:23 p.m.

Kennesaw Mountain, Georgia

The meeting ended.

Much like the previous three nights, there was nothing new. Not enough intel to go on. For the third night he returned to the campsite. Before the fire, Lydia sat cross legged with eyes closed. An oversized green sweater swamped her upper body and lap where only the hint of black trousers were seen. Frustration piqued her features and turned her full lips downward. Unable to focus her gift gnawed at her.

A small, grey tent lay pitched nearby the fire. Inside Blink grunted in irritation as he lay on the tent floor. The kid was young but proven. Followed orders and was a benefit with his gift. Seven seconds of precognition didn't help much, but every little bit helped. A deep sense of loss lay just beneath his surface.

When he was finally ready to talk, Kyle would be there. Everyone was haunted by ghosts and until then, the kid would bear his in silence.

Black tank top and bluejeans with trusty black boots laced over pant legs was Kyle's attire that evening. Though his own features were smoothed from internal emotions, his eyes still flashed at the wait. Fingers ran through his hair as he collected and tied it into a ponytail. Stubble darkened his face.

"I'm going for a ride. I'll be back." A head poked through the tent flap, Blink's youthful face reflected the light from the fire.

"I'm, uh, pretty sure we aren't supposed to leave." A little smirk with steel behind the expression was the only response Kyle gave. Head disappeared as Blink laid back with a retort.

"You're the boss though."

Distracted by the most recent planning session, Kyle neared one of the other campsites. Before he could turn and skirt the group his name was called.

"Aegis!"

Too late to leave unnoticed, Kyle walked forward into the circle of tents where a fire crackled in the night. A burly man of average height beckoned Kyle forward. Brushed back brown hair was streaked with silver. As was the neatly trimmed beard. Hand reached out in greeting and Kyle took it. Strength radiated from the older man as he offered Kyle a friendly, open smile.

"Meant to greet you outside the meetings. But I've been needed for other things. Nice to finally shake the hand of a legend." Head shook side to side as their hands released. A bemused smile crossed Kyle's face as he returned the sentiment.

"I'm just doing my part. The real legend is you, Catch. Since the beginning it's been you that's been making the difference." Champion was the face of the Protectorate, and supers in general, since the initial revelation of super powered individuals. Catch-22 was the renegade who worked outside the system to assist supers that needed help. And policed the supers that needed stopping.

With a shrug, Catch took a drink from his steaming mug.

"Everyone does their part. I'm just glad FedX has been able to make a difference."

"That it has."

"All I know is that every day we wait to strike is another moment we miss our shot. And with how big the mission is and the people needed, the better the chance of a leak. I still say we hit the stash houses and eliminate the criminals we can. Take the money and workers and then they have to move the prisoners."

Each meeting, Catch lobbied to move immediately. The reasons were sound, but the purpose was to free the slaves in the super human trafficking ring. That was why Kyle, Lydia, and Blink were there.

The last two years were dangerous for supers. At first it was rumors. Supers and their families disappeared. Most assumed the missing people decided to move and stay off the grid. Every month brought more supers missing. Several months ago the Underground of Atlanta discovered the missing were being trafficked to a buyer in the south.

Finally the Underground learned that the criminal organization was housing large numbers of prisoners. Not just adults but children too. Soon they would be transported and then there was nothing that could be done. Feelers were sent for assistance for a large scale operation and many groups answered the call.

Despite the pressure that several groups applied for immediate action, the Underground's leader resisted until they found where the supers were being held. The Atlanta group were zealous, following their leader faithfully. Kyle sent Blink and Lydia up a day before he came. At the planning session that night the commander-in-chief made it clear that nothing would happen before the prisoners were found.

And so they waited.

With a shrug of his shoulders, Kyle chose not to choose either side of the argument. All he was there for was to be part of the rescue mission.

"I hear you. However, I also understand the reasoning for patience. All we can do is sit tight."

Neither man was happy to hurry up and wait. But neither could they sit indefinitely. Sooner rather than later the chance would expire.

"You're more than welcome to join us", Catch offered with a gesture.

"Appreciate it but I need to clear my head." With a nod, Catch dismissed Kyle who headed out once again.

As Kyle walked through the woods he paused several times to look behind. The sensation of being followed prickled his neck. Shoulders shrugged as he continued. This wasn't normally his stomping grounds yet a brief call changed that.

Occasionally Sage would contact Kyle. Most often it was with a lead for Kyle to help. As a partner at a software company, Sage often used his abilities to keep an eye out for supers. Sometimes he was able to find them a new life with new identities. Other times there were extenuating circumstances that only Aegis could help with.

When he caught wind of a major operation that needed help, Sage forwarded the information to Kyle. A few days later they were north of Atlanta and waited for go time. It was the waiting Kyle hated most.

The trees swayed in the light breeze as Kyle reached the parking area. As he neared his Monte Carlo, Kyle sensed the presence directly behind him. Having arrived at the car he placed both forearms against the edge of the car's roof.

"Don't know who you are but I don't like being followed", Kyle said as fingers drummed atop the vehicle. The person behind stopped. A gentle voice floated over to him.

"Well, I do know who you are. And I'm curious where you think you're going?"

A sigh escaped Kyle as he turned. At first glance she was beautiful, there was no mistaking that. Black hair lay in short braids back from her face. Silken mahogany skin was flawless. The kind of full lips that looked sexy in a pout and tempted all with their inherent softness. Gray shirt conformed to curves accented with toned muscle. Tight blue jeans left no doubt that the woman was in shape.

"Going for a drive to clear my head. Not that it's any of your business." Arms folded over her breasts as she scrutinized him.

"People are worried about possible leaks and you think taking a scenic drive is going to go over well?" A brow arched over her amber eyes that held strength and expected obedience.

"Listen. I appreciate what you're doing but I'm getting cabin fever just sitting and staying in one place. I need to stretch my legs and clear my head", he said matter of factly. The distance was closed as she moved beside him at the car.

"I could stop you, you know."

"You could try. Wouldn't succeed."

"Oh, I'd do more than try." Both leaned against the car as Kyle looked down into her face. Danger lurked in her cat eye's. Also mischief. With a smirk he crossed his own arms to mirror the small woman who was no more than five feet tall.

"Everybody needs an unattainable dream." Teeth flashed white as she returned his smirk and responded.

"Well it won't do to knock out someone who came to help. But neither can I allow you to drive off unattended."

"More than welcome to ride shotgun and keep an eye on me. Unless you're afraid", he mockingly responded. There it was. An animalistic gleam in her eyes. Power echoed from her smoldering eyes.

"Someone needs to keep an eye on the elderly", she remarked as she circled the car and opened the passenger door.

"Hey! I'm not that old. Early thirties isn't old. And what are you? Early twenties?" She slipped into the car and closed the door. Leaned over she opened his door from the inside.

"It's not the miles that count but the experience. Now come on old man, I won't let you lose yourself." With a shake of his head he slipped into his seat and closed the door. After the engine was started Kyle glanced over to the woman.

"You need your parents' permission for going out this late?" A wry smile touched her lips as she buckled up.

"Are we just going to sit here or are we going already? I knew old people were slow, but this is ridiculous." Head shook as Kyle muttered under his breath and put the car in gear.

ROAD TRiP

Tuesday, September 10, 2041
11:05 p.m.

The car cruised through the city, the lights created a spectacle reminiscent of the holidays. A cigarette was held in Kyle's left hand with elbow resting out the open window. Beside him, the young woman watched him with an unreadable gaze. It would have been disconcerting had he been anyone else. But long ago he stopped caring what others thought of him.

The cool night air whipped through the car. Refreshed, he let out a little sigh of contentment. A barely perceived shiver ran through the young woman's toned arms prickled with goosebumps. An amused smile flickered across his face which caught her eye.

"You enjoying breaking the rules? Is that why you came? To flaunt your reputation as a bad boy?" Her tone was questioning, not accusatory. Almost as though she was truly curious. The butt was dropped out the window before his left hand gripped the steering wheel. Right arm reached into the backseat and snagged a red hoodie to toss at the woman.

"Thanks", she muttered as she slipped it on and zipped it. From his peripherals he caught sight of the woman breathing in the scent of the hoodie.

"You a tracker or something? Or some sniffing fetish?" Barely was he able to keep a grin from his face. Then the feeling of the past gripped him as they continued south on Interstate 75 through Atlanta. A shifting drew his eyes as she pulled her legs up into the seat beside her and raised the hoodie.

"You never answered my question. Why are we out here?" Eyes were hidden from the shadow cast from the hood. An arched brow and entertained smile eased upon his face. The car roared along roadways empty of traffic. Only an occasional traveller. As he stared at the road he sighed.

"When we were kids, my sister and I, our parents used to take us north to visit our grandparents in Illinois. Sandy and I would crawl into the back seats and lay under the slanted back window. It was one of those old station wagons with the wood paneling on the outside. Anyway, we usually passed through Atlanta around midnight."

For a few moments he grew silent. Memories danced on the fringes of his mind.

"We typically left after our dad got off work and we ate dinner. That way it was smooth sailing through Atlanta. My father was not a patient man and hated traffic", Kyle smirked at the understatement of the century before he continued.

"It was always night whenever we passed through. Buildings stretched to the heavens. Lights sparkled different colors. The city always felt magical. Laying in the back during the roadtrips was my favorite part." Shoulders shrugged as Kyle adjusted his grip upon the steering wheel.

"Sometimes just hitting the road is nice. And remembering simpler times. Happier times. It reminds me why the hell we do what we do. Maybe those we've helped are doing the very same thing. Making memories."

The night glittered with hundreds of lights like Christmas. An ambiance of relaxed beauty. Glancing over he saw her eyes study him quietly. Lips curved in a smile as he focused once more on driving.

"Well ... hell", she murmured.

"Maybe I misjudged you. Figured you were like everyone else. An adrenaline junkie. Either that was a great story or the biggest line I've ever heard. Though I'm thinking it's the former", she responded.

Shoulders shrugged as his answer as they drove south, out of Atlanta. Eventually he took an exit ramp and cruised to a gas station. Street lamps illuminated the parking lot as he pulled alongside a gas pump. Both climbed out and stretched, several creaking pops sounding from Kyle as he twisted and bent. Around the front of the car, she walked beside him and held out her hand. The two shook.

"Guess I should introduce myself. I'm Deaton." At her introduction Kyle smiled.

"Nice to officially meet you Deaton. I'm ..." She interrupted him.

"You're Kyle Ross. Also known as Aegis. Told you I knew who you were. Although I think I know the person you are a little bit better now." With a nod of his head, Kyle pulled out several bills from his pocket.

"Mind paying?"

"I always tend to pay", Deaton remarked with a smile as she took the money and headed toward the store. Eyes followed her in appreciation of the view. The subtle sway of her hips were not pronounced or intentional. But damn was it nice to look at. Leaned against the car he followed her with his eyes until she entered the store.

With a glance around the emptied parking lot he saw a little four door car at the edge of the pavement. An older woman crouched at one of the back doors as she spoke to three children in the back. All of them were skinny with worn clothes. A man stood at the road holding a sign, illegible in the dim light. Pinched face and frayed clothing, he attempted to ask for a little help. Any help.

None stopped.

Kyle knew the sort. Displaced and always moving, they were just another example of the country failing its citizens. The wind turned cold, the chill sweeping across Kyle's exposed arms. A glance toward the store showed Deaton was still preoccupied within. Using the keys he unlocked the trunk of the Monte Carlo and shifted several items from a cardboard box. With other items placed inside he hefted the box and closed the trunk.

The walk across the parking lot drew the father from the road and beside his wife as Kyle closed the distance.

"Gonna be a cold one tonight." The father nodded solemnly.

"Yes sir, it will be." Life left its mark on the couple. Faces ravaged with worry and strain, their lined faces were younger than Kyle expected. Hard lives tended to do that. With the box extended, Kyle motioned for the man to take it.

"It's not much. A few blankets and oversized sweaters. And a small tent. Some flashlights and food too." Emotion stole the father's voice but the woman answered with a wavering voice.

"Th-thank you mister. You don't know what this means." Hands stuffed into his jean pockets as Kyle answered.

"Yeah, I think I do. Good luck and god bless", Kyle said as he pulled his right hand from a pocket and extended his arm for a handshake from the father. The man's eyes widened even more as Kyle turned to walk back to the car. Muffled sobs plucked at his heartstrings as the couple hugged, the man showed her the handful of cash Kyle slipped into his hand.

Deaton was back at the car, one hand pumping gas. Nothing was said, but Kyle felt her eyes on him as he slipped behind the steering wheel and closed his door. Finished with the gas, she hung the nozzle and closed the gas tank before joining him in the car.

Neither spoke as he headed back to the interstate to go north.

POTENTiAL POSSiBiLiTiES

Wednesday, September 11, 2041
12:13 a.m.

"That was nice. What you did for them back there", her words intruded on the silence as they travelled back through Atlanta. A shrug was all the answer he gave. Not so long ago he was in a similar situation. Running with nothing and an eye watching the back trail. At least he was alone. The couple were burdened more so with kids.

"It was the right thing to do." Silence hung between them as they cruised north. A chuckle broke the quiet as Deaton giggled softly. With one hand on the wheel Kyle glanced at her in curiosity.

"What's so funny?" A coy smile curled her lips, dimples appeared as she studied him.

"You. The reputation of the great Aegis is a hard man who does whatever is necessary. Wherever he goes innocents are helped and blood covers his hands. You're an enigma. I'm not doubting that you are a fighter. But this other side of you isn't told with the tales of Aegis."

The car cruised up the road without any more conversation. In her seat, Deaton was cocooned within his red hoodie, content to look at him. As the city receded behind them Kyle coughed into his hand.

"The reputation isn't something I care about. If it strikes fear into the hearts of my enemies, then good. As long as I'm making a difference I don't care what's said about me." When Kyle looked over at Deaton he could tell she was weighing his words against his reputation and what she personally witnessed of him. The car turned off the interstate and returned to the parking area where they began.

The headlights flicked off and the car turned off. As he got out there was a group of people who advanced on his position. Both doors closed simultaneously as a large man approached from the front of the group. Anger colored his face as he poked Kyle in the chest with a finger.

"And where do you think you been? No one leaves without permission. We don't know you from Adam! How are we supposed to keep the mission secret when you out of towners think it's fine to flaunt our rules?" With a shrug Kyle raised his hands in acquiescence.

"My bad. I needed to clear my head." The finger jabbed into Kyle's chest again as the bigger man leaned in menacingly.

"Unacceptable. Where were you?" At the second jab Kyle got annoyed.

"Listen friend, I went for a drive. That's it. You want to ground me from leaving again, fine. But you shove that finger at me one more time I'm going to break it. For starters." Thumbs hooked in Kyle's belt as he gave the other man a cold smile. A few of the others in the crowd stepped forward which bolstered the leader. As he was about to go into another rant a voice came from behind Kyle.

"That's enough. Get back to your patrols. Or do you want to ask me where I've been?" Head turned to see Deaton pull the hood back from her face. The big man blanched before he stuttered a response.

"Ye-yes ma'am. I mean, no ma'am I didn't mean to question you. Come on guys, back to guard duty."

The crowd dispersed while they respectfully nodded to the woman who moved to stand next to Kyle. After the last member of the crowd disappeared back into the shadows Kyle turned and looked down at the woman who wore a satisfied smirk.

"So ... you're that Deaton. Leader of the Underground. A little young for the job, aren't you?" Hand reached up and patted his cheek, a thrill flushed through him. With her smirk, that grew larger, she winked those dangerous eyes filled with excitement.

"Like I said, it's not the mileage but the experience that counts. Join me for a nightcap?" It was a question, but the way she said it was a statement. Cocky woman. But as his eyes fell to her hips as she walked away, he let out a low whistle. A drink sounded good right then.

A few quick strides and he walked in tandem with her. Easily they circumvented an unseen path in the darkness as he followed along at her side. Several smaller campsites were passed as the path started up a gentle incline. An realization hit Kyle. With an amused smile he broke the quiet.

"Guess that answers my earlier question. The leader of the Underground here is supposed to be a great tracker and hunter. You were just getting my scent from the hoodie when you sniffed it." Quickly she turned to face Kyle and stepped forward, her chest nearly brushing his own. A mischievous smile danced across her lips as she rose up on her toes.

"That's exactly right." Leaned into his personal space, Deaton took a small sniff before she turned and continued forward.

"Plus you do smell nice." Grateful for the darkness of the night, Kyle felt himself flush with heat. Ruefully he shook his head and trotted forward to catch up.

"Well, my momma did always say cleanliness is next to godliness." A hidden glance was tossed over her shoulder.

"You're momma was right. Now that you mention it, you do remind me of Koalemos." The barest hint of a snicker was heard as once more he shook his head.

"I've been called worse things than the greek god of stupidity." Surprised that he knew who Koalemos was, Deaton appraised him with an arched brow. Laughter escaped him at her incredulous look.

"Hey now, I'm not just a pretty face. I've got brains too", Kyle said as he contorted his face into a goofy expression. The sound of her laughter was magical. The clear notes of a wind chime that transfixed listeners with beautiful melody.

Ahead, light reflected from the newest campsite. There was more than just a single fire. Half a dozen fire pits glowed around as many tents. A few adults around the site gave a shout and wave that Deaton reciprocated. Gone was the woman that rode with him. A spine of rigid steel and eyes so sharp they could cut glass.

This was Deaton, the leader of the Underground.

At the edge of the campsite was a tent that sat before a fire that smouldered. Two lawn chairs stood near the stone encircled fire. As she stuck her head into the tent Kyle bent and fed the flames. Slowly the fire was restored and Kyle placed a few logs into its midst. The tent flap rustled when Deaton exited. A bottle of bourbon and two glasses were held out for Kyle who took them.

"I'll be right back. Need to make the rounds. Are you going to be fine here unsupervised?" The hint of mockery tinged her words even as Kyle nodded and took a seat in one of the chairs. A hand waved in a shooing motion.

"Go, go. I'll manage a few minutes by myself." With a smile she headed out. A glance over her shoulder caught Kyle watching her rear as she left. Instead of being annoyed Deaton purposefully put more swagger in her step. Head shook at her antics as Kyle cracked the seal and poured two drinks. One was placed in the opposite chair while he held the other. Legs outstretched as he enjoyed the heat that radiated from the fire.

A sip of the bourbon revealed a smooth drink. With a sigh he fished out a cigarette and lit the tip, a plume escaping with his exhale. The breeze stole the smoke to distribute it in the darkened trees. While the tendrils of smoke entered the woods, Kyle scanned the shadows reflexively.

Always at night. That was when unseen eyes watched him. A shift in his chair while he took another drink. Briefly he wondered, not for the first time, if he was paranoid. But everytime he decided there was nothing, his skin chilled and crawled. Shoulders rolled as he forced himself to relax.

An older woman approached from a nearby tent. Plaid shirt with the sleeves rolled up and jeans worn white. White hair fell to her shoulders as she stopped and nodded a greeting.

"Nice night out tonight. How long have you known Deat?" Straight to the point, that one. Shoulders shrugged as he answered.

"Not long. A few hours." The woman surveyed Kyle, her gaze appraised then judged.

"Well, she'll be back shortly. Telling her baby boys goodnight. Then she should be back." Eyes scrutinized his reaction. All he offered was a light nod.

"Figured as much. And you're right, it is nice out. So I don't mind waiting." The words didn't seem to have much impact on the older woman who planted fists on her hips. Eyes narrowed as she began her interrogation.

"Are you trouble?"

"More often than not."

"Would you say you're a good man?"

"Good? No, I don't think I would. Necessary? Yeah. Personally I think I try to do the right thing no matter the cost to myself. That doesn't make me good. It just is what it is." Fine lines appeared around the older woman's eyes as she scowled.

"What are your intentions then?" Unsure if he should squirm and avoid the line of questioning, Kyle shrugged once more and took a drag from the cigarette.

"The only intention I have is to help free the poor bastards locked up somewhere. As for Deaton, I was invited for a nightcap." Kyle could see his words didn't impress or answer the question she gave him. So he continued.

"Look, I find her intriguing. And I've seen she has two sides. One is the boss who expects immediate compliance. And I'm pretty sure she can handle herself. The other side is a genuinely funny person with sass who seems lonely. Does that answer your questions?" The woman's face softened and she nodded.

"Good enough. For now", with her piece said she turned and headed back to where she came from. Kyle shook his head and tossed back his drink.

"Women." Another glass was poured before he stoked the fire with a length of stick. A few minutes later he saw Deaton as she spoke with the older woman at the other fire. Laughter rang out before Deaton joined Kyle at the fire. A low sigh escaped her as she leaned back in the chair, her hands cradled her glass.

"Had an interesting conversation with your neighbor over there", Kyle motioned in the direction from which Deaton came from.

"Oh, Pam? She's a mother hen who watches over everyone. Of course every conversation with her is beneficial. Somehow she's able to tell when someone is lying. Comes in handy. What did she ask you?"

"Asked what my intentions were toward you."

"What did you say?"

"To get in your pants." At his response she choked on her bourbon, a coughing laugh escaped.

"You did not!" He smirked at her exclamation.

"Maybe I did. Maybe I didn't. Guess you're just going to have to wait and find out." The two relaxed and enjoyed the quiet punctuated by crackling fire.

"Well, she did tell me you were probably just telling your kids goodnight.

"Is that a problem?"

There it was again. The switch from playful fun to hard as nails. Steely eyed gaze waited for his response.

"Not at all. I'd never hold it against someone for being a good parent. Plus it explains more of the mystery. Another layer." Visibly she relaxed at his words. Once more Kyle was sitting with Deaton and not the leader.

The two stayed up late into the early morning hours as they got to know one another. When Deaton finally crawled into her tent, the flap was left open. Crouched down before the open tent he smirked as she laid down on the mat of blankets and stared at him. A brief chuckle escaped Kyle.

"Get some rest. See you in a few hours." Somehow he managed not to turn around. Back at his own camp Kyle crawled into his sleeping bag and let unconsciousness claim him.

IV
CONVERSATIONS

Wednesday, September 11, 2041
9:05 p.m.

"And this is why we work alone", Kyle muttered to Blink and Lydia.

It was Wednesday night and they were gathered in the pavilion with over a dozen others. The meeting was a replay of the previous night, but with tempers flared. Once again the decision laid before them. To act now in a two pronged attack at the criminal organization's headquarters and stash houses. This would cut the proverbial head off the crime syndicate and bankrupt them by seizing their financial holdings. There was overwhelming support for the mission to move forward.

However, it would cost them the chance of freeing the supers captured.

To act now would doom the imprisoned to their fates. Yet the syndicate would be eradicated and the money seized would be divided between the groups to finance more missions and help those families who fled from their lives.

An impossible decision that demanded to be made.

After hours of arguments a compromise was reached. Twenty

four hours. Tomorrow night the mission would be launched. Whether the facilities holding the trafficked supers were found, or not. Most wanted to immediately launch the attack. That very night. But Deaton was able to convince the disparate leaders of the conglomerate forces to wait a little longer.

It helped Kyle and Catch supported the decision.

Outside the makeshift headquarters Kyle watched as Blink made for the largest area of tents. The kid chafed at not being able to do something. It was one of the basic rules of battle. Hurry up and wait. Eventually he would learn how to handle it.

Next to Kyle, Lydia cradled her head in her hands as fingers massaged her temples. Under normal circumstances the gift of finding a nexus point of importance weighed heavily upon her. Surrounded by the many people around them taxed her greatly. Instead of a singular focus she was assaulted by countless different needs. Lines on Lydia's face aged her at the internal pressure of so many desires. What she needed was peace and quiet away from the throng of people who were, consciously or unconsciously, always looking for something.

Two of the underground led Lydia to the parking lot where they took her to an empty safe house to recover. As Kyle stood there alone he lit a cigarette and returned to his empty camp site. A bed of embers glowed beneath the metal grate that sat atop the stone walls of the fire pit. With his body on autopilot he fed the fire until it lived once more.

A spare blanket was grabbed from his tent and spread out before the fire. Eyes scanned the recesses of darkness in the woods as he sat. Whispers in the back of Kyle's mind told him he wasn't alone. Head shook as he turned to the fire.

"Of course you feel like someone is watching. There probably is. Get a grip."

Amused at himself, Kyle leaned back on elbows and tried to relax. Sleep played the fickle mistress and danced away from his every attempt to claim her. A sigh escaped as he collapsed onto his back.

One day, just twenty four hours, to find the location of the prisoners. Seemed every source or leak from the organization stopped which left the mission in peril. The stash houses and headquarters were not the reason the three drove north from Florida. It was the hope of freeing supers trapped in the trafficking ring.

"You can't save everybody, Kyle." Eyes shut as the familiar sound of his twin echoed in his mind. While he understood why Sandy told him that, it didn't change the fact that without their intercession countless supers would be lost.

"I know, I know. Doesn't mean I stop trying." Almost, he could hear the sigh of resignation from Sandy.

"That's one of your best attributes. Stubbornness. And also one of your worst. How many times were you neck deep in trouble as kids?"

"Well, I always managed to find my way out. Didn't I?"

"What you meant to say was your big sis always saved your butt", amusement colored Sandy's response.

"Not how I remember it."

"That's because you have selective memory. Remember when you argued with Mister Blaine in World History? You almost got expelled over that. It was me that smoothed the edges and the memories."

"That doesn't count. That man was still claiming it was Columbus who discovered the americas."

"True. But how does writing your entire assignment out in elder futhark runes then presenting it while dressed as a viking help your cause? Like always it was me that pulled your butt out of the fire."

"Hey! That was a win. I got three numbers from my little performance."

"Tell me you aren't counting Stephanie Vickers among those numbers. She used to flick her boogers at kids in front of her."

"It's not her fault she was cursed to be a late bloomer. But she was blessed with an above average nasal capacity and uncanny accuracy", Kyle said with a grin.

"That girl was part aardvark."

"Well she did have a pretty big nose."

"Understatement of the century."

With the mood lifted he felt himself relax. Unnoticed before, the tension of the past few days created a low grade headache. Now it was gone. Leave it to Sandy to help him when he wasn't even aware he needed. The familiar presence of his twin drifted away until he was alone once more.

Half an hour later Kyle turned his head as someone approached. Body tensed in preparedness for an enemy. The tension left his body with an exhale. Hand pushed against the ground so he could sit up.

"Didn't wake you from your nap, did I grandpa?" Deaton smiled as she reached the campfire. The flames cast a yellow tinged light that danced in her eyes. The color of champagne and twice as addictive.

"Isn't it past your bedtime?" Both smirked at their verbal sparring. In her hand was a brown bottle of indeterminate liquid that she held aloft.

"Just making sure you got your daily serving of prune juice."

"Well now, I can't say no to prune juice. Take a seat youngling", Kyle said as he patted the blanket beside him. With a chuckle she seated herself with legs unfolded toward the firepit. Tonight she wore black cargo pants festooned with pockets and a short sleeve shirt of the same color. Despite the majority of flacid pockets, she still cut a trim figure.

"How are the kids today? You never said how old they were", he remarked. The sideways glance she gave him almost made him laugh. On one hand he could have asked as a jackass. Or he tried to be nice with the inquiry. The expression she wore said she looked at a two headed cow. Finally she decided Kyle was being courteous.

"Good, they're doing good. And they are four years old. Some days they think they're twenty. Raising them is the most frustrating, difficult, and rewarding thing I've ever done. I wouldn't change it for anything."

There she was again. Proud mother and gentle manner. The real person beneath the mask of leadership Deaton often wore. Yet on both sides of who she was, there was an undeniable primal presence.

"Motherhood suits you. That may be why you're the leader of this bunch. Responsibility, preparedness, and foresight are traits a parent possesses. And that is what's needed for a good leader too." Caramel skin flushed. Or maybe it was just the heat from the fire that reddened her cheeks. The bottle was used as a distraction while she took a draught and avoided eye contact.

The grin spread on his face as he gripped the offered bottle. Their fingers touched for the barest of moments but the contact sent a shiver down his spine. Happily he noticed a similar reaction from Deaton. The bottle was upended once before he handed it back.

"At least that's my opinion", Kyle said while ensnared in her mesmerizing eyes.

"Thanks." Teeth bit her bottom lip as though she stifled more words. The distance between them closed as Kyle leaned in.

"That's cheating." A small smile touched his lips as Deaton also leaned forward.

"What is?" It was Kyle's turn to bend his face closer.

"That. What you're doing right now. I've never met a man who bites his lip. But women do that. And I'm sure you know exactly what it does to the opposite sex." Playful mischief mirrored in her amber eyes. Lips were close, tantalizing in temptation. Their breath mingled. The scent of mint was nice. It reminded Kyle of Christmas candy canes and unbearable excitement to open presents.

"What exactly is it doing to you?" Coyly Deaton played with him as the tip of her tongue moistened full lips. He leaned in for the kiss while Deaton, too, shifted forward. The briefest hint of lips touched before Kyle pulled back a handbreadth. A grin stretched his face as again he moved forward. And just like last time, Kyle retreated just out of reach off her lips. Fire smoldered in her eyes at the teasing. Determined, Deaton invaded his space. Lips caressed in the subtlest of contact.

iMPROMPTU

Wednesday, September 11, 2041
10:22 p.m.

"Boss! We've got a problem!"

The shout combined with crashing from the woods jerked both Kyle and Deaton to their feet. Two men and a woman erupted from the shadows and finished their frenzied scurry to Deaton. Chests heaved while the three attempted to regain their breath. A hand was placed on one of the men's shoulders as Deaton squatted beside him.

"What is it Thomas?" The man's chin lifted by the gentle touch of Deaton's other hand. Eyes swirled with a force of nature, an undeniable primordial presence more powerful than mere emotion. Artists and sculptures attempted to capture the inherent power and righteousness of the gods, yet none came near the majestic grace or fundamental primal authority which radiated from Deaton.

"James called in. That family he relocated is safe but he picked up a tail and can't shake them." Both Kyle and Deaton pulled Thomas to his feet. A scowl pulled at Deaton's lips as she shook her head in frustration.

"That's going to be a problem. Our boy James is a mule. Families that need immediate help are assigned to him and he takes them somewhere safe. There's about half a dozen mules in my group at a given time. And the only ones who know who the people are, and where they've been put, are the mules and myself."

The gravity of the situation settled in Kyle's mind. If James was caught and forced to talk then all the people he helped would be exposed. Even the underground itself. The next question became the most important. Hands framed Thomas' face as Deaton leaned in.

"Remember. Who did James say was after him?"

If it was local authorities then the underground could handle that. Money for the corrupt, blackmail for the self righteous, or officers sympathetic to the cause. If it was the Protectorate then James was done. The only option to keep the secrets safe was to eat a bullet. However, if it was a criminal organization then there was a narrow window of opportunity.

"The syndicate. He said the family he moved were about to be raided. All of them were supers. If they catch James ..." Pain and fear filled Thomas' pale face.

"If something happens to James ..." Drawn into Deaton's embrace, Thomas blubbered. As she soothed the distraught man, Deaton looked to the other two.

"Where is he?" The smaller of the two answered, his limp hair falling in greasy black strands.

"Driving around downtown. Staying near actively populated areas." An idea formed in Kyle's mind.

"What does he look like? What was he wearing?" Despondent, Thomas lashed out angrily.

"Who cares? He needs help, not fashion tips!" Gently Deaton led Thomas away as they headed for the pavilion. James knew too much and couldn't fall into enemy hands. Not just the families moved by him but the current operation. Too much was at risk.

Something needed to be done.

"Kid, come here a second", Kyle spoke to the young man with enough oil in his hair to deep fry a chicken. When the youth neared Kyle planted a hand on his shoulder.

"What does James look like? What was he wearing?" The kid thought for a moment.

"White. Average build. In shape, not fat. Keeps his blonde hair short, like a crewcut. Yeah, and he always has stubble on his face. Says women love it. Um, James was wearing his jeans and boots with a black shirt. Can I go now?"

The boy was released to join the others who were beginning to congregate toward the pavilion. Slowly news spread and camps awakened into activity. It was no different at Kyle's camp. With wild abandon he tossed through his belongings on a search. Behind him, Blink trotted in.

"What's going on?"

"One of the underground's mules is being followed by the syndicate. Gotta get him out without blowing the operation. Where are the clippers?" Several articles of clothing were tossed to the blanket near the fire as Kyle sat and unlaced his boots. The young man thought for a moment before he climbed into his tent.

"Any particular reason you want the clippers", Blink's muffled voice asked from within the tent.

"Yeah, I've got an idea", Kyle smirked as he heard the young man groan. Not that he could blame the kid for his reaction. Many of Kyle's last minute ideas were less than ideal, though they tended to work. Lydia would usually say it was because his plans were asinine. Again, Kyle couldn't argue the validity of her statement.

A few moments later Blink emerged with the clippers to see Kyle as he removed his pants. An open palm reached out in gesture for the clippers. Head shook side to side as Blink handed over the clippers. Activated with a flick of the switch, Kyle buzzed his head, the mane of hair falling in a single clump secured by the ponytail. The clippers then moved to his face and removed the beard to leave a layer of stubble.

"Uh, is there any reason we are playing beautician?" The quizzical expression on Blink's face caused Kyle to laugh as he bent to pull on a pair of jeans.

"All in good time. Did you bring your cowboy boots?"

"Boots. Just boots. Not cowboy boots. And yes."

"Grab them for me", Kyle said while loose hair was brushed from his torso. The small pile of clothes were rummaged through until he found a crumpled black shirt which he pulled on as Blink returned.

"Here you go", Blink said as he tossed the boots to Kyle. A nod of thanks was given to the young man as Kyle hopped on one foot and then the other while he pulled on the boots. A leather belt was threaded through the belt loops as Kyle walked from the camp. The young man scurried to catch up.

"Want to fill me in on the plan?" A hopeful look from Blink went unanswered as they navigated the woods and neared the pavilion. Dozens gathered outside with varying degrees of noisome conversation. The two shouldered through the throng and entered the tent as half a dozen argued.

"There's too much at risk to not get James out", Deaton remarked to the unconvinced.

"One life is not more important than the mission. Sometimes sacrifices need to be made." That was Epstein, a barrel chested man from one of the Carolinas. That particular group was there as more muscle for the operation. For a small cut from the stash houses. A bottom feeder.

"And sometimes you have to do what's right, even if it costs us", Catch responded with a glower. Very clearly divided, the sides grew more boisterous in their opinions. In the center, Deaton tried to calm the other leaders without success.

"How about we replace him with a ringer. Someone who can be followed. There's a fifty fifty chance that person will go to headquarters or where the other prisoners are being held", Kyle spoke up loudly. The cacophony of voices spoke over one another to be heard. Too dangerous. It would expose them. How could they trust the decoy wouldn't break? Why should they put someone else at risk? It was a longshot.

"Enough!"

The roar of Deaton's voice cut through the audio mayhem that filled the pavilion. Every eye turned to her and all remained silent. The glare of her gaze challenged any to interrupt the silence she brought to the unruly group. As she moved through them she stopped before each and dared them to speak out of turn.

Despite her diminutive size, Deaton offered each the chance to bow up in challenge. It was the eyes that caused grown men to pause. A whirlwind of barely restrained aggression swirled in their depths. She wasn't Deaton, the woman who laughed and made jokes. No, she was the leader of the Underground to one of the largest cities in the United States. Perpetual danger lurked within her small frame.

After she passed the others, Deaton paused before Kyle. One hand raised to tilt his chin side to side as she grimaced. Finger twirled as she motioned for Kyle to turn, which he complied. As he looked down at her again, she nodded and turned back to the group.

"This is what is going to happen", she paused to glare daggers at Epstein who appeared as though he would interject. The lumberjack stayed quiet under the withering stare.

"This is the plan. Four of us, Kyle, Catch, myself, and Epstein, are going to load up and head out. We'll tell James to meet us at the destination. That's where we trade Kyle for James and fall back. When they catch Kyle he will either be subdued and taken to their HQ or where the other supers are being held. Either way, he will need to hold out for almost twenty four hours. It keeps James out of their hands and gives us a shot to find the prisoners. The three of you, meet me at the cars in ten minutes."

There were grumbles but no objections as she shouldered free of the group and marched out of the pavilion. Catch sideled next to

Kyle and Blink to shake his head.

"You got balls kid. And guts. Not sure about the brains though." A chuckle escaped Catch.

"Now you sound like my old sergeant", Kyle remarked with a grin.

"Was he right?"

"More often than I like to admit."

VI
ACCORDING TO PLAN

Wednesday, September 11, 2041
11:01 p.m.

The four sat quietly as the Ford Bronco consumed the miles. Behind the wheel sat Epstein, his flannel covered gut rubbed against the bottom of the steering wheel. In the passenger seat Deaton gave him directions with clipped instructions. The back was less comfortable as both Catch and Kyle tried not to cramp in the small space.

The classic, 1980, Bronco roared south on I-75. However, Epstein did remain vigilant and kept the vehicle at the speed limit. The Paul Bunyan cosplay did drive pretty smooth. For a lumberjack. A smile tugged the corners of Kyle's mouth which drew Catch's attention.

"What's so funny kid?" Shifted a bit to keep at least a partially blood flow to his legs, Kyle smirked.

"Figured out where I know Epstein from. The retired Brawny Man. You know, the paper towels. Even has that Magnum moustache." Turned sideways, Catch looked at their driver's profile.

"Na, he's Paul Bunyan." The grin on Kyle's face grew as he

disagreed.

"Can't be. No axe."

From the front Epstein gave an annoyed snarl while he listened to the backseat conversation.

"In the back I do have an axe. I'll gladly show you up close and personal when we stop."

The two in the back burst out laughing as Kyle struggled to pull a wad of bills from his pocket. From her seat, Deaton spied the interaction.

"What was that for", she asked Kyle as Catch looked out the side window.

"Nothing really. Mister Catch here bet me Epstein carried an axe. There was no way that could be true, so I took the bet."

In the rearview mirror Epstein's eyes stared at Kyle.

"How much did you bet?"

"Three hundred", Kyle grumbled.

Subtly Catch shook his head no, the motion almost missed in the vehicle. Eyes narrowed and Kyle looked suspiciously between the two. Not about to let an opportunity pass, Epstein spoke up.

"Of course Catch knew I had an axe. First day here he saw me splitting wood." Accusatory eyes stared at Catch in betrayal.

"Cheater." A guffaw broke from Catch.

The two in front became embroidered in directions as the Bronco took an exit. Legs were cramped in the back which left the two men less than comfortable. A sigh shuddered from Kyle which drew Catch's attention.

"When I said you had balls and guts, I meant it. Pretty sure I wouldn't take this gamble. Taking this other guy's place on the whim they don't want you dead. Then hoping to be brought where the other prisoners are. And then having faith that we could even find you. All of that with being beaten or tortured."

Kyle listened to Catch as the vehicle slowed to speeds prevalent in a city.

"I just want you to know something, Catch. That was the worst inspirational speech in the history of inspirational speeches. Now I'm rooting for the bad guys to bash my head in", Kyle said as he rolled his eyes. A one sided conversation came from Deaton while she talked into a phone.

"Listen to me James. Room 212. Wear that baseball cap of yours, grab the keycard, and hustle to the room." Brief silence then she continued.

"You are one of mine. No job too hard, no sacrifice too great. I always come for mine. Now get to the room." The visor was flipped down with Deaton's gaze on Kyle. It was a promise for James. And Kyle. A sign for the inn welcomed them into the parking lot.

"Listen up. Keep the engine running, Epstein. Catch hang by the front in case things go sideways." The Bronco pulled into the parking spots and backed into an empty space.

"With me", Deaton commanded. First out from the back, Kyle caught the red hoodie Deaton tossed. Arms slipped into the sleeves and the hood went up while he fell in beside the woman.

"That bench is calling my name. Hey kid, toss me your pack", Catch snagged the cigarettes Kyle tossed over his shoulder. The older man eased onto one of the benches and stretched out his legs. A pose of feigned boredom while he smoked.

The front lobby laid bare through pristine windows. Warm air washed over the two as they entered the automatic doors. To the left was the mahogany front desk and on the right a dining area. Feet slowed in anticipation for a check-in. However, Deaton didn't stop and continued for the elevators. Hurried forward he waited beside her.

"No check-in?" Elevator doors opened and the two stepped in. The second floor button was pressed.

"The Underground keeps a few rooms ready around Atlanta. This is one of them", she said while the elevator rose. Amused, Kyle glanced at Deaton.

"Bet you never thought you would be taking me to a hotel room on our second date." A snort escaped Deaton as the elevator chimed and doors opened.

"As if. Haven't even made it to first base yet. And this isn't a date." The gray and black streaked carpet stretched the length of the hall. Taupe walls with an olive shade molding and door frames assaulted his senses. Stopped at one of the doors Deaton used a keycard from her pocket. Inside the same color scheme unfolded.

"After seeing the hotel room, I agree. No scoring for you tonight." The door closed behind them while Deaton walked by the bed and dresser. Using the toe of her shoe Deaton pushed the bathroom door open. Hand fell away from the pistol inside the waistband of her pants. Wryly he smiled at her thoroughness even as she turned to face him.

"It's brave of you to do this. But there's still time to cancel and all of us get out", Deaton said as Kyle flopped backwards and sprawled on the bed. With eyes closed he answered.

"Can't do that. I once chose to do nothing. The price was too high. Anyway, this may be the only chance we'll have to rescue those taken. I'm all in." A chirp emitted from Deaton's pocket. With a glance at the phone she nodded.

"James is here and Catch is watching his shadows. Said they look like syndicate boys. At least they aren't Protectorate."

The bed felt nice which reminded Kyle he couldn't remember the last time he laid in a real bed. With a groan he rolled to the side and stood. At the cracked door, Deaton scanned for James. The elevator chimed down the hall and James trotted forward while Deaton pushed the door open and motioned for him to hurry.

A curse slipped from Deaton's lips when the door pulled shut. With his first glimpse of James, Kyle admitted they could easily pass for brothers. From a short distance it was conceivable they could be mistaken for one another. That was good enough for Kyle who stripped off the red hoodie and tossed it to the other man.

"Wha-what is going on, Deaton? This is an extraction … right?" Bewildered, James automatically slipped the hoodie on while Kyle snagged the ball cap from off his head. Hands ushered James into the bathroom, Deaton following behind as Kyle looked woefully at the hat.

"Getting captured is one thing. But wearing a Georgia Bulldog hat? That's asking too much." From the cracked bathroom door Deaton hissed.

"Put it on and be ready to fight. Remember you want them to think you gave it your all to escape. Just … just don't get away", The bathroom door slipped almost closed, but left a crack large enough for Deaton to watch.

"No self respecting Florida man would wear this …" The hat was pulled on as Kyle continued to grumble. A noise from the door drew his eyes as the handle twitched slightly. With no sign of trepidation, Kyle went to the table beside the bed and picked up the phone.

"Is this the front desk? Yes, thanks. I was wondering if I could order room service because I'm famished. Oh? Yeah, I can hold." The door kicked inward with a crash as two men charged into the room. Both wore dark clothes and short hair. For a moment Kyle wondered if this was a joke as both men could easily pass for male models with strong jaws and flawless skin.

It didn't last as Kyle gripped the lamp by the base and sent it flying into one of their faces who collapsed holding his face. The other man dove forward and bent Kyle backwards over the table. One hand wrapped around Kyle's throat, choking him, while the other rained blows into his midsection. A faint voice echoed from the phone receiver.

"It's … for … you …" With the phone gripped tightly, Kyle slammed it repeatedly into the temple of his attacker who relented and staggered back. Freed from the hold Kyle kicked out into the man's chest which knocked him into the other attacker. Both crashed into the TV. Kyle darted out of the room to run.

A flash of knuckles filled his vision before he was knocked backwards into the room. Eyes blinked several times as he stood. In the doorway was a third man in black trousers and tank top.

Exposed skin possessed a reflective metallic sheen. Behind Kyle the model twins tried to pull themselves to their feet.

"Y'all got the wrong room. I'm a Bible salesman. Can I interest you in an accompanying concordance?" The big man in the doorway seemed to be nearly unmoveable and unfazed. From the sound of things the knucklehead twins finally found their feet. In the bathroom, Deaton and James were secreted only by the door.

"Two choices for you. Door number one, you come with us quietly. Or door number two, we beat you unconscious and you still come with us", the voice of the metal man was quite soothing despite the threats. Shoulders shrugged while Kyle looked at the man barring his exit.

"Door number three. Well, not technically a door ..." The look on metal man's face said he wasn't amused. Too bad. Kyle pivoted on his back foot and charged the two former pretty boys. The action was unexpected. Bodies collided as Kyle thrust forward with all his might. The three careened into and through the window with the sound of shattered glass.

As they fell from the second story window Kyle briefly wondered at the wisdom of his action. Then they crashed through the canvas canopy that sheltered the patio from the elements. Everything flashed white as Kyle's head collided with one of the men beneath him. Screams and shouts echoed distantly.

Hands touched upon a piece of patio furniture not destroyed in their descent. Taupe slabs of granite were pieced together for the walkway, dark red drops marred its simplistic beauty. With the chair, Kyle managed to stand amidst the carnage of twisted bodies. The pretty boy twins were no longer pretty. Nor were they breathing.

The small group of hotel guests scattered from the patio and abandoned half eaten food alongside drinks. Not that he blamed them. A staggered step and Kyle grabbed a table to keep from falling. His knee screamed with pain when he placed weight on it. A perfectly good excuse for being caught.

The boot caught him in the ribs and tossed him over a table and into the street. As Kyle laid on his back the metal man, who punted him, approached. From a black van a woman hopped out. Black hair with blue streaks fell in waves to her shoulders. Dark jeans, leather jacket, and more metal piercings adorned her face than an after school crafts corner.

When metal man stayed back Kyle got the sneaking suspicion he was not going to enjoy what happened next. A pale hand lowered toward Kyle's face. Multiple piercings dotted the hand. Prepared to roll away, Kyle never got the chance.

Electricity flashed from the open palm and washed over his face. Unseen, her other hand pressed into his chest and released another charge. Body writhed uncontrollably as every nerve ending burned in agony.

The pain receded. Head rolled like a drunkard as Kyle tried to roll away. Only partly successful, he managed to flop to his chest.

"He should be knocked out", came a woman's voice.

"Maybe you're losing your touch. Or you just aren't as good as you say you are." That was metal man's soothing voice.

"Like hell. Fried him like an egg. What did you say his power was?"

"Never said. Stop making excuses and knock him out."

There wasn't a response from the woman, or, not a verbal one. Electricity surged through Kyle's body and a final thought floated free as he slipped into unconsciousness.

He should have gone for the kiss.

VII
NOT A GREAT PLAN

There were snippets of clarity. Bouncing around in the back of the van. Miscellaneous light from buildings they passed. The cool moist grass beneath his face. A hint of brightness in the sky from an impending dawn. The hum of hydraulics. Flashes of fluorescent light. A long hall with bars on either side. Figures huddled in corners.

Nothing made sense. Everytime he was close to clarity the witch would dangle her fingers across his face and fry any cohesion he managed to attain. There was only one image Kyle was able to hold in his mind. Through the bars of a cell, two kids huddled together. The oldest was less than ten. And the younger one, a toddler.

Eyes blinked against the blinding light. Head rolled forward and jerked him alert. Bare feet stood on the concrete floor. Walls and ceiling shared the same coloring. Eyes diverted from the white light that cascaded from the fixtures every few feet from the ceiling. The room he was in seemed to be the epicenter of a hub. Five halls led to the central room with cells in each.

Faces spied glances at him. Scared, terrified, depressed, angry, disheartened … the faces of the prisoners shared one belief. There was no hope in this place.

Hands were manacled above his head. A chain ran from the ceiling twice as tall as a man. Shackled securely to the chain, Kyle was forced to remain standing. Boots, shirt, and hat were gone. Only his blue jeans remained. Arms tensed and Kyle put his full weight on the chain. No give.

Mind began to replay the snippets of memory and the last things remembered. From what he could piece together it was now morning, at least. All he needed to do was wait until night fell and the Underground went into action. Oh, and hope they were able to follow him. The idea of being cut off unconcerned him. Lydia found lost things, and nothing would be as pressing than to find him.

He hoped.

The next few hours were spent in an attempt to start a conversation with any of the other prisoners. However, armed guards frequently walked the halls. Several times he received the butt end of a rifle for refusing to remain silent. Time creeped by. Food was brought to the imprisoned while he waited.

"Is this going according to plan", Sandy asked within his mind.

"Of course. When have I ever not followed the plan?"

"This isn't the same as school. Or when you were with the Warriors. Right now you are alone, with no rescue in sight. You need to figure out something little brother." Feet kicked against the floor to swing himself gently.

"Enough, Munin." The voice in his head quieted. These days, when Kyle called her Munin it was because he wanted quiet. A last attempt was made.

"Maybe we can contact Clay-"

"No", Kyle barked. There was no way he would beg Clay for help. For starters it would put them both in a bad spot trying to explain to the Protectorate Kyle was alive and well and that their Excaliber knew. No, it was better this way. The presence of his twin receded from his mind until he was alone with his thoughts once more.

Finally a new sound intruded upon the monotony. The hard

clicks of different footwear. Three individuals walked down the hall before him. Prisoners shied away from the bars and cowered from the trio. The man in the center looked like he may have once been a fighter. Cream colored three piece suit tailored to his body. Wide shoulders and massive arms strained against the fabric as Kyle finally saw his face.

A misshapen nose disfigured from multiple breaks and cauliflower ears confirmed Kyle's first impression. Gold teeth glittered from flat lips peeled back in a smile as cold as the arctic. On the man's right stood electro chick with all her piercings. To the right was an older woman in a long, white sundress with a shaved head. At first he thought she was younger, but despite the lack of lines on her face it was the eyes that spoke of hard earned experience.

Together the three made an intriguing pair.

Three sets of eyes watched Kyle in silence. After a few minutes he sighed.

"I can't hang out all day here guys. Places to go, people to see, things to do." A smirk stretched across his face as he waited.

"You are not James", the man in the suit said plainly.

"You win the 'that's obvious' reward. What does he win Alex?" Snarky commentary flowed from Kyle before electro chick slapped his bare chest and discharged a burst of electricity. Teeth grit as muscles spasmed and he caught his breath. Baldy spoke again.

"If not James then who are you?" Eyes glanced at electro chick for a moment as Kyle felt his pulse slow to normal.

"That's bad manners. As host it falls to you to introdu-" Again an electrical current flowed into his body from the woman. This time her hand maintained contact for a few seconds. Groans emerged from Kyle as he swayed on the chain. A cold smile stretched flat lips to reveal even more gold teeth.

"You are in no position to respond with such glib. Tell me, where is Deaton?" Electro girl walked behind Kyle while the woman in white eased back to watch. Shoulders tried to shrug but with his arms suspended above his head, he failed.

"Okay okay. First off we have a problem. You skipped the first several chapters in the Idiot's Guide to Torture. There's supposed to be a connection between us. Make me trust you." A hand landed on each shoulder as electro girl released a torrent of power. Unable to control himself, Kyle spasmed in agony for what felt like minutes. At a motion from the man in the suit, she relented.

More groans filtered from Kyle as he only stayed upright because of the chain anchored to the ceiling. Head rolled limply as numb feet found the floor and he stood under his own power. Although he swayed more than he did before. The man in the suit smiled again.

"I believe we now have an understanding, yes? Is there something you wish to tell me?"

A glance over his shoulder told Kyle the woman cattle prod was still back there. There might even have been a smile on her face. With a grunt he focused once more on the man before him.

"Yeah … I've got to tell you … that …I can tell you don't shave your head. You're bald. Don't they have hair clinics here?" Hands slapped to his body and this time Kyle heard himself scream.

The scent of ozone roused him. Or maybe it was the slap to the face. The man was standing with his jacket removed. The black shirt beneath accented the cream color of the suit. Hands rolled the sleeves up over thick forearms. When he noticed Kyle was conscious he smiled.

"That is a quick turnaround you have my friend. After you tell me what I want to know you will make me a great deal of money. A buyer down south loves hard cases. And I have a good feeling you are a hard case. Now tell me about yourself." Eyes focused on the man as he finished with the sleeves. Slowly Kyle nodded.

"Yeah, you're right. Might as well tell the truth. I like long walks on the beach. My steak needs to be cooked medium rare. In my apartment I have a tweety bird that constantly tells me it saw a puddy cat. And my favorite color is-" All Kyle saw was a flash as the other man drove a fist into his gut. The chain swayed backwards from the force only for electro girl to place both hands upon Kyle's back and shove him forward. Into a right cross.

Head hung low as he swayed on the chain. The man in the suit glanced at the woman in white.

"He's not dead. Right?" Eyes closed as the silent woman hummed to herself. Electro girl sighed in frustration.

"I'll tell you if he's dead." She circled Kyle to stand in front of him. A hand reached out and raised his chin. Released, his head dropped again.

"I don't know boss, you might have killed him."

Legs that hung limply suddenly encircled the woman and pulled her forward. Instinctively she grabbed his thighs and released a surge of electricity directly into Kyle. Head reared back only to fly forward. Head impacted head as Kyle slammed his own skull against the woman's skull while his legs kept her close.

On the third crack his legs went limp and released electro girl. A single staggered step was made before she collapsed on the ground. As the man in the suit and woman in white looked down at the eye socket and temple caved in, Kyle laughed.

He continued laughing even as half a dozen guards beat him unconscious.

PiÑATA

"In situations like this I find that unique answers deliver the greatest results." The man in the suit spoke while he cleaned his hands of any blood. Greater strength than the normal human aided the former boxer in his assault. Tirelessly he pounded on Kyle, always aware of the danger the shackled man possessed.

All the while the woman in white remained quiet. There wasn't even a flicker of emotion on her face. Only an empty stare normally resigned to the comatose or the dead. A slap bounced Kyle's face back.

"Did you hear me? What do you think?" Unused to being ignored, the man pulled his arm back and smacked Kyle again. Head raised and Kyle stared at the other man.

"Sorry, gotta repeat the question. Wasn't listening", Kyle smirked. A hammered blow connected before the man threw an uppercut. Rocked backwards, Kyle knew the only reason he still stood was because of the shackles.

"That is enough time wasted. Chelsea, would you care to join me?" The woman in white floated across the floor to stand near the prisoner. But not too close. Fingers steepled in front of her chest. With a turn from the woman and back to the suit, Kyle smiled weakly.

"Is she going to pray me free of secrets? Perhaps a confession. Hope you cleared your schedule because I have a lot to confess for." As the final word passed Kyle's lips he froze. Then leaned back as far as he could.

"I quite honestly do not have words to describe how disgusting that is."

From the tips of her fingers, tendrils and filaments slipped from where each nail should have been. Each thread was over a handspan in length. The tendrils undulated and strained forward at Kyle's face.

"Tell her not to touch me and I'll start talking. That can't be sanitary." with a head shake side to side, the man in the suit disagreed.

"I do not believe I can trust your easy agreement. And they will not touch you. They go in you."

With a dancer's grace, Chelsea walked around behind Kyle. A hand gripped Kyle around the throat and held him still. In his weakened state Kyle couldn't wrest free from the suit's ironclad grip.

"Can't we just take a moment, remain calm, and work this out like adults?"

"No."

Soft as loose strands of hair in a summer breeze, the filaments swept from the back of his head toward his face. Hands fought the chain and feet attempted to push away. Yet it was in vain. The thick arm of the bald man held him still. Feathery touches caressed his ears, some travelled within his peripheral vision.

"Chelsea here is an extractor. Capable of integrating into a subject's brain. After time she will know everything you know. No one has ever successfully resisted her."

"And you didn't even buy me dinner", quipped Kyle.

As gentle as a lover's caress, the tendrils probed into ears, nose, and eye sockets. At first there was only pressure. Then it grew greater. Pressure gave way to pain. Eyes felt the friction of sandpaper. Tendrils up his nose threatened to choke him. Sound grew faint until the only thing heard was the pounding of his chest.

"A little distraction for you. Try to fight us both and wear down quicker", the man in the suit whispered before he clenched a fist and rammed it into Kyle's midsection. Each time he was punched the organic threads invaded more. Sensation screamed as though every tendril were a splinter buried deep in flesh.

Sharp pangs reverberated in his skull. Mouth gasped ineffectually for breath. But all he received was another punch to the gut. Skin flushed hot and he shivered while he froze. Like a hand over flame burns and scorches before pure agony takes over, so too was the pulse of misery that fed on his sanity.

Time became invalid. All that existed was the wave of affliction that built to a crescendo of anguish. Gripped in the throes of torment, Kyle held to one thought. Rescue. Deaton would follow him somehow. And when she arrived … payback. But until then he screamed. Throat grew hoarse and slick with blood. And still he screamed.

Through the haze Kyle witnessed the man in a suit yell at several guards before pulling some device from his pants pocket. The cloud of pain dulled his senses as the woman wiggled fingers and pushed the tendrils deeper.

A cloud descended from above. It took a few moments for him to remember they weren't beneath the open sky. Another cloud shoof free from the heavens. White powder settled on the man in the suit. Dust clung as noise erupted from the end of the hall. Again Kyle screamed while the woman pushed and pulled deeper into his skull. Body spasmed uncontrollably.

The man in the suit held the remote more firmly. There was a switch of some sort. Screams down the hall mingled with his own while muzzles flashed from weapons wielded on both sides. Yet the man in the suit held death for all of them in the palm of his hand.

There was nothing Kyle could do. Chained and tortured by the parasitic worms connected to the woman. And the man in the suit so close Kyle could reach out and touch him. If he wasn't shackled.

Why was he here? What possible reason convinced Kyle to be captured? Between bouts of paralyzing pain Kyle's eyes drifted to one of the cells. A young woman huddled in the corner with a child. In front was a man who used his body as a barrier for his family. Malnourished and frightened. The place was filled with cells exactly like that one.

And once more Kyle was drowning in a sea of agony. Deep within his mind a voice echoed faintly.

"Fight."

Hands gripped the chain as Kyle found his balance. Then he slammed his head backwards with as much force as possible. Chelsea fell back, tendrils torn from her fingers to hang flaccid upon Kyle's face. The familiar sound of a limp body as it collided with the ground was one both Kyle and the man in the suit knew.

It happened in slow motion, everything creeped along in that moment. Bald head began to turn as the man prepared to flip the cover on the switch. Legs swept up, right foot connected with the switch and sent it flying. The man in the suit turned for the control even as Kyle's legs encircled his neck.

Muscles bulged and legs tightened around the bald man's neck. Still, the man in the suit struggled for freedom. Enraged, Kyle climbed upward, each handhold raised them higher while legs still coiled about the bald man's neck. Up. And up. Wind whistled in Kyle's ears with the uncanny imitation of his own screams.

When he reached the anchor in the ceiling Kyle relaxed his legs and allowed the other man to crash upon the floor below. Hurt but not dead. Hands released the chain and he dropped feet first onto the bald man's chest. Bone crunched and the feeling of ligaments popped like rubber bands beneath Kyle's feet. The man in the suit laid still with a collapsed chest.

A smile flickered briefly on Kyle's face. Eyes grew heavy with all energy depleted. Darkness embraced him amid the sound of battle.

IX
THROUGH THE LOOKING GLASS

That night the Underground, and their allies, struck. Catch led the strike against the crime syndicate's headquarters and left none alive. Safe houses were raided and demolished under the eye of Epstein. Deaton personally led the team for Kyle and, hopefully, the prisoners.

All objectives were completed successfully.

Vague snippets of faces and sounds swirled around Kyle. Muffled voice and rippled sight reminded Kyle of when he was younger. Completely submerged in water shared similar attributes. Chest compressed against lungs crying for air, head pounded with the crisis of the unknown. Muscles ached and constricted involuntarily in an attempt to escape. The memory of Deaton hovering over Kyle felt like he was drowning while seeing help through the distorted lens of the water's surface. Important and yet insubstantial. For a small length of time Kyle almost believed he was still being tortured, with the criminals managing to break into his mind.

If not for the frequent visits from Deaton, he would have feared the reality of freedom was a charade. After a week Kyle improved enough to know he lived. Men and women passed by and clapped clenched fist to chest. During one of his visits with Deaton he asked what it meant. Softly she checked the wounds that were healed without blemish.

"When we hit them we also made off with hardware. Several hard drives kept surveillance records on the prison where we found you. Your torture session was on there. Some of the footage made the rounds through camp. Everyone knows what you did for James and all those prisoners. What you endured should have killed you. Fifteen hours of torture and you never gave them anything." Softly she ran her fingers through his shorn hair. Hand snared hand as Kyle held her palm near his mouth. Softly he kissed the palm of her hand.

Exhaustion set in and Kyle sagged into the bed asleep. But he swore her lips touched his own before he surrendered to slumber.

Weeks passed and Blink returned to Florida with Lydia in tow. Whether the kiss was imagined or reality no longer mattered. The kisses that followed were real. Recovery was quick and yet, Kyle remained. Soon after, Deaton introduced her kids. To his benefit Kyle played with them in the day and read fairy tales at night.

Once the children were asleep Kyle joined Deaton in her tent. Together they worked with the Underground in the day and laid in each other's arms at night. For the first time in a long time, Kyle was happy.

Yet happiness would prove to be as fleeting as a warm, sunny day in the midst of winter.

A month passed since the mission. The two retired to their tent for the night. When Deaton shimmied from her clothes Kyle couldn't help but steal a glance. A low whistle slipped from his lips as he removed his boots and shirt. The jeans followed. Already under the cover, Deaton enjoyed the view and smiled.

The real Deaton.

Kyle slid between the covers and his hand traced the curve of her hip.

"I've been thinking. Maybe I should make this permanent",

Kyle said while he attempted to decipher her expression.

"Don't you think it's a bit early talking about weddings and marriage?"

"Wait, I didn't mean it like that. I don't want to marry you", even as the words came out of his mouth he knew it sounded bad.

"First you propose and now you are breaking us up. In less than ten seconds?"

"No no. What I meant was stay here with you and the kiddos. The marriage thing wa-" The ramble that wouldn't end was cut short as Deaton rolled atop Kyle. Passionately she kissed him. Fingers ran through his hair as bruised lips pressed against hers. The taste of spiced honey invaded his mouth. Hands drifted to her hips while Deaton trailed kisses along his jaw. Body tensed when she playfully bit his neck. He took it to mean she agreed.

Months advanced past Halloween and Thanksgiving. The cold grip of winter held sway over the snow frosted south.

Smoke rose from the chimney of the small house hidden in the woods. Miscellaneous toys lay scattered on the thick rug between the fireplace and the overstuffed couch. Multi hued christmas lights contended with the fire for illumination to read by. Though it was no longer needed.

Kyle sat in the center of the couch with a child on each side. Both boys slept, cocooned in blankets with a toy loosely held in either hand. Lightly he stroked cherubic faces, the children's book lay unfinished next to his socked feet.

The last Christmas Kyle celebrated was when Sandy still lived. Well over a decade. This time was different. He experienced the holiday through the eyes of adulthood. That morning he sat next to Deaton as the twin four year olds excitedly ripped open their gifts. With each reveal the boys ran to the couch to show off what Santa brought them. Every time Kyle responded with surprised fervor which only made the kids want to show off all aspects of the toy. More than once he caught Deaton as she looked at him with a satisfied smile.

The day flew by as Kyle played on the rug with toy cars, army men, and kid versions of tools that echoed with sound to their flashing lights. After an early dinner the four went outside to play in the snow before the sun set. Snowmen and impressions of snow angels decorated the yard as they finished the outing with an old fashioned snowball fight. To their delight, the twins won every battle and dumped freshly powdered snow on Kyle as he laid in defeat. After Kyle was buried he rose and began another round only to fall from superior numbers of snowballs that collided with his body.

Inside, Deaton gave the boys a hot bath while Kyle made mugs of hot cocoa. Feet pitter pattered from the bathroom to one of the two bedrooms where the kids grabbed their blankets and more than the single book for bedtime. The twins ran back through to jump on the couch. Head shook in amusement as Kyle gave them their mugs of cocoa.

"Don't tell your mom", he said as he snuck them another piece of pumpkin cake. With the boys distracted he went to the bathroom and leaned against the door frame, eyes greedily drinking in the sight of Deaton bent over while she collected clothes and towels. Her head turned and caught him staring. Straightened, she moved over to him.

"See something you like?" Lips curled at her quip.

"Damn right", then he lowered his face to find her lips. The same passionately ferocious warrior kissed him back. Leader of the Underground or mother to twin boys, she always lived to the fullest. A chorus of "eeewwww" sounded from behind which caused them both to grin. Kyle motioned toward the bathroom with his head.

"Why don't you take a long hot bath. I'll wrangle the monsters." Another kiss and she gently pushed him from the doorway to shut the door. An exaggerated huff escaped smiling lips as he joined the boys on the couch.

"Whoa, this is more than one book." A litany of pleas broke his feigned resolve. The boys burrowed under each arm as Kyle began the first book.

When Deaton came out she paused at the scene. Soft lullabies drifted from Kyle while he looked upon sleeping faces. The movement alerted Kyle to her presence where he offered a sheepish smile. Moving to the couch, Deaton scooped up the first boy and transferred him from the couch to his bed. The second boy, little Tye, gripped Kyle's shirt.

"I want Kyle to tell me goodnight." Lips tugged in a smile as Kyle scooped up the light burden and stood.

"Guess I'm laying down this one." Steady legs took him to the room where he gently laid the boy down and tucked the blanket about his body. He was already asleep. On silent feet Kyle slipped from the room and left the door cracked. A voice drifted from the other bedroom.

"I got you two presents. You can open one now." Three steps brought him to Deaton's room where she laid on the bed. One hand pulled the belt free allowing the robe to part, revealing supple flesh. With a grin he closed the door and murmured.

"Best. Present. Ever."

Early the next morning Kyle slipped from the covers and pulled on his clothes. Quietly he exited the room and eased the door shut behind. In the living room he knelt, stoking the fire to life as a light knock on the front door echoed. Easing the door open he nodded to a young man he recognized from the Underground. Out of breath, the man held out a note for Kyle, who took it. After the man left Kyle read the letter.

When finished he crushed it in his hand.

"That didn't look like good news", Deaton said from behind Kyle. A white sheet wrapped her body below the arms. The distance closed as Deaton moved forward and leaned into his body. Fingers ran along his jawline.

The page was offered to the woman who read the letter with a growing frown.

"Obviously I'm not going. I'll just have Blink forward the

information to Sage who can leave anonymous tips." Frustrated, Kyle went to the kitchen and leaned over the small round table. From behind Deaton wrapped her arms around him and leaned her face against his back.

"You have to go. You would never forgive yourself if something happened and you weren't there."

Hands pulled him around to face her. One arm encircled his neck and pulled down. Lips pressed upon lips before he nodded in resignation.

Back in the bedroom, Kyle pulled the canvas duffel from beneath the bed while Deaton collected three sets of clothing from the dresser to hold out for Kyle. The smile on her face contrasted with the sadness in her eyes. Clothes were stowed before he sat on the edge of the bed and slipped on his weathered boots. The habit of packing light was a skill learned while on the run.

Packing was done in less than five minutes. Outside Kyle tossed the lone duffel bag into the backseat of the Monte Carlo. When he turned to face Deaton, he felt the heat of passion as she stole a kiss.

"You still have that other present. When you come back I'll let you have it." Getting into the front seat was one of the hardest things Kyle ever experienced. Their relationship, though brief, was as real as Kyle's friendships with Clay and Sage. Actually, more so. The facade and bravado of Aegis wasn't needed when he was with her. Neither did he worry she wouldn't understand what he fought for.

While valid reasons, the real reason his chest constricted was because he loved spending time with her and the boys. When he woke in the mornings his arms were wrapped around a beautiful, strong woman and at breakfast he was regaled with half remembered dreams from the twins. Whatever he did that day only passed the time so he could return home. Home. A place he was wanted and loved. And where he loved in return.

The car started and the windows rolled down.

"Once this thing down south is settled I'm coming back. You hear me Deat?" Head bobbed, the golden eyes filled with passion almost stopped Kyle from leaving. Almost.

"Be back before you know I'm gone." The car pulled away. Hand fiddled with the rearview mirror where he saw Deaton as she watched him leave. Once the car hit the interstate his foot pushed the accelerator to the floor

"Get this done and hurry back", Kyle said to his own reflection. Little did he know that he would never come back.

PART SEVEN:
iNTO THE WEB

STATUS QUO

Wednesday, April 19, 2045
6:21 p.m.

Those that wanted to lose themselves in Gainesville went to the Grid. What was once Morningside Nature Park was now the Grid. Trailers, campers, portable sheds, busses, and vans were laid out like a scattered caravan through almost three hundred acres. Generators ran on local moonshine stills and lights powered by a plethora of solar panels were the only form of electricity on the Grid.

Absolutely no internet.

Signal jammers were scattered about the Grid. Nearby towers often had the tendency of malfunctioning. Electromagnetic pulse generators near the center of the park released random pulses to disrupt and disable sensitive electronics. In the skies the 'Net' floated over most major cities. Sky drones, nicknamed 'Sk-Eyes' were aerial drones with digital cameras that kept constant vigil surveillance over their quadrant. Thousands hovered above Gainesville in near permanency due to solar panels built atop that constantly recharged the long lasting power cells.

But not over the Grid. One way or another, any Sk-Eye that was assigned to the stretch of land over Morningside Nature Park quickly became disabled through 'mysterious' circumstances.

Nomads were what they were called. People who wanted to live off the grid and not be under constant surveillance by 'Big Brother'. Or they didn't want to be around supers. Or, more likely, did not wish to be around 2.0s, the human Upgrades. It wasn't just a localized event but a mindset felt in every country of the world. Almost every major city also offered a grid. A place to disconnect. Where the individual was judged based on action and decision instead of DNA.

The haven also offered amnesty through anonymity. Not designed for criminal activity, the Grid were for those who sought freedom and a modicum of peace. Aware that no law equalled lawlessness, the Grids shared unbreakable rules. No violence, no lies, no free rides. Their law was always handled internally. If a community could not come to an agreed consensus it fell to a Grid Ranger, Granger. Grangers acted as law and order which included executions if deemed necessary.

It wasn't perfect. But what was?

The Grid, outside of Gainesville, was quiet. School aged children gathered near two school busses with faded letters and chipping yellow paint. A massive patched tarp anchored from the roofs between the vehicles for shade. Children sat scattered in groups upon stretched out quilts while the teachers continued their lessons. Divided by ages, teachers taught their selected groups. The alphabet mingled with multiplication tables while details of Sumerian civilization drifted into the mix.

A smile twitched his lips as he leaned against a tree. The groans coming from homework announcements were all too familiar. And so distant that it was a different life. Smoke curled from his face with an exhale. Returned to his lips, the hand rolled cigarette dangled for a moment. Another plume of smoke drifted on the afternoon breeze. Finally he sighed deeply and moved away on a meandering walk through the nomad encampment. Black boots moved effortlessly through the downtrodden paths. Deep scouring and abrasions gave the boots character and more than a little history. The footwear revealed what the man did not.

A navy blue jumpsuit covered his body. Black boots laced over pant legs up to the knees. Unzipped to the navel, the arms of the jumpsuit were tied snuggly around a narrow waist. The cobalt tank top form fit his muscular torso as a second skin. Patches of sunlight danced on shoulder length golden hair and wiry beard. Calls rang out in greeting from different campsites. Some shouted "Aegis" while others beat their breast with a fist twice before holding the clenched hand into the air. Nods of acknowledgement were shared yet the dark blue eyes remained aloof.

Scattered through the woods were plants grown for food. Certain areas were cleared of forest vegetation for gardens while others were found along paths. Surrounded by life, Kyle relaxed with an iota of peace. It never lasted. Eventually the faces of those he failed filled his peripheral vision. Accusation etched deeply on the apparitions' faces. Guilt would bubble, a spring of free flowing water that drenched him in their blood. Blood that stained his hands.

"I know that look boss. Self punishment again?" Kyle turned to where the voice came from. The man was young, appearing in his twenties. Blue jeans and black shirt with sneakers, Blink looked normal. Even the dark brown hair that curled around his ears and easy going smile testified he was normal. The only sign he was more than he appeared came from his brown eyes. Weary loss echoed from his stare.

"Someone has to punish me", Kyle whispered. A shrug of his shoulders was followed by the inclination of his head, a gesture for Blink to follow. The two continued the walk, the younger man falling in step.

"Atlanta was close. Too close. We got lucky. Next time we use our own crew. Picked by either you or me. Can't go off half cocked again." The words fell from Kyle matter of factly. Almost like they were conversing about the weather or a favorite sports team.

"Man, it was tight but we did it. Helps that I always have an ace up my sleeve and you don't stop."

"We were tight, the crew was sloppy though. Could have gotten people killed. No more outsiders."

A resigned nod from Blink and Kyle gave a grunt of confirmation.

The path widened as the two entered their camp site. An old fifteen passenger van sat to one side, more rust than white paint etched on the exterior. Opposite sat an eighty seven SS Monte Carlo. White with red pinstripes, the car managed to get Kyle out of more than a few bad situations. Sunlight was blocked by the green tarp strung between trees and covering the central area.

A plastic folding table sat covered with miscellaneous equipment. With his boot he hooked a metal chair over and sat. Elbows leaned against the table as Kyle began cleaning the tools of his trade. The fire was nearly out so Blink went to a stack of firewood they collected the previous day and returned with an armful. Slowly he stoked the fire before more kindling was added and then a few pieces of split wood.

Silence drifted between the two, broken only by the pops from the fire and the disassembling of firearms.

"When is it enough?"

Kyle glanced up to see Blink who knelt before the fire, eyes unfocused and seeing through the flames. Unthinking muscle memory took over while he slipped the slide over the receiver, the two halves of the pistol joined. Just enough pressure was placed on the spring within the slide to slip the takedown lever back into place. The slide was racked to ensure everything was smooth. Gently he set the pistol down before he turned to Blink who still stared into the nothingness of his own mind.

"It's different for everybody. What you did was self preservation. Instinct. You say I should stop punishing myself but you are the one that needs to let go." As he spoke Kyle stood and walked over to the younger man, his hand placed on the shoulder in semblance of comfort.

"You can't carry that burden and move forward", solemn words escaped him softly while he tried to console Blink. A rasp filled cough and the younger man stood with a nod. Without a word he left the site to disappear into the trees. The kid needed time, a concept Kyle understood completely.

Everyone had 'what-ifs'. It was the nature of life. Pure vision of twenty twenty was always seen when looking to the past, never in the present. Hindsight was a bastard. That was part of the problem.

Blink was a precog.

The way he described it was confusing. Every moment of every day he was bombarded with second sight. For him it was actually seven second sight. Overlaid on his sight were ghostly apparitions that revealed the future of what would happen next. Or, at least, what would happen if he didn't do anything to alter the future. What Blink saw was a seven second window in which he could alter the outcome. Kyle couldn't imagine living with the ability twenty-four seven.

The biggest complaint Blink often griped about was not being able to cheat at cards. There just wasn't enough time. Not for anything important. And no do overs. It wasn't a constant loop like the movies where people were allowed to try scenarios repeatedly over until it ends the way you want. No. One shot and that was it.

Three years earlier he and his little brother stopped at a convenience store in Smyrna Georgia. Just a normal day. Waiting in line with two drinks, one for him and the other for his brother waving from the car. Then a man pulled a gun on the store clerk. Hyped up and high, the robber flinched from a drug induced hallucination. Ghostly form raised the revolver, sighted at Blink's chest. The hammer fell and released the fireball that fired the bullet that tore into his heart.

Seven seconds. Muscles tensed and locked at the realization he was about to die.

Six seconds. Head turned on a swivel, the robber yanked the revolver from the black hoodie.

Five seconds. The arm raised, the revolver aiming at the clerk whose eyes widened in fear.

Four seconds. The clerk jumped back, his back rocking the shelf behind laden with packs of cigarettes.

Three seconds. The squeak of Blink's wet shoe on the linoleum floor was the culprit. The sound that drew the gun wielder's attention.

Two seconds. The arm turned, the revolver moved ever closer.

One second. The rush of adrenaline moved his legs as he dove away from the counter and down one of the store's aisles.

Time was up. The gunshot was unnaturally loud. Glass shattered and fell sounding like crystal wind chimes before they smashed to the ground. The thief sobered with the shot and staggered away as he ran careening against aisles and racks, giving an impersonation of a pinball. A ghostly figure ran in and screamed for an ambulance. Blink didn't need seven seconds to know.

It took half a dozen officers to separate him as he cradled the dead body of his little brother on the blood splattered seat of the car..

Most days the young man was fine. Sometimes he wasn't. Everyone had regret.

The kid bounced back fairly quickly. At least one of them did.

Every year that passed just gave Kyle more faces to haunt him with. A full bottle of moonshine sat on the tabletop. It didn't stay full for long. Mind drifted backwards to a small house in the woods. Sacred memories created free of darkness, despair, or fear. A place which evolved into home. Kyle wished he never left.

One job in Florida called him south. A family needed help. Once the job was done, two more rose. Defend a super from an anti-super group, move a family to safety, stop a murderer, protect innocents, find children kidnapped. The list went on until Kyle realized he needed to choose. His own happiness in Georgia or the fates of faceless innocents who needed Aegis.

Four years. Four years of dedication to the cause. A long time ago Kyle swore to himself to never be a bystander. If his actions made a difference then he would follow the lonely road. Most days he told himself the right decision was made. Other times the liquor became a salve against the fear, the fear he made the wrong choice.

Today was such a day. The liquor flowed freely as Kyle forced himself to believe he chose right. A duty to put others' needs and wants before his own.

That was the scene of their reunion.

DESPAIR

Wednesday, April 19, 2045
6:55 p.m.

Shadows stretched across the grass as the sun lowered into treetops. Branches played shadows across the stretched tarp ceiling like marionettes. Breeze rustled bringing life to the shadow puppets that danced above Kyle who held the bottle like a lifeline to sanity. Liquor never brings sanity and rarely brings peace of mind. Regardless of the potential attributes offered by the alcohol, neither sanity or peace awaited Kyle.

Two new shadows stretched before him before they detached from the tarp. The thought that ghosts formed into corporeal beings came to drag him to a hellish punishment both frightened and was accepted by Kyle. Slowly Blink drifted into focus which brought him back to his senses. Then his eyes fell upon a face from his past.

Sage Winters.

The same shaved head but with a new beard that hid half his face. However, there was no denying the eyes of one of his best friends. Even if they were haunted by a depth of pain and hatred that sobered Kyle. Blink looked between the two before he stepped backwards slowly.

"I see you two know each other and have some catching up to do …" The weight of the moment wasn't lost on the young man who eased away, a nonchalant wave to a few men deeper in the trees who led Sage into the Grid upon his arrival.

Alone, the two men merely stared at one another in silence. Slowly, so as not to startle his friend, Kyle pushed to his feet and stood waiting. Fingers easeed the bottle of moonshine to the tabletop by its neck. Unsure if a handshake was appropriate, he paused. His trepidation was unwarranted as Sage surged forward and wrapped heavy arms around him. Great sobs shook from deep within Sage's chest as tears ran freely into the bushy beard.

Uncertain, Kyle returned the hug as he felt hands grip tight as though he was a buoy in a sea of helplessness. Knees buckled and Sage's legs gave out causing Kyle to direct him into the chair before he crouched beside. Minutes of uncontrolled emotion spilled from Sage until finally he regained his composure.

The bottle of moonshine was offered and accepted, several deep draughts taken while Kyle stood and turned his back to offer a moment of composure. Another chair was collected and he returned to the table to sit across from Sage. Life left evidence of difficult journeys through miles of perilous terrain. For both men.

Gone was the blonde, meticulous crew cut and clear blue eyes. Golden skin once glowed with health and vitality and a strong jaw clear of stubble. Strong and quick, he remembered there was nothing too great for him to overcome. Back when he was young. And dumb. Now he was old. Equally as dumb, but old age gave you the benefit to think about the stupidity of the moment.

And then he did it anyway.

Maybe the true blessing was the immediate action of youth versus the contemplation of older age. Better to just react than to actually think about it and still choose to leap in front of a locomotive. Benefits of the ignorance of youth. A term that could no longer apply to him. The mane of hair lost its luster, the beard having gone from thick and wild to limply resigned. Gold highlights once shimmered in the sunshine instead sat a dulled tan, lost between tawny and grey.

The eyes that looked up after another swig from the bottle were far from the piercing blue of youth. Once his eyes were compared to the brilliant hue of a cloudless summer day sky. Now they resembled a stormy winter day. Overcast by the season, then darkened by shapeless storm clouds that threatened neither rain nor snow, but sleet. Freezing pellets that stung the skin accompanied by slush that brought to mind melted snow that oozed down a grimy gutter. The worst aspects of either form of precipitation. All were seen in the eyes of the superhero turned vigilante called Aegis.

For a long stretch the two sat in silence. Afternoon eased to evening as Blink silently returned and lit several small tiki torches that offered light and an area free from roaming mosquitoes intent on draining the blood from the nomadic campers. The occasional swat by the young man in blue jeans was the only sign of life at their camp as the youth settled down nearby to wait. Eventually one of them had to speak. Or die. They were both pretty old afterall.

The smirk that stretched across Blink's face drew Kyle's attention. They spent enough time around one another that the young man sheepishly avoided eye contact, somehow sure Kyle knew precisely what amused him. Lips parted, cracked and dry, as Sage spoke with a voice made raspy by liquor and emotion.

"I came home early. No reason. I just finished checking a few receipts turned in by a client and figured I'd surprise Naomi with flowers. The door was open when I got home. I know I should have called building security but … I was drawn in. Something slammed into me and I crashed into the table in the foyer. I must have hit my head because I only have glimpses of what happened."

Domed head dropped as Sage fought to retain control of his emotions. So engrossed in his friend, Kyle didn't notice Lydia arrive. He wasn't truly surprised. She was always quiet when that was needed. Always three steps ahead of him. A steaming tea pot was held in one of her strong hands as she collected and poured four cups of hot tea. Thick, brown waves fell unbidden down her shoulders, never able to be tamed. Silvery sheen of white glowed from strands in her hair, the only evidence of her age.

She knelt near Sage and carefully held out a warm mug, the warmth of the cup and the sincere look of pained understanding deep in her olive eyes, won the wounded man over. With a curt nod he took the tea with a mumble of gratitude. She stood and handed Kyle the other mug. Hands brushed absently at the tan button down shirt she wore before Lydia handed the third mug to Blink before collecting the final mug and retreating across the campsite to the van where she busied herself out of ear shot.

"Life has just been so busy. I got busy. Now it's too late", Sage dropped eyes to his cup as words drifted off. A thickness entered his voice as he continued.

"I remember seeing Mary dragged by, tied up and gagged. I can still hear her muffled cries for me. Why didn't daddy save her? You know she made the marching band?" Eyes looked up with a glimmer of light before the darkness within extinguished the hope.

"I don't know what was worse, seeing her dragged by while I was helpless or seeing my wife pulled along. Dead." Choked sobs wracked his shoulders before he threw the mug to the ground in impotent rage. Despair flowed from the broken man with Kyle uncertain how to help. Once again Lydia was there, her form moving gracefully to wrap Sage in willowy arms. His head rested against her shoulder as his shattered soul mourned. A nod from her was all Kyle needed to excuse himself and join Blink in hasty retreat to the woods.

Moss hung from trees, old and young alike, draping down in curtains as the two men moved a short distance away. With a grunt Kyle squatted with his back against a pine. Meanwhile Blink paced to and fro. It was evident Sage's story affected the young man. Hit too close to home. Irritated, Blink kicked the ground twice before he flopped onto the ground, legs outstretched.

"I think I know the answer but, does this ever stop", Blink questioned in futile frustration. Leaned back against the tree trunk, Kyle closed his eyes with an equally disgruntled sigh.

"If supes and upgrades didn't exist people would still be using, abusing, and killing one another. It's human nature. To destroy ourselves."

"Then why try, if it is a never ending cycle?"

Lips tightened as he silently admitted to wondering the same thing. Everything done, all the differences he made in his life, what did it amount to? If he saved someone from being killed today, there was always tomorrow for a second attempt. There was no way he could be everyone's shield all the time. So why try.

You couldn't cheat death. At the end, Death always won. One day or one year, it mattered not.

"You don't believe that Kyle. If you did you wouldn't have stayed on the beach with the boy and his mother. Or chased after Henry when he took the kids. Every single moment of life is a treasure. Don't you think I wish I had one more day?" Sandy's voice echoed in his head and struck chords deep within.

Everything he did now was to make sure other kids got the chance to grow up. To allow parents time to raise their children and know one another. He didn't fight for money, or the law, or for himself. It was for those around him. Eyes opened to look over at Blink.

"Every second we can steal from death is another moment an innocent gets. Maybe one day the world won't need a shield or a seven second seer." Fingers found a pinecone which he tossed at Blink's head. Unsurprisingly he dodged easily. Seven second bastard. Footsteps neared them with Lydia's careful stride. The pace slowed as she approached. Unreadable features and crossed arms warned both men that something was amiss. Both stood and waited.

"If you go back there to your friend you will decide to help him.

If you do, that will be the end of our mission. You won't come back. Neither of you." The heavy words wrapped the three with the weight of importance.

"So. What do you say? Should I go and talk to him", Kyle questioned her. Rough times were shared between the two and he trusted her opinion. Wordlessly she reached into her khaki pants and pulled out a piece of paper. The note extended in her hand as Kyle paused. Briefly he wondered how a piece of paper possessed the power for him to decide.

Reluctantly he took the page and unfolded it. Both sides were empty. A brow raised as he looked to Lydia who merely pointed once more at the note. Narrowed eyes were given to the woman for the silent treatment. Again he looked at the paper but this time held it up so the dying light brightened his view. A gasp escaped him and he dropped the paper to purposefully return to the camp and Sage.

The wind tossed the abandoned paper down the path. With the final light of day a pattern of fine dots were seen drawn across it.

FROM THE PAST

Wednesday, April 19, 2045
7:17 p.m.

Returning to the campsite felt like a dream. Feet followed one after another as his mind reeled. The symbols haunted him since he first saw their engravings. Carved into the dock. It seemed as though every single point in his life was haunted by the symbol. And now it reared its head once again.

What did it mean?

The sun was set, the flames danced in the light breeze casting its glow about the clearing. Unmoving, Sage sat at the table with the bottle that hung limply between his fingers. Head was bowed, warmth from the fire brightened the bare skull. It was a corpse that didn't know he was dead. Yet.

The pained loss his dear friend suffered from was impossible to comprehend. While he lost Sandra, she was still with him. And she was his sister, not a wife and child. He couldn't fathom the depth of desolation that afflicted Sage. And he didn't know how to comfort him. But he had to try.

Slowly he circled to squat next to Sage. If it wasn't for the slight rise and fall of his chest Kyle would question if he lived. Carefully he pulled the bottle from unfeeling fingers. The action stirred the man who straightened in his seat. Empty eyes looked to Kyle.

"What can you tell me about that symbol?" Raising the bottle Kyle took a draught.

"One of the men knelt down in front of my face. I can still smell his breath. Garlic and liquorice. One of those neural links in his bald head. A big brute. He stuffed that paper in my shirt. He only said two words. 'For Henry'. I still don't have any idea who Henry is." Hands cradled his face as Sage gave into tears.

Kyle rocked back on his haunches. For Henry. Henry Abernathy. The man he beheaded with the shield now sitting wrapped in the trunk of the Monte Carlo. The misfortune and tragedy that befell Sage's family was on him. Naomi's blood was on his hands. Mary's abduction was on him.

The bottle was tilted and Kyle finished the moonshine before he threw the empty vessel into the fires. Fire licked upon and within the bottle, flames greedily consumed the remains of the flammable liquid. The shadows deepened giving angular lines a severity that did not exist during the day. There was only one man who would act in the memory of Henry Abernathy. And he possessed all the resources to do so.

Samuel Abernathy. The elder brother of Henry.

Even before today's visit Kyle was looking at Abernathy. Rumors circulated about what went on in the Heresy. Witnesses prepared to testify vanished like the morning dew. Atrocities and vile acts echoed from within the fortified building. Disappearances plagued the entire southeastern region of America. Crumbs of intel led back to Abernathy, yet with little enough substance for the authorities to act on.

Instinctively Kyle knew.

Mary was alive.

His hands gripped Sage's shoulders and raised him to his feet. They say the eyes were the windows to the soul. If true then what looked out from one of his oldest friend's eyes was tortured damnation. Hope needed to be rekindled.

"If the person I believe is the one behind this, then I'm confident your daughter is alive. I will not rest until I find her. I've got some out of state friends who will help. But you're gonna have to assist too. Illegally." As Kyle spoke he noticed his words ignited a spark of life. An ember of hope.

"I'll do anything to get my Mary back. Anything." There was steel in Sage's words. A promise that there was no line he wouldn't cross. Arms reached out and grabbed Kyle in a hug. It wasn't a gentle hug. Kyle was the buoy of hope that Sage clung to with all his strength. For without hope he would drown in an ocean of misery and guilt.

They parted company some minutes later. Back to the car to sleep. Meanwhile Kyle broke open another bottle of moonshine. Lydia was right. There wasn't a choice. The suffering Sage endured was because of Kyle's actions. The death of Henry painted a target on those Kyle cared for. He was the reason Sage and his family became targets. The past couldn't be changed. But maybe he could save Sage's future by rescuing Mary.

Hours later Lydia guided a drunken Kyle to his tent. With his head in her lap he listened to the melodic voice as she stroked his fevered brow. Nightmares claimed him.

"I'm sure you must be weary, dear, with soaring up so high; Will you rest upon my little bed? Dear friend, what can I do? To prove the warm affection I've always felt for you?"

Her gentle words crooned as sleep stole him away. The last thing he remembered was the shadows of branches across the tent tangled as a web.

HARD CHOICES

Tuesday, April 25, 2045
11:08 p.m.

Frosted breath exhaled into the night air. Strong gusts of wind blew through the city stirring trash to dance upon the wind like ghosts. Heavy clouds hung low from the heavens, portent of rain imminent. A hush clutched the city in thrall. The moment breath is held awaiting release at some pivotally, emotional revelation.

And, yet, sweet relief was not forthcoming.

Several blocks west, on University Avenue, stood the Heresy. She was not like her brethren built round about her. Heresy was more than just modern architecture. From technological advancements pioneered to living quarters, from the ability to remotely work from rented digital couches or avatar cocoons, to on site dining facilities, from theaters, parks, arcades, bars, and clubs … Heresy was its own city. The price of a day pass was steep. A weekend getaway? Astronomical. To live there? One would need to bleed gold. The building catered to any need, desire, or vice. Within the walls of Heresy the law no longer applied.

Evil grew and flourished under the watchful eye of Samuel Abernathy. Influence and control spread from the Heresy throughout north central Florida. A network of interconnected strands that led back to one man. Abernathy. Lines of affiliation wove through criminal organizations and local politicians. Even the Protectorate were unwilling to pressure Abernathy and his empire, so well was he connected.

Then there were the whispers none gave voice to. Genetic manipulation. Biotechnology. Abominations. Amalgamations of evolution and technology. Unwilling subjects supposedly pooled from beneath the umbrella of the web. Untouched at the center rested Abernathy, the Spider.

Several blocks east rested the Golden Towers of Gator Nation, gateway into Gainesville. Regal and weathered, the Seagle Building overlooked the northside of University Avenue. Set opposite was the Sentry Building, a reimagined modern revitalization of the older Seagle. Twins born in different centuries and eras. Bronzed exteriors lit like torches at dawn and dusk, reflected flames of the sun dancing across the surface of the Golden Towers.

It was on the Sentry's roof that he stood watch in silent contemplation. Stone gargoyles perched on the parapet, wings outstretched as garish faces snarled down upon the city. Inhumane and uncaring, the statues were not meant to succour the faint of heart but to defend the inhabitants from evil. A low whistle hummed from the frozen creatures on the roof as the wind blew steadily. A mournful wail reverberated in the night.

"Not long my friends. Soon your empty howls will be filled with rain. And my coffers will overflow in blood", Kyle whispered to stone confidants. Palm patted the stone side of the beast as his eyes looked upon the monolith that pierced the heavens in erroneous hubris. Certain zealots called the building the Tower of Babel. They were wrong. Abernathy and his ilk didn't reach to the heavens in search of god. They believed they were god and, thus, deserved their place in the heavens.

"Pride comes before the fall", he whispered to himself. The sound of shoes scraped the rooftop behind Kyle causing him to glance backwards.

"Pride goeth before destruction, and an haughty spirit before a fall." White teeth flashed amidst a black beard. Slowly Kyle shook his head at his friend. Time was unkind to Sage Winters. Life, even more cruel. The three men, Kyle, Sage, and Clay, escaped the Dead End of Lake Gem Estates for a better life. The community of fearful bigots who believed they created a haven away from the supers and the version 2.0s, the 'upgrades', were blissfully ignorant that some of their children could potentially be one of the undesirables. Most recent media outlets revealed the juicy new details that Jim Stevens Jr, heir to Stevens Constructions, was in fact a super. The founder of Lake Gem Estates and countless other, equally segregational communities, now floundered under new direction as Jim Jr fought for equality for all.

With a final glance at the technological monstrosity Kyle turned and leaned against the wall, a silent survey of one of his best friends. Just a year older than his own thirty seven years, Sage tasted a life of love with a beloved wife and daughter. All that remained was the taste of gritty ash and salted tears. Crows' feet gathered at the corners of his eyes and refused to relinquish their hold. Deep lines crossed his forehead. Not a thousand small cracks but three deep valleys furrowed in permanency across his head from temple to temple. A gloriously unkempt beard likened him to a pirate upon the seas. All that he needed was an eyepatch to complete the ensemble.

There was no need for an eyepatch.

Eyes, so dark they were nearly black, looked upon the world with a heaviness untold. If the gaze by happenstance were to fall upon you, a weight would settle upon your shoulders. Emotion and memory imparted with a single glance shook all to the center of their being. Forlorn lost rage, impotent against the inevitable grind of desolation assigned him by fate, conveyed in eye contact the immutable reality of life. Life was grief, pain, loss. And life sought to return us to the ethereal existence of the afterlife in equal manner of our arrival. Cold, crying, helpless, and alone.

"What happened to us?" The quiet query was rhetorical. Mainly because Kyle was reluctant to look in the mirror.

"Sandy died. With her death went our purity and virtue. Now the world is bereft of innocence." Dismay colored Sage's words. Shadows of defeat clung to him like a parasite. And with every moment passed, he surrendered hope, joy, and love. Darkness enveloped his hunched shoulders. The spark of his soul died a week earlier. And his heart only continued to beat for one thing. Not hope. Closure. Judgement.

PORTENT

Tuesday April 25, 2045
11:23 p.m.

The upgrade lay stretched out on the queen sized bed. Striped of all but the bedsheet, each corner post was secured to a limb. The upgrade was disrobed and laid only in his white cashmere boxers. All hair was removed, tattoos covered his body in grey spirals that gently flowed into another in dizzying patterns. An IV was connected to either arm covered in ridges that ran across his torso. Subdermal implants. The knuckles were three times their normal size.

A brute.

To the side stood Blink. His normal attire of jeans and shirt were forsaken for the uniform of the night's activities. Like Kyle, he wore the cobalt jumpsuit made of titan-steel fibers, one of the strongest and lightest metals created. Used as a base ballistic nylon, the titan-steel is coated with polyurea which is especially protective against kinetic force and piercing. A dusting of aerogel coats the exterior while a foam variant of aerogel is utilized within the suit for regulating extreme temperatures. Inside the jumpsuit were various layers and trauma pad inserts along the arms, legs, and especially the chest and back which assist in shock absorption.

Over the jumpsuit went the plate armor. Polyurea coated titan-steel breastplate and back plate. The same went for the greaves that connected to the knee high boots and the cuisses protecting the thighs. Vambrace and rerebrace were for the forearms and upper arms. Due to the desire to remain light and mobile the plates of titan-steel were thinner and hence, lighter. The idea was the titan-steel would stop the damage while the jumpsuit would soften the kinetic energy of the strike.

It wasn't always the case. On more than one occasion, Kyle watched as others died while his abilities made any wounds suffered survivable. It wasn't necessarily fair, but that was life.

The brute shivered uncontrollably, muscle spasms trembled his body. Behind, Sage waited in the doorway. Shock and regret flickered across his face only to have the chilled determination win through the emotional, morale war within. With an incline of his head, Kyle motioned for his old friend to leave. The door closed with his departure.

"We don't have time for this", Kyle said simply as he leaned over the brute to look into his eyes. The eye speculum peeled the lids apart like legs of a metallic arachnid, forcing the eyes to remain open in a disturbing appearance.

"Come on, this is the quickest way to extract the info we need. Plus it's so cool."

"I miss the old days where we just beat the information out of them", he turned his back to the brute as Blink pulled out an odd looking visor. In the center of the hollows were several glistening needles. Kyle looked over his shoulder and watched as the visor slipped on the brute's head, fastened to the temples securely.

"The only problem with the old way is anything can be said to stop the pain. You can't believe them. My way lets us see what we want to know."

"Your way makes my eyes hurt."

"He's not conscious so he won't feel a thing. And if he was awake, he'd only feel pressure. No pain."

"It still looks wrong", he shuddered as the needles lowered from the visor and pierced the cornea of the brute's eyes. The idea of watching something pierce your eye caused a shiver to run down Kyle's spine.

"We both know he's not going to survive. I don't understand you sometimes. You can bash people with your shield, toss bad guys from roofs, and blow them away. But a little needle going in your eye makes you turn green." As he spoke Blink pulled a pair of goggles over his eyes, one wire running to the laptop in his hands and another plugged into the makeshift visor currently connected to the brute.

"I still don't see why you don't just use the Neural-Net Interface", Kyle grumbled while he folded his arms across his chest. Thin, flexible electrodes, so small they couldn't be seen by the naked eye, slithered through the needles and into the retina where they entwined and followed the axons through the back of the eye to the optic nerve.

"Too many possible problems with the Neural-Net. Not the least of which we could trigger an alarm by combing through the interface without clearance. You can't tell what kinda software is in there until you're in. Or what system the device is connected to. Then it's too late."

Made sense, even though Kyle didn't want to admit it.

Around a third of the world's population had the Neural-Net, short for Neural Neuron Electrical Transference Interface, implanted in their craniums. Where the Neural-Net succeeded where so many others failed was the simple realization that no matter how small or what coated the electrode, they were still foreign bodies that would corrode with age and risk host rejection.

News reports and media stories were filled with dead heads, the term for the defective outcomes from the first generation of neural interfaces.

This is where the Neural-Net succeeded.

Within each interface was a miniscule bioprinter. Using the

organic material that the device was exposed to, allowed the Neural-Net to create dendrites which grafted into the preexisting dendrites. From the created dendrites came new myelin coated axons specifically grown as an interface between organic and machine. New axons were then inserted into the nodes of Ranvier, intermittent openings in the myelin sheath. However none of this would be possible without stimuli.

When the interface is implanted, a second phase occurs. Fibrous electrodes are extended around the exterior of the skull, beneath the epidermis. Within the Neural-Net exists a stimulator which converts an electrical pulse through a magnetic coil into a precise point along one of the electrodes around the skull.

Acting very much like Transcranial Magnetic Stimulation, directional pulses result in depolarization and an excitability of action potential. Concurrent and repetitive pulses can strengthen and grow the long term potentiations.

In short, they stuck a chip into your head that shocked your brain into playing nice with the computer now sharing the same space.

Kyle watched some of the procedures and always felt unease. Scalpels cut incisions before the drill bored into the skull. The part that disturbed the most was needing to remain conscious during the operation.

"I'm in."

Just like that Kyle was drawn from internal reverie, eyes turned to the small screen which flickered random images as Blink burrowed deeper into the brute's grey matter.

"Find the passcode yet", the question echoed from Kyle, breaking the silence that filled the room.

"This isn't like finding your lost keys or remembering if you turned the headlights off to the car. It's a bit more complicated." The strain in Blink's voice reminded him that what the young man was attempting was difficult. Perhaps quiet was needed.

With care Kyle moved around behind his seated compatriot and glanced between the flashes of images and the sedated brute who twitched as the unseen filaments probed deeper. Seven second flashes of the future rarely helped, but in this situation it gave enough warning of wrong pathways chosen. Still, the seconds ticked by agonizingly slow.

Pixelated images became clearer if not more random. Patternless glimpses of unfocused life grew dizzied. Relentless determination etched on Blink's face as he drove furiously deeper in search of information that flashed by too quickly for Kyle to identify.

"And ... got it ..." Breath came between clenched teeth as the young man visibly relaxed. Kyle grasped his shoulder tightly as he bent down over his companion's shoulder in concentration at the screen.

"That, stop! What is that?" Blink enlarged the random image, fingers flying over the keyboard as he attempted to bring the frozen picture on screen into focus. The goggles were pulled from Blink's face while he hunched over the laptop trying to decipher the pixelated image as it slowly focused.

A rasp escaped the brute, his mouth opened wide.

"Kyle Ross ... Finally you enter my web ... Soon you are mine ... forever ..." The unrestrained head was raised from the bed, eyes with needles embedded deeply latched onto Kyle in a stare as unhinged jaw flapped open in a death head's grin. Then the body sagged into the bed, a muffled exhale signaled his death.

The picture finally focused on the screen.

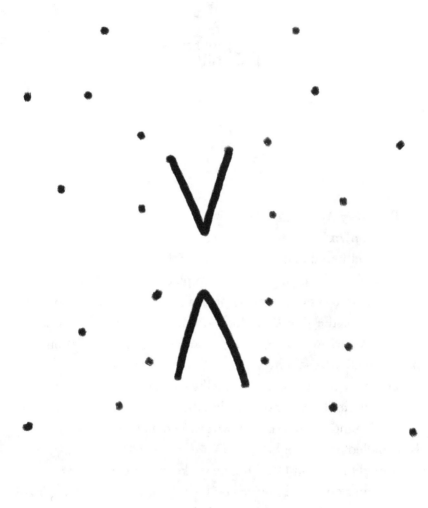

VI
PREPARATION

Tuesday April 25, 2045
11:52 p.m.

They gathered in the living room of the penthouse suite. Arms crossed, Kyle waited near the gas fireplace. Flames danced within on an unending line of fumes. The beautiful danger of the fire drew his gaze. To the side Blink looked out the window lost in silent reverie. A narrow groove of carpet suffered under Sage's constant pace while Lydia sat enveloped within an armchair.

The noise of someone entering the room drew Kyle's attention. Dressed in similarly armored attire, the woman walked straight for him with hand extended. The two grasped one another's hand and Kyle pulled her into a hug.

"Good to see you Deaton", he spoke in her ear.

"Damn right it is. How've you been, oldman?" The two broke the hug and Kyle shook his head at her in mock rage.

"This old man can still knock some sense into you."

"Well, everybody needs a hobby", she smirked while looking up at Kyle.

"How are the twins?"

It was four years since first they met and Kyle was instantly intrigued. Flawless caramel skin and close cropped hair was accented by her toned five foot frame. Despite her beauty and small size, it was the eyes that mattered. Golden honey so lightly hued they appeared enhanced. However it wasn't their unique color that set her apart.

An uncaged primal power burned in their depths.

A ferocious fighter, yet she retained a mother's gentle touch with a caring, empathetic nature.

But the cause pulled them in different directions. The underground needed Deaton and Florida's lawlessness needed Kyle.

There was a weighted pause as she looked into his face.

"The twins are good. Started school. Maybe after this little mission you come back for some R and R? They missed you", she reached up and placed a dainty hand against his bearded cheek.

"I missed you", she whispered.

"I missed you too", his hand covered hers for several moments. Emotion and connection lasted eons within the brief moment that passed too quickly. Withdrawing her hand, she swung the previously unnoticed knapsack from one shoulder and unzipped it. A crimson jacket was pulled out and tossed to Kyle who caught and unfolded it.

"I know how you like your red hoodies. This is a ballistics titan-steel weave with a kevlar lining. It also has ceramic composite plates that are replaceable."

The jacket was swirled around his body as his arms slipped in. Straightening the jacket he nodded at the weight.

"Thanks Deat." As Kyle turned and twisted in order to get a feel for it Deaton smiled a toothy grin.

Now that their moment was over Kyle looked to all of them, their eyes drawn in readiness.

"So the plan is simple enough. At midnight a group of the underground are hitting several police and fire stations in Pensacola. No casualties. This is just to draw the Warriors from the Citadel. Between twelve fifteen and twelve thirty several Sk-Eyes will be forcibly taken out. The net will compensate by shifting all the other Sk-Eyes until replacements are launched. Surveillance will become compromised and gaps will appear in the net. One gap will be right here."

Even though everyone knew the plan, they all still listened.

"At twelve forty a large contingent of the underground will breach the first floor and begin ascending. Now we know the bottom elevators and stairs end on the tenth floor. The only way to climb higher is to transfer to the upper elevators and stairs there. And they are heavily guarded. If anyone tries to fight their way through security from the lower levels, they will be decimated. That's where we come in."

Blink interjected.

"This is when I fire the harpoon from our roof to the tenth floor", he said excitedly.

"Yes Blink. That's when you shoot the line across. We just simply go across and hit the tenth floor security unaware. We now know, thanks to our dead friend, that the eleventh story to the forty fifth story has no bearing on our mission. That is the public area. The next four stories is where we believe the cages and illegal laboratories are located. We can help clear potions as we make our way to the fiftieth floor where Samuel Abernathy resides."

The seriousness of the situation was etched on each of their faces. Blink worried on a pen, teeth gnawed absently. Both women crossed arms over their chests and tensed. As for Kyle, the weight of responsibility for the mission laid on his shoulders.

"We won't have a lot of time. We need to bust in, free the slaves and test subjects, then get out. All before local authorities or the Warriors arrive."

An alarm beeped from around the room.

"Midnight. Time to get ready and move into position. Remember to cover your faces. We really don't want to become famous. It's bad for business. Blink, hit the little boys room before we go." Grins spread as Blink looked dejected.

"Come on man, it happened one time. One time! And they never forget …" The mumbles followed him while he left to use the restroom. His voice raised once more.

"It was one time!"

The shield was tossed over his shoulder while he picked up the Salazar air rifle and connected it to the gunsling. Deaton left the room as she contacted her groups throughout the city. Slowly Lydia walked over to Kyle who was double checking equipment.

"Don't face him Kyle. You don't escape if you do. Don't hunt him for vengeance."

Hands fiddled with the kevlar mask in his hands. She wanted him to turn to her, look in her eyes, and tell her it wasn't personal. That wasn't possible because it was personal.

"You know as well as I do that he was behind those kids disappearing. When I killed Henry he did that out of spiteful anger. So I'm gonna kill him. Not for the greater good. Not for what was right. Not for judgement. No. I'm gonna kill him because I want to."

As Kyle walked away she knew he would never be the same. A small smile crossed her face.

VII
POINT OF THE SPEAR

Wednesday, April 26, 2045
12:07 a.m.

"Happy birthday Kyle", Sandy whispered in his mind. The panes of glass in the french door reflected his image back to him. A critical eye scanned the man before him. A birthday was just another day. Literally. It was supposed to feel different on your birthday. But it was just another twenty four hour period that slipped by.

"You too sis." Back in the day, when they were still youth, he used to say that having your sibling share your birthday was a perk. You never forgot theirs. Twenty years without celebrating it helped to bury the day and the emotions that went with it.

"Why didn't you tell Sage about me", she queried.

"He's got enough on his plate without saying hi to a ghost. After. I'll tell him after."

For the fifth time in as many minutes he checked the time. A quarter after midnight. The selected drones would now be out of commission. For the next fifteen minutes.

The kevlar mask turned in his hands while he cleared his mind for the upcoming thrill of madness. At the fore stood the enigmatic recluse, Samuel Abernathy. Brilliant and cut throat, Abernathy was known for his odd tastes and eccentric behavior. And for taking care of his baby brother, Henry. That lifelong hobby ended quite abruptly five years earlier.

Over the last five years the symbol his sister once drew on a dock kept appearing. Always with rabid mutts. And somehow they were always connected to Samuel Abernathy. A web of evil stretched from the Heresy and the man perched at the center.

Another chirp of the alarm tolled twelve thirty.

The french doors were pushed wide open, swinging freely. With the mask held up for his final inspection he noticed a few peculiar irregularities. What felt like depressions were on the top and bottom of the mask's face. With a shrug he put it on, securing it firmly. One of the windows swung back on the gust of window. Catching his reflection he shook his head ruefully. An orange outline for the face while the eyes were glowing x's. The nose was a small line above slashed teeth. Hands reached back and raised the red hood overhead.

Time to go. The frayed boots carried him across the gravel roof to the parapet. Hands braced on the parapet as he studied the Heresy a few blocks away.

Feet crunched the rood behind him prompting him to turn and look. At the harpoon, Blink inspected the weapon to ensure it was still in good working condition. Satisfied he gave a thumbs up.

It was going to be an unpleasantly long zipline from the Sentry. They would make due. Eyes carefully kept track of the countdown as Deaton came out in her black leathers arrayed with armor plates. A smirk stretched his bearded face as he turned once more to the Heresy.

"This is going to be the biggest, most daring, mission for the underground yet. You know that?" The question floated between them as Deaton waited for Kyle's response.

"Yup."

"That's it? That's all you have to say? We're making history tonight and making a difference. And all you can say is 'yup' about bringing down another statewide organization profiting off of human trafficking?"

"Yup."

"God, you're incorrigible."

"Yup." By the last 'yup' he was grinning. Even when she roughly shoved him.

Behind them, Blink shouted.

"Ready to fire and harpoon me a skyscraper!"

The alarm beeped a final time even as the sounds of vehicles screeched to a halt ten floors and several blocks away. From the vehicles swarms of underground fighters hastened into the lobby and beyond. Several vehicles blocked the roads and prepared for the inevitable arrival of law enforcement.

"I'm starting to regret this plan of playing Tarzan", while Kyle muttered he took the Steyr ACR from Deaton. Another bullpup rifle, this one fired flechettes, small darts, coated with a tranquilizer. The specialized round also ditched a large amount of propellant which slowed the flechette. Instead of a quickly accelerated dart capable of fully imbedding in the target, the slower charge made the rounds less deadly and optimal for non lethal scenarios.

The Steyr ACR was slung over Kyle's shoulder which allowed the rifle to hang below his right arm. The 1911 fortyfive caliber pistol sat on his right hip, the straight edged dirk in a sheath in his boot, and the cutlass in its scabbard on his left hip. Momentarily he wondered if he was carrying too much equipment. Then he remembered Henry and suddenly, he now questioned if he was carrying enough.

Too late to second guess now.

"Blink, fire." The command was given with all uncertainty gone from his voice. A chuckle of excitement escaped Blink as he lined up the shot on the concrete floor between the tenth and eleventh floor. The whoosh of air as the harpoon fired rustled the red jacket. Breath was held until the spike embedded in the concrete of the Heresy building.

"Nice shot", Deaton congratulated the young man as Kyle

attached his mechanized trolly pulley. With a glance back Kyle watched as Blink shouldered the launcher for the shaped charge.

"Don't hit me."

With that he ran toward the wall on the roof and leapt, pulling his legs up as he cleared the wall. Then he was hurtling over city streets. Traffic and pedestrians below continued on their typical night, unaware individuals hurdled through the air over one hundred feet above them.

A random thought materialized in his mind. From this height would he die or turn into a meat bag of jellied organs. Idle thought didn't last as the window of the tenth floor rapidly approached. He could see a flurry of activity as the Heresy's security bustled in response to the underground rebels that climbed from beneath.

The sight of two security guards freezing at the sight of a man zipping toward them was amusing. Mouths opened in slack jawed confusion. A whistle went by Kyle's head to impact the window. Upon contact the charge exploded inward, a shower of glass shards launched at the unsuspecting guards.

Rather than applying the break, Kyle continued forward with neckbreak speed. Timed just right, he released his hold on the trolly and flew into the Heresy. Arms and legs tucked in as he bowled into several of the guards then skidded across the floor. Before he stopped sliding he raised up onto his knees while he raised the ACR. Switched to three round bursts he pulled the trigger, spraying the guards still before him.

Several impacts rocked him forward as some of the guards he barreled over took shots at him. The shield across his back either deflected or stopped the barrage though the kinetic energy still felt like heavy blows. Right arm raised the rifle up as he removed the spent magazine from the mag well to slap a new magazine in. Finger toggled to single fire while he rose to his feet, shouldering the rifle to fire more carefully before him. More blasts impacted his shield which staggered him which caused him to miss his first shot.

The second didn't miss.

Before him was a long hallway with elevators on either side. To the right were the bottom floor elevators and on the left the upper elevators. Over two dozen guards fired before him. Mixture of pistol and submachine gun fire unleashed toward Kyle. Rounds punched his torso and legs in lethal damage.

Despite the pain from the hits Kyle continued to fire. Two and three guards fell. Another impact hit him just above the left knee which instantly numbed his leg. Dropped to his injured knee Kyle continued to sight and fire. Four, five, and six went down. A round hit the back of his hood to crack against the kevlar coated, titan-steel mask. Stars shone in his vision as he stumbled forward, left hand catching him in his fall.

Seven, eight, nine more guards hit the floor unconscious. Pushing off the floor to straighten himself, Kyle ejected the spent magazine and slammed another home as his body took more hits than his pain-addled mind could count. The rifle aimed down the hall once again to fire at the double visioned guards. A round ripped through the armor of his left side to carve a blood furrow beneath his floating ribs. To add insult to injury a round hit him in the seat of his trousers to bite deeply into the flesh of his left cheek.

And then Deaton arrived.

Her entrance was graceful. She hit with left leg extended before her while her weight rested on her right knee. The Benelli shotgun rose to her shoulder as she fired. Flechette rounds on minimal charge to make it less deadly. The flechettes were also coated with tranquilizer. The shotgun barked repeatedly at the guards behind Kyle which gave him a momentary respite.

Staggered back to his feet, his left leg dragged somewhat, he renewed the push. He was the shield. He was Aegis. He could take the punishment. And the guards obliged as more appeared from the end of the hall. Halfway down the hall, between the elevator banks, stood a circular security desk. If they could reach it and take it, that would allow them to take cover until reinforcements arrived from below.

New arrivals at the end of the hall disembarked from the upper elevators on the left. These were no mere security guards. Assault rifles in their hands and body armor, they were ready for a fight. Ducking his shoulder dropped the shield, his left arm snagged the grip and raised it before him as the ACR began to fire again.

Behind, Deaton finished dispatching the guards at his read. Using Kyle as a human shield, she grabbed two double stacks of shells from the caddy and slammed in each pair. Another set of four were snagged and slammed home in two more swipes. The reload lasted less than three seconds before she fired again while she bounced side to side while most of her body remained protected behind Kyle.

Flechettes and darts skipped from body armor as their non lethal alternatives became useless.

"Switching rifles", Kyle shouted over the echoing din of gunfire.

"Green", was Deaton's reply as she weaved side to side releasing shotgun blasts around Kyle and his shield. The strap was shrugged off as he dropped the ACR to the floor. Right hand grasped the Salazar rifle grip as he shouldered it and braced the barrel against the edge of the shield.

"Switching ammo", was yelled into his ear.

"Green", was his response as he continued firing down the hall. This time with fifty caliber rounds. An impact sounded behind and then Blink shouted.

"Snake!" A short sprint and then he was behind Deaton. Neither rifle or shotgun was part of his arsenal. Instead he wore four Beretta M9s with thirty round magazines. Two in shoulder holsters and two, grips forward, on either hip.

The first time Kyle saw Blink's loadout he questioned the efficiency of them. Dual wielding pistols looked great in the movies but were rarely a good idea in real life. After the first time he saw him in action, Kyle changed his mind completely. For Blink at least. When you have a seven second head start on the enemy and knew where they would be, knew where your bullet would hit, and knew if you needed to correct your shot, it made all the difference.

Both Blink and Deaton wore full combat helmets with bullet proof face shields and armor. Notwithstanding the protective gear, even a few rounds to armored plates would knock the wind out of them, if they were lucky. Possibly they would have cracked ribs and more than likely trauma and contusions.

Every step forward was filled with agony. The shield remained impenetrable yet the kinetic energy was taking its toll on Kyle. However, he continued to push. It was imperative the three arrived at the relative safety of the security counter. The three discussed previously the need to reach the barricade because sooner rather than later enemy reinforcements would arrive from the elevators behind them.

At that point they would be cut down in a lethal crossfire.

"Rear incoming!" The words Kyle didn't want to hear were shouted from Blink. Seven seconds before they were cut down. Always have a plan for every contingency, especially FUBAR scenarios. Thankfully the trio planned for that as well.

Blink smacked Deaton on the right shoulder. In turn she hit Kyle on his right shoulder. As the punch registered Kyle already caught sight of Blink sprinting past his right side headed for the counter. The strategy was Blink would take lead and draw enemy fire while dispatching any hostels between the three and the safety of the security desk. It wasn't a great plan, but it should do the trick.

Seven Second Seer. To have the capacity to see the future only seven seconds ahead of the present was almost a worthless ability. Yet in this situation it worked to their advantage. Add the fact that Blink was an ambidextrous marksman and it made all the difference.

It was a dance. Run, leap, spin, slide. Blink knew which bullet would hit him and where. Relying on instinctual reaction to his foresight he moved like a graceful dancer that delivered death with every pull of the trigger.

While Blink swirled in a beautiful, dangerous, and deadly

rhythm Kyle drew on his reserves of energy and sprinted. Left leg moved stiffly as every time he stepped down a thousand needles stabbed at his nerves. The throbbing matched the thunder of his heartbeat. Ahead Blink reached the counter and leaped nimbly to the top.

Faintly he heard the ding of elevators behind as he came abreast of the security station. Another punch on his right shoulder and Deaton dove over the counter. Another barrage was released from in front caused Blink to drop below the desktop. With his left leg still weak Kyle flopped to his side and rolled across the countertop to hit the floor in the safety of the security station.

"That was fun, can we do it again", Blink laughingly said as he reloaded the pistols.

"If I didn't see two of you I'd shoot you." Kyle shook his head attempting to clear the cobwebs.

"Well you better do it now, you might not get another chance", retorted Deaton with a healthy dose of gallows humor. As she lay on her side she pulled her knapsack off and pulled out a radio. The arrival of the underground rebels was needed and she was the one picked to coordinate their arrival. Returning fire was left to the seer and the shield.

Reloaded, Blink began to play a deadly game of whack-a-mole. Crouched beneath the top of the counter, he would pop up and fire a few shots as his body weaved like a boxer. Return to cover, pop up and fire some more. Grimly Kyle slung the shield over his back once more while he got his legs back underneath him. When he popped up he fired without flinching, trusting the durability of his armor and his body.

While Blink covered the west side of the hall, Kyle began taking out those that spilled from the elevators on the east side. More than one shot enemy fell backwards out the shattered window. That would be a disturbing scene. A pedestrian out for an evening stoll just to have a body splat in front of you. Just before they screamed thinking it was a possible suicide another would hit like an over ripened watermelon.

It truly would be raining men.

Ducked down from a particular intense strafing of gunfire he chuckled to himself. Then he was up again to fire. Rounds hit his upper torso, mostly stopped by the titan-steel plates. Although a few slipped between the gaps to bury in his flesh. Now those hurt. Without hesitation he always returned the sentiment.

Dropped down he yanked the empty air reservoir and top magazine to slide another one in. Behind Blink continued to drop the enemy with accurate shots allowed by his seven second prescience. Despite not actually taking fire, the constant use of his ability wore him down. Again Kyle popped above the countertop and took several shots. Satisfaction filled him at how well they were holding up. Then another round hit the gap between chestplate and rerebrace on his bicep. Return fire took out the shooter and he ducked down with a swear.

Bulletproof he was not. While his skin was much tougher than any humans, rounds could still penetrate. However, the dense fibers of his musculature were able to stop rounds. Still hurt like hell and he would need to remove the bullets.

Deaton motioned to get their attention.

"The first floor is clear and they are headed up the elevators. We need to distract these bastards." The radio was dropped and the benelli collected.

"I thought we were distracting them", Blink muttered.

"Actually I was taking a nap", Kyle grinned at Blink's mock horrified expression. Turning his head in either direction Kyle felt a welcoming pop that alleviated most of his headache.

"Shall we?" Hand motioned above and Blink nodded while he turned back to his side of the hall.

The two men returned to their offensive as Deaton raised up just enough to fire a few times and then ducked to slam fresh reloads in.

"Seven seconds until friendlies", Blink shouted over the deafening gunfire.

The shield was swung from Kyle's shoulder where he fit his arm through the straps and gripped the handle. Several deep breaths and then he hurled himself over his side of the counter to openfire. The sudden emergence took the enemy momentarily off guard. He took full advantage of the lull with devastating fire from the Salazar rifle. An inaudible ding heralded the arrival of the underground rebels who were more than willing to throw themselves into the fight.

The arrival of overwhelming reinforcements sent the enemy into retreat up the stairwells. Rebels dove into several of the upper elevators before they could close and return to the upper levels. Quickly the level was cleared and parties of rebels took the elevators to the levels with the prisons and laboratories. Taking the breather, Kyle reloaded the rifle and moved back to where the three played the Alamo. Leaning against a wall near the elevators Blink ate a handful of energy bars. Using his ability as proactive as he did, drained him.

Tossing back the hood he removed the mask and gingerly rubbed the back of his head. A nice sized goose egg met his probing fingers. Thank god for good equipment and hard heads.

A flurry of activity within the alcove of the security desks drew his attention. Then he noticed he didn't see Deaton. Fear clawed into his throat as he hurried over and saw a group of rebels leaned over a body. The boots and legs that were exposed caused his throat to constrict.

Deaton.

ATROCITIES

Wednesday, April 26, 2045
1:01 a.m.

When Blink saw the expression on Kyle's face he quickly returned to the outer edge of the security counter. Kyle's hands gripped the riddled countertop and he bowed his head as emotion threatened to overwhelm him. Not another friend.

Each time he managed to grow close to someone, life intervened. Burying people left its toll on him. Every night the souls of the dead came to him and haunted his sleep. The truth was Kyle was worn thin, exhaustion from saying a final goodbye. He was tired of losing people.

"Get off me and help me up!" The familiar voice prompted Kyle to hop the counter as several of the rebels assisted Deaton to a standing position. Gauze and bandages wrapped her left shoulder, blood already stained them. Her left arm was cradled to her chest and wrapped securely to hold it in place.

When she saw Kyle's grit streaked face she pushed from the rebels and placed her right hand on his cheek.

"I'm good. Some bastard shot me in the back. I don't think I'll be able to keep my date on the fiftieth floor." The pained expression on her face brought a smile to his.

"I think we can manage, You just find Sage's little girl."

"Speaking of Sage …" With care she moved gingerly around the counter as her former caretakers encircled her as bodyguards.

"When we got him plugged into the system he hacked it and locked them out. We now control Heresy. He also found a lot of files that he's dumping on the internet as we speak. Abernathy and all his compatriots are being revealed to the world. We'll find his daughter and get them somewhere safe off the grid. Times ticking so you better go."

Before Kyle could respond she reached up and grabbed a handful of his hair to pull his face down to hers. Lips pressed together hard for moments before she released him.

"That's a promise that you better come back to pay." Head shook with a rueful grin on his face.

"Yes ma'am."

Bending he retrieved the shotgun and looked at Deaton's one arm.

"Keep it. It's got eight in there. I have my trusty nine mil", she patted her sidearm.

A nod and the group followed her to one of the elevators. As the door closed he caught a final glimpse of her. Grime and soot covered her bare skin. Blood stained bandages and a useless arm. But it was her eyes that always did him in. Ferocious and hungry for more.

The doors closed.

"Times tickling", Blink reminded him.

"I know. Time for Abernathy to have some judgement."

The two men entered one of the waiting upper elevators. As the doors closed they looked at one another as music gently piped in from the speakers in the ceiling. The button to the forty ninth floor was pressed. There was no sense of motion despite the elevator's ascent. Another energy bar was pulled from one of the pockets that festooned Blink's pants. Tearing it open with his teeth he quickly consumed it.

The elevator chimed and the doors opened.

Immediately they were assaulted by a cloud of smoke. Coughing, they exited and looked around the hall. Rebels were moving to and from. Some were leading kids and adults in various states of dress to exits. Most staggered with glassy eyes. It was heart wrenching to see but it made herding them easier.

"Which way?" Kyle asked as he covered his mouth and nose with his hand in vain attempt to mitigate the smoke inhalation. Gunfire caused both men to spin, weapons at the ready. The sound echoed down the white washed walls. The lights flickered and the floor trembled. Somewhere beneath them an explosion shook the building.

"That can't be good", Blink remarked.

"No shit Sherlock. No which way?" Suitably embarrassed, Blink tilted his head toward the end of the hall where the smoke seemed to dissipate somewhat. With Blink in the lead, Kyle shouldered the benelli and followed with a head on a swivel. The deeper they went the cleaner the air became until the smell of disinfectant grew strong enough to burn their noses.

As they went Blink checked rooms where the doors were open. The beretta rested in his right hand prepared just in case. At one such door he froze with mouth agape. Catching up, Kyle looked over his shoulder and felt his stomach churn. Stretchers littered the room with dissected bodies strapped down.

Easing past Blink wasn't difficult as the young man stood aghast in shock. Metal trays littered the lines of stretchers. The first one Kyle came to made him nauseous. Some kid, barely a teens, lay on cold steel without a shred of clothing. Horned protrusions covered his skin. What was appalling was his chest was opened up. It looked as though they were implanting some sort of device.

Picking it up he shook his head. No idea what it was. Electrodes ran from the device and inserted into several organs. Finally Blink approached with rage and helplessness fighting for control of his face. Reaching out he fingered the straps on the boy's arm.

"Why did they restrain him? He's dead."

Taking several steps back Kyle surveyed the room and its macabre inhabitants. Quietly he answered.

"Because they weren't dead when they did this. And they were probably conscious."

The two men left the room, quietly closing the door to the mass tomb. As they continued down the hall the men chose not to look at one another. Tears welled in both their eyes. Near the gold gilded elevator Blink choked out a statement that would haunt Kyle for some years.

"I hope they all die."

IX
THE FALL

Wednesday, April 26, 2045
1:10 a.m.

"Moment of truth", Kyle said to Blink at the elevator. Only a single button existed, which the young man pressed. A portion of the wall hissed and retracted to reveal a triplicate security system. Thumbprint identification, iris scanner, and verbal password. The knapsack was pulled free of Blink's back as he delved within.

Two chromed boxes were removed and opened. With a grimace Blink removed a severed thumb and a lone eye. Each was held in opposite hands and raised to their corresponding scanners. After a mere moment both scanners chimed, leaving only the password. Leaned in, Blink spoke clearly.

"Arachne."

A third chime sounded and the hidden compartment closed as the doors opened. With a gesture the seven second seer motioned for Kyle to enter first.

"Age before beauty", Blink grinned as Kyle stepped in. Following closely the young man entered. The doors closed slowly. Inside every surface shone with a golden sheen. The shotgun was adjusted against Kyle's shoulder as Blink unholstered his pistols. Silence accompanied them until the doors began to open with a soft beep.

First to exit, Kyle looked around the empty expanse of darkness. Large marble columns rose to meet the glass ceiling above. The doors closed behind them, their world once more bereft of light. Forked lightning split the sky above which illuminated the morose fiftieth floor. Slowly they crept deeper into the malevolent top floor.

A yellow light softly breathed into life as the men made their way through the forest of massive pillars. The light grew stronger as Kyle eased past another long line of columns. As he passed a final upright marble monument Kyle laid eyes upon Samuel Abernathy.

A marble dais rose at the end of the room. An obsidian throne rested above all. Abernathy leaned back in repose, his skeletal form gaunt. Two braziers burned below the throne and on either side of a stone tomb. A glass sarcophagus rested on the stone work. The dancing flames cut severe lines in Abernathy's face as he rose.

Black trousers and shoes were the only clothes he wore. Painstakingly slow, he descended down the dais one step at a time. A shaved head revealed multiple neural links embedded in the man's skull. Upon his bare torso were familiar symbols. The dots that plagued Kyle for decades.

The two entered the clearing, twelve pillars arranged in a half circle before the throne and tomb. Lightning flashed above as the heavy clouds broke to send a torrential rain against the clear ceiling above. Every step they took brought them closer to the skeletal form of Abernathy. Only the dark eyes moved as he watched Kyle and Blink come closer.

"Finally. I meet the one responsible for my brother's death. A heroic feat. And to climb my cathedral? I see why the gods look upon you with favor."

The shotgun aimed without waver at the bare chest of Abernathy. In a flash Blink grabbed hold of Kyle's shoulder. Worry creased the young man's face as he closed his eyes to see the next seven seconds.. A cackle escaped the monstrous form before the throne.

"You see death, young seer. You fail to understand that your mission was a success only because I allowed it. Every step taken has led you into my web. Do not think to fire upon me Aegis. Or she will pay for your actions."

At his words the glass sarcophagus retracted into the stone it rested upon. A still body laid unmoving upon the tomb.

Mary.

A pristine white gown embraced her in silken fabric. One side of her head was shaved, the glinting metal of a neural interface ran from her temple to the back of her head. A snarl escaped Kyle as he raised the shotgun and took several steps forward.

"What did you do?"

Once more Blink pulled at Kyle in an effort to restrain him.

"I have done what my goddess has bid. Every decision you have made has brought you to this moment. I shall be reborn immortal!" The bone protrusions of Abernathy's arms raised. At his gesture the glass within the ceiling above parted, each pane receding. The storm pelted them with rain. Each drop a needle that froze exposed skin.

"You're mad", muttered Kyle as rain ran down his face and beneath his collar. Lightning pierced the sky and thunder shook the top floor. A dull rumble filled the room as the twelve pillars retreated from their heights to disappear into the floor. When the final meters of each column finished retreating into the floor, statuesque beings stood revealed. The two men turned, keeping their backs together.

"Mad? I am a visionary. Once I was only a man, but then the gods came to me. The age of man has ended, the age of gods returned. Humanity looks upon the mythos of the past as allegories of man. But they existed. The gods. Now the gods have returned."

The dozen statues moved, swords leaving scabbards and pointing at the two men. With their movement came the realization that the twelve were avatars. Somewhere nearby were twelve people in avatar couches, their neural links allowing them to control the robotic figures. The rain matted clothing and hair as the twelve advanced on Kyle and Blink.

The shotgun shifted to the nearest avatar as Kyle grimaced. Beside him, Blink only sighed. Then the dozen avatars charged.

The benelli barked twice into the face of an avatar, the slugs tore through eyes and dropped the machine disabled to the ground. A small pivot and he repeated the action twice more. The fourth avatar lashed out with its sword, cutting deeply into the shotgun with such force the weapon was torn from Kyle's hands.

With a leap forward Kyle slammed into the avatar and wrestled to control the sword. The strength of the machine proved too great as the sword slowly inched toward Kyle's neck. The blade lightly pressed against his throat, the sharpened edge drawing a line of red that quickly was washed away by the rain. Inexorably he was forced to his knees as the sword relentlessly strived to slice through his throat.

Thunder barked and the avatar fell back, sparks erupted from its eyes. Sputtering Kyle climbed to his feet realizing the thunder was actually Blink firing his pistols. The kid saved his life. Again. Two more avatars charged Kyle as Blink danced between the swords of his own half dozen foes. With a shrug Kyle slipped the shield from his back and onto his left arm, his right pulled the cutlass free.

As Blink danced gracefully with his opponents Kyle clashed with shield and sword against his two. The flames rose higher within their braziers on either side of the tomb while Abernathy moved to stand directly over the unmoving body of Mary.

"Millennia ago the gods were entertained as the most fit of the ancient world competed with one another. A tournament for Zeus. The victors were the strongest, fastest, smartest. By becoming victorious, these mere mortals were offered the chance to be the vessel of a god."

The monologue echoed as Blink weaved about, avoiding the deadly attacks of the avatars. Well placed shots rang out and destroyed half his opponents. Sword clashed on shield as Kyle narrowly ducked a sword that nearly removed his head. The cutlass flicked out and removed the offending arm with a following strike that beheaded the avatar.

"Humanity grew prideful. And the time of the gods ended. Now … now the time of the gods beckons once again. Immortality whispers its promise. And I have answered. I will become the first of the modern gods. Already I have become omnipotent."

The maniacal laugh echoed with the roaring thunder. Feet splashed through water as Kyle rammed the final foe. The cutlass was ripped from his hand at a particularly powerful riposte. The shield raised to crash into the avatar's face, sight momentarily blocked. Hand palmed the 1911 as the shield dropped. Two squeezes of the trigger launched the bullets into the avatar's face. A turn to assist Blink wasn't needed as the younger man finished off his own foes.

Sudden applause from frail hands drew the two men forward.

"Good. Good. You have proven your worth. Now all that remains is your surrender." A red slash of lips amidst pale face met the steeled determination set on Kyle's face. Again Blink grabbed Kyle's arm.

"We can't. This floor is rigged with explosives. If we attack we die. All of us."

The malnourished form of Abernathy turned and climbed the steps to his throne. A sigh escaped as he lowered into the seat.

"Your seer speaks true. Now you see that your actions are not your own. You acted according to my plan. And into my web have you become ensnared."

As he spoke, one hand probed his bare chest. Sharpened nail drug across flesh, red lines appearing on his torso as he carved into his own body. When the wizened hand dropped to Abernathy's lap, a design was seen. A spiderweb bled in ghastly revelation.

"Drop your pitiful weapons and surrender."

A sideways glance between Kyle and Blink and the young man shook his head. Eyes returned up to meet the empty eyes above as Kyle stood a single step forward.

"If you kill us, you die too. Are you willing to lose it all?"

The raspy laugh shook frail shoulders as he leaned forward upon his throne.

"I am immortal. The first of the new gods. My mind lingers in all that wear my neural link. They are my children. All are connected in my web." Yellowed teeth flashed in lightning.

"Lord Zeus approves. Now drop your weapons." Hands opened to spill shield and pistols from the two men. Windows behind the throne rescinded into the floor and powerful gusts of wind buffeted the room. As they watched, Mary sat up.

The silken dress clung to dark skin as legs swung over the tomb. The eyes looking back were malicious. The eyes of a monster. The eyes of Abernathy.

She slipped from the stone and walked toward the open window even as her body swayed from the storm.

"No!" Kyle stumbled forward onto his knees with outstretched hands. Nightmares became reality. Another person he cared for walked toward an impending demise. And there was no amount of fighting that could be done to stop it. Sometimes all that could be done is surrender. The death of Henry put Sage in the crosshairs. His friend already lost a wife. There would be nothing left if Mary died.

"Please! Tell me what you want but just … let Mary go. Let Blink and Mary go and I'll give you whatever you want." Tears mixed with the rain that cascaded down his face. The only reason Mary and Sage were involved was because he killed Henry Abernathy. Naomi was dead and that blood was on his hands. If there was a chance to save Mary, Kyle would take it.

A glance at Blink's drawn face cemented his decision. There was no hope reflected in the young seer's eyes.

"Good. Now you see the fruitlessness of resistance. You will be my first to ascend."

From either side of the throne, avatars emerged from recesses within the dais. The fire danced within the braziers where they framed the tomb. It was then that Kyle realized the stone wasn't a tomb.

It was an altar.

The avatars moved to Kyle and reached down, lifting him to his feet. Behind, Blink slipped slowly to where Mary was even while Kyle was pressed onto the altar. One of their hands turned Kyle's face where his eyes looked back the way he had come. The elevator sat empty. A whirring sound heralded the lowering neural interface. Hand flashed up to halt the device.

"Let them go first. When I see them go then I'm all yours."

The interface paused and the guttural voice washed over Kyle. "They may go."

After a few moments Blink trotted into view with Mary in his arms. Only once he reached the elevator did he turn and look back at Kyle. As the doors closed, Kyle gave the young man a sad smile. And then they were gone.

Resigned to the inevitable sacrifice, he closed his eyes as the neural link lowered.

"You will become my Aegis. My shield. My child, fear not, for I am with you."

Pain lanced into his temple as the drill pierced. Teeth clenched against the invasion. Long seconds counted in his head as excruciating agony filled his being. Lightning flared across the sky and illuminated the rotting face of Abernathy hovering just above his face.

Dark eyes pierced from the sagging depths of hollowed eye sockets. Long fingers caressed across Kyle's face. Putrid breath escaped open mouth as Abernathy leaned in to reveal a secret.

"The gods wished you to be their rebirth. Now I take you for myself."

A blinding light roved over them as the heaven's were split by a new power. The thump of a heartbeat shook the room. Abernathy rose and stared into the night sky, his body ringed in pure light. A hiss escaped his lips.

Grinding of the drill against his skull sent Kyle's body thrashing as the avatars continued their installation of the device. But as he screamed, two glowing ovals of blue bounced at Abernathy's feet. A shockwave of invisible force lanced out causing the two avatars to collapse. Even Abernathy fell, hands cradled to his head.

With a grunt Kyle rolled and fell from the altar to splash in the water on the floor. A glance up at the heavenly host above blinded him by the light. Blood trailed from his temple as he gripped the sides of the altar and pushed upright. The blinding light moved to silhouette Abernathy from above.

After a moment Kyle knew what it was. One of the jets of the Protectorate. The skeletal form clawed over to his throne even as Kyle gave chase. A stumble almost saw him landing on the ground but he managed to stay upright. That was more than could be said for Abernathy who floundered with unintelligible shrieks.

From above descended a pair of Warriors on a rappel line. Two more landed behind them even as Kyle's hands found Abernathy and hauled him up to a standing position. The front Warrior pulled off his mask to reveal the features of Excalibur. Clay Issacs. Bionic arm extended as he shouted over the storm.

"We have it from here Kyle! Those EMP flash grenades should have scrambled his neural net. We have him, so let him go!"

Several more lights flashed into the room as news stations sent their reporters to cover the story. Hands gripped Abernathy and dragged him backwards until they stood framed by the open window of the fiftieth floor. Where minutes earlier Mary once perched. Yellowed teeth grinned as Abernathy shouted into Kyle's face.

"They can't stop a god! In two minutes my interface resets and I will not be contained! You will be the sacrifice!"

Kyle looked between the monster he held and the Warriors where Clay slowly closed the distance. Shaking his head he shouted at his old friend.

"Some dogs you have to put down."

Simple words surrendered to simple action. Releasing Abernathy, Kyle shook his head before he lanced out with his leg to kick the monster out the window. The spotlights followed the falling body all the way to where it collided with the pavement below. Arms wrapped around Kyle and yanked him from the window. As the restraints tightened on his arms and legs Kyle just laughed into the water on the floor.

And laughed.

And laughed.

PART EIGHT: BROKEN

SHATTERED IN DESPERATION

Sunday, April 25, 2055
12:03 p.m.

"Let the monsters govern themselves."

For a long time Kyle believed he was lost. The mental break as the drill burrowed into his temple led to him throwing Abernathy from the fiftieth floor. With his lawyer arguing that Kyle was not in his right mind, the death penalty was removed. Under the Uniform Code of Military Justice, Kyle could have received the sentence of death. However, the extenuating circumstances and his defense were enough to remove the ultimate punishment of execution. Afterall, who would convict a former superhero that acted immediately after brain surgery?

Some nights he woke laughing from the memories of tossing Abernathy to his death. Other nights Kyle muffled the screaming cries into a pillow as he faced the monster he had become. It was on those nights he admitted Lydia was right.

"Don't face him Kyle. You don't escape if you do. Don't hunt him for vengeance."

And he didn't escape. Some days he feared he would be trapped in the penthouse forever laughing as Abernathy hit the pavement fifty floors below. Other days he knew he would never escape. The shadows in the night reached out to him with gnarled hands outstretched. Eerily the face in the darkness was his own.

The face reflected from the stainless steel mirror in his cell was one he no longer recognized. The soft voice of Sandy tried to console him, yet he blocked her out. Nothing could stop his self flagellation. The specters of the dead, snuffed by his hand, clawed relentlessly at his soul. Only the visage of those he saved kept him from complete madness.

Even then, the faces of those he failed waited their turn to bring accusations to Kyle. If Kyle was able to be honest with himself it wasn't the lives taken by his hand that broke him. The knowledge that his choices and decisions cost the lives of innocents chipped at his resolve. Hindsight offered many paths he could have taken to spare lost lives. The knowledge haunted him that there were other ways.

Kyle fell victim to his own reputation. Aegis could shrug off attack and push through any adversity. And he did. But those at his side were not as lucky. Family and friends paid for his own hubris. Selfish pride ignored the cost those around him were charged with. They died while he lived.

Damnation was the inheritance extorted upon Kyle's circle of allies while he continued onward. At night he tossed and turned as visions of spiders crawled over him to sink their fangs deep into his flesh. Sandra, Naomi, Tank, Frank, Gabriella, Champion, and countless others watched from the shadows. Earnest expressions painted their faces as Kyle suffered, screamed, and cried. He was a blight on those he cared for.

When mornings came the nightmares receded. Yet at the corners of his vision Kyle swore the damned followed his every move from shadows. With each day he surrendered to the guilt and accepted the fate he earned. Of all the inmates in the prison it was Kyle who knew he deserved punishment.

From the very first night in the prison, he knew he belonged there with the other monsters. Afterall, he was the worst of them all.

Taurus Island sat in decimated ruin ever since the terrorist attack in 2030. The very same event that was the catalyst for Aegis turning his back on the Protectorate. A decade later saw the island turned over to the federal government. By that time it grew apparent that a new facility was needed to hold the criminal super population.

And so demolition wiped the island clean and a new prison was created. This one specific to those with abilities.

It was there Kyle Ross was sentenced.

An agreement was accepted between Kyle and the Protectorate. A thirteen year sentence without possibility for early parole. Once completed he would be remanded to Anastasia Island to serve no less than ten years with the Protectorate. Specifically, the Warriors. Thanks, in no small part, to the intercession of Clay Issacs, codenamed Excalibur, Kyle would once again wear the symbol of the Spire as a Warrior.

If he survived thirteen years with criminals he helped put away.

The prison was run in a unique way under the warden named Kohn Keyes. A different approach was used for supervising miscreants, delinquents, and the criminal. Plagued by a high mortality rate among the guards, Warden Keyes chose to pull the guards back to a supervisory role outside of the fences and gates. Towers were erected that allowed a certain amount of overwatch. The use of lethal force became approved.

All cells were located on the first floor as the second floors were blocked off. Prison guards made the rounds on the second stories, their rifles easily able to fire from above. Fights were frowned upon but not broken up. Instead the guards made sure to keep the relative peace. Although, orders to stand down and lie on the ground were never repeated more than once.

Under these circumstances Kyle Ross was released into the general population.

The stone cell was shared by a man known as weasel. In the prison your birth name didn't matter. Only your super name. The first night in his cell, Kyle was forced to live up to his name. Aegis. Only this time it was he who needed the protection.

Three men slipped through the open cell door intent on ending Kyle's life. The struggle was brief as Kyle dispatched each through brute strength.

When morning came with roll call there were three less inmates in the prison. Their bodies lay stacked in the center courtyard.

The following night was a replay.

On the third night he lay in his bed in false countenance of slumber. Shadows stretched across the courtyard and into his cell as the moon set. Morning rapidly approached. As Kyle decided he would be unmolested and finally sleep, a shadow detached from the static darkness. The figure crept forward with nary a sound. Body lay in repose as Kyle prepared to leap into action. Barest glint of light off the shiv was all the warning Kyle got.

Hands intercepted the arm that thrust out as the man pounced to the bed. With a roll Kyle flopped both himself and his attacker from the bunk and made sure all his wait landed on the arm beneath his side. Through their clothing the sensation of shattered bone reverberated in Kyle's side. The makeshift dagger was snatched from his opponent's nerveless hand. Left hand clapped over his enemy's mouth while Kyle drove the dagger deep into flesh. With a twist the blade snapped off inside the fiend.

The strike was true enough because the man died in less than a minute. Much like the previous night, Kyle drug the body from his cell by the legs to deposit in the center of the courtyard. A strobe of light flashed across his attacker's face for a brief moment. Smooth brown hair and the hint of peach fuzz adorned a face not yet devoid of youth's chubby cheeks.

It was just a kid. And now he was a dead kid. Kyle staggered back as unseeing eyes looked through him in surprise. Mouth hung open as it did in the cell. But no words escaped, much like in the cell during their skirmish when Kyle silenced the kid. And now he would forever remain silent, life snuffed out at the hands of Kyle.

Numbly he found his way back to the cell and sank onto the bed. Hands stained red with the blood of a kid grew tacky as they dried. When morning arrived Kyle shuffled out with empty eyes and unwashed hands. He was a monster among monsters. This was where he belonged.

Every night for two weeks Kyle was attacked in his cell. And every morning there were several more bodies found in the courtyard of the first floor. After that Kyle was left unmolested, but not accepted by the other prisoners. Once a law dog, always a law dog. Weasel slipped out one night to bunk in one of the empty cells. That worked out just fine for Kyle.

In the silence of the nights he blocked the voice of his sister from his mind and shut her out. Eventually Sandy stopped trying.

News played from a projector during the evenings. Each day another scene of unrest and turmoil. Crime skyrocketed to new heights as law enforcement fought to maintain peace. New attacks unfolded and the nation changed as fear lived freely.

Evil was winning.

Days blurred into one another as Kyle willed himself to die.

Until the day Abe Francis arrived.

REFORGED

Sunday, April 25, 2055
12:12 p.m.

There was no recreational yard or mess hall. The courtyard of each wing operated as both. Once you entered a wing you only got out if released or dead. Kyle was trying for the latter. A klaxon reverberated in their wing. Three times the klaxon trumpeted. The prisoners knew from past experience that sixty seconds was all the warden allocated for them to return to their cells. Before the cells closed and the guards above began to fire.

Slowly Kyle meandered to his cell and went to sit on his bed. A concrete slab with a mattress was all the comforts they could claim. Collapsed on the bed he rolled to the wall and closed his eyes. It was Sunday which meant new recruits arrived. There was no desire to witness the jockeying for position that was to come.

Not for the first time was he reminded that this prison felt more like a gladiatorial school in ancient Rome.

The sound of hydraulics whined as the walkway lowered to catcalls and shouts that echoed in the wing. A hush fell on the prison wing. Unnatural silence filled the atmosphere. Eyes opened as a shadow laid across his form. Turning, Kyle was unprepared as a massive hand grabbed his mane of hair and dragged him from the cell. A toss sent him to the concrete floor with a crash.

With a shove Kyle pushed to his feet and turned to lay eyes upon the man who assaulted him. A fist connected with his face which caused him to stumble back. A grip on the chest length beard hauled him up short. Barely did he have enough time to register a massive form before another punch knocked him flat on his back.

"I thought you were something special."

The bearded face remained unfocused even as the knuckles dropped once more.

When Kyle regained consciousness he realized he missed dinner. Prisoners were already returned to their cells. Forcing himself up he staggered to his cell to collapse on his bunk. Since his arrival in prison time caught up with him. Body aged and lines engraved on his face. Even his abilities began to wane. Even superheroes got old. For once he slept fitfully.

The next morning he stumbled to the water basin and washed the matted blood from his face and hair. The scab over his eyebrow fell into the sink and swirled with the pink tinged water. Grabbing the towel from his bed Kyle dried his face and exited the cell. Breakfast was in full swing. Limping, he went to the conveyor belt that circulated between the first and second floor.

With his breakfast tray in tow he went to an empty table and sat. Cold steel bench leached his warmth even as he picked at the food. When Sandy and he were kids they knew when it was going to be a bad night. Their mother started drinking early. And then, like storm clouds their father swept in a force of nature. They could always feel the change.

Quietly he chewed the unevenly toasted piece of bread. He felt the storm approach. The man was as wide as a wall, just as thick. Black beard didn't hide the brick jaw beneath. A horse shoe of dark hair circled his head though the light glared off the bare patch on top.

The mountain sat across from Kyle and stared. Massive forearms rested on the tabletop as Kyle chewed while keeping his eyes downward. A sweeping motion sent Kyle's tray from in front of him to clatter across the floor. There was no flinch as Kyle continued chewing the toast.

"You've got sand, I'll give you that", Abe said as he moved from the table. That wasn't the end and when they grabbed Kyle from behind he didn't fight back. Fists and feet rained across his body until only a fog was left in his mind. A grip in his hair jerked his face up so he could see Abe's face. Distantly in the back of his mind he recognized the metal sheen of the mountain's eyes. Cybernetics.

"With this long hair and crazy beard you look like an old lion. You aren't a lion, not anymore. Shave him." Hair pulled from follicles as the men roughly shaved him before dumping him on the floor. Guard allowed the beatdown while money exchanged hands with bets on the outcome. An hour later he limped to his cell and collapsed on his bed.

Months of abuse rained down upon him. Eyes sunk into their sockets and the wrinkled skin and crags upon his face testified that Kyle Ross was no longer a young man. Strength faded and speed disappeared. Every day he healed from new atrocities.

And still he begged for death.

The news reports of the real world revealed a battle between authorities and a shadow organization called the Red Spider, named after a distant constellation. It wasn't long before their members made their way to Taurus Island. By this time Abe was the king of their wing and welcomed the new prisoners under his rule. A prominent tattoo was inked on Abe's chest that declared he was now a member.

And still Kyle refused to fight. Rather he accepted the punishment doled out as penance for his sins. When Kyle felt the urge to fight back, the faces of his dead watched him with empty eyes that conveyed their accusations. And so he accepted the punishment. Death hovered near but refused to welcome him in her loving embrace. At times Death's caress trailed across his skin in freezing shiver. Yet she failed to beckon him from the state of perpetual hell that became his existence. Though Kyle longed for death he lacked the courage to end his own life. With every week the face in the steel mirror grew more haggard.

Another Sunday came, the klaxon tolled the alarm of new prisoners. Normally he stayed in bed until it was meal time, only to venture out for a few bites and his beating. However, for unknown reasons he limped to the bars of his cell and looked out. The walkway lowered from above and six convicts eased down. Several were called to empty bunks while one young man slowly circled the courtyard, eyes seeking someone particular.

Their eyes met and a shock of recognition travelled through Kyle. Though he was sure he never met the man before, it was the eyes he knew. Golden eyes with the caged spirit of a predator. Shouts rang out as the young man walked to Kyle's cell and entered. The kid, for he wasn't even twenty, hopped onto the top bunk and looked down with curiosity upon the weathered old man he now shared a cell with.

"Listen kid. You need to go find another bunk. Here with me you are a target. I can't, I won't, protect you." Bone deep weariness claimed Kyle and he slipped onto his bunk. The springs in the mattress above depressed as the kid lightly hopped down and stood. Kyle was determined not to respond. Unaffected by Kyle's lack of communication he began to talk.

"The world is going to hell out there. I remember when I was a child there were those willing to stand up against evil. Ready to fight to protect the people. I remember stories of a man, larger than life, who did what he needed to do to protect the world. His name was Aegis." The kid paused expecting a response. The only one he got was a huff as Kyle rolled over to face the wall.

"Aegis fought. And he fought. He never gave up. Even when everything was stacked against him, he still fought. Can you imagine the like? He was a hero. He still is." The mattress dipped behind Kyle as the kid sat next to him.

"My mother told me tales of him. A ferocious fighter not afraid of anything. He fought with his heart. That is why she loved him. And why she loves him still." Slowly Kyle rolled over to look at the young man. Dark skin and shaved head, the kid had the barest stubble of a goatee. Smaller than the average man, it was the eyes that spoke of danger. An untamable, wild quality he shared with his mother.

"Tye?" The youth grinned a set of pearly whites.

"In the flesh." Sitting up, Kyle looked into his face even as the young man wrapped his arms around the frail old man.

"How … why are you here", Kyle questioned as he eased from the embrace and searched the young man's eyes.

"I got nicked ripping off one of the Spider's politicians. Two years to think about my contributions to society", the kid grinned before losing the smile. Fingers lightly touched Kyle's face.

"What have they done to you?" Hand enveloped the tender probing fingers as Kyle shook his head.

"Nothing I didn't deserve. How's your mom? Your brother?" Tye jerked slightly. Perhaps it was in remembrance that it would be a long two years before he would lay eyes upon them again. Reality was a heavy thing in prison.

The dinner bell rang and Kyle pulled himself to his feet. As he looked out the bars of his cell he watched the other inmates stream to the conveyor belt to select their food trays. Concern etched the wrinkled valleys of Kyle's face deeper.

"When we go out there don't intervene if I'm approached. Just let what happens, happen." Kyle limped into line with Tye behind him. They both grabbed their trays and moved to an empty table. Old habits kicked in as Kyle sat with his back to an empty cell. Unenthusiastically Tye flipped the meat patty on his plate and grumbled.

"What the hell is this?" A smirk creased Kyle's ragged face.

"Don't ask. You don't want to know." With a shudder Tye began to shovel the food in as he chewed extensively. As expected, Abe waddled to their table, the muscles of his chest strained against the grey jumpsuits they all wore. A hand reached down and picked up Kyle's meat patty to shove into the maw of Abe's mouth. As he chewed he looked down at Tye with interested eyes.

"You going to introduce me to your new friend, Aegis?" Without looking up Kyle answered as softly as he could.

"Just a kid looking to do his time until he's released. Like all of us." A look of surprised mockery filled Abe's face.

"Is that so? I guess we are going to have a lot to talk about aren't we kid? Starting with why I shouldn't rip your arms off. I know who your momma is, boy. When I get out I owe her a visit. But until then I'll keep myself busy with you."

Massive hands swatted both trays to the floor and Tye stood with fists up at the ready. A loud roaring rumble of laughter escaped Abe's massive chest.

"A fighter? Now isn't this a treat."

The mountain turned to face Tye but a hand landed on his bicep. Head turned in surprise that the broken shield was able to muster enough gumption to touch him, let alone rise and stand opposite him.

"I can't let you hurt him." A swell of laughter rolled through the crowd who formed up at the possibility of a fight. Fingers jabbed down into Kyle's chest as Abe shoved.

"For that I'm going to make sure you are conscious when I break his arms and legs." A ham shaped fist launched out and smashed Kyle in the face. The shield crumpled even as the other prisoners laughed. Looking back at Tye with arms still up in a fighter's stance, Abe took a step forward.

"That all you got? My dead grandma hits harder." Surprise filled Abe's face as he turned back to see Kyle pull himself upright. Blood flowed from his nose as he smiled at Abe. Rage overcame his countenance and Abe slammed a meaty fist into Kyle's midsection before he chopped down behind the older man's ear to drop Kyle to the floor. Not done, Abe put the boots to Kyle as he lay writhing upon the ground.

"Now that old Aegis is finished, where were we little one?" The massive man moved around the table near Tye who retreated a few steps. The crowd turned their attention behind Abe. A scowl filled the mountain's face as he snarled at the other inmates.

"What are you looking a-", Abe screamed.

Kyle pulled himself to the bench as Abe advanced on Tye. The spark inside that went out a decade ago, the spark he smothered, ignited as Abe advanced on Deaton's son. Memories filtered through his mind of picnicking and watching the twins collect wild flowers. The twins slept in their bed as he stood in the doorway while Deat gently covered them up.

The same kid that now retreated before the mountain.

Hands pulled Kyle to his feet and he jumped forward to dive on Abe's back. One arm snaked around the thickly muscled neck while his other hand thrust into Abe's face. Fingers clawed down the forehead and burrowed into mechanical eyes.

And Abe screamed.

The mountain spun, casting Kyle to the ground in a heap, as unseeing eyes searched for the broken shield. Hands gripped the table and flipped it in rage as Abe screamed for Aegis. Slowly Kyle stood and circled the blind man with arms windmilling violently. Behind the mountain Kyle kicked out to connect with the back of Abe's knee. The big man dropped to his hands as his shouts of anger turned to pleas for help mixed with enough cursing to peel the paint off a pulpit.

"You wanted me, asshole", Kyle spoke as he leaned down close to Abe. Straightening, Kyle looked to the crowd, who chose not to interfere, before turning to the fallen mountain. Ruthlessly he lashed out with boot to connect against Abe's temple which sent him over to his side.

Kyle drove the toe of his boots into the mountain. Over and over. The warning klaxon blared the sixty second countdown for the prisoners to retreat to their cells. Unswayed by the sound Kyle knelt on Abe's chest and delivered devastating blows upon the ruined face below. Bony knuckles split raining blood with every determined strike.

Tye grabbed Kyle from behind and dragged him off and to their cell just as the bar doors slammed shut. The walkway descended from above as the medical team rolled Abe onto a stretcher to take to the clinic. Prisoners shouted and struck the bars, raising a tumultuous noise at being locked down until the following day. Threats were shouted to Aegis, promises of payback.

"I'm gonna skin ya alive" echoed with "nobody crosses the spiders" and Kyle's personal favorite "I'll take pleasure in guttin' you boy."

Seated on the bottom bunk Tye watched Kyle quietly. At the wash basin the water ran over bruised and swollen knuckles. The split skin already began to knit as he splashed water on his face. A look at the reflection in the mirror revealed an older man ravaged by forty-seven years of hard living.

Before the eyes looking back were flat, empty, and devoid of life. Now, there was a spark of flame. Purpose. Reason.

"Tomorrow is going to suck. You know that right? All his friends and his gang are going to want retribution", Tye whispered worriedly. The water was turned off and a towel mopped Kyle's face dry as he turned to face the twin.

"For ten years they wanted a fight from me. They wanted to face Aegis, Shield of the gods. Today I came back. Tomorrow they will realize the error of their ways."

The next day when the cell blocks opened it was Aegis first to the breakfast conveyor. Each tray was taken by Kyle and he held it out for the inmates to take. The first several took their food trays without incident. And then one of the Red Spider gang spat in Kyle's face as he attempted to hand him his food.

With a grin Kyle slammed the tray into the prisoners face and was tackled by several. Slammed against the conveyor sent all the other food trays crashing to the ground and enraged the entire wing. Mass riot ensued as all became embroiled in a heated fight.

Only the warning sound of the klaxon returned a semblance of control as inmates retreated to their cells before the bars slammed closed.

Half a dozen more were removed to the clinic while the inmates remained in lockdown the rest of the day. Raging threats were tossed about the entire day and through the night. Seated on the lower bunk, Kyle pulled several meat patties from the pocket of his jumper and handed half to Tye. The inmates rattled the metal bars of their cages and shouted obscenities and threats. One prisoner went on a poetic tirade describing the breeding decisions of Kyle's grandmother.

Late that night Tye spoke from his bunk.

"They aren't going to let what you did today go unpunished. Messing with their food is just going to make them want to kill us even more." After several silent moments Tye leaned from the top bunk to look at Kyle below.

"They're going to make us pay." Deep even breaths was the only response Kyle gave. A few more moments and Tye returned to stretching out on his bunk in quiet contemplation. Below, Kyle finally spoke.

"Our cell opens first which lets us arrive at the food conveyor first. Every day they want blood I'll give it to them. But it will cost them their food for the day. When you're locked up like an animal there are very few things that we can be deprived of. Food is one. Right now hunger is gnawing at their insides. A few more days of this that will become fear gnawing on their guts." Quietly he rose and moved to the wash basin. The reflection looking back appeared healthier. Natural skin color returned. Deep wrinkles smoothed out. Gauntness filled in. A smile returned.

"Soon they will be afraid. Soon they will be filled with fear. They will learn that I have the power to destroy a thing. He who can destroy a thing, controls the thing."

The next day Kyle once more handed out the food trays. They nearly made it a quarter of the way before the fight began anew.

That night the threats weren't only aimed at Aegis. The other prisoners were starving and began to blame the Red Spider gang.

The following day almost half the wing was served before breakfast was interrupted by another riot. This time the inmates turned on the attackers themselves.

Afterwards, breakfast was a quiet affair. There were still fights and attacks, but they were smaller incidents. And Kyle and Tye found a modicum of peace. Briefly.

Until the day Abe Francis returned.

THE COMING CLASH

Sunday, May 30, 2055
12:45 p.m.

A little more than a month passed since Tye arrived. A month since Aegis awakened. At his table Kyle ate quietly as Tye stood nearby speaking to a few inmates. Laughter rang out in response to a bawdy joke. Eyes glanced furtively in his direction making sure the Aegis was fine with the interactions with his young ward.

Other areas of the courtyard rang out with activity. Some inmates worked out and others played a game of wall ball. A few returned to their cells to read while others watched the Sunday news broadcast. It was an interview that drew Kyle's attention.

The screen was a bare wall with a sheet tied between cell bars. The projection from the second floor danced in wavering motion due to the circulating air in the wing. The Protectorate clashed with another Red Spider group that laid waste to parts of Jacksonville. The battle destroyed two major bridges in the waterway of the Trout River. Both the Main Street Bridge and the Trout River Bridge were destroyed as the confrontation spilled into the Saint Johns River.

Clips of the fight played on a screen behind the news anchors who spoke about rising tensions between supers, biomechanical upgraded humans, and regular humans. Discussion about the agendas of the Red Spider group that was quickly gaining traction seemed to be the most prevalent.

"Let the flatliners and upgrades kill themselves", was the common sentiment shouted at the screen. A close up on the esteemed leader of the Warriors revealed a haggard and worn Excalibur. Fate proved to be unkind to Clay. Rising, Kyle returned his emptied tray to the conveyor as the klaxon sounded.

With practiced motion the prisoners returned to their cells. The doors closed before the walkway lowered to welcome new inmates. And the return of an old one. Seated on his bunk, one leg stretched out, Kyle opened a book to continue reading. At their cell door Tye scanned the infusion of new inmates that arrived. A warning tone inflected his words.

"Kyle … Abe's back."

Unimpressed Kyle continued to read. A page turned without pause. The young man glanced behind him before continuing to speak.

"Looks like he's got new eyes. And new ink. And … he's staring at us."

Still uninterested, Kyle didn't even glance up with his retort.

"Figured he'd obtain new replacements. And it's prison, new ink goes with the territory."

Backing away from their cell door, Tye pointed out the bars.

"Looks like he got a promotion while he was gone. He's wearing the lieutenant tat now", gripping the edge of his bunk Tye climbed up to lay on his bed. With a sigh, Kyle closed his book while he rose from the bunk and moved to the cell door. Unmistakable by his girth, the mountain glowered across the courtyard.

"Yep. That's definitely old ugly. I don't see a new tat." Even as he spoke the massive man turned to face in Kyle's direction. The top of the grey jumpsuit was unzipped, the arms tied around his waist which exposed his upper body. Etched in black ink was a symbol that was all too familiar with Kyle.

Hours later Kyle sat on his bunk trying to understand what it all meant, what the symbol represented, and how its importance still reverberated after Samuel Abernathy's death. Tye was able to fill in some of the gaps. The Red Spiders used the symbol which brought about its resurgence. There was even thought that the 'Web' organization was merely a precursor to the Red Spiders.

If that was true it meant that there was a chance that Abernathy wasn't the originator, but a follower.

The two men remained distant from one another, though the glares bridged any distance. Conflict never came to fruition as the evening ended and the inmates returned to their cells for the night. Posted to the cell door, Tye kept an eye and ear out as Kyle mended broken pathways and reconnected with old friends.

IV
MISTS OF THE VEIL

The grey stretched out before him, indistinct as a foggy morning at sea. There was no source of light in the mists, only a storm cloud covered sky. Indistinguishable shapes drifted on a windless breeze. An empty desolation that filled the unseen landscape in afflicted smoke without the promise of fire.

A realm bereft of light and life.

Hands clenched as he looked down. Unlike the last time when he sojourned in the mists of the veil, Kyle was a physical presence. Instead of the prison jumpsuit, he wore the armored uniform of the Spire. Even his shield lay across his back. While his steps still sank into the spongy ground there was a tangible feeling to his form.

Slowly he turned to look in every direction. There was no difference that he could ascertain. Every facet was cloaked in an impenetrable haze. With a shrug he started walking. Minutes or hours stretched with no way to discern the passing of time. Only tendrils of mist that coiled and writhed in his journey.

Several times he called out. The fog stole his echo leaving him deafened at the silence. Unperturbed he continued forward. Always forward. More than once a shadow grew in the mists only to dissipate before becoming corporeal. A haunting emptiness that went on for eternity. The atmosphere sought to drain him of determination.

He would not be broken.

Weariness tried to wrap him in embrace. Surely he could pause and rest. Perhaps sleep. A brief respite. Lids grew heavy as the mist thickened. Visibility shortened where he couldn't see one foot before another. A weight gently pressed his shoulders, the thick blanket of fog upon which he tread beckoned him.

"Fight her Kyle! Resist! Find Sandy, Sage, and Clay! Don't let-"

The voice wisped away as Kyle's eyes slowly closed. What was Blink doing there anyway? The fog in his mind tried to clear as his hands pressed against a cocoon of mist. Fingers clawed at cohesive tentacles restricting his limbs. Mouth opened to shout and slimy strands invaded his mouth to seek his throat.

Choking, Kyle bit down to sever the strands even as his hand searched valiantly at his waist. Just as real darkness dimmed his vision his fingers found the handle of the cutlass. With defiant roar he unsheathed the blade and sliced free of his cocoon to fall upon his hands and knees. Coils spewed from his mouth as he angrily lurched to his feet.

Several swipes of the cutlass freed him up the web that clung to his body. The mists thickened even as Kyle wandered about searching for the source of Blink's voice.

"Hey kid! Blink! You seven second seer! Where are you?" Minutes of the search stretched, blending and bending with time until he wasn't sure how long he stumbled about. The cutlass slid home in its sheath as he wandered about. Eyes searched about as he tried to decipher where he came from. And where to go.

"Sandy, it would be real nice for a little help right about now." The statement was scattered by the nonexistent wind that tossed his plea into nothingness. Nonetheless he persevered forward into the grey. Hunger gnawed at his gut and thirst parched his lips. Swallowing harshly he forced himself to remember that the physical aspects of his body possessed no power here.

Only the mind.

Eventually the landscape began to change. The terrain changed as mounds appeared in the ground and wispy trees made entirely from thickened fog condensed into solids. Above the branches of the formless trees entwined in an impenetrable canopy. Even the grey light dimmed in the forest of mist.

Unfazed, he continued. Though his hand crept to the pommel of the cutlass unconsciously. Deeper he journeyed until all he knew was the endless trees and the tendrils of moss that swayed low from unformed branches.

Motion drew his eyes. It wasn't the ethereal wind or the swaying trees. Something moved. Consciously. He felt the nearness of conscious thought. Not a creature or inanimate object given life by randomness. Not something.

Someone.

The blade slid free soundlessly. Careful steps brought him forward as he turned his head left and right. Always keeping his eyes unfocused on a single point. The motion of the ghostly forest moved with a rhythm he sought to match. It was the unnatural that he searched for. A mere flicker of movement that did not belong in the apparition filled density he now lived and breathed.

There.

The corner of his eye caught a flicker that was not of the place. With willpower he forced himself to remain calm, to not react.

There.

Again movement. This time closer. It approached from his left. Unconsciously his left hand clenched as he mentally berated himself for not sliding the shield onto his arm. Too late now. A few more slow steps forward and pause.

There.

So close he could almost taste it. A silhouette of a figure, grey in composition, but not the same hue. Foreign to the forest he now hunted in. The barest hint of a human outline could be seen. But it wasn't time to strike. Almost. Muscles quivered with restrained power. Skin vibrated with lack of action. One more step, just one more step.

There.

The being was now on his left and finally close enough. His left forearm struck out at the things chest while he drew his left leg across where the backs of the figure's legs should be. If it was human. Arm and leg connected with substance and the figure crashed down on its back as Kyle grasped it by the neck and followed downward onto his knees. His right arm reared back and the tip of the cutlass was prepared for the lethal strike down into its chest.

"Kyle stop!"

The mist withdrew from the figure to reveal it was Sandy he pinned to the ground with hand around her throat. Quickly he released her throat and dropped his sword to pull her into his embrace. Mouth opened to speak. Before the first word escaped she clamped her hands over his lips and shook her head no.

The danger fraught in her eyes caused Kyle to retrieve his dropped cutlass and glance around warily. There was nothing perceptibly wrong, just a prevalent sense of danger. The two stood slowly. Eyes wouldn't stop returning back to his sister. Unable to contain himself any longer he reached out and pulled her into a hug.

Sandy was solid. Real. Tears leapt unbidden to his eyes and she reached up to gently wipe them away.

"I'm so sorry sis."

"Stop little brother. You have nothing to feel sorry about. No apology."

"But if I was there on the boat maybe i could have-"

Dainty hands covered his mouth stopping further words from escape. Sorrow filled a face Kyle had only ever seen filled with life and joy.

"There was nothing you could have done. It was too late. I thought I was so smart, so powerful. I thought I could protect you. Protect everyone. And I failed. You should forgive me", Sandy dropped her head to his chest as his arms instinctively went around her. A harsh laugh escaped him.

"I don't even know what that means." The twins looked into each others' eyes and Sandy nodded once.

"I'll tell you all of it, I promise. But first we need to get to Sage and Clay." A sarcastic smirk stretched his face.

"I can't exactly help with that sis. I'm in prison, remember?"

"So are they."

Releasing her, begrudgingly, he sheathed his sword and looked around the grey forest.

"Funny. Last I saw Clay, err excuse me, Excalibur was on the news in Jacksonville. And Deaton promised to move Sage and his daughter away somewhere safe. So the only one in prison is me."

A pause as he looked at her.

"And maybe you."

Fingers jabbed him in the chest as she stood on her tiptoes.

"God! You never change! Just as stubborn and bullheaded at sixteen. You're almost fifty!"

With a sigh she deflated and withdrew her arms to fold over her chest. Not in defiance but almost self supplication.

"You're so blind. That's partly my fault. Always trying to protect you. And by protecting you I think I sheltered you too much. Hid the truth for too long. We need to get to Clay and sage. I'll tell you what I can on the way. The rest you have to figure out on your own."

With that she led while Kyle followed in frustration. Careful steps, Sandy made sure to avoid the trees and branches of grey. A word of caution was spoken over her shoulder.

"See that moss? Yeah, that's not moss. Don't touch it." A brow arched as he moved between mossy tendrils that swayed without wind. Some things never changed. Sandy was always bossy. Following her deeper into the dark trees he couldn't help but ask.

"What is this place?"

"Hell."

"What?" Laughter trailed from her.

"Okay then, heaven."

"I swear to god I'm gonna make myself wake up and go back to prison."

"Don't even joke about that! This is it. The final play in the game. No more timeouts. No more second chances. This is it." The somber and frightened tone sobered Kyle to the inherent danger in her words. Never in life did she ever speak that way. Not once.

"Yeah … sorry. Bad joke. So, uh, where are we then?"

Pausing she turned and shrugged slightly.

"The afterlife. The before life. Purgatory. The next step in reincarnation. The collective unconscious. The Asphodel meadows. The line before the judgement seat. Honestly, I don't know. What I do know is that everything that's been, everything that will be … all of it, breathes here. Everything is interwoven together into a beautiful tapestry."

Slipping between shades of grey and greyer he shook his head at her words.

"You call this place beautiful? I keep expecting an axe murderer in a mask to pop up behind every turn", he muttered darkly. Another sad smile creased her face as she motioned for him to keep up.

"It wasn't always like this. When I was a kid I still remember fields of green and skies so blue you could almost swear you saw another color just beyond the horizon. But even then the mists of the veil grew like an infection. And you're the cure."

Head shook in utter disbelief at her words. Welcome to heaven. It's sick and going to hell in a grey handbasket. But hey, you're the one who can save it. It didn't seem real.

"How am I supposed to save this place from this?" Hand brushed a string of moss in gesture of his incredulous words. She leapt forward to stop him but was too late. Fear etched on her face as she cowered into the ghostly grass.

Concern touched him and he almost bent to crouch next beside his sister. But shadows writhed from the trees. The shield slipped from his back and the sword filled his hand as he watched the small shadows descend slowly. Moments later he realized the small shadows were easily the size of his Monte Carlo. Crouching low he whispered into Sandy's ear.

"Now what?" Breathless in terror her words squeaked.

"Now we run."

ENTER THE GREY

Feet flew without wings as the twins fled the gargantuan entities that lowered from lofty heights. While Kyle didn't know what they were, there was one thing for certain. He didn't want to find out. Deeper they fled. Every step extinguished the levels of brightness until the landscape possessed new levels of dreariness.

Despite their large size, the disembodied entities were soundless in their pursuit. Without a direct line of sight there was no feasible way to identify what followed them. Only the prevalent unknowable knowledge that tobe caught was one of the worst fates possible.

And so they ran.

Time blurred without meaning. Minutes became hours and days became seconds. Heart pounded in his chest at a rapid tempo that feet tried to match. Having already run into a branch, Kyle made sure to avoid every low hanging clump. There was no desire to face a second summoning of the terror inducing presence.

Eventually Sandy slowed before collapsing upon the misty ground. With heartfelt gratitude Kyle sank down beside her. Great gasps wracked his chest while limbs trembled at their exertion. Laying there panting reminded him of the days where they explored forests, creeks, and abandoned buildings. Then, just as now, they ran until their legs gave out.

The only difference was the fear that prodded their hasty flight. The cold surface of the shield cooled his fevered brow as his face laid upon his arms. Lips parted to ask about the things from the trees. No words escaped as they both froze, the swirling fog outlined an approaching figure. Half shielded from view by the ghostly mist, Kyle grew watchful.

There were eight of them.

Cloaked in the neverending grey, each figure appeared as an indistinct column of formless smoke. Opposite beings moved in tandem with their opposing counterpart. Leapfrogging. Each separate pair advanced only to pause as another set then moved forward. Basic movements that allowed a unit to move forward while providing cover for bounding forward.

All movement from Kyle and Sandy stopped as the two lines passed a good distance away on either side. At least with this scenario he could understand what occurred. Until he felt a presence grow above him. Only eyes moved to search the shadows. What he saw was unexplainable and nearly impossible to comprehend. What could only be described as the bottom hull of a ship passed over them. A carapace of dark grey marbled by pits and scars. The hull smoothly transitioned past them until the rear became visible.

A large opening the size of a man glistened as morning dew upon blades of grass. Mucous fluid dripped malignantly from the porous opening. Wet coils of rope-like substance puckered in pregnant expectation. It was only then that he realized the eight figures on either side were the thing's legs.

The monstrous spider passed by leaving the two drenched in sweat.

With the creature passed from sight the two lay still. Sweat drenched Kyle's body as he lay unmoving and waited for Sandy's signal. After an eternity she stood and offered her hand. Taking it, Kyle stood shakily and sheathed the cutlass once more.

"That is the largest spider I never dreamed of." A resigned smile and shake of Sandy's head argued against his statement.

"I've seen bigger. Much, much bigger." The look on Kyle's face vehemently denied opposed the idea of a larger creature. A bemused smile flitted across Sandy's face as they began their journey anew. Again he followed while continuing their quiet conversation.

"That … that was a spider", the disbelief was not yet suspended from his voice.

"Yes little brother."

Nothing more was offered as he trailed Sandy. Briefly he wondered if this was one of those things she alluded to. A trip to self enlightenment. It was utter bull. Nothing like teaching a starving man to fish sentiment. Nonetheless he honored her wishes. For now. That deal didn't extend to Clay and Sage.

"How are those two trapped? Prisoners is what you said", his slightly confused questions searched for answers.

"I guess it all depends on where we are."

"Don't give me that wax on wax off crap. Where are we then?" The shadowy figure of his sister paused which allowed him to catch up.

"Did you know evolution takes thousands of years?"

"What does that have to do with any of this!?" Hands reached up and grabbed him by either ear to drag Kyle's face to hers.

"I'm trying to tell you, if you would just shut up and listen. And be quiet. You can't listen if you're talking", she twisted his ears which caused him to jerk away. Silence was maintained.

"Sorry sis. Go ahead." A quick gesture waved Kyle down. Crouched in the eternal mists, half submerged, several shadows scurried across their pathway ahead. More spiders. However these were much smaller. Only the size of cows with legs that skittered their chitinous forms swiftly through the darkened forest. Only the size of cows.

With their passage the two continued forward while they

maintained silence for several moments. Finally Sandy considered it safe enough to speak again. Though in a hushed voice.

"The old myths are true, or at least their basis. The gods did exist. In some form. They were the first to exhibit powers. That's why they so often intermarried. To continue their bloodlines. But they were far from immortal. But they learned how to attain longevity in a fashion."

They eased through a small clearing and paused to rest.

"In a similar manner of how humanity has tried to elongate life now through technological means. If memories, thoughts, and brain waves could be replicated then they could live on in a way. That's where telepaths come in."

The moment of respite ended and Sandy led them onward even as Kyle kept unquestioned queries to himself.

"Telepaths, like me, can slip into another person's head. Not only can we do that but with enough determination and will we could imprint ourselves onto another. Almost like a separate identity. And then we could, conceivably, erase the original mind and memories. A kind of immortality. Like a replication."

A pause allowed her a chance to choose an unseen path. Finding it, she headed off again.

"And so the gods lived lifetimes. Until a powerful telepath decided to bring about their downfall and form a new hierarchy. With herself at the center. Arachne. Through her power she made herself immortal and linked versions of herself throughout the world. By taking control of new telepaths. Every generation she took the most powerful as host and made the others satellites to herself." Hand reached out and Kyle stopped Sandy.

"Wait wait. You mean the gods like Zeus and Thor were real?"

"In a fashion. Keep up."

Bewildered at the turn of reality Kyle continued to chase his twin.

"This place is like a repository of all conscious and unconscious. The older the mind, the more powerful the mind, the longer they exist. Before you ask, I don't know what happens when the pieces of who and what we are disappear. Maybe we are reborn. Maybe our souls merge into each other and we become something new from the shades of disparate parts." A grin broke across Kyle's face as she answered his unspoken musings.

"This place though, we who are empaths or telepaths, precogs or seers, we can see this place. Enter this place. A realm of beginnings and endings and a myriad of possible what ifs."

Finally she stopped and knelt beneath a hazy tree and gazed into the unseen murkiness.

"That's where I messed up. For thousands of years Arachne has existed. The shades of her reflections infected this place. And slowly she consumed it. Minds were assimilated in her greater consciousness as she's leapt from body to body over the generations. And here she stalked her prey. This is where she hunted me."

Understanding dawned upon him. Eyes opened to the reality of this realm as her words echoed in his mind. Once the mists of the veil were alive with greens and blues. But inexorably it changed. No, not changed.

Terraformed.

A metamorphosis. The coils of mist. Grey formed tree trunks. Fogged canopy of branches and limbs.

It wasn't a forest. It was a massive spider web. The forms of the trees were the victims of consciousness trapped within cocoons that nourished the spider at the center. Minds or souls, whichever, ensnared by an omnipotent evil. An evil that murdered his sister.

"I'm going to kill her", he swore as he leaned his forehead against Sandy's.

"Not yet. You aren't ready. There's so much more for you to know. And no more time." Her fingers drifted down to trace along the scarred and beaten boots he still wore. Dropping his hand, Kyle covered hers.

"These boots have seen me through my life. Always there, always a reminder of my big sister watching out for me. And not even death could stop you at that." Tears fell from her eyes. Softly he brushed them away as she shuddered..

"All I can do is help from here. When I died I lost my powers in the real world. And that's the problem. When I linked with you and the others I left a psychic link that opened a window for Arachne to spin webs and snares for you. For all of you."

The mists shuddered, the tendrils of grey shaking as though the lungs of a great beast breathed in. The canopy dilated like a living organism. Somehow, he thought, perhaps it was. With squinted eyes into the darkened shapes of the web, Kyle tried to identify anything of worth.

"Why is it so much darker here than where we came from?" A quiet whisper against the things that bumped into the night. With an equally hushed voice, Sandy answered.

"This was the beginning of her web. The forms lost to the mists, these are her earliest victims. This is the seat of her power here. And where some of her most prized catches sit as trophies. This is where we free Clay and Sage. Once freed all three of you need to escape to the real world and take the fight to her there."

A brow arched on his face.

"What about you?"

A grim smiled stretched across her face.

"This is where we will fight her. Only in both planes of existence, simultaneously, can we defeat and destroy her." Kyle was about to question who the 'we' were that would fight her there in the misted veil. Then he saw them.

It began with a few forms that eased into his eyesight. But quickly the numbers grew into the dozens. Some wore garb from centuries and millennia ago. Others wore modern clothing. All possessed some form of weaponry. And all wore the same hungered determination on their faces.

"Are they all like you? Some form of mental ability?" A nod was her response.

Nearby a figure appeared. The man looked familiar. It took

several moments before his body tensed and his hand closed on the cutlass pommel as reaction almost took over. Never would he forget the face before him.

The visage of Samuel Abernathy.

Quickly Sandy grabbed his arm to stay his hand.

"No! He's here to help."

"How the hell can you be on the same side as Abernathy?"

"The enemy of my enemy. He almost did to Arachne what she did to the old gods. Almost replaced her. The neural links distracted her long enough for any hold he possessed on the real world to get eradicated. Plus he didn't take kindly to being used as a tool to distract and break you just to be tossed away like trash."

Abernathy waved with an evil maliciousness that was palpable. And nauseating. But this wasn't just Kyle's fight. Though he disliked the idea immensely, Kyle begrudgingly acquiesced. As he looked about he wondered what they waited on.

"Is there going to be an alarm? Dinner bells? When does this start?"

"We're waiting on Earl."

"Earl? Who's Earl?"

"Earl is one of the first of us. Not just of those with mental abilities. He's one of the first generations of our evolutionary birth. Straight up O.G. Here he comes."

Kyle turned his head and saw the figure slowly emerging from the mist. The first thing he noticed was the green mohawk, smoke rising from a corncob pipe to frame a bronzed face with a shaven square jaw. If only that was the only oddities noticed.

A bare, heavily muscled torso covered with tattoos caught his attention. As did an incredibly detailed tat of hello kitty. Slung across his back looked to be what could only be a bazooka. Around his waist was an ornate gun rig with silvered studs. On his left hip hung a katana that would have made any samurai proud to own. On his right hip rode a butt forward Colt Peacemaker.

To finish the amalgamation of Earl's outfit was a scottish kilt combined with greek greaves and vambraces. A banjo was held lightly in the man's hands.

Dumbfounded, Kyle could only ask one sentence.

"What … the hell … is that?"

The banjo was held lightly in the new arrival's left hand as his right was extended.

"Hey mate. I'm Earl."

VI
BATTLELINES DRAWN

Instinctively he took the other man's hand and shook. Firm and steady. The memory of one of their father's sayings danced across Kyle's mind. Never trust a man who won't shake your hand. And always take a measure of a man by their handshake. Too weak and they were men who conformed to others or possessed no central tenet of identity. Too strong and they were most likely opinionated bullies that forced their ideas and personality on others.

Or they were firm without being aggressive, lenient without being weak.

Earl was one such handshake. Solid without being overbearing with just enough give to be equal.

Immediately Kyle liked him.

The other man took a knee beside them and exchanged nods with Sandy. It appeared the beings gathered around were prepared for a war. However, Kyle couldn't figure out why they were ready when he was just learning about the offensive. He mentioned as much.

"I don't understand. If this has been in the works for so long, as it apparently seems, why am I just now getting read in?"

The mohawked man nodded to Sandy to answer. Yet there were

guarded undertones in their non verbal exchange that drove Kyle mad.

"We couldn't. You can't have known before you were ready and before it was time. Battle lines needed to be drawn without tipping our hand. Plus you shut me out." Head shook with Kyle's inability to accept the excuses.

"Who would I have told to be overheard? Also, there's no way I could keep you out of my mind. Even if I Wanted to. Your powers are too strong."

"I already told you. My powers disappeared when I died. And I think you perfected your stubbornness in your old age. It was-" Words stopped and the nearly imperceptible shake of Earl's head. Turning to face the other man, Kyle scowled.

"Don't censor my sister. If she wants to tell me something, she can." The cold smile on Earl's face chilled Kyle to the core. A killer's smirk. But just as quickly as the face turned glacial, it warmed.

"Listen kid. There are just certain things you can't know yet. And other things you need to discover on your own. And before you're all butt hurt, understand this. Every single one of us that have gathered here, we failed when it was our chance. Arachne beat us. And because we were unsuccessful she has gotten one step closer to game, set, and match. Our shortcomings have pushed us to the brink. And you are the only thing standing between free will and checkmate."

Like there wasn't already enough pressure on him, now Kyle was told the fate of the world somehow rested on his actions and decisions. An unbelievable twist of fate. It wasn't Sandy, the most powerful telepath of her generation. It wasn't the mongrel of stereotypes or Abernathy. For some unknown reason, they believed it was his destiny. Or Kyle would be the final loss.

No pressure.

"So … what do we do then?" Straight teeth flashed as Earl motioned to Sandy to field the question.

"The only thing left to do. We go to war." A bemused grin

stretched over Kyle's face.

"So what's the plan. Or at least what do I need to know?" The head bob from Earl said he was now asking the right questions. Sandy leaned in.

"The first part is the most dangerous aspect. And the most important. We rescue Clay and Sage then you will run out of here. Run like hell. She'll chase. Especially since Earl will be with you. All the way out of the web. Once free you return to jail. Earl will talk you through at that point. Arachne will follow. And that's when we attack. Try to give you time to get to her physical vessel and take her out. While we do the same here."

Head shook as Kyle sighed.

"This sounds like the least thought out, asinine plan I have ever heard. Let's do it."

A rough shake of Kyle's shoulder from Earl was made in earnest camaraderie.

"Then let's save your friends."

Leading the way, Earl moved forward while remaining crouched. A glance at Sandy revealed she was staying.

"This is the end of the line, little brother. My fight is here. Yours is out there in the world of the living. Do it. And remember. We will meet again, in this life or the next." Arms wrapped her in a squeeze. The empty feeling of finality gripped him as he embraced her in farewell.

Choked by emotion Kyle released his sister and followed the visible mohawk through the forest of spider web.

Caught up to Earl, Kyle followed silently. Extra care was given not to touch a single strand of the web. A biology lesson from the past reminded him that spiders could feel the vibrations from contact with their web. There was no desire to meet the spider before he must. Of course it may not have been a desire to learn more about the other man so much as a way to keep his own mind off the terror briefly approaching.

"How long have you been stuck here?" They paused as the forms of several lesser spiders passed. Exoskeletons gleamed dulling in the absent light. Once the threat passed they continued.

"I'm actually not stuck here. My gift is a form of astral projection. So I can travel between grey as I please. And anybody empty of a soul is a potential vessel for me. So I've been coming and going for thousands of years." The shock was written on Kyle's face which made Earl chuckle beneath his breath.

"Yeah. I'm that old. But I also never had enough power to challenge Arachne up front. I just pester the outer fringes and lend support where I can." Finally they reached an open area within the forest of the web. Several pillars stood near the center of the clearing. There were no identifying marks to discern which two cocoons were the ones Kyle needed. The overwhelming sensation must have been written on his face.

"Once we get over there you will have enough time to free two, maybe three, before we are swarmed. Just go on your gut instincts. The three of you have shared a common thread with your sister. That commonality is still there and open. Find your center, find your friends."

It was guru mumbo jumbo. But it was also the only chance he was given to find the needles in the haystack of cocoons. So he focused on his sister. The memories of her laughter and the thoughts of who she was. Oddly enough it seemed to work. Two of the dozens of faceless victims called to him.

A brief nod was given and Kyle sprinted forward alone. Only after splitting the distance between the immobilized forms and where Earl remained in seclusion did Kyle realize he was on his own.

Screw it. He was Aegis afterall.

At the first pod of tightly woven spider silk he pulled the cutlass free and sliced through the thickened wall. A figure fell free as the blade rose and fell once more to split the second swathe of spider encasing open. Both, Clay and Sage, fell free of their bonds. Trying to rouse them failed so Kyle grabbed each from beneath their arms and staggered to a jog pulling their disoriented forms toward the escape route.

A shriek of rage shook the ground nearly causing Kyle to stumble under his burdens. Through a combination of luck and instinct he maintained his feet while dragging the two. Behind them a powerful presence lowered from the web. Great was the consciousness that Kyle felt burrowing within that he likened it to a colonoscopy of the mind. An invading presence where it shouldn't be.

Ahead a massive spider dropped to the ground the size of a small garage. Right in their passage to escape. There was nothing left to do but continue to charge forward. As glistening fangs dripped in anticipation of sinking into Kyle's face. Earl stepped forward and pulled the revolver to fire two rounds into the arachnid's face.

The creature collapsed as the trio passed. A shout came from Earl as he holstered the revolver and began to strum the banjo.

"Keep running! I'll catch up." Fingers strummed upon the strings as the other man shouted out catcalls to Arachne. The last glimpse of Earl was him swinging the banjo directly into the face of the widow spider that settled to the ground in the clearing. The groaning sound at the impact heralded the destruction of the banjo while accompanied by a shout from the odd warrior.

"Now we're making some music!"

Refusing to slow by looking back, Kyle continued to drag both men along with him. At some point along the way each man began to run in staggered steps with Kyle. The nightmarish landscape haunted them with each step. Every materialized tree form initially seemed a spider prepared to attack.

The frenzied run to escape the forest passed faster than his entrance. And yet it still was an eternity. Finally ahead there was a break in the canopy while the mists of the veil lightened. Nearly free, Kyle couldn't help but laugh.

Until one of the spiders the size of his monte Carlo crashed to the ground before them and blocked the final distance to freedom. By then both Sage and Clay regained their equilibrium and strength.

Releasing them, Kyle prepared for a hopeless battle with the massive creature.

"If this is the end you're going to have to earn it", Kyle snarled through clenched teeth. The cutlass was drawn and the shield slipped onto his left forearm as Kyle prepared for a final battle. The Spider rose up on hind legs and prepared to strike as a shout echoed from behind the three men.

"Fire in the hole!"

The rocket launcher fired the explosive directly into the spider's midsection. The explosion tore the creature in two and launched bright green ichor across the area. Trotting past them, Earl dropped the smoking launcher to the ground and spurred them to catch up.

They escaped the gloom of the web and reached the neutral greys free of the canopy of trees. Spinning on his heel, Earl grasped the men.

"Remember this, when you wake. Clay, take a ship and get Sage. Sage, hack the prison so there are no defenses when the two of you arrive. Kyle, stay alive. And while you're at it, try to kill someone without destroying the body. Now go! Wake! I'll see you on the other side!"

Even as the three men began to lose their hold on the grey existence they watched as Earl attacked the pursuing hordes of spiders with the ferocity and tenacity of a mad man.

And then Kyle saw nothing.

JAILBREAK

Monday, May 31, 2055
12:57 a.m.

Kyle woke with a start. Sweat drenched his grey jumper as muscles cramped from frozen exertion. At the cell door Tye glanced back to ensure Kyle was fine. When it was apparent he was Tye went back to overwatch duty. Slowly Kyle rose from the bed and moved to the water basin. Water ran cold through the faucet and he quickly splashed his face.

Wiping the excess drops from his face with his towel, Kyle moved to the door beside Tye.

"How long?" A bewildered expression flicked over the young man's face.

"Two minutes. Maybe. Go back to it. I've got this." Surprised, Kyle shook his head.

"It's already done. The rescue party is already alerted and hopefully headed this way." WIth an indifferent shrug both men returned to their visual diligence.

The wing grew quiet in the semi dark. Above on the catwalk, guards made their circulatory rounds. Most of the prisoners retreated to their bunks. Across the open courtyard in an opposite cell stood Abe who stared transfixed. Upon his chest was the finished tattoo. An open declaration of allegiance.

The dots connected each long, tapered leg of the widow. At the center, the odd lines placed within the symbol became the hourglass representation. Finally, at long last, the true monstrous depiction came into crystalline focus.

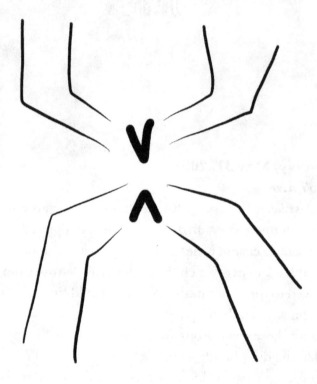

There was no denying the battle lines drawn so vividly into flesh. While the mechanical eyes glaring across the prison did not possess physical intent, the presence that echoed conveyed malicious purpose. The mountain was but a physical manifestation of the evil sensed in the realm of grey mist.

The two men locked eyes in a battle of will. The mountain claimed total annihilation and subjection. The man known as Aegis radiated determined hope and resistance. There were no miscommunications. Bitter rivals and complete opposites. When the cell doors opened next, there would be a confrontation that only one would walk away from.

It would be a lie if Kyle didn't acknowledge a modicum of excitement.

The night lengthened. Each hour strike merely promised an immediate showdown, as of yet unrealized. Time flowed differently in the mists of the veil and Kyle hoped that they would not fail in the physical world.

Yet there was nothing left to do but wait.

And wait.

The wait ended with the activation of cell doors.

Arms were pulled back from the cell bars as the doors rolled back. The bunk creaked behind Kyle as Tye slid from the mattress and landed on the floor. Creeping behind Kyle the younger man looked out with concern.

"Is this us?" Over a dozen inmates slipped out of their cells and crowded behind Abe who stalked out of his own cell with singular intent.

"No, I don't believe this is us. This looks to be the other side. It's never easy. Nothing worth doing ever is." The mountain moved to the center clearing of the courtyard as his compatriots formed a half circle around him. Some of the other prisoners were rousing. Yet they chose to remain within their cells to watch. Uncertain glances rose to the guards above as they wondered what prompted the decision to let tonight be the showdown between the Mountain and Aegis.

Kyle knew.

The war began in the grey mists were drifting over to the physical plane. The final battle to determine if Arachne would be triumphant. This was just one of her moves. To ensnare a pawn before Kyle got the opportunity to cross the battlefield and become a dangerous hazard to herself. And he was more than ready to mess up her plans.

A final glance at his reflection elicited a smug grin. As the once birthday boots from his sister carried him from his cell Kyle couldn't suppress the smirk. The prisoners gathered only saw the broken Aegis who surrendered to his fate and denied his power. The image seen in the mirror confirmed he was no longer that man.

Natural color returned to chase away the sallow hue of his flesh. The weathered skin ravaged by wrinkles and deep crevasses across his face smoothed and tightened. Atrophied muscles slid smoothly beneath the grey jumper with hidden power.

Gone was the shattered shield, the broken hero, the lost vigilante.

Aegis stood reborn in the fire of diversity.

As Kyle approached Abe the bigger man opened his arms wide and turned his head to rabble rouse the crowd who grinned in anticipation. Kyle didn't give the man the chance to speak. A left lanced out to crack against Abe's jaw. An immediate right haymaker followed smashing the face the other direction to meet another swift left jab.

The mountain staggered back and raised his hands to defend his face. Unconcerned, Kyle followed with several blows to the midsection. A delayed left hook was swung at Kyle's head. Easily he ducked beneath the flailing arm and drove several punches into the mountain's kidneys and another to the liver. Left leg kicked out with Kyle's toe connecting with the back of Abe's knee which dropped the bigger man to both knees.

With a leap forward, Kyle wrapped his arm under the thick jaw of Abe and locked his other arm around the back of his foe's head in a rear naked choke. The mountain tried to lean forward to bring his chin to his chest however, Kyle wasn't going to allow that. Legs wrapped around Abe's midsection as Kyle lunged backward to pull the bigger man in the opposite direction.

Sandwiched between the concrete floor and Abe wasn't the most comfortable feeling but there was no escape for the mountain whom's thrashing limbs slowed. Even when the much larger man ceased moving Kyle refused to let go. Long seconds stretched into a minute before the half circle of Red Spider members acted.

Hands tried to pry Kyle's arms away as several more attempted to strike him. A perk of having the mountain laying on you was that he became a decent shield. Half the blows bounced harmlessly off the larger man. Finally a boot heel crashed into Kyle's temple and he released Abe to roll away to his feet. A handful approached as blood dripped from his chin where the split flesh of his head wept crimson, a minor annoyance.

Blood slowed as an itching sensation afflicted his head. A cautious hand gingerly touched the wound to feel as the last edges of split skin knitted together. That was what happened when your body got used to a certain type of injury or attack. Kyle's body evolved to protect him. The rapid healing of flesh dissuaded a group of the spiders but the others were unswayed.

Kyle wouldn't have it any other way.

The reforged Aegis leapt into their midst with a frenzied attack. Behind him Tye advanced into the fray to join the fight. Easily the two men incapacitated the handful of attackers to leave them motionless on the cold hard ground. Or screaming at limbs suddenly torqued in unnatural directions.

However the other half of the group were reinvigorated as the mountain slowly stirred before he rose to stand once again. A bellowing laugh escaped Abe's bloodied lips as he turned to face Kyle as the shield prepared for round two. The mountain raised his hands to forestall Kyle as he spoke with a gravelly voice.

"This is a big'un. I haven't wore a meat suit like this since the last sons of Arba! And just superficial damage. One second Kyle…"

The mountain turned and looked upon the bewildered faces of the other red spider members. A cold smile stretched upon his face as his massive hands reached out. A throat was taken in either hand and the man bashed the makeshift clubs into their fellows until bodies stopped twitching. With what remained released from massive hands the mountain turned back to face Kyle and Tye.

"Don't tell me this ugly face ever looked so good." Hands dropped to sides as Kyle only shook his head in slight amusement.

"I think I liked you better with the mohawk. Good luck trying to grow one on that body. Tye, meet Earl. He's some of our back up. Where's the rest?"

While Earl grew distracted, and disgruntled, with the lack of hair on top of his head, he did hear the last question. With a grin he pointed at the ceiling.

"They're already here."

The lights flickered and died as the power went out. Then suddenly the roof and part of the second story collapsed. A Protectorate jet kicked debris and dust around the courtyard. Several lights illuminated the trio of men as the ramp lowered and Excalibur himself appeared to wave them onward.

"Come on! We ain't waiting all day!"

The mountain led while Kyle and Tye followed closely behind. The jet rose on thrusters to escape the prison.

PART NINE: THE WIDOW

OLD FACES

Monday, May 31, 2055
3:11 a.m.

It was a small reunion.

As the jet cut across the state headed for their final destination there were plenty of handshakes, hugs, and introductions. Tye ran up the aisle and hugged his mother. Deaton looked ferocious and relieved as she clutched her son. Mother nature did right by her. Meanwhile Clay pulled Kyle into a bear hug only to release him as Kyle introduced the mountain as Earl, their guide through the grey.

Over the intercom hissed the voice of Sage.

"Welcome aboard Rebel One. The premier air service for all the escaping convicts. The flight will be short so there will be no in-flight movie or snacks tonight." The cockpit door opened and Sage climbed down. In the copilot's seat was a young woman Kyle felt he should know. Before he could ask, Sage gave him his next hug.

Following Kyle's line of sight Sage released the embrace and nodded. Voice came out husky from emotion.

"Mary. After you got her out, Deaton got us away and safe. That's a real woman there you know?" Kyle glanced over to see Deaton look away. A knot formed in his throat as Kyle swallowed against it.

"Yeah, I know."

Again Clay steered Kyle to an older woman of sleight size. Long grey hair in a tight pony tail and a lined face could not hide her beauty. Or her identity. Hand extended from Kyle.

"Been a few years, Starburst." The former Warrior teammate took the offered hand and shook it. A twitch of her lips was all the emotion the hard woman allowed.

"Call me Ellen. You earned it. Plus I'm retired. But when Clay called I knew I still owed you one for pulling me out of that wreckage. And even disconnected from the Protectorate, I knew something was wrong. Now we know. Don't make me regret becoming a criminal." She released his hand and turned to take one of the vacant seats. Kyle grinned at her retreating back.

"Yes ma'am."

Eyes turned back to where Deaton and Tye were speaking with another man and Kyle prepared to move over to them when Clay stopped him again.

"I should introduce you to one more of the team. This here is Jack Sawyer." Another young man reached out and shook his hand adamantly. Extracting his hand Kyle nodded politely.

"Nice to meet you." The man was just a kid. A mop of brown hair and peach fuzz on his chin. The kid didn't let his youth stop him from gushing.

"Thanks! It's a real honor to meet you again. You're one of my heroes." A glance was shared between Kyle and Clay as the latter shook his head in resignation. Confused Kyle questioned.

"Again?" Before the young man could launch into a response Clay mercifully distracted the man by sending him over to sit next to Starburst. The piercing gaze from the older woman shared her displeasure as the chatterbox began to talk to her. A bemused shake of his head before Clay answered Kyle.

"Yeah. Last time you saw him you rescued him out in Ocala." Shocked recognition spread on Kyle's face as he turned to look at the young man again.

"That is one of the kids? From Henry Abernathy's abduction?"

"Yep. Turns out he's a super too. A first year at the academy. He may be young but he makes up for it with his power."

"The ability to talk someone into a coma?" Restrained laughter from Clay as he shook his head.

"No. He can create and control electrical currents." Impressed, Kyle shrugged. Clay knew best what was needed. And he should as most of his life was spent with the Protectorate. Finally Clay released Kyle so he could go speak to Deaton.

As he approached Kyle realized the young man with them wasn't a man but a kid. Big boned with wide shoulders, but still a kid. The few steps between them disappeared when Deaton moved into Kyle's arms. In that moment he felt whole. For the first time in a very long time. When she went to pull back he only held her tighter. She melted into his arms.

Finally Deaton leaned back with a pained smile on her face.

"Don't hate me."

"Never."

"Remember Christmas? You never got the second gift. I was going to tell you after Gainesville. After rescuing Mary. But everything went to hell. And I couldn't tell you while you were locked up." His arms released their hold but maintained a tether on either side of her hips.

"Tell me what?" Pulling free of one of his hands she reached out and beckoned the youth forward. As the young man approached Kyle looked between their faces.

"Let me introduce you to Brick. His birth name is Mason Deaton Ross. Your son."

FAMiLY

Monday, May 31, 2055
3:21 a.m.

"My son?" Shock filled Kyle's face. The one thing he never expected in his life. To be a father. Then to find out after a decade locked up. It was almost too much to handle. However, Deaton kept hold of him as she drew close.

"When? How?" Confusion still shown on his face. A light chuckle escaped Deaton to whisper along his cheek.

"When is easy. When we first met and brought down the slave monopoly in Atlanta. We had that fall in the caravan. Winter at the house in the woods. Made more than memories. As to the how ... surely you aren't that old?"

With their faces so close Kyle whispered even as his eyes were unable to leave the figure of his son. His son.

"Why didn't you ever tell me?" The tone wasn't accusatory. It just made the regret even greater for Deaton. Of all the men walking the planet, here was the one who would never blame her for the decisions she made. Not over her children. Or theirs.

"When I found out I was going to tell you that night. But then the next morning you headed back to Florida. And when we came down for the job at the Heresy in Gainesville, I was going to tell you after. But we never got the chance." Fate was a fickle creature. And she enjoyed making his life difficult. He was the one to make it hard.

"Does he know …?" The question of whether his son knew he was his father lodged in Kyle's throat as his mouth dried and tongue thickened.

"Of course. Brick, come meet your father." As the young man stepped forward, Deaton moved to the side. Unsure, Kyle extended his arm prepared for a handshake. The boy, young man, moved past his hand and wrapped his arms around Kyle's chest with face burrowed in the grey jumper. Instinctively Kyle embraced him and felt his chest ache.

Deaton turned her head in an attempt to hide the tears that glistened. Tye ushered from behind her and slid them in for a group hug. A smirk stretched Tye's face.

"Brick here is all mellow and kittens. Sandy? Now she's a junkyard dog. Only her way or the highway."

Eyes widened as Kyle looked down into their faces in even more shock. Deaton laughed and cried as Brick hesitantly spoke.

"Sandy is my sister. And my twin. I'm older but she thinks she's in charge." With a shake of his head Kyle chuckled.

"Some things never change. And you … why didn't you tell me? Ah, but I understand", Kyle said to Tye who wore a sheepish grin.

"Mom might have killed me if I spilled the family secret. I was little last time we met, but I still remembered you. Even though Brick and Sandy never met you, they knew you. Recollections of two little boys and stories from our mother. Strangers passed through the underground and every now and then we would hear new tales about you. Maybe you weren't with us, but you never left."

Tears swam in Kyle's eyes as Tye hugged him tight then released to give them space. Under his left arm Deaton held to him while his right hand gripped Brick's shoulder. His son. Eyes searched his son's face as questions bubbled at the surface.

"Tell me everything."

Minutes stretched into infinity while Deaton and Brick told snippets of stories spanning almost fourteen years. Every word flowed like water and Kyle was dying of thirst. Their area of the jet rang with laughter and watered by tears of joy and regret. A bubble of reminiscence which Kyle refused to pop.

Yet time waited for none.

Behind him Clay lightly rapped Kyle's backside. When Kyle turned Clay smiled sadly.

"Congratulations brother. You deserve some good in your life. But right now we need to get ready. I've got your gear in a foot locker. And your shield. Fifteen minutes until we arrive."

Regretfully Kyle disentangled from his family. His family. Moving slowly he raised the lid of the container to look at the dark plates and uniform. Kneeling down he moved the armor and gripped the curvature at the bottom to pull out his shield. Without looking up he asked the question.

"Where we headed?

"Back home."

"Ah, so back to the Spire and Anastasia Island."

"No. Home. Back to the Alcove and Dead End."

HOME

Monday, May 31, 2055
3:45 a.m.

The jet lowered on repulsors to settle deep within the sands of Lake Gem. The two, Kyle and Clay, were the first down the ramp to the beach. Moist sand clung to his boots reminding him of the past. Dark memories swirled in his mind for a few moments before he looked at the others descending. This wasn't about the past, but about the future.

"Home sweet home." The mutter escaped Clay as he looked down the beach to where a few lights sparkled from the Alcove. Turning he spoke to the group.

"We know why we're here. And we know what we have to do. All that's left is to do it. Mary, you stay with the ship. Brick, you stay with her and keep this jet buttoned up."

Both youth merely nodded. There was no back talk or begging to come with them. It spoke volumes to their maturity as well as the level of gravitas that gripped the scenario. The two retreated up the ramp and closed it.

The darkness of the night enveloped them. Above, clouds blotted out the moon and stars to wrap the group in a deep gloom. Ominous silence clutched tightly onto the group. Every shadow writhed despite no wind caressing the trees. Earl snorted and Kyle merely nodded. It felt a bit like the grey mists of the veil. Clay continued.

"The Widow is here. She broadcast it through enough free psychic mediums. If that wasn't enough there were enough clues left in the digital world. That's how we know at least Wizard, Hallan Branch is here. And under her thrall."

Pointedly Clay looked at both Ellen and Kyle, as Wizard was once a teammate of theirs. The power to control was worrisome, but to control a Warrior … Faces pinched with the cold rasp of fear.

"The point is we know the Widow is here. And protected. There could be more people we know who are forced to do her bidding. It doesn't matter. Right now they are our enemies. There are two objectives. We need to remove Wizard because he can control everything from tech to satellites to potentially weapons of mass destruction. For that I'm taking Sage, our hacker, Jack who can fry what we can't hack and Tye who can sneak us close enough to do what we need to do."

The names called nodded to one another, yet their faces asked a silent question. Was sneaking upon the clueless enemy even possible when the Widow operated in anonymity for decades? Regardless, the names of those called slid closer to Clay as he continued.

"Kyle, you've got Deaton for the same reason I've got Tye. You also have Ellen who wants some payback and Earl as a shock troop. The Widow is yours. At least Kyle and Earl should be immune to the Widow. And if your other teammates become liabilities, you have to take them down or take them out."

The remaining four looked at one another with grim sets to their faces. Determination became tempered by regretful possibilities. They did not have the luxury of relative safety. If the choice came to saving a teammate or saving the world, then they would mourn their dead. One life was precious but even more so was the fate of billions.

Clay finished up.

"We'll move out together. But when things start going to hell remember the objectives. Watch each other's backs. And don't get dead."

The group milled about for a moment as the situation sank in. Former Warriors grimly looked between one another. Experience told them of the dangers and likelihood some would fall. Parents felt the cold hand of fear as they looked at the younger generation. The youth of the group looked uncertainty at the expressions of the elders, guts churned in fear.

The shield was moved to Kyle's left arm and the straps tightened as he walked up to stand next to Clay. Their fear was tangible, which the darkness fed on.

"I'm just saying what the rest of us is thinking. That was the worst pep talk we've ever heard."

Several laughed out loud as Clay grinned tightly and nodded at Kyle who shrugged.

"But the night isn't getting any earlier and Clay ain't getting any prettier. Let's do this."

With the moment of levity over, uncertainty returned as trepidation festered into unease.

The eight moved together down the beach.

Memories threatened to assault Kyle at the familiar landscape. It wasn't far from where they currently trudged that the four skipped school and played hooky on the beach. Both Sage and Clay glanced at him showing they too remembered. Tonight was as much for Sandy as it was the rest of the world.

Tension mounted the longer they walked. Sweaty palms slicked their weapons. Several times they paused at strange sounds or the flicker of movement. On the fringes of the woods shapes moved and caused most of them to grow shakily pale. Apparitions of spiders followed their progress. Breath shuddered from the group as they each fought to subdue their terror. Tongues sought to moisten dry lips only to fail as the teams drifted back into a single group.

"They aren't dangerous here. The Widow's minions can't affect this world, only appear", Earl spoke with a shrug of his shoulders.

"That may be true, but right now I'm feeling a bit affected", whispered Jack unconvincingly. Vigilant eyes kept track of the spiders as they continued onward.

It became evident what house they were approaching even before Sage stiffened. More time was spent at Sage's childhood home than all their others combined. The back door swayed open in the breeze with a spine tingling creak. The old screen door lay trampled upon the back porch. A splash in the lake caused a few to flinch. A scream from the woods made all of them flinch.

Two hands raised and halted the group silently. Both Deaton and Tye warned them from their extended senses. Meanwhile Kyle turned left and looked into the black forest of trees that ran on their left. Beside him stood Earl who stared into the inky shadows. They both felt it. A heavy presence that beckoned them forward to smash upon the rocks at the siren's call.

Hands gripped rifles at the ready as Deaton slowly approached the edge of darkness. Behind, Tye crouched at the water's edge and copied the concentrated expression of his mother. Slowly Deaton shouldered her trusty shotgun and whispered.

"Contact. Two are approaching. One on the ground. One from the trees."

Earl stepped up to put himself in front of Kyle who grimaced. Carefully Ellen crept beside Deaton as both waited. Briefly reflections of green were momentarily seen from the forest depths. Opposite of them, Tye called out.

"One in the house, just inside the doorway. Another on the other side of the house. No, wait …"

Head raised and he breathed in deeply as he turned his head.

"No, that one is on the roof now. I caught the scent of another … but I lost it. I can hear a heartbeat near though." The sound of Clay drawing his sword rasped from its sheath. Copying, Kyle drew his own cutlass with his right hand.

A silent pause gripped the night as though all waited upon the forceful exhale all knew was imminent. Utter stillness broken by the rapid beat of their hearts and irregular breathing while struggling to find their calm amidst the darkness.

Then the night erupted with blood, gunfire, and screams.

BLOOD AND TEARS

Monday, May 31, 2055
4:04 a.m.

The attacks occurred almost simultaneously. Silk webbing sprayed from the heights of the trees like a madman with two cans of silly string. Taking his position literally, Earl leapt in front of Kyle and was hit with sticky strands that enveloped his arms. The coils yanked the man forward into the darkness where he thrashed through the woods.

Reflective green light sprang to life as a lithe form leapt from the woods and crashed into Ellen who managed to squeeze off a few rounds. The bullets ricocheted from body armor as Ellen turned the rifle sideways to wrestle with the female attacker.

Bullets whizzed from the house as the group scattered and returned fire. A silhouette flapped from the roof like a monstrous bat. At the water Tye screamed as a beastly being launched from the lake. Massive flat jaws opened wide and latched down upon the young man's arm to drag both beneath the broiling surface.

A cushion of air pressed them from above before the figure arrived, clawed feet slamming into Sage with bone crunching strength. The sword was knocked from Clay's hand and a giant leathery wing sent the man flying. Jack dove into the water to assist with wrestling the being to the shore.

Tye limped to the sand and collapsed as liquid pumped from his severed arm. A flash of vibration shattered the rifle Elen used as a bludgeoning tool only to have a shimmering hand shove into her chest. With a dive Deaton tackled the woman new revealed to be Gale Tanaka, aka Vibe. Another former Warrior fighting for the widow.

Electricity sizzled blue on the shore between Jack and the enemy who resembled a humanoid alligator. Unmercilessly the Gargoyle being rained down attacks upon Sage. Before Kyle could charge forward Clay dove into the winged villain causing the men to roll across the sand.

"Go find the widow and stop her! We have this", yelled Clay even as the Gargoyle flapped it's massive wings taking them into the sky.

Indecision momentarily kept Kyle rooted. Friends and family were fighting in a deadly battle front. Some were down unmoving while others fought valiantly. But as Clay said, Kyle had a job to do. Without a second look he charged into the darkness to follow the sound of chattering wood and grunts of conflict. Visibility disappeared within only a few strides into the forest. A veneer gauze gripped Kyle's face as he plunged deeper into the woods.

Gossamer strand clutched upon his armor as Kyle relentlessly tracked the sound of battle between Earl and the unseen assailant. He felt the pair before he saw them. Half cocooned in webbing, Earl struggled vainly with the creature over him.

Splay legged, the being stood hunched over Earl as its six arms held the mountain down. Fangs glistened with blood and venom over a maw in the center of the face. Two black, bulbous eyes protruded from its forehead the size of saucers as multiple other sets ran along either side of its head. Devoid of hair, only rough whiskers decorated its head and upper torso. From the center of its mouth a fleshy hollowed tongue lay embedded in Earl's chest.

Sprinting forward, Kyle tackled the creature to the ground

leaving Earl convulsing behind them. Landing on top, Kyle slashed down with the cutlass and severed one of the upper legs before the other arms struck him which launched him off and away. A groan escaped as he found his feet and turned once more for the human spider. Who happened to disappear.

"Of course it poofed."

Slowly he turned while listening. There was no sound from the branches above but he could feel it as it watched. In the distance he felt the pulsing call in his mind as the Widow beckoned. On the ground Earl began to rouse and rip swaths of silken web from his body with various degrees of success.

Stay and fight or continue forward and draw the monster away from Earl? It wasn't much of a choice. The sound of the mountain's curses followed Kyle as me moved deeper into the darkness. Twice the creature attacked.

Dropping unseen from above on strands of webbing, the spider struck Kyle both times with crushing blows of enhanced strength. However both times Kyle managed to remove another arm despite the immensely powerful blows. In the distance the sporadic firefight echoed to reveal at least some of his people were still fighting. And so were their enemies.

Each step moved him into the unearthly realm. Ribbons of silk web fell from the heavens like otherworldly banners to the Widow's kingdom on earth. Trees became ensnared by delicate gauze. Even the blades of grass were interconnected by the glistening satin strands. Boots became wrapped in web as he pushed forward determined.

Mist floated through the woods dampening the now glistening interweaving web. Small forms barely registered upon the outskirts of Kyle's peripherals. Ghostly shouts and screams echoed and small detachments of spiders skittered about as apparitions. The veil that separated the physical realm from the grey grew thin. A clearing in the treeline birthed a frightening image.

A massive pontoon houseboat hung suspended from the

centralized web. Along the keel was the stenciled name of the vessel. Charlotte's Web. This wasn't merely a random ship, but the one where Sandy lost her life.

The cycle of events became completed as the widow moved from the recesses of the cabin to look down upon Kyle.

Lydia.

The cold smile upon her features revealed a hint of warmth at seeing him. Almost a wry acknowledgement. Around her the spectral vision of her otherworldly form encompassed her. A shadow detached from the darkness underneath the boat. The face of the man was emotionless, only the great weight of reflection in his eyes revealed he was only a puppet. Aghast at their identities, Kyle almost dropped to his knees.

"Why Lydia? And why do this to Blink? He was always your friend."

The presence of a near immortal minded pressed against Kyle and pushed him to his knees by the sheer encompassing timelessness of the consciousness. From his left the deformed spider crept into view.

"You should understand now. I saved mankind from the rule of the gods. Me, Arachne, born a weaver in ancient Lydia. I crushed the gods that sought to rule mankind. And I have been reborn every generation within the mind of the greatest telepath every century. I am salvation. Should I not receive my just reward? Should I not now truly become immortal and rule my subjects?"

Slowly Kyle forced himself to his feet in defiance.

"You don't just choose to be god! It's not your place to rule and subjugate us! You're murdering people so you can steal their lives! If you can't understand that's evil then you deserve your fate!"

Lydia waved one lithe hand, the ethereal vision of her spider manifestation in the grey mirrored her gesture with one massive appendage. Legs buckled beneath him from the force of her mind. Body spasmed and muscles cramped as she tightened her web. A battering ram of consciousness slammed into his mental walls. Pain filled Kyle with every stroke of her attack. Defenses crumbled and the debris of his mind fell away. The barrier created by his mind cracked, pieces of his soul eradicated from the onslaught. Her might buried him in inept resistance.

"The gods were right. Mankind is unworthy to chart their destiny without guidance. However, it was not their fate, but mine. And you will be the successor to this failing, mortal host."

The spider fired strands from his mandibles that ensnared Kyle's arms to the ground. With uneven gait the creature advanced ungainly upon missing limbs.

From the partial sight of the mist of the veil ghostly figures attacked the apparition of the Widow, gaining her attention and ire. A host of small spiders crawled across Kyle's body, their incorporeal forms assisted in his restraint as the spider closed on him. Five arms and three ichor glistening stubs wrapped around his uncooperative body to hold him fast. Fangs dripped a foul smelling gelatinous fluid near his face as the maw of its mouth opened to eject a fleshly tube.

Vainly Kyle struggled to free himself but failed to counter the overpowering strength of the creature. The Widow's attention turned once more to Kyle.

"Oh yes. I came for your sister. Truly she was the most powerful of her kind in a millennia. However her purpose wasn't to become my host. No, her true destiny was to lead me to you."

Still he squirmed and yet her words pierced him.

"For that you killed her?"

"I will murder thousands to attain what I seek! An immortal host! A being able to regenerate and evolve to cast off the inherent weakness of mortality. Even now your body fights the disease of time to become undying! In time your body will not succumb to death! You are the perfect host to a god." The spider chittered and reared back its head prepared to drive its venomous fangs into Kyle.

Suddenly arms wrapped around the creatures head, fangs pierced through a forearm. With mouth open in silent scream Earl yanked back and squeezed. Veins popped from his arms as the spider released Kyle and flailed backwards in an attempt to bring its great strength to bear on its attacker.

With a single minded drive. Earl squeezed and twisted until the spider's exoskeleton cracked and the neck and head deformed in his unrelenting grip. The spider dropped lifeless. For one brief moment the mountain swayed until Blink squeezed the trigger of his pistol to remove the top portion of Earl's face.

Red mist coated Kyle's face as Earl fell dead at his feet.

The thirty round magazine was emptied into Kyle's chest. Every round battered his armor and bruised his body until he fell forward on hands and knees. The sound of the magazine released and Blink slammed another home which racked the open slide forward to chamber another round.

With a primal roar, Kyle surged to his feet and attacked his friend. Cutlass slashed for the body while the shield was thrust for Blink's face. A leg lanced out from Kyle seeking to crash against Blink's knee while a cut flew for the other man's face. A stab for the chest and another swing of the shield to shatter ribs.

Yet none landed.

The abilities of the seven second seer allowed Blink to avoid every contact while firing his pistol at point blank range into Kyle's body. Round tore through reinforced fabric and burrowed into his flesh. Every missed attack was countered with the dagger in Blink's left hand that bit deeply through articulated plate armor and scoured flesh.

For several minutes Kyle fought ferociously. And yet minute by minute, shot by shot, and slice by slice, Blink shredded Kyle's flesh to wear the older man down until he collapsed in exhausted pain. The seer moved forward to finish Kyle but the Widow raised an arm and ghostly limb forestalling the final strike.

"Enough. I don't want him dead, only beaten."

Somehow Blink sliced the straps from his shield and it now lay several body lengths away. The nerveless fingers of his right hand dripped blood upon the fallen cutlass. One of the strikes sliced through the nerves of his right forearm. Hands yanked Kyle's head back as Blink looked upon his mistress and god.

It was in that moment that Kyle understood.

Every attack he suffered, every loss he accumulated, was designed to weaken him for the moment she would take his body. Each betrayal of her carefully planned out ministrations was formulated to crush his spirit. All the maneuvering of his path was methodically laid out by the masterfully architectured widow. But she failed to grasp a fundamental aspect of who Kyle was.

Laughter sprang from bloodied lips as Lydia starred at Kyle.

"You forgot two things woman. One is that I need diversity to evolve, to grow even stronger. And secondly ... I'm never alone."

The ghostly images of the green mohawked Earl and Sandy tackled into and through Blink's physical body. As they wrestled across the ground, they quickly subdued the spider-like specter that possessed Blink's body. The katana fell and dismembered the ghastly creature.

As Kyle climbed to his feet the billowing figures of dozens in the grey advanced on the Widow's dual forms. Both forms of the nightmarish being shook with laughter.

"You think I do not know you? I whispered sweetly in your ears as I delved into your mind. I slowly poisoned your spirit and watched with glee as you surrendered to depression and helplessness. I prepared for just this moment in time, I have seen all the possibilities through seers more powerful than that weak fool Blink could ever hope to be. Every prophesied scenario has led to this moment. The birth of a true god. And the death of the shield of the gods."

The widow spreads all her limbs. A maelstrom of psychic energy cascaded out in torrential gale winds that threw all away and shredded all that managed to remain in defiance.

All that remained in the woods of the physical realm and the mists of the veil were Kyle and the Widow.

GODS AND MONSTERS

Monday, May 31, 2055
4:43 a.m.

Lightning forked across the skies. Gone was the woods around Lake Gem. Erased was the grey forest of the web. Shattered stone laid under his boots as in all directions existed nothing but darkness. The gargantuan widow raised upon massive legs before a stone altar. And Kyle stood alone, weaponless, shieldless.

"You won't win", even to his own ears the words sounded hollow. The widow cackled as thunder rolled from the storm.

"I already have. Watch as your friends fail and die."

The air between them shimmered and Kyle watched the scene back at the house on the lake. Ellen lay still as blood pulled from the wound in her chest cavity. Deaton struggled against Vibe, arms deflecting the vibrating strikes from the older Warrior. Sage lay still, a peaceful expression on his face that he lacked in life. On the bloodied sands Tye lay shivering as he tightened his own belt upon the stump of his arm.

Water lapped at Jack's knees as he wrestled against the gator, blood leaked from several minor wounds. Across the roof Clay struggled against the vastly more muscular Gargoyle who ripped and tore at Excalibur. Wizard slowly emerged from the house, a rifle in his arms as he moved in the direction of Deaton and Vibe.

The Widow's cackle wracked Kyle's spine.

"When you take control of a person, you kill their soul. Because nothing can challenge and permanently overcome the will inherent within the body. Your faith in your slaves will be your downfall."

The widow cackled to the lightning that flashed upon the canvas of night.

"You trust in fallible, mortal creatures will prove to be misplaced. Watch."

And so they observed as with every moment Vibe drove her hands closer to Deaton's chest. Jack was forced to his knees as the gaping maw grew closure to his face. And Clay was overpowered by the Gargoyle. The Wizard stopped and shouldered the rifle preparing to fire upon Deaton.

The vision shimmered and then the jet crashed atop Wizard, pancaking him from existence. The Widow screamed in rage as the back hatch opened and out ran Brick. In his hands were held one of Clay's spare swords. With a mighty swing Vibe was beheaded. The gator opened jaws wide to engulf Jack's face but, with one hand, Tye shoved the end of the rifle into the reptilian man's mouth and pulled the trigger.

The two men fell from the house with Clay landing on top of the Gargoyle's wings. Bone shattered and the monster screamed until Clay climbed upon it's back and grabbed his head. With immeasurable strength the Warrior twisted with a jerk that echoed out the snap of the spine.

A scream of rage shredded the vision and lightning struck all around Kyle as he hunched against the absolute power of the storm. The Widow reached out and collected Kyle bodily in her limbs to slam him against the altar where he laid stunned.

"It matters little. When I am you I shall tear them apart while wearing your face. The last thing they will see is your visage as they die!" The widow roared and reared back upon her legs before striking forward with massive fangs that sought to spear Kyle through the chest.

The physical attack was merely a representation of her mind as it invaded Kyle's. Darkness surrounded him and crushed him immobile as fangs lowered to his neck. Globs of venom rained upon him as the massive spears closed on him. Pain flashed in his mind as the Widow gained entry into his mind and froze him with a thought.

"You never possessed the strength to stop me. Alone you are less than nothing. And soon you will not even be that."

Like a toddler with a book, she shredded through the pages of his memories. Excruciating agony filed his being as all he could do was watch. The reunion on the jet. The revelation of a son and daughter. The fight with Abe in prison. The years of surrender. Samuel Abernathy. Henry. The deaths of Frank and his family. The dead woman on the beach. The puppet Vibe, even then, at the academy. The first visit at the grey where her fangs tasted his neck all those years ago. The subtle machinations the Widow weaved through his life.

And the loss he suffered every step of the way.

The ghostly image of the first encounter in the grey when the Widow was poised to take him filled his mind at the first touch of her fangs. A fire burned where they brushed burning him from the inside out.

Images flashed too quick to stop as recollections drained into and through him. Sandy opened communications in the woods between Kyle and Clay when they hunted for Henry. The reveal to Clay and Sage that Sandy existed within their minds and allowed mind to mind talk. The memory of Sandy as she protected Kyle from the Widow's mind after death. And then words spoken not long ago.

"When I died I lost my powers in the real world."

The truth dawned slowly but with frightening reality.

Sandy lost her power when she died. All the years she communicated with his mind caused a different evolution within

Kyle.

It awakened his own telepathic powers.

Every incident he accredited to his sister was his own innate abilities manifesting.

The fangs stopped their advance and retreated as the Widow screamed in rage.

The night Sandy was murdered she was tossed away by the storm in the grey, scattered by the power of the Widow.

It was his own power that pushed the Widow back.

Now he understood what Sandy wouldn't, couldn't, tell him. The power was his to give. Or to use to destroy the Widow. The gargantuan spider retreated from Kyle as he stood upon the altar. Fear glinted within her eyes.

One foot eased forward, his weight almost sent him to the ground. Only the realization of what he was, who he was, kept him upright. The fates of all those he loved hung in the balance. The spark of fear within her eyes bolstered his spirit and confirmed what he finally knew. He was not a helpless sacrifice upon the altar, unable to resist and escape the fate of the damned. Neither Sandy, the Protectorate, nor the Widow controlled his destiny.

Life or death. Freeman or slave. Marionette to unseen machinations of the puppeteer or master of his own destiny. The choice was laid before him, honest and without guile. Burden of responsibility for his life and the lives of the world versus surrender to the Spider and a life freed from difficult decisions, duty, and the inevitable loneliness of a life unending.

An eternal proposition made with a single breath upon a single step.

"My turn."

Shadowed features watched from the edges of his consciousness. Countless victims observed with stoic faces as their freedom from the eternal web became possible. A sea of souls silently urged Kyle forward. Those embraced by death, yet denied the afterlife, offered unheard pleas while those souls yet to be born prayed for a future of wondrous possibilities instead of the cruel, iron rule of the Widow.

Leaping forward Kyle sank his teeth into the fangs of the Widow and released the storm within.

Memories flickered by in his mind too fast. He spun like a turntable as scenes played in his mind. The widow's memories laid bare before him. The woman slinking through history killing and taking what she believed was hers. Death that spread like the plague through supers for generations. Vile plans and even darker deeds.

The age of heroes and the gods unfolded as he watched the Widow murder and slay with impunity. Old gods passed judgement and took Lydia's hands in punishment. Through which they sought to control her. All their actions did was birth the vile creature that warred throughout the ages because of the talent of her hands.

In the darkened room of an ancient home Kyle looked down upon the broken and sobbing Lydian woman. Sympathy panged his heart even as his hands reached out and surrounded her neck and squeezed.

On the altar the widow writhed as he strangled her ethereal form. In the woods his hands crushed the life from her beneath the shadow of Charlotte's Web still suspended above. In hundreds of minds scattered around the world he snuffed out the lingering traces of her soul that infected the living. In the grey, the webs crumbled and cocooned beings floated free.

Under the darkness of the forest around Lake Gem Kyle heard her mind cry out in denial.

"It was prophesied the new god will be born and rise!"

Coldly his hands retained their viselike grip as the light left her eyes.

"I am. The shield of the gods is gone. You ushered me into this life. But instead of a world of darkness subjugated to the will of an evil woman, a new future has come where fate is not written. I won't rule this world or its people. But I will protect it from the likes of you. Welcome to the new age. Bitch."

The body of Lydia lay cold and stiff even as he laid down beside her. The night was at its darkest, just before the dawn. But instead of heralding a reign of unimaginable terror that could have lasted for an eternity, the world woke anew. A new beginning.

Kyle closed his eyes.

EPILOGUE

The green hills rolled into the horizon. Trees dotted the landscape with branches stretched to the heavens. The blue sky was unending and achingly beautiful. Odd creatures never before seen pranced through the fields gaily. Upon the updraft soared eagles beside doves. Scattered about were figures in various states of repose.

It was a place of rest and rejuvenation.

He laid on the downey soft carpet of greenery with hands behind his head. The loose fitting black tank top ruffled with the light breeze. Blue jeans and worn black boots laced to his knees completed his attire. There was no worry of danger or scenarios fraught with unrest. Just a man enjoying the peace of the moment.

Off his right a young woman approached. The flower of womanhood was in full bloom as her hair drifted off her shoulders and swayed with each step. The billowing sundress could not hide her athletic runner's build. Nor could it hide the soft curves.

Upon reaching the reclining man she joined him. Lazily she stretched out on one side, a fist perched upon her hip. The two were siblings by their shared features. Even more so, they were twins. Flawless complexion and skin that radiated life. Easily they could have been in their early twenties.

Except for the pale white hair that fell to the man's shoulders.

The man was muscular without appearing as a bodybuilder. Pale blue eyes, several shades lighter than the sky, glanced at the woman. A weight pressed upon the soul behind the eyes, yet it was happiness and a sense of tranquility that radiated from them. Despite his flawless skin there were scars layered upon the man.

The gravitas of experience and memory.

Nonetheless he smiled, which grew as another figure approached in equally relaxed attire. Lifeguard orange swim trunks and flip flops that smacked with every stride. He, too, appeared in his early twenties. Face was as free of hair as the top of the man's head. As he reached them he sat cross legged and enjoyed the cool sweep of wind across his face and torso.

"He's taking long enough. I've got places to go", the bald man said with a neutral tone.

"Give him time. And stop complaining, I've waited more than most", the woman replied in a melodic voice.

The large man sat up and leaned over his drawn legs with a smirk across his face.

"Sage, remember. Patience is a virtue." The other man sighed with mock exasperation. Then a somber mood struck him while he picked at non-existent lint of his orange shorts. Quietly Sage spoke.

"Hey Kyle. I never thanked you. For looking after Mary when I was gone." All three thought of that night, a decade earlier. The night they were victorious against the Widow. The triumph came at a steep cost. Ellen Paige. Earl. The marionette Blink. Hallan Branch. Gale Tanaka.

Sage Winters.

The battle was fought with each knowing the stakes and possible mortality rates. And all were willing to pay the ultimate price.

"You never need to say those words brother. That's what family does. It's what we do", Kyle muttered solemnly even as a bewildered look crossed Sage's face.

"I think you got confused at what was said. I said I never thanked you, I never said the words though." Waiting for a few moments,

Kyle grunted amusedly as Sage looked to the skies as though the subject was closed.

"You're a cheeky bastard." That elicited a smile from both Sandy and Sage as Kyle merely shook his head in feigned outrage. Once more they fell into the comfortable silence of best friends. There was no need to fill the empty minute with unnecessary chattering. Head tilted as Kyle closed his eyes sensing something in the grey.

"He's crossing over now. It was peaceful enough. There. There he is."

Over a hill walked Clay Issacs. The limp was there, as it was ever since the fight with Gargoyle. Bone fractures and nerve damage plagued him. One arm was bare of synthetic skin, the mechanical limb a reminder to his sacrifices. Scars adorned his flesh and his face was worn as old leather. Even resembled an old catcher's mitt.

But as he grew closure the wind blew against Clay. Dust clouds floated from him as the road map of life, written across his figure, drifted away in rebirth. The cybernetic disappeared along with the scars and ravages of old age of a hard life.

When Clay reached them the final vestiges of the Warrior known as Excalibur was gone. What remained was Clay Issacs, the young man who possessed dreams of a future with the woman he loved. The three stood in greeting as Sage went in for a full embrace. Then the four looked around to each other with smiles written upon their faces.

"It's been a ride guys", Kyle chuckled as they grinned.

"That it has. One helluva ride." Sage lightly punched Kyle while agreeing.

"I wouldn't have done it with anyone else", Clay laughed.

"That's cause no one else would take your sorry butt!" A punch was thrown and Kyle danced away from Clay who was still laughing even as he missed.

Another hug from Sage drew them all in. Tears glistened on his face as he smiled.

"I love you guys. Never forget that. And a part of me will always remember you. But time for me to go. The last great adventure."

Tears welled in every eye as they bid farewell to Sage. Slowly, Sage disintegrated into glittering dust that danced away on the breeze. Kyle shook his head in wonder.

"He waited around here for you Clay. Course the moment you show up and he can't wait to leave." That time Clay did smack him. As he rubbed his shoulder Kyle avoided their eyes and asked a question.

"What about you two? Going to become sparkling pollen and give some poor folks an afterlife hayfever?" There was a light laughter but Clay broke the serenity.

"We missed so much when Sandy died. We figure we have time on our hands. Going to earn back those lost moments." Throat was thick with emotion as Kyle nodded and tossed another query at them.

"Y'all aren't coming back are you?" Sandy ran into Kyle's arms and hugged him tight.

"It's time we moved on. Together. You don't need us anymore. But I will always love you little brother. Plus I know Deaton is watching out for you. Along with your kids, with Mary, with Tye and Mary's baby boy. They will look out for you as you look after the world. This isn't goodbye. It's until next time." Feigning a bravado he clearly didn't feel, Kyle nodded.

"Well … about time. I'm tired of having to clean up y'alls messes. Plus I need to keep an eye on all these crazy people who are still breathing."

The other man moved in and the three shared a long, final hug.

"I left you my sword. It should pair nicely with your shield. What are they calling you now that Aegis is officially gone?" The embrace ended as Kyle smirked.

"I'm using my middle name, Aeneas. Has a nice ring. He was a Trojan warrior and many royal houses claim a lineage from him. Plus it pisses off Earl who keeps crying about copyright infringement."

With a sudden urge, Kyle leaned down and kissed his sister softly on her forehead.

"Now get out of here sis. Be free. And take this dolt with you." Horrible at goodbyes, Kyke turned and walked away. After only a half dozen steps he paused and turned back to see the couple watching as they held hands.

"Go on Cassandra. Release your burden of the sight and find peace."

Even as he watched, they disappeared into a rainbow and arched away transfigured into something completely new. A sad smile stretched on Kyle's face as he closed his eyes.

"Never the end dear sister. Until we are reborn."

Kyle Ross faded from the grey and returned to the realm of existence.

R.L. ARENZ III

www.rlarenziii.com

Who is R.L. Arenz III? (Otherwise known as EEEEARRRRLL)

He's a single father of five. He's a man of faith. He's happy on a river bank with a line in the water and a book in his hand. He's endured hardships from life and made too many mistakes to count (seriously, he ran out of fingers and toes). He's been knocked on his butt and gotten up to ask for more. Sarcasm and annoying wit escape him at every opportunity. But beneath gruff appearance and gallows humor hides a man who cares for others.

A long time ago in a state far, far away, the third R.L. Arenz was born.

Okay, the 80's wasn't tooooo long ago.

Born and raised in Florida, R.L. (EEAAARRL) got the privilege of living in both rural and urban settings. Everything from cow tipping and roman candle freeze tag to Chinese fire drills in the middle of University Avenue and walking through the Taco Bell drive through late at night for those wonderful 3-cheese burritos (Bring them back!). Working a very wide assortment of jobs allowed him to experience employment environments in almost every atmosphere. Yet it was the love of books, inspired and ingrained by his mother, that whispered dreams of one day completing a novel of his own.

Life, as it is want to do, intervened and distracted the aspiring author. Combined with a long streak of procrastination, his dreams were continually placed on the back burner, while dinner for his kids was on the front. Yet it was creating fantastical stories to tell his children, the foray into a variety of play-by-post sites (Star Wars of course), and the voices of unsung characters screaming to have their stories told that finally prompted him to crack his knuckles and dive into writing.

And never forget hosting his very own Science Mystery Theater 3000 episodes alongside his cousin and the oft powerbombed, Mr Moose. God rest his soul. The moose not the cousin. In the end, three things saw him through.

To show his kids to follow their dreams.

To fulfill a passion that beats in his heart.

And the hope that, once the books are published, the characters sharing his brain would return his sanity. Or the little which remained.

R.L. currently lives in Florida with his five children, the entire race of mosquitos, and the often reported 'Florida Man'. And no, R.L. isn't the Florida man. Just a man. That lives in Florida. Still.

R.L. continues to work on two novels, a horror-sci-fi called Wraith, and a sprawling epic.

MORE FROM VRÆYDA LITERARY

Can You Hear the Angels Sing?

978-0-9921188-0-8 / 978-0-9921188-5-3

Rev. Prof Seth Ayettey

Usurper Kings

978-1-988034-04-1 / 978-0-9921188-1-5

Son of Abel

978-1-988034-06-5 / 978-1-988034-07-2

Neon Lieben

978-1-988034-15-7 / 978-1-988034-14-0

Sapha Burnell

MacroMicroCosm

ISSN 2368-979

www.vraeydamedia.ca/literary

@macromicrocosm | @macromicrocosmlitjournal

Available on Amazon, Barnes & Noble, ChaptersIndigo,
Bookshop.org & Indie Bookstores worldwide.